Under Shadows

Born and raised in Upstate New York, Jason LaPier lives in Portland, Oregon with his wife and their dachshund. In past lives he has been a guitar player for a metal band, a drum-n-bass DJ, a record store owner, a game developer, and an IT consultant. These days he divides his time between writing fiction and developing software, and doing Oregonian things like gardening, hiking, and drinking microbrew. He can be found on Twitter @JasonWLaPier and he blogs at jasonwlapier.com

Also by Jason LaPier

The Dome Trilogy
Unexpected Rain
Unclear Skies

Under Shadows

JASON LaPIER

Book Three of The Dome Trilogy

HARPER
Voyager

Harper*Voyager*
an imprint of HarperCollins*Publishers* Ltd
1 London Bridge Street
London SE1 9GF

www.harpervoyager.co.uk

This paperback edition 2017

First published in Great Britain in ebook format by
HarperCollins*Publishers* 2017

A catalogue record for this book
is available from the British Library

ISBN: 978-0-00-818106-2

For Jennifer

CHAPTER 1

There was no doubt Jax had seen more in the past year and a half than he'd seen in his whole life, but in spite of all those new experiences, it seemed there were even newer sights waiting for him throughout the galaxy. Such it was that afternoon, when inside a half-constructed domed city on the third planet out from the star Epsilon Eridani, he found himself in a venue that was both a library and a bar.

"Welcome to the *Bibliohouse.*" The greeter was a pink-skinned young woman with a small smile and brown hair long enough to be tied into a tail. She wore a navy-blue suit that matched the color – and gloss – of the floor tiling. "Is this your first visit?"

Jax found it hard to speak as he gawked around the space. It was large and circular with a central bar that curved around for dozens of meters. The ceiling rose a good ten or twelve meters above his head, and along the outer walls stretched high shelves dotted with scores of books. Real, paper books, though the shelves were far from full.

His partner, Stanford Runstom, Public Relations

representative for Modern Policing and Peacekeeping, answered the waiting question with an affirmative grunt.

"Delightful," she chimed. "Are you here to write or to read?"

"Um, we just wanted to have a drink," Runstom said.

"Well, naturally, sir," she said with a cock of her head.

"What is this place?" Jax managed to blurt. "Is it really a library? And a bar?"

She smiled. "New to EE-3, aren't you? Yes, the *Bibliohouse* is a library. I'll put you in the reader section and set you up with the introduction."

They followed her to the central bar, which Jax could see curved around in a full circle, but was only seated on the front half by well-padded stools. Every few seats there were short walls, like dividers, and affixed to these were page-sized datapads on thin, bendable arms. Past the bar, he could see the back half of the space was occupied by long tables, and seated sporadically at those were men and women of various backgrounds, tapping at keyboards, faces lit blue by screens.

Once they took a seat, the hostess tapped at a small wrist-pad and the screen next to Jax's head lit up. He pulled it to get a better angle on it and started skimming through a document titled "Welcome to the *Bibliohouse*".

"When you're ready to order," the hostess said, "just tap the icon at the bottom of the screen there and a bartender will come by."

"Thank you," Runstom said for both of them.

Jax was already nose deep into the intro. With all the new construction going on across the planet, it was important for everyone to document their work. Evidently, some visionary higher-ups also wanted stories collected as well, so that someday in the future, when some wealthy Double-

E-Threer wanted to know the rich history of their world, they'd have a massive repository of materials to draw on.

Therefore, a percentage of every workday was dedicated to writing: either more formal documentation around the plethora of projects, or the informal recitation of interesting stories, tall tales, legends, and anecdotes. Workers were encouraged to do their writing wherever it felt comfortable, and the owners of this particular library thought some would find it comfortable to make their recordings in a place where they could access any information – technical, historical, biographical, and even fictional – about EE-3 as well as imbibe a well-crafted libation.

Clearly, they were onto something. Jax thought that if he ever made it back to Terroneous, maybe he'd try to convince the Stockton Public Library to allow him to open up a bar in the back.

"You fellas know what you'd like to drink?"

And with that, the magic of the place had worn off. It wasn't the arrival of the bartender – Runstom must have hit the button on his pad already – but it was the thought of that little library back in Stockton. The thought of Terroneous, a moon orbiting a gas giant in the Barnard system, impossibly far away from this bar on a small planet in the Epsilon Eridani system. The only transportation they had access to was Runstom's small ship, which was only capable of Warp; it'd take years for that thing to make it from Eridani to Barnard's Star.

Of all the things they needed to figure out, the most important for Jax was getting back to Terroneous. How strange that such a place had become home to him. But he couldn't have known it until they'd taken him from it. Had ModPol done him a favor by illegally extraditing him from the independent moon? Forcing him to realize his connection to that place? Maybe so. He didn't care how it had become his home, just that it was. And he needed to get back there.

Back to her.

"Ale," Runstom said. "The brown one."

"Mucksucker Brown, comin' up. And you, sir?"

Jax looked at Runstom, then at the bartender. The man could've been the brother of the hostess, he looked so similar. Perhaps it was a family-owned place; or maybe it was just the identical glinting blue suit. Jax had no idea what to order, just that he needed something with alcohol in it.

"Brandy?" he said, then added, "If you have it?"

The bartender cracked half a grin, then glanced at the rounded wall behind him. There were shelves reaching as high as the bookshelves around the outer wall, but these were populated by bottles of all shapes and colors. Jax flinched as he watched the man turn his head upward. They must've had a ladder to reach those upper rows.

"We've got some," he said, still looking up. "Not easy to get out here, but we have some fine brandy imported from Poligart."

"Oh, uh," Jax started. He felt like an idiot when it came to money anymore, never having any for one, and never knowing what anything cost anyhow.

"Go for it," Runstom said, laying out a card. "Someone told me I need to get better at spending the company money."

The bartender let the rest of the smile appear. "Comin' right up," he said, then left them.

Jax could only imagine what they looked like to these people: a tall, lanky man from the domes of Barnard-4 with skin as pale as the foam head on the beers they were drinking, and his companion: the broad-chested, oddly well-dressed

Runstom, whose skin was dark olive in color. No one here was from "around here", because they'd all arrived within the last decade or so to begin construction and pick up other necessary jobs to support the development of a new civilization on the once primordial planet. But Jax had learned that he would be an outcast among outcasts anywhere he went that wasn't Barnard-4. The domers on the planet of his birth never left home, and there was little chance of encountering one in his travels. Likewise, Runstom never really fit in anywhere he went. He was just too weird.

Plus he had the green skin.

"Alright." Runstom's tone pulled Jax's attention away from the deliciously information-dense pad. "So where the hell is my ship?"

Runstom's company-issued ship, a luxury thing called an OrbitBurner-something-or-other, hadn't been at the docks. The issuing company being the same Modern Policing and Peacekeeping that had wrongfully extradited Jax from Terroneous. Though technically Runstom worked for the Defense division, his ties with Justice strained.

Jax blew out a long sigh, trying to determine the best way to break the news about Runstom's ship, then just decided to blurt it out. "Dava took it."

"Dava?"

"Space Waster."

"Sonova—"

"But she'll bring it back." Jax leaned in a little closer. "Look, Stan, I know you're going to be pissed about this. But I promise you, they'll bring the ship back."

"They?" Runstom's eyes burned and his lips drew taut. "How many are there?"

"Just three," Jax said quickly. "They stowed away. Look,

I'm sorry I didn't tell you before. Please understand – I just didn't want any more violence. They promised me they'd keep to themselves."

Runstom looked down and away. "Violence."

The drinks arrived and Jax knew he'd have to sit in silence for a few moments while Runstom processed this. He always had a way in his head, a way that things *should* be done, and when they weren't done that way, he had to reason out why. In this case, he probably felt that Jax should have alerted him right away that there were stowaways on board, so that he could summarily arrest them. But that's not what happened. Jax knew that Runstom would have to ponder why things didn't go the way they were *supposed* to, and that it meant he would have to take a moment to see it from Jax's perspective. But he would, eventually. Or at least he'd try.

Jax took a sip of his brandy. It was like sweet fire in his throat. It reminded him of the last conversation he had with Dava, stowed away and pilfering Runstom's liquor supply. Threats had been exchanged, but they were all just trying to survive. Despite Space Waste being a pack of bloodthirsty gangbangers, he owed them. Sort of. When ModPol had picked him up on Terroneous, it was Dava and her crew that had intercepted him. *Rescued* him from wrongful imprisonment, but not to grant him his freedom; instead to recruit him for their own purposes. A harrowing experience, if temporary.

"Three of them and two of us," Runstom said. "If you hadn't made a deal, they'd have taken it by force."

"Probably," Jax said after a burning swallow. He decided not to remark that *two of us* was an exaggeration, given his uselessness in any such altercation. None of the various custodian, technician, and operator positions he'd held in the domes required anything remotely resembling combat training, and even during his short time on Terroneous, he'd stayed as far away from trouble as possible. Or had tried to, anyway.

"And they were supposed to disappear once we landed."

Jax frowned and nodded. "Well, that was the deal."

"What makes you think they'll be back?"

He shrugged. "That OrbitBurner doesn't have a Xarp drive, so no FTL. Space Waste has zero presence out here in Eridani, and these three are on the run. So they'll need another way back to Barnard or Sirius."

Runstom seemed to turn that over in his mind, then he took a pull of his dark beer. "That won't be easy."

"No, I don't suppose so."

"What's the other reason?"

Jax hadn't alluded to a second reason, but Runstom wasn't going to let him get off that easily. "I gave them something."

"You gave them—" Runstom started, then stopped and his eyes narrowed. "You mean information."

"Yes," Jax said. "On our way to the docks, you were telling me about something your mom said. About someone going into Space Waste, someone who was undercover."

Runstom flinched slightly at the mention of his mother. They'd only talked to her a few hours ago, and it had definitely changed the man. Jax was pretty sure they hadn't seen each other in several years, at least in person. And with her being in some kind of witness protection relocation deal, the communication between them had been poor to say the least. Her name was Sylvia Runstom, though she was now going by Sylvia Rankworth, and she was Assistant Director of Agricultural Systems on Epsilon Eridani-3. Jax got the impression that she still kept up with some of the networks she'd acquired while she did undercover work herself, back before her son Stanford was born, well over three decades ago.

"Yes," Runstom said, glancing over his shoulder. "You said you might be able to identify one or two Wasters that didn't fit in."

"There was definitely one guy who was up to something," Jax said. "His name was Basil Roy. He was a programmer – not an operator like me, but a real engineer."

"Doesn't sound the gangbanger type."

"No, he wasn't." Jax took another sip, hoping the brandy would lubricate his memory. "They were having him write software to interface with this special detection equipment. Stuff they lifted from somewhere."

"Vulca."

"What? Yeah, that sounds familiar. What's Vulca?"

Runstom sighed. "One of the moons around Sirius-5. There's a big research base there. And I was there when Space Waste attacked it."

"What, really? You – were there? Doing what?"

He nodded. "Same thing I'm doing here. Selling ModPol Defense services." Before Jax could ask more, Runstom waved dismissively. "I know, Sirius-5 is already a ModPol subscriber. But ModPol wanted to force the moon – Vulca – to get a separate contract. Figured they had money to spend with all the research funds pouring into their facility."

"And did they?"

Runstom looked at Jax in silence for a moment. "Well, yeah. After Space Waste attacked them, they realized the value of having ModPol around. We had a trial unit of Defenders there. Not a large one, but enough to rout the Wasters."

"I see," Jax said. "But not before they made off with some equipment."

Runstom laughed for the first time all day, though it was

more of a short huff than anything. "All this new equipment. The techs just installed it. They put the old gear in the empty boxes so they could ship it out for resale."

Jax thought about it. "So the Wasters stole what they thought was brand-new equipment, and what they got were new boxes with old stuff in it?"

"Yep."

"So it was never going to work," Jax said. "Which didn't matter, since Basil Roy spoofed the detection software. It led them right where he wanted it to."

Runstom took another quiet pull. "There's still a question of why."

Now it was Jax's turn to huff a laugh. "To make them think they could get the jump on the ModPol transport. They thought the stolen tech helped them zero in on it when it Xarped into Eridani space. The Wasters thought they had the easy score, but they were walking into a trap."

Runstom's brow furrowed. "I should feel good about that. That gang has taken a lot of lives. Civilian and ModPol. People I worked with. Friends of mine. I should be saying, lock them all up, whatever it takes."

"But you don't feel good about it?"

Runstom sighed. "Something doesn't sit right. I'm glad we made so many arrests, of course. But it was ..."

"It was bloody," Jax said. "A lot of people died."

Runstom nodded. "On both sides."

He went quiet and Jax tried to figure out what was going through his head. He had no love for Space Waste, there was no doubt about that. So what if someone went in undercover and tricked them into walking into an ambush? Even as vile as those gangbangers were, it was still a crude trick. Dishonorable even. Did that matter to Runstom?

"It wasn't justice," Jax said.

Runstom's head picked up and he met Jax's eyes. "No. It wasn't justice. It was closer to ... to war."

And there it was. Stanford Runstom worked in the Defense division of Modern Policing and Peacekeeping, but his heart was where he started, in Justice. Jax knew his friend would always have the mind of a cop. And part of that meant that he wanted things done by a certain code of conduct, by a procedure. That there was a fair way and an unfair way, and even the lowliest of criminals deserved the fair way. If they were guilty, it should be determined by a trial.

But if this had been an act of war, hadn't Space Waste charged into battle willingly? And there was the big question: would they have made that kind of attack if they hadn't been led into it by deception? Their intention hadn't been so warlike, they just wanted to steal stuff.

Of course, the stuff they thought they were going to steal was a weapons cache.

Runstom sighed and glanced at the WrappiMate around his forearm. "So when do you think we'll get the OrbitBurner back?"

Jax fidgeted. How the hell could he know? Dava probably flew it out to the site of the battle; it was the only place of interest in the whole system, aside from EE-3 and a ModPol outpost in some secret location. What she might be doing out there, he couldn't guess, but then again, he never could work out what motivated that assassin.

"Soon," he answered quietly.

CHAPTER 2

Tim Cazos was fucking sick of Space Waste.

Everywhere he looked, that goddamn logo with the twisting arrows. What did that even mean? Three arrows, curving along a circular path as if to go one into the next, only to bend awkwardly outward at their heads. It was on every wall, on every ceiling, even on every floor.

Not that there were that many walls, ceilings, and floors on the dropship. It was basically a big box – a bay – with a smaller box – a cockpit – mounted to the front of it. On the outside it looked less like a box, given the massive Xarp drive thrusters at the rear and the high-burn crash-landing gear underneath. But where he was inside the loading bay, it was just a box. And all six sides had that goddamn logo splashed across them.

Cazos was strapped into one of the hanging personnel cages. Not for any reason but the lack of gravity; he was sick of floating around the awkward space of the bay. A few dozen cages, a handful of deflated spacesuits – also decorated with the bent-arrow logo – and weapon racks, mostly empty save the occasional particle blaster or projectile firearm. Healthy paranoia had caused Cazos to stuff himself into a suit and seal it up, despite the bay being completely capable of maintaining pressure and oxygen as normal. At least he hoped it was capable. How many missions had this heap of junk seen? Before and after it fell into the hands of Space Waste?

He itched to wake the handypad strapped to his arm, but it wasn't time yet. He gave himself a count to wait. Long enough to know the Space Waste command ship, the *Longhorn*, had fled the system, and long enough to wait out any ModPol sweepers. He knew the *Longhorn* had already Xarped away, because Rando Jansen was a fucking tool. But any blip of a signal now, and he'd get himself roasted by trigger-happy ModPol fighters.

Just a few more hours, then he could check the contact monitor. In the meantime, he was just a derelict dropship, drifting at the outer edge of the remains of a nasty battlefield.

So he spent his idle time cursing Jansen. *Underboss Jansen.* Cazos had never met the fucker until he got the Space Waste assignment. By that point, some plan had already been running full thrust ahead. Cazos – the "hacker" – was just decoration. *Make them think you wrote this program. Make them think you can make the detection equipment work. That you can find the target when it comes out of Xarp.*

And so he'd done what he was told, though he didn't believe anyone was stupid enough to buy it. Apparently he'd overestimated the collective intelligence of Space Waste. He'd whipped up a phony user interface with lots of graphs and maps and numbers swirling around, and everyone took him at his word. And why not? He was the unassuming Basil Roy, software architect.

And besides, it had appeared to work; because Jansen

knew right where that ModPol transport was going to pop out of Xarp. He didn't need a real detector.

Cazos was sick of thinking about it. Whatever Jansen's plans were, he didn't want to know. He was obviously toying with Space Waste, but to what end? The ambush had taken the old boss out of the picture, and that put Jansen at the top of the food chain. Why take command of a band of gangbangers? Why not just arrest them all?

It made no difference. Cazos knew a clusterfuck forming when he saw one, and this was one he needed to stay away from. As far as he was concerned, his debt was paid.

A distant beeping wormed into his ear, slow and persistent. He blinked away heaviness in his eyelids. He looked at the heads-up-display in his suit's helmet. He must have drifted off, because the hours had rolled by.

"Goddamn zero-G," he muttered. He could never get used to it. He would do anything for a planet under his feet again.

He shifted his limbs around, trying to drive the numbness from them. Another part of his HUD was blinking in time with the beep. The oxygen had burned down to twenty-five percent and was giving him a subtle warning that the tank needed changing.

It was time. The itch to check his datapad could finally be scratched. He switched the piece on and it winked to life. Diagnostics scrolled by for a moment, then he was flicking through the interface, seeking out the contact app.

Desolation. The battle had gone poorly for Space Waste, that was for sure. Pieces of ships – most of them Waster fighter craft – drifted about the three-dimensional space. No signals of any kind, other than the auto-emergency beacons here and there. And the little camera drones that the Wasters liked to use to record their battles. "BatCaps," he said aloud when he remembered what they called them. There were a few dozen of those still.

"Shit." One more signal. A scanner. Well, if he was caught he was caught. He got ready to turn off the datapad and play dead, but stopped himself. "Just one second." He zeroed in on the scan signal and ran it through the database, just for the hell of it. A lot of scanner equipment contained a signal inside it, like a serial number. This one came up right away. It was civilian.

This information gave him pause. He could continue to hide, but it seemed foolish to hide from a civilian ship. Unless they panicked and somehow reported his presence back to ModPol. He could get on the open comm and threaten to blow them to pieces if they attempted any transmissions. Really though, what difference did it make? Once the Xarp drive was warmed up, he'd be gone.

It was his plan all along. Well, there hadn't been much of a plan, not really. The primary goal was to get a ship with Xarp capabilities. He'd altered the fleet manifest back before they left the Space Waste base, including the dropship on the carrier. Once the conflict started, only the raiders and fighters were deployed, leaving the lone mistaken and useless dropship in a bay, just waiting for him. Then all he had to do was to escape just before the *Longhorn* Xarped away. No one would miss him in the heat of the moment. After that, he would play dead. What to do next, well, there the plan got a little fuzzier. He had a handful of caches, two in the Barnard system and one in the Sirius system. A few thousand Alliance credits in hard currency. The stuff was traceable, but only if someone took the time to do it. Something he never worried about, because he had the equipment to scramble the hidden etchings inside the money, inside those slim, rectangular cards printed with algorithmic ink. It made it harder to spend – especially anywhere that wanted to keep a reputation – but not impossible.

"Scrambling Alleys is what got you in this mess, asshole."

His brain told his mouth to shut up so he could think. The analyzer in his handypad wasn't much information to go on. He needed to scan that civvy and find out what it was, maybe where it came from.

The O2 level on his HUD dropped another percentage point. At the very least he needed to get out of the cage and turn on the air. So he did, drifting from the wall over to the panel that hung from the ceiling in the center of the room. He was going to light up on the other ship's contact map any moment now, since he had to power on the reactor to generate oxygen and nitrogen. He tried to move quickly, but a part of him wanted to linger just to see what the civilian would do. Just to tempt fate.

He must have been in a good mood. Maybe it was the dawning realization that he'd actually escaped those bloodthirsty bastards.

A sing-song tone trilled throughout the bay, signaling that pressure was nominal. He removed his helmet and climbed out of the suit. Getting undressed in null gravity would have been hard enough for him, but wrestling with the bulky suit added a few more minutes to the process. Finally he got free of the thing and pulled himself over to the cabin door. Pressure inside the small cockpit was already good, so it slid open as he touched the panel.

Floating around without a suit was somehow more nauseating. Probably because most of his body thought everything was normal, allowing the confusion in his inner ear to dominate. He closed his eyes and took a few breaths, his chest swelling, causing him to become all too aware of his increased heart rate. He opened his eyes and shook his head in a failed attempt to shed panic.

He strapped into the chair in front of the main console. Having the screen to anchor his focus on seemed to help. He fired up a few subsystems, letting the proximity scanners and other sensors come to life. This activity would most definitely make his presence known; so be it. He charged the auto-turret but set it to remain in its locked position. This way it remained non-threatening, and anyway, if he opened it up, he'd have to lock it again before he could kick into Xarp. Having done all that, he set the Xarp drive to pre-charge.

All this would be generating a lot of noise, signal-wise. So it was time to deal with the civilian ship. He did a full scan on it, and whistled. An OrbitBurner 4200 LX. A wasteful but sporty propulsion system for showing off, plus a Warp drive for making it to an event only fashionably late. No weapons, and a hybrid hull good for stopping rocks and radiation, but not much else. Chock full of the best AI-assisted systems, which meant it might be a crew of one, or it might include a small party of guests.

Those caches Cazos had, how secure were they? There was no telling if they would even be there. Maybe they'd be there but they'd be bugged. His ticket to freedom could be his ticket right back to prison.

But here was a luxury machine, just out for a cruise in the Epsilon Eridani system. A largely uninhabited system, except for a ModPol outpost and a brand-new colony, still being constructed, on EE-3. A colony with a very specific customer in mind: the richest of the richest domers.

It was a brilliant idea, to build an out-of-the-way colony and sell residency at a premium; thus ensuring only occupants that have too much money to spend. A population of pure consumers, locked into a controlled economy. Sold on exclusivity, their stockpiles of cash could be slowly bled away from them. It was like counterfeiting, but without all the legal trouble.

This OrbitBurner, it had to be one of those richies who'd come out to Epsilon Eridani for an early look at the new domes. And now he was out flying around the system, showing off his shiny rocket to whomever. Maybe a whole party of richies. Right there in front of him.

They wouldn't have much hard currency on board, no of course not. But they would have valuables. Cazos wished he could take the OrbitBurner itself, but without Xarp, he'd be stuck in this mostly-empty system. He could strip it though. There was a fair amount of room in his dropship's bay. He knew how to pick apart the processing systems – all that AI would be worth a good trade somewhere. And there were bound to be other luxuries onboard. Food, clothes, personal electronics. Alcohol. Well-aged, expensive shit.

He just needed to find out how many people were on it. He would have to board. And there were a few guns in the back, so he'd be well armed. The question would just be a matter of whether he could restrain them. He didn't want to have to kill anyone, but the sheer amount of death he'd witnessed a few days prior out-scaled anything he could have ever imagined. When he stepped back and thought about it, what was the death of a few rich assholes out flaunting their luxury spaceship?

"No," he said. He wouldn't let his encounter with Space Waste corrupt him. Well, he was already pretty goddamn corrupt. But it wouldn't make him a killer. He'd just go aboard, flash his guns, and make them tie each other up. If they gave him a problem, he could always retreat to the dropship and threaten them with the auto-turret.

Cazos pointed the comm laser at the OrbitBurner and hailed her with an SOS. Just text, no voice or video.

* * *

Ten minutes later, he floated around the bay, trying to decide on a gun. He was torn between practicality – the smaller weapons, like the shock-pistol – and menace – the larger weapons, like the pulse machinegun. He also debated briefly on whether or not he should don the spacesuit, but decided it wasn't necessary. The message he'd received back from the civvy was a friendly invite, and they'd set up a ship-to-ship dock plan that would mean no need to spacewalk.

Cazos went for the big gun, the pulse machinegun. If he had to fire it in zero-G, he'd probably lose control. But he didn't want to fire it, he just wanted to do a little terrifying. He strapped it over his shoulder and extended it in front of him, holding it with one hand so he could hop from handhold to handhold with the other. The zero-G was a good thing, he realized: he'd never be able to lift this gun one-handed if there were any gravity. He grabbed a shiny space blanket out of a cabinet and wrapped it around the barrel.

He slapped the controls at the door and slid open the inner airlock. He made a move forward, then caught himself, pulling back to the controls. As a final precaution, he decided to force the inner door to stay open. If something went down, he needed to know he could get back to his boat.

Normally this meant he wouldn't be able to open the outer door, but since they had established a seal between the two ships, it wouldn't be a problem. The OrbitBurner had a universal airlock that could change shape as necessary to fit any other docking module. The readout on the panel at Cazos's outer door showed a perfect seal, with optimal pressurization on the other side.

He flipped to the camera, wondering if he'd see a grinning welcoming committee on the other side. No, of course not. They'd opened their outer door, but not their inner. The small bay between the doors was empty.

The outer door of the dropship was less compromising than the OrbitBurner's universal. In fact, it was more or less *invasive*. When he opened it, it pushed six triangles outward, wedging itself into the other ship's airlock. The consistent pressure would allow his new friends to open their inner door, but they couldn't close their outer door on him.

He waved his free hand at the camera next to the door, then lifted the blanket-shrouded weapon. "Hey there!" he said, forcing what he hoped was a friendly smile. "I got that busted drive coil I told you about. I sure appreciate you folks giving me a hand."

"Of course," came a woman's voice from the tinny speaker. "Stand by, I'm opening the door now."

Cazos felt his cheery grin turning darker as the door began to slide away and the painted and posh interior of the OrbitBurner appeared before him. He slid away the blanket and pulled himself through, barrel first.

"I hope you have something to drink on this beautiful boat," he said. "Because—"

Then he closed his mouth as something cold, hard, and flat materialized against his throat.

* * *

"Welcome to the party, Basil." Dava pulled lightly on Basil Roy's shoulder, rotating him to face her. Her blade turned too, so that the point of it poked into his throat. "I was really hoping to find an ally on the other side of that door. But this is even better."

She could feel the others come into the foyer without seeing them. It was the change in the air, the energy. Thompson-Gun, one of her best soldiers, and Lucky Jerk, the pilot with ninety-nine lives. She could feel the tension they brought. Dava had been running on fury since the ModPol ambush that got a bunch of her Space Waste family killed, and most of the rest captured. Including Boss Moses Down, the single person in the universe she truly gave a shit about.

So she really only had two things on her mind at any given moment: get Moses back was the first. The second was to find those responsible for the setup and murder them.

And in her pocket, there burned a handwritten note from Psycho Jack, also known as Jack Fugere, also known as Jax. Fugere, the Fixer. Jax, the hacker.

A note that read: *Basil Roy faked the detector.*

She didn't know what it meant, not exactly anyway. They had stolen fancy new detection equipment from a research station on a moon named Vulca, orbiting a planet called Sirius-5. That equipment was supposed to allow them to detect a ship incoming from a Xarp jump anywhere inside a single star system, from one end to the other. Only it needed the right software to make it work.

And along came Basil Roy. Another hacker, or as he preferred, *solutions architect* or some shit. He had made the equipment work.

They had a target: a supposedly lightly outfitted ModPol transport ship that would Xarp from Barnard to Epsilon Eridani. The ship itself was barely armed, but its cargo was to include a number of experimental weapons to be delivered to a ModPol base where they could be tested in a largely empty system.

The detection equipment had seemed to work, finding the ModPol transport coming out of Xarp. Space Waste moved in, swarming the ship with fighters and boarding it with raiders. And then they found themselves waist deep in a shitstorm of an ambush. ModPol ships came out of hiding and flanked the fighters, while hordes of ModPol Defenders poured out of cargo holds and splintered the boarding parties.

So although she still didn't quite understand how it all went wrong, she knew that the job was a setup. And she knew that the detection equipment's software had to be part of it.

And she knew that the fish wriggling at the end of her spear was the one who forged the software.

"Lemme take that for you," Thompson-Gun said. Dava watched the other woman as she drifted around Roy and gently tugged the pulse rifle from his hands.

"Whoa, whoa, whoa," he said, his hands reflexively going palms out. "I'm on your side. It's me, Basil Roy. The uh, the hacker."

"I thought you preferred *solutions architect*," Dava said.

"Right, that's what I prefer." His eyes rotated to meet hers. "You're Capo Dava, right?"

"What's the story, Roy?" she said. "Got left behind?"

"No. I mean, yes. Rando – I mean, Underboss Jansen – he wanted me to stay behind and um." His right hand twisted through the air. "To collect up the BatCaps. You know, the Battle Capture camera drones."

"We know what BatCaps are," Lucky said.

Dava withdrew the blade. It was a good story, and she thought she might play along. He wouldn't be going anywhere. "So you've seen the recordings?"

"What? Um, no. No, I haven't, uh." He seemed uncertain as to what to do with his hands with the knife no longer at his throat. If there'd been gravity, he might have let that take over and lower them for him, but instead they drifted in front of him limply. "I was supposed to play dead. Just sit in the ship with the systems powered down until it was all clear, then I could go grab the BatCaps."

"Play dead," Dava said. A new level of discomfort crossed Roy's face as his brain struggled to determine whether that'd been a question, statement, or command.

"They left you in a dropship, by yourself?" Thompson said. "To collect up BatCaps?"

"Well, it was the only ship on the *Longhorn* that has a Xarp drive. And I need to get back home after ..." He trailed off, then attempted to puff out his chest a little. "After my mission."

Dava turned her head. If she had to look him in the face while he spouted lies any longer, she would cut his throat too soon.

Thompson picked up the conversation. "Basil, do you have any idea what kind of clusterfuck happened here?"

"Well, I don't – I'm just a computer guy, here," he said. "I mean, I know we lost the fight. But what else would I know about it?"

"Lost the fight?" Thompson said. "We got slaughtered out there!"

"I'm just a computer guy," he repeated, his voice going small and weak. Then it turned curious. "Hey, how did you all get this OrbitBurner?"

Dava turned back to him. "No. No questions from you."

"What? I," he started, then swallowed as he looked at her eyes. "Dava – Capo – we're on the same team. We're all Space Waste here."

At this she closed her eyes. She buried deep the rant about what Space Waste was, and why someone like Basil Roy would never be a part of it. She pushed it down and out of the way, because there was no time to explain these things to a dead man floating. Her family was scattered, and she and two companions were stuck in the wrong fucking system. She needed to push forward.

"Basil, I know the detector was a fake," she said quietly, opening her eyes.

"What?" Lucky said. "What the fuck does that mean, Dava?"

"Shut the fuck up, Lucky," Thompson said. Then she leaned in close to Dava. "What *does* that mean, Capo?"

Roy's mouth went open and closed a few times before any words came out. "Why would you think that?"

"I don't think it, I know it."

His hands went palms up again. "Why, though? Why would anyone fake the detector? And why would you think that? We found the ModPol trans—"

"Because we found the ModPol transport," she said evenly. "We found it so easily, we didn't need a goddamn detector. We found the transport and walked right into an ambush."

This statement stunned the room into silence. She brought the knife back up, not pointing it at Roy, just bringing it to her eye-line so that she could inspect the edge. She'd been sharpening it to pass the time while they drifted about the battlefield in the OrbitBurner. When she sharpened a blade long enough, she wondered how thin that edge could get. Was it possible to get it down to a single layer of molecules? Would that make it so that the blade could cut through anything, any material in the universe?

"It was Jansen!" Roy blurted. "It was his plan, it wasn't

mine. I had nothing to do with any of this! I was a tool, a pawn – don't you see that? I'm nobody!"

"So Jansen knew about the ambush," she said.

"I don't know," he said. "Honestly, I really didn't know what was going to happen. All he told me was to make it look like the detector was working."

"And he gave you the location of the ship?" Lucky said. "The ModPol transport?"

"Yes! Exactly. He told me where it was going to come out of Xarp. All I had to do was make it look like the detector software saw it there. Right place, right time."

"You're not really out here collecting BatCaps," Thompson said.

Roy swallowed. "No. I'm sorry I lied about that. I didn't – I don't know who to trust. But I did my job for him. And now I want out."

"For Jansen," Thompson said.

He hesitated a moment. "Yeah. For Jansen," he said. Then he added quietly, "Now I just want out."

"What a clusterfuck," Thompson said with a sigh.

"People are dead," Dava said. "Because of some fucking game that these pricks are playing. People are dead. And people are locked up."

"I'm sorry," Roy said. "I really – I didn't know. I just did what he rRRRKK—"

The blade went swiftly across, slicing clean through his throat. The momentum caused him to spin slowly, the blood streaming like a fan in the lack of gravity.

"People are dead," she repeated quietly.

* * *

"We need to get Moses back," Dava said. "And the rest. We need to get them back."

Thompson was trying to wrap some kind of plastic cloth around the oozing neck of Basil Roy. "I know, Dava. We will."

Dava shook her head and reached out to steady the stiffening body so that Thompson could accomplish her task. "And we need to get Jansen. I never trusted that guy."

"Yeah, but you don't trust anyone."

Dava tried to aim a scowl at Thompson, but her soldier was focused on tying the plastic tight. "I trust people," she muttered.

Lucky Jerk floated past them carrying a box. "Well, you were right about this guy anyway. He was lying about that stupid detector."

"And if he was lying," Thompson said with a huff as she tugged on the corpse, "then that means Jansen was lying."

Dava drifted silently for a moment, watching them work. Thompson was stuffing the body of Basil Roy into the perishable cold-storage freezer and Lucky was transporting anything of strategic value from the OrbitBurner to the dropship.

She'd been too quick. Too quick to kill. She should have slowly bled him dry, bled as much information out of him as she could've. Jansen, that snake. She wanted to paint him as the ultimate villain in her mind, but she didn't know what the hell he was up to. And she'd slit the throat of the only man who might've had a clue.

She tried to process the situation. ModPol had taken a bunch of Wasters into custody. What they would do with them, she didn't exactly know. And then there was Jansen. He'd fled the scene along with Captain 2-Bit and the rest of the Wasters onboard the carrier – the *Longhorn* – that had brought them to Epsilon Eridani. Who else was in on Jansen's plan? If she had him pegged right, very few. He was playing a role, and that role was as a Space Waste underboss.

What she needed to do was get back to Barnard's Star – that's where the *Longhorn* would've fled – and get to their base in that system. Jansen would be there, but he wouldn't suspect Dava knew anything. He didn't expect Dava to be alive, but then again, he probably wouldn't flinch at her survival instincts. She could let Lucky spin a yarn about their daring escape; he'd already built a reputation for mythical fortune. And they'd say nothing about their encounter with Basil Roy. That missing person would be on Jansen's conscience and no one else's.

She watched the spherical drops of blood quiver and pulse in the air before her. While her mind churned through paranoia and conspiracy, her two companions were focused on the present.

"Okay, body is secure," Thompson said.

Lucky drifted in. "I pre-programmed the autopilot to head back to EE-3 with its emergency beacon on. Someone will pick up the signal near the planet and the docks can override the guidance systems and bring it home."

"Good," Dava said. She thought about leaving Jax a note, but then she wasn't sure what she would say. She could thank him for the tip about Roy, but it was a battle too late. The body would have to be message enough. "Let's go home."

CHAPTER 3

Almost a full week of going through the motions. Playing the part of the public relations officer. Runstom had been supplied with well-edited footage of the battle, composed in some distant marketing cube. Everyone he talked to seemed to be impressed by it, though he suspected some were more impressed by the production quality than the content. He was making progress as far as the job went: administrators were at least willing to schedule further meetings with ModPol Defense. Still, he couldn't shake the sense that they looked at him warily. A salesman. Or worse. Something dangerous, to be kept at a safe distance.

He considered going downstairs to the recreation room to occupy his mind with a game or something to drink, but decided against it. The OrbitBurner had just come back that morning. The Wasters had taken it out, then sent it back on autopilot. He was looking forward to doing something – what, he wasn't sure. It's not like he could arrest them. ModPol didn't even have jurisdiction yet on EE-3, and aside from that, he wasn't a cop any more. He could turn them over to the local constable, but they would be more trouble than the locals could handle. So when the OrbitBurner came back with no one aboard, he admitted to feeling a little relief. They got away with taking his ship for a joyride, but it was better for everyone that they'd gone on their way.

The comm unit blipped and he stepped over to it and looked at the screen. Though the face had become more commonplace in the past week, he was still unused to seeing it. "Sylvia," Runstom said into the mic. "I'll open the main hatch."

Part of him didn't want his mother here. And part of him did. Maintaining a distance had become necessity for them. A physical distance as well as an emotional one. Not that Runstom was much for emotions. Yet seeing her again threatened to open wounds, feelings of shame and abandonment. As he grew older, he learned to understand the reasons why she did what she did: it was the only way to keep them both safe. Her gift to him was that he had a normal life.

Well, a life without a mother, but normal otherwise.

Jax was making good progress with the sketchup application. Runstom tried not to look over his shoulder for too long; the pressure seemed to slow him down. They were on the small bridge of the OrbitBurner. While he waited, Runstom didn't have anything else to do but sit at a terminal himself and peruse flight log files. The Wasters had taken the ship out to the site of the battle. Bounced around for a few hours there. Then a new contact was registered. A military dropship, similar to the model that Runstom and Jax had commandeered back when this whole mess had started. Back when they were on a prison barge, when Jax was being transported off Barnard-4, where'd he been accused of murder, out to a deep ModPol outpost. The barge had been attacked by Space Waste, intent on rescuing one of their own who'd also been arrested on Barnard-4.

Runstom and Jax had barely escaped with their lives, and only because they stole a Space Waste ship. An old military model, retrofitted for modern crime. The thing was a flying box of nothing. It'd been originally built for a single purpose: hurtle soldiers across space quickly and drop them onto a surface. Its most welcomed feature was a Xarp drive, necessary for making the long interstellar distances in a somewhat reasonable amount of time.

The same type of ship had appeared on the site of the battle, according to the OrbitBurner's logs. Stood to reason that it belonged to the Wasters. The two ships had docked together. The other departed. The OrbitBurner was set with an automated course back to EE-3, where it had switched control over to a station that had guided it down to the dock. No passengers.

Why the Wasters had bothered with the courtesy of returning his ship, Runstom didn't know. He suspected Jax had gotten close to them. Not friendly, but close enough to earn their respect.

"Hello, boys," Sylvia said as she stepped onto the bridge.

Runstom stood. "Jax is just working on a sketch of someone he met while he was with Space Waste."

"Basil Roy," Jax said. "A programmer. I'm just about done."

She smiled faintly and nodded. "And this Basil Roy?" she said. "He didn't fit in?"

Jax laughed. "No, not so much."

"He wrote some code that was supposed to scan for the ModPol transport ship," Runstom said.

"But he faked the interface," Jax added.

"So it led them to the right spot, just as the ModPol ship came out of Xarp."

She looked from one to the other. "Ah, so the software didn't need to work. This Basil Roy knew the expected coordinates that the ship would drop into all along."

Runstom's hands didn't know what to do with themselves. He wished Jax would finish already. "Can I get you something to drink?" he said to Sylvia.

"Oh no, Stanley dear, I'm fine."

"Uh," Jax said. "I think I got it."

He stood up and stepped back to admire his work. Sylvia strode toward the screen. The movement created a buffer that kept Runstom from leaning in to have a look for himself.

"I noticed that you were connected to the local network through the dock," she said, sitting down at the console. "I'm going to route you through to—" she started, then paused and looked from side to side. It was a small amount of movement, and a small pause, but Runstom took the gesture for what it was.

"Now I see where Stan gets his paranoia from," Jax said with a grin. Runstom shot a glare at him.

Sylvia chuckled. "I'm going to route you through to a more secure network. Once I establish an encrypted tunnel, we'll have access to a few databases that might have the info we're looking for."

Jax's smile faded as he leaned closer. Runstom wasn't sure if the other man was growing more fearful, more curious, or both. He knew there would be questions later on. Questions Runstom sure the hell couldn't answer. Like what databases his mother was talking about. How she got them. Who else had access to this so-called secure network.

Now that Sylvia was planted in front of the terminal,

Runstom and Jax had no choice but to let her work. Runstom pulled the B-fourean back so they could talk without disrupting her. He didn't have a solid plan, but he was working through some possibilities in his mind.

"When she figures out who this guy is," Runstom said. "We might know why he's inside. What his mission is."

"*When* she figures out who he is?" Jax said, whispering so as not to offend Sylvia, though she probably heard anyway. "He could be nobody."

Runstom's brain wasn't ready for that. "He's somebody. He's undercover. It's the only explanation."

"Maybe." Jax shook his head, then his posture slumped in submission. "You're right. It's the only explanation that makes any sense."

Runstom reached up to put a hand on the taller man's shoulder. "Listen, Jax. I need you to go back in."

He pulled back, glaring. "Back into what?"

"Into Space Waste."

"You're fucking insane." Jax no longer made any attempt to quiet his voice. "No way. No, no, no."

"Listen, Jax. This guy could be one of us. If he's undercover, he's there on a ModPol mission and he may need our help."

"Forget him, Stan. You promised me I could go back to Terroneous—"

"I know," Runstom said, his voice stern. He worked to soften it. "I know. And you will. But something is really wrong with this whole thing and I think this Basil Roy might be the only clue we have. He led Space Waste into a slaughter. They could be hunting for a mole right now, and it means he doesn't have much time. And I know he knows a helluva lot more than—"

Jax took a step back, shaking his head. "What is it with you? If this guy is undercover, then that's his choice. There's no way I'm going back in that den of psychopaths to find out if he needs a hand!"

"They're not psychopaths," Runstom said. The statement shocked himself as it came out of his mouth. "They let you live. They even sent back the OrbitBurner. They trust you."

"Dava let me live," he said firmly. "Dava might trust me – well, to be honest, I don't think she trusts anyone. And even if she did, don't you get what's going on here? Space Waste is falling apart. They're going to be at each other's throats trying to find out why they were ambushed."

"All the more reason to get in there now and—"

"Why do you even care?" Jax said, extending his arms to their full wingspan, nearly banging them on the low ceiling of the OrbitBurner's bridge. "Seriously, Stanford! Tell me why it matters to you."

"Because I'm sick of not knowing what the fuck is going on!"

They stared at each other in silence. Runstom hadn't shouted, but when he replayed the words in his head, he could hear the frayed edges.

Jax's mouth opened and closed. His eyes narrowed at Runstom, then he simply shook his head. He left the bridge through the stairwell that led to the recreation room below.

And there it was. What was it that Runstom was really after? He stood alone at the back of the bridge, his mother Sylvia working quietly through her databases on the other side. She heard all, there was no doubt. What would she say? He suspected she might be the only one that could understand his motivations. His desire to put the pieces together. His inability to cope when they didn't fit.

Then again, she had a mind for the gray, and Runstom's mind sought black and white. He frowned at himself, his stubbornness rising from within. So what if he just *had* to know what was going on? So what if he was looking for an explanation? For a case to solve?

So what if that wasn't his job?

* * *

Jax paced around the recreation room furiously. How much more could he take of that blockheaded Stanford Runstom? The man was in constant detective mode, and he wasn't even a cop any more. He was a goddamn public relations officer.

"Sick of not knowing what's going on," Jax muttered. "How about sick of running for your life? Sick of being in hiding? Sick of never …"

He was alone but even still, he couldn't finish the thought. His eyes caught the liquor cabinet. It probably wasn't the best way to cope with his souring mood, but it was a way.

The bottles in the cabinet sat in cozy-looking mounds of fluff, with a pair of stylish straps crossing over each. Designed to hold everything in place in zero-G, Jax realized, with the benefit of appearing plush and expensive. Looking at them made him think of his last encounter with Dava and the other Wasters. They'd hid down in this rec room, Runstom none the wiser, focused on piloting from the bridge above.

The thing that stood out most in Jax's mind was Dava's claim over experience with fear. Jax had been living it for a year, always on the run, always looking over his shoulder. He'd thought he'd earned a mastery over the subject. Dava reminded him he knew nothing about it.

He knew very little about her; the first thing to come to mind was always that she was a bloodthirsty assassin. The number of times she hadn't killed him was growing uncomfortably large. She was black, that was the next obvious thing. Which really meant she was born on Earth. In the colonized systems, Barnard and Sirius – and now Eridani – that made her almost as rare as a greened-skin space-born like Runstom. Dava and Moses were the only Earth-born people Jax had ever talked to. He'd seen a few on holovid of course, and had even seen a few in passing while on Terroneous. He tried to imagine what that was like, to be so rare. No, to be so outnumbered. Maybe that was the fear Dava was talking about.

If Dava lived in fear, she certainly hid it well. And just because she had grown up worse off than Jax, he decided he'd definitely gained some knowledge of fear in recent times.

"So fuck it," he said, and unstrapped a bottle of something brown.

He was going to insist on getting back to Terroneous; that's what he decided as he took a gulp of something spicy and fiery and in a distant way, a little like rotten wood (a fragrance he'd never known living in the domes, but had recently learned while living in a tiny, shoddy apartment in Stockton). The distance from Eridani would be measured in weeks, even at the highest Xarp speeds. He had no money himself. Runstom carried a company card, and that was taking care of expenses while they were on Eridani. He didn't know how to get back home, not without Runstom's help.

"Home." He tried the word aloud since he'd caught it popping into his head. The idea was starting to sink in. Or perhaps worm in, chewing its way through his mind and body and rooting there: *you can have a home again. All you have to do is go back to Terroneous and call it home.*

He took another swig. Surely Runstom would see reason. Jax's part in this whole mess was over. Couldn't he just go in peace?

And that's when the rest of that conversation with Dava came back to him. When he'd asked her how she managed to live her whole life alongside fear, her answer was *anger*.

A small part of him fed on that. He'd been wronged time and time again, by criminals like X and Jenna Zarconi, by ModPol, by Space Waste. He was a tool, a playing piece, a disposable nothing to all of them. They took advantage of people like Jax, and it wasn't fair.

And that's why he'd given up Basil Roy's mischief to Dava, because he wanted to stir things up, to help make a mess of it. Runstom wanted to solve the mystery, to unravel and decode all the games that the galaxy was playing, but Jax just wanted to break them.

He could go back in, go back and play the malleable fool, the timid operator. He could use his gift – the invisibility of the weak – and wreak havoc.

He put the brown bottle back and selected another one. This time a clear liquid, that burned with just as much fire – probably more so, since he expected it to taste like water – and an aftertaste that made him think of medicine and fruit. Where did all this stuff come from? He looked at the label for an answer: *Ethereal Vodka, distilled in Nuzwick.*

Nuzwick. Another town on Terroneous. It was one of the many that Jax visited when he and Lealina Warpshire traversed the entire moon, resetting the configuration on hundreds of magnetic field sensors. Lealina, because she was the acting director of the Terroneous Environment Observation Bureau, and Jax because he was the mysterious B-fourean who figured out that millions of lives were not in danger from a flux in the satellite's magnetic field. That in fact, the reason the TEOB's sensors were all entering an alarm state was that they were running out of memory due to a shared default configuration that was created by engineers who never had to use their creations in the real world.

There was a terminal at a polished wooden desk off to one side of the room. Jax capped the bottle and secured it back in its cozy case, then made his way toward the terminal, only tripping twice. It turned out the desk wasn't real wood, just high-quality plastic colored with a wood grain. It would have fooled him a year ago, but on Terroneous, everything was really real wood. Warping, rotting, insect-infested plant matter. It was not as glamorous as rich domers liked to believe.

He slumped into the chair and flicked the terminal on. He wasn't sure what to expect, but after poking around for a few minutes, he found a messaging app. If he could get a note to Lealina, somehow everything would be a little bit easier to deal with. But that meant he'd need to send something via drone mail. Did they have d-mail on EE-3 yet? Of course they would. Establishing a d-mail station would be one of the primary goals of a new settlement. Yet the few moments Runstom had left him alone, he'd been unable to find any public d-mail information. Despite being a library-bar combination, the *Bibliohouse* only offered access to a local mail system.

This settlement was about as secretive as it could get, and Jax wondered if there were some clandestine restrictions about sending mail off-planet. It was secretive enough that he'd only heard about it in passing in the last few years, but he had no idea how far along it was in development until he arrived about a week before. It was technically part of the Earth Colony Alliance, like the domes of Barnard-3, Barnard-4, and Sirius-5. With thousands of workers already living on-site, it wouldn't be long before an exodus was made: the richest of the population making the trek out to the brand-new, state-of-the-art domes.

He found the dock portal on the terminal, which gave him access to a few local resources. He felt a thrill of electricity tingle through his chest when he saw a d-mail messaging system. The feeling quickly slipped away as he was unable to access it.

He sighed and rubbed his eyes with his palms. The stuff milling around in his stomach was not helping him think. It was probably an even worse idea to mix the brown and the clear. The two liquids, thrashing around in the same system—

Before a dizzy spell forced him to slide completely out of his chair, he grabbed the edges and bolted upright. He stared at the screen. A crude interface, with a few icons and small patches of text. But that was just the interface. He had found the dock access. The terminal was just a thin screen and an input scanner. The scanner could be toggled between a few different input modes: swiping holographic icons, hand signals, and touch-typing. It wasn't an independent computer – the few months on Terroneous had him thinking that way, that there were uses for computers that ran on their own, without servers – it was a ship terminal. The actual network of processors would be buried somewhere in the bowels of the OrbitBurner. The terminal on the bridge and the terminal in front of Jax were essentially the same computer.

Which meant that if Sylvia set up access to any external systems, Jax should be able to find them from this terminal.

He switched to full typing mode on the input scanner. He stabbed at a few key combinations he knew of until one of them worked, causing the screen to display the version information for the interface and the underlying operating system. "Star Sprinter Systems, OS 19.4," he read aloud. Nothing he'd ever used, but a lot of operating software was derived from the same base code. Based on the key-combo that worked to bring up the version, he was guessing it was a Phoenix OS derivative. He hadn't worked with that since school, but he'd been immersed for a few years back then, so it was just a matter of dusting off a few brain cells.

After some misremembered key-combos and lots of trial and error, he brought up a command prompt. There he was at least able to fail, but fail in a way that gave him semi-useful error messages and help text. It was technobabble to the average person, but if Jax read an error a few times, he could make sense of it, or at least take a guess. After he'd groped his way around the system for a few minutes, he figured out how to see the external mappings. The dock portal was clearly labeled as *dock-portal-618*, but there was another more cryptic mapping called *sr-2896*. Jax checked it for activity, and there was definitely a bunch of traffic running through it.

He opened up another channel on the same mapping, which took him a few tries. Once it was done, he found a common command-based text editor, usually used for system administration, but sometimes used for d-mail composition. Sure enough, the editor's mailer plugin was able to scan the channel he created on *sr-2896* and find a d-mail service. Now all he had to do was type up a message.

At that point, he was a little more thankful for the liquor, because it helped lubricate his words. He had two goals: the first was to let Lealina know that he was okay and that he was trying to get back to Terroneous by any means possible. The second was to disguise all of that so that it didn't sound like a personal d-mail from Jack Jackson, alias Jack Fugere, the fugitive from ModPol and Space Waste associate.

He just needed a couple of details. During his short time with Lealina, he'd learned they'd both attended the South Haven Institute of Technology on Barnard-4. On a more intimate level, he'd learned that non-domers found dome life *claustrophobic* – a concept that was a bit foreign to Jax, and really only sunk in when he had to hide deep underground beneath the TEOB Magma Center, where networks of tight tunnels were carved out by geology researchers and their robotic assistants.

To the Director of the Terroneous Environment Observation Bureau —

Your recent trials concerning the malfunction of Pulson Integrated Sensor Systems magnetic field detection equipment has made news all around the known galaxy, including out here to Epsilon Eridani-3. As we're in the process of establishing our own environmental observation agency in this newly developing colony, we wanted to ensure we learn from the near tragedy that you and your team managed to avoid there on Terroneous. I just wanted to reach out and thank you for your work and for not being afraid to share your story with the rest of the galaxy. As my Life Support Systems professor at the South Haven Institute of Technology used to say, if you can't learn from history, then what the hell are you doing in my classroom?

I must return to the work of establishing our underground research center, though I must confess I popped up to write this d-mail partly to get out of those tunnels. Quite claustrophobic, indeed!

Wishing you the very best,

— Kay Klosky

The name at the end would be his last guarantee Lealina would know the message was from him. If she were to look it up – and she would, if he piqued her interest with such a bizarre d-mail – she'd find that there was a Kay Klosky employed as a librarian at the Stockton Public Library, one of Jax's favorite haunts.

He re-read the message a few times and then tapped the send command before he could change his mind. There were no errors, and a confirmation came back letting him know the message was enqueued with some d-mail facility in some unknown location on EE-3. It was out of his hands. Depending on the facility's capabilities, the message could go out on a drone within a day, and then it would be another day or two for the Zarp-capable micro-ship to zip from the Eridani system to the Barnard system.

There was a small amount of relief flowing through Jax in that moment. He felt purged. He also felt thirsty, but not for anything with alcohol in it; for once he felt thirsty for some honest nourishment. He stepped away from the terminal and wandered around for a moment before he came across a heavy door with a warning sign about the importance of keeping the seal due to perishable goods within.

The door came open with the touch of a button. The first thing Jax saw inside the refrigerated pantry had already perished.

CHAPTER 4

"This is him," Sylvia said, leaning back from the terminal.

Runstom stopped pacing around the bridge and came up behind her to get a look at the screen. "He looks just like the sketch. Don't they usually do some facial surgery or something when they send someone undercover?"

She leaned back and quirked a silver eyebrow at him. "*I* didn't have surgery when I went in."

His face grew hot. "No, of course not. I just – well, I've heard sometimes they do."

The corner of her mouth bunched in a smirk and she turned back to the screen. "Yes, you're right, of course. They often do facial surgery. Sometimes it's just temporary, but that can be detected. Other times it's permanent. That's when they really need to conceal an identity. But it wasn't so much the sketch that found him." She pointed to the screen.

"Tim Cazos," Runstom read. "You're saying you found him by his name?"

"The man's alias is a crude encryption of his real name,"

she said, tut-tutting. "Tim Cazos, alias Basil Roy. The database scans for aliases when it's matching facial properties. Part of that alias-matching algorithm looks for patterns like re-used letters or similar word segments, things like that."

Runstom sighed through his nose. "I don't see it."

"Don't feel bad, most wouldn't." She tapped at the screen and a small window opened with an explanation. "Take all the consonants in his name: T, M, C, Z, S," she read. "Shift them back one letter, so T becomes S? That makes S, L, B, Y, R. Mix in the vowels: A, I, O. Jumble them around and you get B, A, S, I, L, R, O, Y. Basil Roy."

There was a low burn in Runstom's gut. He'd skipped lunch when he found out the OrbitBurner had returned, and he hadn't been eating much anyway, once he'd found out that the planet's main source of meat was slippery, tube-shaped, many-legged aquatic creatures endearingly called muckbugs.

An encryption of a name – was this the kind of thing he was supposed to be looking for? If he were a detective? "For fu— uh," he coughed. "I mean, really."

"Mmm," Sylvia said. "For fuck's sake is right. Obviously, he's a software engineer. Or was."

"And now he works for ModPol."

"Yes and no." She swished some windows around, obscuring the face and pulling up a dossier. "He's a hacker. He'd been an engineer for years, but started to dabble in illegal activities a few years back. Cryptocurrency fraud. He got too greedy, as people do, and trifled with the wrong crowd. Landed himself in a sting. He flipped on some of his mates, in exchange for a reduced sentence. But there were strings attached."

"They wanted him to go undercover?"

"Exactly. But they didn't tell him it would be Space Waste."

Runstom shook his head. "No, of course not. He probably thought he'd be going in to bust some other hackers."

"Naturally, he'd think so." She tapped at the screen again. "Note the objection to the assignment."

He looked, but the language was so vague, it didn't really say anything. The actual assignment had to be secured, and even in this confidential file, it was obscured. "It doesn't say, but it must have been the Space Waste assignment."

"Must have been."

She eased the chair away from the terminal slightly and turned to him. Her eyes pierced through him silently. It was an old game. One he couldn't believe he even remembered. There was a detail he was missing, and she was prompting him to find it. *Use your eyes, Stanley.* This is what she was saying. Even when he was younger, when he was her little cop-in-training, he hated this game. Knowing that he was missing something somehow made it even harder to see.

He broke from her gaze and looked at the screen. The photo, partially obscured by the dossier. Crimes, arrest, trial details, sentencing, known accomplices. And there it was.

"What the fuck."

She smiled, though there wasn't much amusement on her face. "Jenna Zarconi," she said.

"Which means he's probably one of X's." Runstom turned from the screen, clutching the stabbing in his temples. "How is it possible? What does X have to do with this whole mess with Space Waste?"

"I don't know, Stanley. With X, it goes deep. It's several rounds into a long game. Could be a favor to be repaid, or the repayment of a favor."

He slumped, his shoulders like sacks of sand. Somehow in all of this mess, X was involved. Mark Xavier Phonson. The well-connected crooked cop. The man who'd tried to kill Runstom and Jax on Sirius-5 to cover up his own messes. Messes created by Jenna Zarconi when she'd spoofed those same connections and pulled off a mass murder by asphyxiating an entire subdome block. A crime she'd almost gotten away with, given that the whole thing had looked like the life-support operator on duty was responsible for the slaughter.

"Stan!" Jax appeared suddenly, as though aware that Runstom was thinking about him. He doubled over and panted, managing to point at the stairwell. "Body. There's a body. In your freezer."

Seconds later, they stood in front of the cold-storage unit. A man was hanging from a large shelving unit. Strapped to it with lengths of all-purpose elastic ropes. Clothes bunching oddly against the restraints.

"He was bound while in zero-G," Runstom realized aloud.

He glanced down. The floor under his feet. Turned slightly to scan the rest of the room. Something caught his eye and he knelt. Small, rust-colored circles. The body was bleeding when they moved it.

He stood and went into the store room. He wished he had some gloves. Instead, he glanced around the room and found a rectangle of stretchy plastic used for sealing up food. He wrapped it around one hand and lifted the head on the body.

He'd seen the sketch and the matching photo from Sylvia's database. "Jax," he prompted.

Jax took a cautious step forward, but didn't come much closer. "Basil Roy."

Runstom lowered the head. "His real name is Tim Cazos. I guess we can thank your Space Waste friends for this."

"Is he – he's dead?"

Runstom looked at Jax, ready to burst at him that yes, this man was dead by those Wasters' hands. But there was enough fear on the B-fourean's face. He turned back to the corpse. "Looks to be a laceration across the throat. It would have been quick."

"You'll have to get rid of the body," Sylvia said from behind them. "Off planet."

He stared at it. The storage had kept it from decomposing, or even bloating much. His brain didn't seem to want to process the words of his mother. This was a murder victim. A murder victim on his own ship. She expected him to make it disappear?

There was a burst of static from somewhere in the recreation room behind him. A speaker came to life.

"Uh, this is the control room of the EE-3-618 docking facility. We have, uh, orders to override your controls. Um. Do you want to say something?"

"What the hell?" Jax said, his voice rising. Runstom held up a hand to still him.

"This is ModPol." A different voice. *"We're coming aboard to inspect the ship. Do not attempt to depart. The maglocks have been engaged."*

Runstom strode toward the nearest wall-mounted comm unit, passing Sylvia as he went. "I thought ModPol doesn't have jurisdiction here yet."

"Not really," she said. "But for some people, they believe it's just a matter of time. They figure they might as well start developing trust by giving ModPol some 'professional leeway'."

He switched the comm to broadcast on all-call. "Whoever is out there, you have no jurisdiction here. You will *not* board this vessel."

"What's the matter, Stanley? We're supposed to be on the same side, you know."

The static and the tinny speakers had obscured the voice before, but now it registered. "McManus."

* * *

Jax watched Sylvia spring to a nearby terminal and whip through the interface. "They have everything locked out. Even the door."

"The maintenance hatch?" Runstom said.

"Can't be locked remotely."

"A safety feature," Jax guessed. He could feel his muscles tensing in anticipation of bursting for this one known exit.

Runstom gave them both a look. "Then that's where they'll be coming in."

Sylvia stood. "Then we hide Jax. And the body. Quickly."

"Where?" Jax said.

"This is an expensive ship," she said. "There must be safe-rooms. Something well hidden."

"No," Runstom said quietly. His face grew taut.

Jax wanted to shake him. "No, there are no safe-rooms?"

"No, we're not hiding."

There was a pause, the space of a breath, and Jax couldn't stand the silence. "I'll give up." He heard his voice crack as he spoke. "You don't need to go down for this. I can tell them I stowed away on your ship during the raid."

"No, goddammit!" Runstom's eyes narrowed with a ferocity Jax had not seen before in the man. "This *ship* is not their jurisdiction. This *dock* is not their jurisdiction. This goddamn *planet* is not their jurisdiction. Maybe it will be someday, but not today."

He stood there for a moment and Jax didn't know how to react. He felt frozen in place, his skin running cold from the open storage unit. Then Runstom moved, striding with such purpose that Jax and Sylvia were swept up behind him.

When he reached the maintenance hatch door, he cranked the wheel and opened it. The airlock was stained oddly, and Jax thought it was like some abstract art piece or something for a moment, before he realized it must be Basil Roy's blood. What had Runstom said his real name was? Tim. Tim Cazos. That's whose blood had sprayed into the airlock in zero-G, hanging there until the craft accelerated, at which point it drifted to one side and splashed against the inside of the outer hatch door.

"What are you going to do, Stanley?" Sylvia asked carefully.

"Stan, it's not worth it," Jax said, lightly touching Runstom's arm. "If you have to turn me over, just do it."

He couldn't believe he was even saying it. Only moments ago, he was arguing for his freedom, fighting to get back to Terroneous and as far away from this mess as possible. But hearing that ModPol was here now, coming after Runstom, with his mother in the room, Jax felt something he hadn't felt since his last day on Terroneous. They were after him, and he was going to drag the people who meant most to him in the galaxy down with him. He couldn't let that happen, as terrified as he was of being taken into ModPol custody.

Runstom turned and gave him a shove, hard, his strong hand into Jax's chest. Jax stumbled back, almost falling, bracing himself against the corridor wall outside of the airlock.

The flat fingers curled into a point. "You stay back."

He glanced at Sylvia who took a step back herself, not from a place of fear, but something else. Jax tried to read her face and the best he could come up with was that she was showing respect. This ship belonged to Runstom. It was his house. His rules.

The wheel on the outer hatch turned and the door swung slowly inward.

"McManus," Runstom said through gritted teeth. "What are you doing on my ship?"

Jax felt the energy draining from his body and his spirit. "This motherfucker," he mumbled. There was no giving up with these people. They wouldn't rest until they dragged him in. They were never going to forgive him for his part in the giant fuck-up that ModPol created when they wrongfully arrested him and forced him to become a fugitive.

"It's Sergeant McManus," he said. "Remember, Stanley? I'm a Sergeant now."

"ModPol has no jurisdiction here," Runstom said evenly.

McManus huffed. "ModPol is everywhere. Haven't you heard? Or have you not been watching yourself on the holovid broadcasts?"

Runstom's stance got even more tense. "Jared. I want you off this ship."

"Of course, Stanley." He pointed at Jax. "Give me Jackson and I'll be on my way."

Runstom was quiet for a moment, and Jax could practically hear the wheels turning in his head. "You came alone."

McManus's face contorted and he stiffened. "I have a pilot with me."

Runstom took a step forward. "The premises of this ship are private property. You are an intruder. I'm going to give you ten seconds."

This caused McManus to flinch and cock his head slightly. "What's supposed to happen in ten seconds?" When Runstom didn't answer, he waved dismissively. "You know what? It doesn't matter. I'm not leaving here without Jacks—"

"Ten."

Runstom launched himself at McManus, slamming him into the wall on the left side of the hatchway. Jax felt himself tense, but he couldn't get his body to move. They grappled for a second and then their bodies collided to the floor, though through which man's force, Jax couldn't tell. They were both solidly built, but by Runstom's own admission, he'd not kept up his cop physique since leaving Justice for his public relations position in Defense.

Sylvia took a step forward, as though she might do something or say something, but her mouth went tight. Runstom freed an arm from the tangle and slammed a fist into McManus's cheek with an audible pop. He reached back for another punch, but McManus shook off the first hit and managed to block the second.

Runstom grabbed the blocking arm and hooked an elbow up and under it in some kind of locking move. McManus responded by lowering his body and heaving his shoulder into Runstom's midsection, whose back bounced against the wall, forcing out a grunt. His hold loosened slightly, just enough for the muscle-bound McManus to wrench his arm free.

The two straightened up then and traded blows, jabs and hooks crossing between them. Jax had only ever been in a fight once in his life, back in the domes on B-4, and he had been too drunk to remember exactly what happened, only that the following day his hand hurt and his eye was black. The way Runstom and McManus moved – ducking, punching, swaying – suggested they knew much more about what they were doing. Jax felt like he should step in, use the numbers advantage against McManus, but hesitated. Would he just be in the way? More likely to hurt than to help? To get hurt? He glanced at Sylvia, who seemed to be going through the same deliberations; though her flexing hands suggested a different thought process than Jax's raw fear.

Runstom took advantage of an overzealous swing from McManus, hooking the arm and spinning him around. He grappled McManus from behind, placing him in some other kind of hold that bound up his arms. For a moment Jax thought it was over, perhaps because the action had come to a standstill and Runstom had the upper hand. But then suddenly their combined forms compressed as McManus bent down, and Runstom's legs swung out. They sprung upward in a swinging motion and Runstom flipped over the top of McManus, slamming down onto the floor on his back with a yelp of pain.

Jax's fear evaporated in a puff and he lunged forward, reaching his long arms for McManus's throat. The cop spun, whipping a gun from his holster and aiming it at Jax's face in one motion. Jax froze, some part of his brain locking in fear for its life, another part lost in studying the sudden but intricate details of the weapon's design. Tiny valleys carved into a mixture of metal and plastic. A tunnel that quickly blurred into darkness. The gleam of the overhead lights against the sheen of the surface.

Distant movement jarred his paralysis. Runstom was flipping himself over, lunging for McManus. He tackled him through the gut, and both men hit the floor beneath Jax's feet. The gun hung loosely in McManus's hand, his arm extended to one side. Jax reached for it, but it moved quickly, the butt slamming into the back of Runstom's head. It drew back and Jax flinched, then tried to grab it a full second too late. It slammed down in the same spot again.

They rolled over, Runstom dazed, McManus in control. The gun swung around in Jax's direction again, and though it didn't fire, he flinched again and slid back onto his ass. McManus pressed his advantage by standing to his full height and aiming the weapon down at Jax.

Runstom groaned and rolled over, putting one knee against the floor to prepare to stand. McManus's gun swung to meet him.

"Have you ever been shot by a stungun?" he said. "Do you know how much it fucking hurts?"

Jax scrambled to his feet, but not before a bolt of white shot forth and struck Runstom, his body jolting against the wall in a fit of shaking. Jax grabbed McManus by the wrist that held the gun, but the cop's elbow shot out sharply, landing in Jax's midsection with a painful and staggering shock unlike any he'd felt before. He fought to draw breath and fell to one knee.

McManus swung the gun around the room with narrowed eyes, seeking out other targets. Jax managed to turn his head and though his vision wavered, he could see Sylvia was gone.

The cop grunted in apparent satisfaction and holstered his weapon. He came up behind Jax and grabbed his shoulder. Jax tried weakly to resist, but the ground came suddenly up to meet his face with a painful smack. He felt his arms get pulled out from under his body and yanked behind, then felt some kind of binding slide over his wrists.

"Don't worry, they aren't shock cuffs," McManus said. He hooked his hands under Jax's armpits and with a grunt, hoisted him to his feet. "I decided to go back to the old-fashioned style. Strict-cuffs. The more you pull against them, the tighter they get. They're not standard issue anymore. Too many broken bones."

Without resisting, but just through the shifting because of the unnatural position his arms were in, Jax felt the oddly-warm straps constricting. He tried to breathe, to relax his muscles, but he was still having trouble from the blow that landed just below his chest. The walls blurred by as he felt himself pushed and pulled through the outer airlock hatch and into the space beyond.

* * *

Runstom bathed in pain for eternity. Every nerve screaming electric. His vision stuttered like a video on a short loop. His ears were full of a swirling buzz, a living, organic noise.

When he could feel anything other than pain, it was numbness. It felt as though ages had passed, but he knew from his training that the effects of a standard stungun lasted about a quarter of an hour.

"Never," he coughed when he could get his throat to do anything more than grunt. "Felt."

"There was a time when everyone coming up through basic training had to get zapped." His mother's words. Understandable, but distorted. "They wanted every cop to know how it felt. They stopped doing it though. Better not to know, then you won't hesitate to use it when you need to."

"Fuck." Bright shapes punched their way into his head whenever he opened his eyes. "Mick ... McManus."

"Take a deep breath, Stanley. Not into the chest." He felt a warm pressure on his stomach and realized it was her hand. "Here. Pull the breath into the belly. Slowly. That's right. Now hold. Four. Three. Two. One. Now out, slowly. Push it out from the belly. All the way out. Again."

He wanted to brush her away, get to his feet, get after McManus. But he humored her. Breathed like she told him to. The pain became less like fire and more like ache.

"McManus," he said when he thought his voice would work. "He'll get away."

"At the Department of Agricultural Systems, it's our job to scan the surface of EE-3. We measure everything. There's a small fleet of satellites up there." He tried to interrupt her with a wheeze, but she waved him quiet and continued. "Inside the satellites are brigades of these tiny drones that we can program on the fly – like in case we need to track down a specific anomaly, or even just send a message. There are hundreds of these innocuous little buggers floating about in low orbit. I have a subroutine that tells a drone to track a ship, attach to it, and begin pulsing a beacon."

"I didn't know you could do that," he whispered through measured exhalation. He held back on asking *why*.

"Naturally, I coerced someone into creating the original routine for me," she said. There was too much left out of the word *naturally* and he wanted to press her, but he was occupied with the breath-holding and counting after an inhalation. She swept away the opportunity for further inquiry with a wave of the hand. "All I have to do is upload the signature of the ship I want to track. It has to be in EE-3's orbit for me to reach it with a drone."

"So you've done this before?"

"There are people I've felt an urge to keep tabs on, yes."

He laughed, or rather made the motions of laughing, expelling a small hiss. "Still paranoid."

"Still alive."

"So wait." He was still in a lump, half-lying on the floor, half-propped against the wall. He tried to shift his weight around so that he could look more directly at her. "You're saying you can track McManus's ship?"

"There was only one ModPol ship in the public traffic reports. An intersystem patroller."

"Intersystem. Special ops ship?" Most of ModPol's Xarp-capable ships were the big ones, large transports. Patrollers in general could only do sub-warp, but there were a few special models. Oversized patrollers that weren't much but guns and engines. Runstom had only flown one once, unsimulated. McManus on the other hand could barely fly a standard patroller, but he'd admitted that he had a pilot with him.

"He left the ship in orbit and came down in a shuttle. The same shuttle is heading back up now."

Runstom strained to get his legs to cooperate. "We need to get up there, now."

As he moved to get up from the floor, she pushed him into a sitting position. It was a demonstration of his weakened condition: a woman in her sixties dominating him physically. A lightning strike of pain flashed through his head. His reward for making the effort to stand. He sucked in a breath to chase away the black clouds at the edges of his vision.

"We're still mag-locked," she said. "The dock controller told me they're on a timer, so we can lift off soon. But not right this minute. So just sit still."

He closed his eyes. Tried to slow his breathing. Slow the blood pounding heavy through his chest and into his temples. He allowed himself to feel the comfort of her hand on his shoulder. "Okay, Mom."

They were both silent for a few moments and Runstom tried to empty his head, tried to think of nothing. Finally she spoke. "You're going to be leaving soon."

"Well, the work here is done anyway," he said unenthusiastically. "Next steps are outlined."

"Everyone loved you."

He rolled his eyes. "It was too easy." There had been several meetings with various administrators. He showed them the polished recordings of ModPol Defense in action. Evidently it had been more convincing than the previous attempts from the marketing department of ModPol Justice. Still, it wasn't that everyone was enthusiastic. It was more that they simply didn't question any of it. Nodding heads and handshakes. "Did you have something to do with that?"

She shrugged. "I may have convinced some people to hear you out. I knew this visit was going to be short – with Jax here with you – and I didn't want you to be delayed."

He swallowed. "I have to go."

"I know," she said. "I know. I wish you didn't have to, but you do."

There it was. The fear he'd been fighting for the past week. Fear that at any moment he would leave and then he wouldn't see her again for some unknown length of time. Months, years. Maybe never. Never was always a possibility.

"You're going to be here for a while," he said, hopeful. Just knowing where she was, it was something.

"Probably," she said. "Nothing is ever certain, especially not ... well, you know."

Not for someone in witness protection. "Well, in any case. Maybe I can make it back here sometime. And maybe you'll still be here."

She took away her hand and his arm felt cold from its absence. "Listen, Stanley. We don't have long, so I'm going to talk to you about something."

"Are you sure—"

"Just listen." She stood, partially turning away from him. "You're being used."

"Mother," he said weakly.

"To some, there are many pieces on the board, and you are just one of them. You're not a person, you're a piece. You're useful, but you're disposable."

"What do you mean by that? Disposable?"

"I don't mean they'll kill you. They aren't killers. They're always working the long game. Always the long game. And their game never stops changing, never stops evolving."

"Are you talking about ModPol? Defense?"

"Defense, Justice, all of ModPol, all the rest," she said. "Anyone who is securing their position in this galaxy. Because it's not as safe a place as the domers would like to believe."

"Yeah, no shit." Runstom's head was still thick, but it had lightened enough for him to stand, using the wall to brace himself.

She turned to him. "X is different."

He pinched the bridge of his nose, squeezing his eyes shut tight. "X. I don't want to hear about X. He should be in prison for life."

"Mark Xavier Phonson is good at the game, but only out of necessity. He runs on survival instinct. Through raw coldness and manipulation – and pure luck – he is still out there. Doing what it takes to stay alive."

"He's a real scumbag," Runstom said, feeling his lip curl up as he said it.

"He's probably afraid of you."

"That's good."

"No, it's not good." He opened his eyes as he felt her touch again on his arm. She drew close. "Fear breeds desperation. And when men like X become desperate, blood spills. That cop – McManus? You knew him?"

"Jared McManus. We used to work together. He was on B-4 with me. First day on the murder scene."

She nodded. "He was probably supposed to kill you both. That's how X would want it done. But he's still a cop, that McManus. He's no killer."

"So he'll drag Jax to some ModPol outpost."

"No," she said, shaking her head and looking down. Like she was disappointed something wasn't getting through to Runstom. "He's under X's thumb, that's why he came all the way out here. He'll take Jax directly to X, most likely. Someplace secret."

"Damn it." With a groan, he pushed himself away from the wall. "I need to move."

She walked him to the bridge, which was an arduous journey since they had to go up the stairs. He cursed the over-fashionable ship for the millionth time. They could have put a lift down the middle of the thing, but no doubt the designers thought a lift would have sullied their vision or some goddamn thing. The twisting stairwell wound around an open space through the middle large enough to float through easily when there was no gravity. But when there was gravity, the winding of the stairs made the trip up them four times longer than it needed to be.

After she'd deposited him into a chair in front of terminal, she reached over him and tapped at the interface. "This is the tracking protocol. The drone is small and low power, but the radio waves will travel through space easily. But only at the speed of light, mind you. It won't do you much good until you get close enough."

"And he won't notice his ship is sending out a beacon?"

"It'll blend in with engine noise. The beacon is randomized to further obscure it. It'll pulse only once every few minutes."

He frowned. "That doesn't sound easy."

"Just use the protocol and your sensors will pick it up." She reached over again and tapped some more. "Here, I'm making you a copy of it in case you need it."

She ejected a tiny disk from some unseen port when she was done and gave it to him. "Alright," he said. "If he's got an intersystem ship, he's going to Xarp off as soon as he breaks gravity."

"I suppose that means you want me off your ship."

He looked up at her to see a wry smile. He tried to return it, but her words from earlier resurfaced. He was being used. A disposable piece in a game.

"I don't want to be used," he said.

"And what *do* you want?"

He turned the question around in his head. "I guess I want to be useful."

Her smile faded and she put a hand on his shoulder. "Useful people get used, Stanley." She squeezed him briefly, then turned quickly and headed for the door to the main hatch. "I know I don't show it, but you're everything to me, Stanley." She spoke without turning back to look at him. "So be careful out there."

He mumbled assent, and then she was gone. He watched one of the terminal screens that showed the hatch opening and then closing. The dock's magnetic locks had released.

He flexed his fingers trying to worry away the numbing residual effects of the stunner. A hollow emptiness burned through his stomach.

He could only do what he needed to do.

* * *

Jax had tried to reason with the cop on the shuttle ride up, but even when using the autopilot, he was so skittish that Jax figured he'd better not distract him or they'd be smashed to pieces on their way to the main ModPol ship. He remembered hearing McManus say that he had a pilot with him, but that pilot was busy keeping the ship in orbit, leaving McManus to handle the shuttle himself. Finally, they managed to dock with only minor bumps accompanied by a groaning crack, and then Jax was being hauled out of the shuttle with dizzying alacrity. As always, the transition to a nearly null gravity environment disoriented the hell out of him. He'd never get used to it.

"I don't know why you people just can't let me be," he said finally as his captor closed up the shuttle and jabbed at a console. "You know I'm not a criminal."

"Oh, I know." The response came with a mirthless chuckle. "I've heard this song before."

"Sergeant McManus, right?" Jax said as the cop came back from his bout with the wall-mounted computer system. "What is this, like some kind of career move for you? To be the cop that brings in a wrongfully accused citizen? For the crime of being afraid and running for his life?"

McManus grabbed Jax by the arm and tugged him across the tiny shuttle hangar. "I wish."

"What does that mean?"

He ignored Jax and slid open a door that led to a narrow chamber. Jax could see sleeping tubes beyond it, similar to the one he'd been locked inside the first time McManus captured him.

"What does that mean?" he repeated, doing his best to pull back. The small resistance was equaled by a small tightening of the bonds around his wrists.

McManus shot him a glare and then pulled him toward the door. "Just shut up so I can get you into a stasis pod."

"What's going to happen?" Jax said. "They're going to give me a trial and find me innocent. They're going to just let me go, right?"

"If you believe that, then why do you keep running?"

"Because I shouldn't *have* to go on trial. I'm innocent and everyone knows it!"

An unseen audio unit sparked to life. "Sergeant, there's a contact."

McManus sighed. He floated to a nearby wall and found a comm unit. "There's a planet, Ayliff. There's gonna be some contacts."

"This one's got an intercept trajectory."

"What the fuck," McManus muttered to himself, before speaking directly into the comm again. "No. What is it?"

"Civilian ship, Sarge. Hold on. OrbitBurner 4200 LX."

Jax felt a twinge in his chest. Simultaneously he felt hope and fear.

"Goddammit," McManus said. "That lunkhead Runstom

just doesn't know when to quit." He spoke into the comm. "Ayliff, is it powering up any weapons?"

"Uh, no, Sarge. I don't think it has any weapons."

"No, of course not."

"He's coming in hot though, Sarge. Time to intercept, eight minutes."

"Time to Xarp?"

"Eleven minutes, forty seconds."

"Wait, whaddya mean, time to intercept?" McManus said after a moment of quiet thought. "He's got no weapons."

After a pause, the ship's pilot came back on. "Current trajectory suggests a collision course."

"No fucking way." McManus shook his head and pointed a finger at Jax. "That crazy friend of yours is going to ram us."

"He is crazy," Jax said. Maybe he could convince these cops that it was better to just leave them be. Runstom was a wild card that no one wanted to deal with. Calling him crazy wasn't really all that much of a stretch. "Just let me go, McManus. I told you, it's not worth it. I'm innocent. Let me go before Stanford kills us all."

"I don't think so," he said, his eyes narrowing.

McManus pulled his way toward the bridge, tugging Jax along by the elbow. It was awkward progress, but the cop seemed adept at yanking himself from one handhold to the next in the absence of gravity.

"Ayliff, where is he?" he said as they billowed through the hatch. "How close?"

"Six minutes, thirty."

"He's catching up to us," McManus said. "Why is he catching up to us?"

"That little OrbitBurner is a mover."

Jax felt helpless. He was useless when near weightless, even if the microgravity caused him to slowly sink. McManus's grip on his elbow was like a winch, and if he resisted, the cuffs constricted. He could feel his breath growing short and sharp with the rising panic.

McManus directed his attention to a silver-haired, pale but solid-looking woman seated along the right side of the cabin. "Granny, heat up the auto-turrets."

"Sergeant McManus, you know I can't fire on a civilian vessel," she said with a shake of her head. She motioned at her controls. "The auto-guns won't do it."

"Dammit." McManus let go of Jax and floated to a wall terminal, mumbling as he tapped at it. "I thought we had override codes installed on this thing."

"Five minutes," the pilot said.

"Stop counting down and take evasive action, Ayliff!"

"You got it Sarge, but there's no way we can outmaneuver that baby."

"Just keep him off us long enough to break gravity so we can Xarp out."

"Ah, shit." The woman McManus had called Granny turned in her half-tightened restraints. "We're not really gonna do a hot Xarp, are we?"

Jax felt the floor meet his feet with the smallest amount of pressure. Somehow the contact made him feel even less stable. His body, drained from long-gone adrenaline, wanted to collapse, but there wasn't enough gravity for the act.

"Depends on whether you can keep this crazy bastard away from us," McManus said. He stabbed the terminal a few more times, then leaned back with a grunt. "There. Auto-turret number six is unlocked. It's manual now."

"Manual?" she said, her head sliding back and her

eyebrow crooking. "Like without the targeting computer? How the hell am I supposed to hit anything?"

"Granny, you're the goddamn gunner!"

"I'm the defense system operator," she said, her brow furrowing. "And I don't shoot at civilian ships."

"Well you don't gotta kill him," McManus said, propelling himself away from the wall and toward Jax. "Just keep him from killing us."

"Tighten those straps, people," Ayliff called out. "He's getting close. And if we hot Xarp, you don't wanna be caught loose in the cabin."

McManus grunted as he shoved Jax against a cushioned wall at the back of the cabin. "Sorry, Jackson. I was going to put you in a sleep tube. Hell, was looking forward to a nice nap myself. But your buddy Stanley is complicating that plan."

"It would get a lot simpler if you just let me go." Jax grunted as McManus drew thick straps across his chest. "You could even tell ModPol I'm dead. Tell them you saw my body. I'll go deep and never come up again. I'll disappear."

The cop looked up at him and for a moment Jax thought he was considering the option. Then he looked back down, reaching behind Jax to loosen the wrist restraints. "Ain't taking you to ModPol."

"Where are you taking me?" Jax said, his voice suddenly going weak.

McManus didn't answer. He just pulled down a mask and strapped it to Jax's face. Then he floated to an empty chair and began strapping himself in.

Jax tried to repeat the question, but he couldn't get his mask-muffled voice to rise above the tension in the cabin. What was McManus hinting at? It couldn't be good.

"Here he comes," Ayliff said.

"Give him a few warning shots, Granny."

"Alright, Sarge."

The gunner – or rather, the defense system operator – tapped at a screen, then held a finger down, swirling it in a circle. Jax couldn't make out the visual, but he imagined she was aiming the sights of the gun somewhere in the direction of Runstom's OrbitBurner. She stopped the motion, and with the other hand she tapped once. A stream of distant high-pitched shrieks came from somewhere below the bridge.

After a few moments of tense silence, McManus barked, "Report!"

"No hits, no damage," Granny said.

"Contact has taken evasive action," Ayliff said. "I think that bought us some distance."

"Good," McManus said. "If he gets any closer, take another—"

"Shit," Ayliff said, silencing the rest of the room.

There was a din of ambient noise throughout the cabin from engines, life support, and whatever else, but now Jax could hear a distinct sound off to the left side of the ship. It sounded sinusoidal, like a wave pulsing to a steady beat.

"That thing has some bad-ass afterburners on it," the pilot finally said.

"Granny!" McManus shouted.

"I can't find him!" The gunner's hand swirled around her pad. "You gave me one of the turrets on the bottom of the patroller and I can't get an angle up to him."

"I'll get 'im back," Ayliff said.

As soon as the words came out, the ship lurched, and Jax imagined it spinning on the center axis, a line that drew from the rear to the front. Which meant that Jax was rotating along with it, being strapped to the middle of the wall perpendicular to the center axis. He coughed and sputtered, and something hot forced its way from his mouth and into the mask. He started to panic that his gastric ejection had blocked his airway, but there was a light sucking sound and with a sickening feeling that spread through his body, he suddenly understood the mask's purpose.

The ship twisted again, then shuddered with a jolt. "Holy shit!" Ayliff called out. "The crazy bastard clipped our nose cone!"

The turret shrieked again. "Not even close to a hit," Granny said. "But that gave him something to think about."

"If you say so," the pilot said. "Looks to me like he's coming back around again."

"Are we out of the gravity well yet?" McManus said through gritted teeth. Jax could see the pink skin on the cop's hands going white from gripping his chair so hard.

"Hold on," Ayliff said. "There. Yes. All hands ready for Xarp?"

"Just hit it," McManus yelled.

The only thing Jax was thankful for in that moment was the mask that captured the contents of his entire stomach.

CHAPTER 5

The thick material of the guard uniform flexed tightly around Runstom's stomach as he bent to lace up his boots. It had been made for someone who didn't have the surplus that had been invading the territory around his midsection. The spendy, flashy nonsense in his wardrobe as of late had been better at hiding it than any official uniform could.

Not that he was going to allow such an intrusion to smother his fire. Gut or not, he was going to get back to Barnard's Star and find Jax. Whatever it took. Before it was too late.

The image flashed in his mind whenever he allowed it to drift. Xarp wake. The trail was invisible to the naked eye but had lit up the scanners like a glowing highway. The OrbitBurner was speedy, but had no Xarp drive. Just a showy, useless hot rod for flitting between planets.

He needed a ride. McManus would have gone to Barnard. Runstom's gut feeling, and the computer's analysis of the Xarp wake confirmed it. Jax had been checking the launch schedules obsessively, so Runstom knew there was a transport leaving EE-3 for Barnard but it was a slow model, and worse, it wasn't scheduled to set off for several weeks.

While Runstom had been trying to ram McManus's inter-system patroller, the OrbitBurner comm network had traded data with it. Standard protocol for the ModPol mesh network. Every ship registered to ModPol was a node. Whenever nodes in the mesh got close enough for transmission, data passed between them. Any information was always going to be stale, but stale information was better than no information. Everything had been encrypted and Runstom didn't have clearance for all of it of course, but he got the highlights.

No details for anything outside of the system, but there'd been plenty of chatter about recent events within Epsilon Eridani. Most of the activity revolved around the cleanup after the battle that ensued when Space Waste attempted to hijack an interstellar ModPol transport. The same transport Runstom had hitched a ride on, ferrying his OrbitBurner from Barnard to Eridani. Reports of massive casualties on both sides, though the numbers for ModPol losses were obscured. With uncomfortable pride, the report had stated that twenty-six Wasters were killed. Thirty-one had been taken into custody. A newly retrofitted prisoner transport barge had been dispatched to transport the prisoners back to a maximum-security facility in deep-space orbit around Barnard's Star.

The prisoner transport barge had been fueling up at ModPol Outpost Epsilon, so Runstom had kicked the OrbitBurner into overdrive to catch it. When he'd reached the ModPol outpost, he sent his ship back to EE-3 on auto-pilot. He wished he could give it to Sylvia, but it was dangerous for them to be connected in any way. They'd already risked much by spending a small amount of time together while he was on her planet. So instead, he included a message that the ship was to be a gift to one of the other higher-level administrators. A thanks from ModPol Defense for their time.

But not before he'd ejected the stiff body of Tim Cazos. Unleashed the scrubbers on the rust-dry blood that adorned the walls around the maintenance hatch. It'd hurt, to purge evidence. But what would he do with it? Call Justice? Launch a criminal investigation against certain members of Space Waste?

It was last rounds before the ship went on lockdown in prep for Xarp speed. With a grunt, he adjusted the unwelcome gut inside the tight uniform, stretched his legs, and holstered a stun-stick. His quarters were made for two, but the transport had come over with a skeleton crew. He left the room alone.

The differences between ModPol Justice and ModPol Defense were less noticeable in the backwater space of Eridani. The presence of Justice on the outpost was minimal, but the Defenders didn't seem to mind the slowly increasing invasion by would-be police forces. Runstom wondered if the cops that made it to Eridani were ambitious, looking forward to moving into EE-3 as soon as the door was opened with a contract, or if they were there for the complete and total lack of action.

He'd checked in and reported to the local marketing administrators about his progress with the E-threers and their mild interest in Defense services, then hurried to make contact with anyone who knew if there was room for him on the prisoner barge destined for Barnard's Star. Endured several unfunny jokes about there being empty cells. And then finally someone had let him know there was an open spot if he didn't mind putting on a guard uniform. Someone had gone absent. Something about an asshole sergeant who had landed guard duty as penance for incompetence. A patroller had shown up to give him a lift.

So Runstom got to take McManus's place. It seemed the only option for getting back to Barnard in a timely manner.

He made his way down the lonely corridor, pulling at the ill-fitting uniform. The barge was the same one that Runstom was on when he was transporting Jax from Barnard-4 to ModPol Outpost Alpha, back when all of this started. It was there that he had confessed to Jax that he believed the operator was innocent of the murders he'd been charged with. The same barge that Space Waste attacked while they were in transit, in order to free some of their higher-ranking goons. The support systems on the barge had been severely damaged and many ModPol officers and guards lost their lives that day. Runstom had barely managed to escape by stealing a Waster ship, dragging Jax along with him.

And here it was again. All put back together, at least partially. According to gossip among the guards and staff, the cell blocks had been salvaged and retrofitted into another type of transport, originally designed for transporting raw materials mined from asteroids. Which made this version Xarp-capable, unlike the last.

The effect was that much of the interior was the same. The familiarity of it unnerved Runstom. Like walking through the memory of a bad dream. Every miniscule jounce the ship made as it maneuvered jolted through his nerves. Every shudder jarred loose memories, recalled fears of gravity in flux. Bodies bounding. Normal things like provisions and handypads becoming dangerous debris. And then the cutting. Knives through the metal skin of the hull. The projectile fire. The laserfire. The whole barge bleeding air, losing pressure, losing oxygen. Losing a partner, a fellow cop, the closest person Runstom had to a friend.

He gripped a handhold that ran along the narrow corridor. There was only a gray ambient light to see by, and it made him nauseous to stare down the length of the passage. An unnatural, shrinking point, like losing consciousness. The handrail felt sticky under his gloves.

His arm buzzed with a warning. Runstom had one shift to serve before the Xarp jump and he was going to be late. He pulled himself forward by the wall handle, bracing himself against it. The artificial gravity was only a half G, but his legs felt heavy. They'd turn it off completely soon. Not until after the shift. Not until everyone was secured.

If he lost Jax, it would all have been for nothing. All his efforts, all his justice. It would be meaningless if an innocent man was killed by an unchecked monster. Mark Xavier Phonson. X.

Runstom reported to his post.

The cell block was mostly empty. Thirty-one prisoners, and the capacity was several times that. Most of the guards were younger. Fit, strong-looking, but babies. He tried not to think about how short their lives would be if there was another attack. He dodged their small talk with nods and grunts and thousand-yard stares. Sometimes they called him McManus, and he couldn't tell if it was some kind of lame joke or if they really were just confused. Runstom didn't allow himself to spend the energy on anger in either case.

An attack seemed possible. If the Wasters would go after a prisoner barge once for just a couple of their mates, wouldn't they do it again for thirty-one? But they'd been routed, sent home to lick their wounds. And the barge was going straight to the zero-G maximum-security prison, deep in Barnard space. Special delivery. Not like the predictable route it was on before. It would come out of Xarp in the vicinity of the highly-protected prison. Even if the Wasters knew its schedule, which was unlikely, they'd have no window for an attack.

Runstom reminded himself of these details as he walked his round. The prisoners were unsettlingly quiet. Each one he passed was either lying or sitting on their cot. Dejected. Tired. There was a difference, he realized, a difference in the violence he'd witnessed the first time on this barge and the violence he'd witnessed most recently. The first was ruthless, to be sure. A cold-blooded assault on a Justice ship. A purpose of breaking prisoners out of custody. But the most recent incident, it was an attack, met by an ambush. He'd been lulled into thinking the Wasters' purpose was theft. They thought there were weapons to steal. But the attack and the ambush, these things felt more like war than crime. And perhaps he should assume that the Wasters didn't just want to steal from ModPol, they wanted to cripple ModPol. A move driven not by greed, but by strategy.

The main difference of the cells in this version of the barge was the addition of a sleep tube in each. It was part of Runstom's job to ask each prisoner if he or she understood the directions for operating the tube. They were required to get in themselves when the signal was given. There was a timer. And then the tubes would close. Anyone not in a tube was going to ride Xarp in real time. Runstom had done it before. A slow, sick, painless torture. The human brain didn't know what to do with it.

"Ain'tchu got any D?" A voice calling out from the level below Runstom. "I don't wanna get in the tube, I just wanna ride with some D."

He heard the young guard respond with practiced patience. "Do you understand the instructions?"

"Fuck the instructions, lady. I want some D. It's inhumane to Xarp without D."

"Please answer the question," she tried firmly.

"How about you answer my question?"

"Listen, Waster – if you don't get in the tube, you're going to have to ride raw."

Runstom looked into the cell in front of him, ready to recite his own questions. The man in the dark corner spoke first. "*Waster.* Always found that distasteful."

"Aren't you with Space Waste?" Runstom asked, then cursed himself for engaging.

"Aye, I know we're prone to wastin' stuff." His voice was deep, and though it was soft, there was a strength to it. "Laying waste. But that's what we do, not who we are."

Runstom stood quiet. Watched the man step forward. He was tall, as tall as a B-fourean, but not nearly as skinny. And his skin was a rich, dark brown. An Earth-born. The lines in his face were obscured by scars, but the eyes showed age. Runstom glanced at his pad to read the name. *Moses Down.*

"What we are is waste," he said. "The waste discarded by domes. And domes – domes are built for creating and discarding waste. They are systems of perpetual hunger and consumption. You weren't raised on a dome."

"No," Runstom said, though it hadn't sounded like a question.

"But your job has taken you to domes. Many times, I'll

bet. You ever approach the domes in a shuttle with windows?"

Runstom had. Shuttles rarely had windows or even screens that anyone but the pilot could view. But on occasion he'd seen the domes from an approach. Such as the time he was called to work on a case on Barnard-4. A multiple homicide. He'd watched the entire time, the way the storms swirled around the stacks that rose from the processors.

"Pollution," Moses Down said, as though he were looking at the picture in Runstom's mind. "Sometimes it looks natural, like clouds, like rain. But it's unnatural. Corrosive. Toxic. Domes burn everything. Burn it down to molecules and blow it into space."

"Those planets have no atmosphere," Runstom said. His voice was weak. Making someone else's argument.

"No, of course not," Down said with a half grin and a shake of his head. "Don't let my old Earth skin fool you. I could give a shit about what domers pump into the void outside of their domes. I just wanted to make the point. See there – the domes – there, the polluters win. There's no environment to save, not like the doddering, fragile Earth. Domes sit on dead rock. That's what allowed them to establish these systems."

Runstom's hand moved toward his handypad, trying to do the job that his mind and mouth wouldn't. Trying to move him on to the next prisoner. "Systems," he heard himself say.

"Intake and excretion." Down made a motion with his hands, one waving in, one pushing out. Then he dropped them to his side. "Me, my family, we are not wasters. We are waste. Human waste. The unwanted byproduct of dome life."

Runstom stared up at the dark man in silence. There was something about him, about those burning brown eyes. He swallowed and blinked. Flashes of the things he'd seen Space Waste do. The people that died. He felt his forehead crease when he reopened his eyes. "You're murderers."

Down's smile faded and he nodded solemnly. "Ain't nobody perfect."

Runstom looked down at his handypad, staring through it. "Do you understand the instructions?" he mumbled.

"I ain't trying to antagonize you, boy," Down said. "I just wanted you to know where we came from."

Without looking at him, Runstom felt a gesture in his direction. "What do you mean, *we*?"

The prisoner stared at him for a long, cold moment before turning away. "You've been shit out of the bottom of the system," he said idly as he drifted to the back of the cell. "Just like the rest of us, Mr. Runstom."

* * *

He finished his assignment and went to the center of the block to wait with the other guards. Most of them had gotten the point that the sour, green-skinned man wasn't worth talking to. And only mildly worth talking about, in hushes.

The chief came around eventually, asking each to check-in with a report. "McManus," she said about halfway down her list.

Runstom's face grew hot. "With all due respect sir, would you please not call me that?"

The chief was as young as the rest of them, a tall B-fourean with short-cropped pale hair. She crooked an eyebrow at him. "Um. Well. What do you want to be called?"

"My name is Stanford Runstom," he said through gritted teeth, tapping at the name badge just left of his sternum. "The chief of the watch should know that."

"Oh." She flicked at her pad for a moment, then looked back at him. Pointed a finger in the general direction of his chest. "Sorry, Runstom. Your badge says *McManus.*"

Runstom frowned down at the name affixed to his left breast. He hadn't noticed it when he put the uniform on. A simple detail. Did he even care that he got stuck with McManus's uniform? No. The disappointment came from missing the detail. He was drifting away from the goal of becoming a detective, both in title and in spirit.

"All prisoners checked in," he said softly.

As soon as she dismissed them, he strode toward the door as fast as his legs could work in the half gravity. He could hear the voices behind him, a traditional pre-Xarp celebration being planned. The guards would be required to tube-up, but the sleep would be in shifts; a fraction of them would be in a semi-stasis, half-sleep, ready to be jolted awake if necessary. Whatever the shift, most of them would get as many drinks into their system as possible in the next hour. Xarping sober was reserved for the highly disciplined or the self-torturous. Runstom was one of those; which didn't matter.

Back in his room he went through his own pre-Xarp ritual: programming his entertainment module to scoop up any transmissions of bombball games as they came within range of sportscasting relays. There were always a few hours of post-Xarp downtime and he liked to use that time to catch up on the season. It was something to look forward to. Something trivial. But one of the few rewards he gave himself.

As he prepped his tube, exhaustion pulled at his bones. He shrugged off the oppressive uniform and frowned one last time at McManus's name staring him in the face as he tossed it aside. Missing details. Amateur. Like a rookie. What else had he missed?

* * *

Accelerate. Accelerate.

The human mind wasn't meant to travel this fast. So fast, light can't keep up. How can a brain that spends most of its day trying to decode visual signals into something meaningful cope when it's moving faster than light?

The human mind wasn't meant for a lot of things it's been subjected to.

Speaking – or thinking – of which, Jax pined for Delirium. D-G, the little vacation he'd taken a few times before. The Wasters had a new kind called D-K that was supposed to be more potent. He knew he shouldn't, but he couldn't help but be curious. Not that it mattered; no drugs were available to him in this damned ship.

It was his fourth and final trip between stars, and his eighth time experiencing faster-than-light speed. Each time it happened, his mind rewound to the beginning, replaying each memory in slow motion. As though he were traveling so fast that he lapped himself in a loop of time, and now watched only the moments where he broke laws – natural laws – not meant to be broken.

The first was his escape; from a prison barge, and from certain death. Some military dropship that Space Waste had repurposed, and Jax and Runstom had commandeered. Runstom piloted, Xarping in one direction, stopping to turn,

Xarping again, and again and again. Multi-routed hops, like a hacker covering tracks on a network. Not that Jax had ever known any actual hackers. Well, except the ones that hacked him and framed him for murder. Fortunately, the original gangbanger pilot that they restrained in the cargo hold had a cache of Delirium-G. He'd revealed it to Jax on the condition that they'd both get a dose. The drug made the jagged trip bearable as Runstom tracked down the superliner that they would dock with and board.

The second was thankfully shorter, though drugless and sleepless. After weeks on the superliner investigating the murder that Jax had been accused of, they took the dropship for a hop across the Barnard system to the moon Terroneous. Runstom and Jax had survived the trip, but the ship had not, crash-landing into an empty field of grass. It was the first time Jax laid eyes on plant-life that had not been gardened or engineered.

Then he took a third trip, a long haul out to the Sirius system to chase the last of their clues. It was an interstellar commercial flight, which included stasis pods. Sleep was inescapable in the warm dark tube that droned with a soft, enveloping pulse of white noise that obscured binaural beats designed to quiet the mind. A light hypnotic gas ensured the sleep would hold for the duration of the trip, slowing his breathing and heartbeat. Most people wouldn't dream, he'd been told, but some did. Jax dreamt of his flight from justice, replayed over and over and over, an inescapable loop.

And then only a few days since he'd arrived on Sirius-5, they'd found their killer, Runstom had made his arrest, and Jax needed to go. They'd solved the crime, but were under no illusion that Jax would be immediately exonerated. So he was back on one of those same commercial flights, returning to Barnard, in another sensory-depriving stasis tube. Upon boarding, his last and final companion was fear. He was alone, more so than he'd ever been in his life. His only ally gone off to make things right, with Jax's remaining responsibility to stay out of the light.

Trip number five was a hitchhike, a soulless ride from the interstellar port back to Terroneous, but Jax drew few memories from those days. A shell arrived on that moon – a destination that some distant part of his mind desired, but once his body arrived, such desire was difficult to rekindle. Nevertheless, he trusted his inertia and slowly began piecing together a new life.

The sixth Xarp flight was when he was stolen away from that freshly planted home by this same sonova bitch, Jared McManus. They'd tubed him so again he'd gone into sensory-deprived sleep. Thinking back, he knew it'd been a short trip, but in those endless moments his frightful dreams of fugitivity slammed into fresh nightmares over the loss of his new home and his new friends. Lealina. She was not some true love, some mindless magical romance. She was real. She had made him feel real in a time when he'd forgotten what that was. She was what his life could be.

He'd been thrown into the tube by ModPol – by McManus – and when it opened, he'd been in the hands of Space Waste. Maybe it would happen again. When it happened before, he'd been given no choice but to join the gang's ranks. They were planning an attack, and they needed his so-called hacker skills. And so the seventh Xarp trip Jax had taken was another leap between star systems, from Barnard's Star to Epsilon Eridani, for the purposes of assaulting a lonely ModPol transport. He'd expected the

Wasters to distribute Delirium-G or even the harder D-K for such a brutal trip, but their leaders were strict about limiting narcotics use before a fight. Instead, the Space Waste carrier had Xarp lounges: virtual rooms where passengers could congregate and take in limited forms of entertainment, such as storytelling or gambling. Breaking the laws of physics the way Xarp does, the mind can't handle much input, so the data that flowed through those lounges was limited in bandwidth. It was the equivalent of a text-based chatroom, similar to the kind that Jax and his fellow operators frequented to pass time during long shifts at the life-support terminals back on Barnard-4. Although in the case of the Xarp lounge, the signal was a bit different, spiked into the brain through a helmet, in a way that made input and output seem like a spoken or typed conversation.

He had tried to play games with his fellow Wasters on that seventh Xarp trip, but the rules were usually not in the system, and instead only known to the participants who would send requests to bots to manage virtual decks of cards or random number generation as necessary. Most of the games seemed to Jax to be rooted in either luck, deceit, or both. They'd let him play as long as he was losing, but his first win had made them suspicious, given his role as a hacker. Again, their label, not his. Again, he'd never even known any hackers in his life, except those that were involved in murdering a block of domers and framing Jax for the crime.

So this was trip number eight for Jax. It would be his last, either because he would be thrown in prison or killed when he arrived to see the light of Barnard's Star. And when this final trip started, all the others came flooding back, just like they always did. All the memories, the prison barge, the superliner, Terroneous, Sirius-5, Terroneous again, the arrest, the Space Waste base, Xarping to Eridani. The whole string kicked off by the haunting tragedy of those suffocated souls, Jax too concerned with his own false imprisonment to remember to mourn them. Damn Jenna Zarconi for her blind revenge streak. And damn Mark Xavier Phonson for driving her to it.

The thought of X was something Jax didn't want in his head any more. The corrupt bastard had his come-uppance when Runstom arrested him back on Sirius-5. But nothing had stuck, and Jax never heard word of what became of him. He pushed the thoughts away.

The ModPol intersystem patroller had a similar lounge system to the Space Waste carrier, and Jax hadn't noticed the apparatus that had slid around the back of his head until the interface spiked through the black clouds of his mind.

They could have left him in the blankness of Xarp. Days, weeks – endless *nothing*. Body slowed but not stopped. Mind useless but not asleep. It would have been torture. But they didn't do that. They plugged him into the lounge. A shred of compassion from these thugs with badges.

The cops had lounge games of their own, which Jax had no choice but to play in order to keep his sanity. Most of these games were conducted by Ayliff, the pilot, and Granny, the gunner, as McManus managed to grumble his way through the text-like interactions and drifted in and out of the exchanges. After a while, Jax switched to some of the other channels that were available. These were one-way inputs, some of them being obsolete news broadcast recordings, others fiction. He sampled a few of these, but they all seemed to be poorly-written drivel about adventures through space.

With enough probing through the system's help interface, he figured out how to open a private channel with McManus.

"Whaddya want?"

Even through the pseudo-text, pseudo-voice, mind-fuck interface, Jax could detect the cop's disdain. "You said you're not taking me to ModPol."

"Did I?"

"Yes."

There was an infinite pause. "Don't remember."

Jax wondered if the spike would pick up his exasperation somehow. "What's going to happen to me?"

"Look, man. You might as well forget about what's going to happen and just let it happen."

Jax boiled. He wasn't going to let the cop off that easily. "It's a long flight, Sergeant, and we've got literally nothing to do for, what, days?"

"Ten days."

"So talk to me. Obviously I'm not going anywhere."

"You just don't get it, do you Jackson?" the reply snapped back. "People like you and me, we're just tools, okay? We're not in control. They are. We do their will. Most of the time without even knowing it."

"Speak for yourself—"

"No, I'm speaking for you, domer. You were born to work and eat and sleep. Part of a herd. Like an animal from Earth."

"You're from Barnard-3, aren't you?" Jax said, but it felt like a desperate comeback. "You're as much of a domer as I am."

"I *was*," he said. "I started to see it, when I joined ModPol. Getting out of the domes. Seeing the world from the outside."

"And now I see it too," Jax tried. "I've been out for—"

"Sure, yeah. You've been a fugitive for a little while. Bouncing around the stars, making a big fat mess wherever you go. But you don't know what a real life outside the shelter is like."

But Jax did know. He didn't know from his own experience, but he became close with people who grew up on Terroneous. He tried to understand, tried to feel what it was like for them, how hard it was, and yet their ability to push through. He needed to understand that drive, that hope in the face of hopelessness. "It's survival," he said. "Survival above everything."

Another infinite silence, then McManus returned. "Yeah. Sometimes to survive though, it means someone else doesn't."

The suppressed thoughts crawled their way forward through Jax's black mind. He fought them, but he was tired, weak. *X*, they demanded. *You never really escaped.*

"Do you know Mark Phonson?" he transmitted.

There was a brief pause before McManus replied, "No."

"Mark Xavier Phonson," Jax said. "To some only known by the initial of his middle name."

"What is this, some kind of riddle?"

"That's what this is, then?" Jax could sense the hesitation in McManus's transmission. He needed to push. "I die, and you live another day?"

There was a break so long that Jax almost checked the connection to see if he was still part of the lounge network. "Yes," McManus said finally. "It's X."

In the midst of Xarp-sickness, Jax didn't think his stomach could get any hollower, but there it was. A hole rolled throughout his insides. And he understood why McManus couldn't go back empty-handed. X would want to see

Jax – the eternal thorn in his side – disappear for good. He'd want to see it with his own eyes.

"You can't," Jax said. "You can't take me to X."

"So you know who this X guy is," McManus said. The transmission carried mirth. "I don't. I don't even know who he is. But I know when someone has enough power to destroy. And to do it without anyone knowing who he is."

"He's—"

"And I don't want to know."

McManus left the channel.

In the emptiness that followed, Jax's mind conjured worst-case projections. He was not going to be arrested and thrown in prison for an extended period of time. He was going to be killed. Possibly tortured. It was possible that X wanted him for information, wanted to know what Jax knew, as if Jax knew any goddamn thing anyway. Why did someone so strong have to spend so much effort on someone as weak as Jax? He was perfectly willing to crawl under a rock and let the whole thing go.

But X wasn't going for that. A man that powerful must be sufficiently paranoid, and whether Jax was a threat or not didn't matter. He would err on the side of caution and assume Jax could be the piece that brings him down.

For an immeasurable time, Jax wandered the channels of the lounge interface. Flipped past the old recordings and replays, past the bad fiction, past the mindless games. There were some historical entries, something akin to school-age education, and there were dreadful trainings on banal police procedures. Out of sheer boredom, he sifted through the trainings until he found one that was a basic overview of the local computer operating system. Specifically, it was Roscorp Common Machine Integration Operating System,

4.5.2.g.13, with a laundry list of management modules installed. Jax didn't recognize most of these, but based on their cryptic names, decided they must have had something to do with making an interstellar ship work. A few he did recognize, and with a little more prodding – listing and scanning files – he realized that Roscorp must license life-support operations from Vitality Systems. The very same Vitality Systems that built the life-support equipment that Jax operated back on Barnard-4. The equipment that managed to fail spectacularly when hacked, performing its function in the exact opposite manner than designed.

The training would have been numbingly boring if Jax weren't already numb and bored, but he suffered through it anyway. His reward was the quick aside that the command interface could be accessed by the lounge system if necessary. This access was apparently out of scope for the basic training, but once it ended, he had some ideas about what to poke next.

And that was how, by combing through help pages and trial and error, he found the command interface. It wasn't protected – and Jax wasn't really surprised. It was the local-network protection fallacy: systems like this were designed never to be exposed to anything outside of the ship, so what need was there for protection?

The engineers who built the system didn't envision a scenario where cops take a computer operator into custody, then connect him to the lounge system for several days with nothing better to do but poke around. And poke he did.

CHAPTER 6

Nine days in Xarp space, in a damn dropship. No sleeping tubes. Lucky Jerk, always prepared, had packs of Delirium-G hidden in pockets all over his flight uniform. But when he dug them all out and pooled them together, there were only a handful of doses. Dava, Lucky, and Thompson had to share them. Which meant rationing. Which meant going for hours, riding Xarp raw, pulling spacetime out of reality and into some mindless dimension where nothing meant anything, pulling it thinner and thinner until that point where they wanted to just die and end it all. Open up the windows and suck out to the black. Welcome oblivion. And just before reaching that tipping point, popping a pill and zonking out. A different kind of mindlessness. One of acceptance. Of disconnection.

And with the mindlessness, with the emptiness, old ghosts came to fill the void. They came because they'd been dodged too often. Sidestepped with the day-to-day fight for survival. They came because in the emptiness, they could not be ignored.

"Lay down now, Davina." Her father. The tang chemical smell of oil that never left his skin.

"Where's Ma?"

"Right here, Davina. We'll be right next to you." Her mother wore a perfume, what was supposed to smell like flowers. It was a special occasion for her to not have the familiar scent of damp dirt. The cough that accompanied her sing-song words. The cough that made them all flinch.

"How long is it?"

"It's far," her father said. His voice was musical too. It was how her parents had met; folks sang together in those days. "So far that we have to go to sleep."

"Why do we have to go so far?"

"It's what people do," her mother said. She always had this answer, no matter the question. "People move. There are better places out there. A better home for us."

"We had a home."

"This one will be better."

"Why?"

The cough again. The collective flinch. "You trust us, doncha, Davina?"

"Yes." Said too quickly. To cover the lie.

"What we had was not a good home." Her father hung his head, spoke into his chest. "Maybe it was at one time, but ain't no more."

"So everyone is going to leave?"

They looked at each other. Then her mother looked away. Her father frowned and met her eyes. "No." His face darkened, his voice became smoke. "We have to leave them."

"Why?"

A bad energy grew in the space around her. Rows of beds like the one she was sitting in. Beds that were cylinders, beds that had covers on them. Anxiety in the air. In the hurried voices, the commands in the distance, echoing around the massive chamber. Drawing her parents' attention. Causing them to glance. To fidget. To cower.

"Lay down now, Davina," her mother said. "Don't make no trouble, just lay down and it will be over fast."

"Why do we have to leave them?"

Her father's strong hand on her chest. Flattening her into the tight cylinder-bed, like stowing something into a cupboard. The eyes bearing down, pinning her into place. The eyes that would not be argued with.

"Because we're lucky, Davina."

She hadn't trusted them. All they did was lie. Lie to her about how things would be okay, how things would get better.

Her mistrust had been justified. When she woke up, they were gone. And there was no home.

Nine days with those ghosts. Nine days of seeing them and losing them. Crossing and re-crossing the border between their presence and their absence.

To hide from them, Dava thought about the more recent betrayals. The snakes in her own house. Kindled that fire, forcing it to grow, refusing to let it fade. Then they docked with the base and took the first step out of the ship, and there it went. Smothered into smoke by the heavy air of failure and loss. The half-gravity of the slow swing of the station's arms pulled heavier than the fattest of planets.

The welcome from Space Waste was not warm. Which was just fine by Dava, since she'd come looking to pick a fight. But it was so cold there, she was unable to rile anyone she came across. Those that had survived the assault had become living dead. No one was excited to see that she and

Thompson-Gun and Lucky Jerk were still alive. Nor were they disappointed. They were just nothing.

As the coals smoldered, she pushed herself to storm for Rando Jansen. She wanted explanations. But he was locked away. Planning another attack, was the word. And Dava wasn't allowed in, according to the malaise-laden guard posted outside the war room. She'd been demoted. No longer a capo. For her failure in the assault, though the guard didn't reveal that much out loud.

Finally, she managed to corner Captain 2-Bit at the drinking hole. He blinked when he saw her – it'd been the biggest reaction she'd gotten since her arrival.

"Captain," she said, drawing close under the dim lights. "Tell me what he's planning."

He frowned at her, then motioned to the bartender. "Sorry about the demotion, Dava." He glanced at her glass.

She was drinking a well-aged whiskey. "Yes, the demotion came with a diet. But Moora didn't have the heart to enforce it."

Moora the bartender silently slid a skinny glass of yellow ale in front of 2-Bit and turned away.

"There's D-K," he said after taking a small sip from the top. Eyes still on his beer. "Lots of it around."

That would explain all the disconnected faces. "What happened in the war room?"

He sighed, trying to hang his shoulders heavy with the weight, then snuck a sideways glance at her and winced. "Top secret."

2-Bit was a good leader, always looked up to by the grunts and the flyboys, but he was naive – almost intentionally so. It was a quality Dava respected: she knew he preferred everything to be straight. But 2-Bit wasn't stupid, in that he was well aware of his own weaknesses. So he played along with games of deceit as best he could. Given the choice, he'd prefer bold truth over subtlety or riddle.

"Captain," she said. "We've known each other a long time."

"Eight years," he said without hesitation.

"Moses was taken prisoner."

He blew out a sigh and took a hard drink. "We figured."

"A lot of us were taken prisoner," she said. "Are we going to get them back?"

He stared into his beer until she touched him on the shoulder. He looked at her and looked down. "RJ," he said. "Underboss Jansen says it's time to press on. That ModPol ain't expecting us to make another move right now."

"So it's a good time for us to make another move." Against the warning in her chest, she prayed this meant a move to go after Moses.

"Yes."

She drained her whiskey and tilted the empty tumbler at Moora. "Captain, I know I got busted down."

"Dava ..."

He shriveled as Moora came by and refilled her glass. "You can still tell me anything, Captain. Look around at who's left. You and I have been here the longest."

He glanced up at her, then took a swallow of beer. He nodded and looked up to the ceiling and became suddenly lost in some unseen clouds. "Of course, girl. Of course, Dava. Such a young girl when I met you. But always strong. So strong. Should be you leading these people. Not me, not RJ. Not Moses."

"Hey," she said, feeling her face grow hot and her hands grow tight. "Moses—"

"Moses," 2-Bit said back to her with an unexpected fire

in his eyes that stunned her into silence. The rare anger faded quickly and he looked up again. "He's just a little lost, is all. He's old, like me. We don't know what to do any more. We don't know what it's for sometimes."

She caught herself trembling as she raised her glass to her mouth, as the warm liquid graced her lips. Anger, or fear? Moses could preach. Had she mistaken a gift of the tongue for drive, for purpose? No. He always had a plan.

"I want you to tell me what RJ is planning," she said firmly.

2-Bit took a deep breath. "It's another assault," he said. "This time, on the mining colony of Ipo. A little moon. You know it?"

"No." She leaned back slightly. "Captain, look at what's left of us. How can we do another assault?"

"Fresh crop," he said, bobbing his head in a rehearsed compliance. "More recruits just come in."

"From where?"

"Jansen convinced the Misters to join us. Convinced them that it's better to be united."

"United."

"Against ModPol."

She nodded heavily, halfway between uncontrollable raging hatred for the Misters and respect for what actually sounded like a good idea. The Misters. Rival gang of nobodies. And yet they'd almost killed her a few months ago. More concerned with turning a profit than anything, peddling drugs and weapons.

But the point had been made. Space Waste was damaged, and in no condition to continue petty squabbles with other gangs while at war with ModPol. Even still, shoring up the ranks and immediately going on the attack was risky.

She watched 2-Bit's hands quiver by mere micrometers as he lifted his glass. "How's he going to be sure this next attack is going to pay off?"

His eyes dropped sheepishly. "Intelligence," he mumbled into his beer before taking a long pull.

"Like the kind of intelligence Basil Roy gave us." She decided not to waste time making up a story about how she knew he wasn't on the base. "Where is our illustrious hacker anyway?"

He looked at her, his voice cool skepticism. "He disappeared."

Damn 2-Bit. He was going to make her spell it out. "So we go on this mission, Basil Roy giving us directions. We run into an ambush. Then he disappears."

2-Bit cocked his head slightly. "Ambush?"

"Did you really think we just lost a fair fight?" She drained her whiskey and stood up. "I have to show you something."

She found a quiet corner of the station and recounted the details of the breach-and-board to Captain 2-Bit. The army of ModPol Defenders camped out in the cargo bays. Anyone they didn't slaughter, they'd captured. She watched the concern spread slowly across his face, but he was only going on her word. Then she showed him some of the BatCap footage that she and Thompson-Gun and Lucky Jerk had retrieved. As he saw with his own eyes the clearly prepared ModPol fighter ships disguised as asteroids reveal themselves and pinch into the Space Waste ships, his concern turned to fear. Eyes widening, breath catching.

2-Bit was no idiot, and although he wanted to trust Jansen, the evidence was stacking up. Basil Roy was Jansen's man, and Roy had clearly deceived them. The hacker's disappearance fed 2-Bit's distrust. And yet she couldn't bring him around to fully distrusting Jansen. 2-Bit wanted to believe that Roy had deceived all of them, Jansen included.

In the end, Dava got 2-Bit to agree to stay on his toes and keep a watchful eye on things. And to look the other way while she went about her own business. He'd let slip that the next attack was going to be on Ipo; apparently the miners there had struck a vein of some material ideal for packing into torpedoes and hurling at other ships, exploding spectacularly whether they made a direct hit or not. Whatever kept him busy, she didn't really care.

Thompson came around to find her eventually, once 2-Bit had stumbled away, half-drunk, half-confused, all useless. They walked around the outer corridor toward their old barracks to see who or what might have moved in during their absence.

"These Misters," Thompson was groaning. "Place is crawling with them. Flighty bastards. Not much good except for fodder."

"Something tells me Jansen sees us all that way."

The old hallways felt like home, but not like home at the same time. Everything had changed, and now it was like she was walking through a memory, a twisted museum commemorating something that once was, now no longer.

Thompson was carrying a case, and Dava nodded at it. "Got yourself a replacement Tommy-Gun?"

She frowned down at it. "Yeah. It's my only spare. Not as good as the one ModPol lifted off me."

Dava knew how much Thompson-Gun's namesake meant to her. She'd watched her friend customize the piece over the years. It had been a work of art as much as a weapon. "Better hold onto this one," she said in a mirthless attempt at teasing her.

Thompson shook it off, changing the subject. "I heard a rumor," she said in a low voice. She must have held her tongue until she felt they were out of earshot of anyone important. "About where they took the prisoners."

"Heard from who?"

"It's a rumor, Dava. There is no who."

"Then what?" She tried to keep her voice low, but it wanted to leap out of her chest. She clutched the handholds tighter as they drifted in the low gravity. "Where?"

"The Pollies have that new lockup. The zero-G place. In the outer belt."

She took this in. It made sense, except for the fact that there weren't Pollies on the ModPol transport, they were all Fenders. Military, not police. "Must be the Fenders didn't want to deal with the prisoners."

"Or they had a deal, made a trade or something."

"Aren't they all ModPol?"

Thompson laughed. "Yeah, but they're like factions, you know?"

Dava couldn't draw those boundaries in her mind, couldn't fathom what the cops and the soldiers would trade for. "This rumor – it's making its way around the base?"

"Of course."

"Anyone asking why we're not hitting the prison?"

They stopped, and Dava realized they'd reached the hatch of Thompson's chamber. "Of course," she said again. "But RJ is saying they might be expecting that."

"RJ," Dava muttered. He was probably right about that. Or he was right in the words he was feeding to the grunts. Spinning the rumors to tell the story his way. Was he capable of that level of manipulation? He'd fooled Moses.

She could kill him. He was probably well guarded and

plenty paranoid at this point, but she was the best. She could find a way.

It was strange to admit, but she'd never killed without being on the job. She'd never taken it on her own volition to assassinate. Although Basil Roy might count. No one had ordered to spill his blood.

What would Moses want her to do? She was so certain of Jansen's deceit. She didn't need hard evidence. She didn't need a confession from the late Basil Roy. She just knew it. If Moses knew something as strongly as she did, would he order the hit?

He would weigh it out. He would lay all the cards on the table, flip them over into proper piles, see all the players, the moves, the outcomes. She couldn't see any of that. She couldn't see the consequences. She never had to before, but now that she had the option to take things into her own hands, she was stuck. How was she supposed to predict the consequences of assassinating the underboss of Space Waste?

Every one of those empty faces she'd passed drifting through the empty base. They burned her. They fled, those that lived, those that were uncaptured – they were all guilty of leaving the rest behind. But in the end, Dava had fled as well. Those faces, she hated them for being so stupid, for being used, but then Dava had been used as well. Those faces were mirrors. Reflecting what she hated about herself.

"Who can we get to go with us?" Dava said, barely in control of the words as they came out.

"Go where?"

"I don't know yet." She just knew she needed a crew. That was the first step. Mutiny against Jansen wasn't going to pay off, and she had no idea what might happen if she managed to kill him. Who was loyal to him? It was a sure bet the newly arrived Misters were. No, before she could do anything, she needed to find out who could stand with her. "It doesn't matter where we're going or what we're doing. Who can we trust to join us?"

"How many do we need?"

Dava bit her lip. "A small crew. They have to be solid. If you're not sure, they don't make the cut. I only want ringers."

Thompson nodded and pulled open her hatch. "Give me a couple of hours. I'll send you a message and we'll meet."

* * *

By the time they gathered together in the dark shadows behind the tanks in the recycling pod, the seed in Dava's mind had grown into a full-blown plan. She looked around at her posse.

"Alright, Tommy. Who are these piece-of-shit bastards?"

Thompson-Gun's face twisted into a snarling smile. She slapped a lean, muscular woman on the arm and nodded. "This here's Seven-Pack. Close-combat specialist. She and I used to run under Professor One-Shot." She frowned. "Until Poligart."

Dava had heard the story about Poligart, though she hadn't paid much attention. The one habitable moon of Sirius-7 and location of a small but strong colony. The incident was one of the first encounters with some Misters. A small crew of Wasters, lead by One-Shot, got into some kind of shootout. They'd been outnumbered and came out on top, but One-Shot didn't make it. "Yeah, Seven-Pack," Dava said, looking the woman up and down, recognizing her from around the base. She had blood-red skin and matching red hair and had probably been born on Poligart. "I heard you took out a bunch of those bastards yourself."

"She did," Thompson said. "Got her leg all fucked up in the process. Missed the attack in Eridani, but now she's good to go."

Dava nodded. "Close-combat specialist. And what does Seven-Pack mean?"

With a quiet shudder, a revolver appeared in the woman's hands, the barrel pointing skyward. She flipped open the cylinder, spun it with a flick. "Six," she said, then flicked it closed and triggered an unseen switch. With a tiny pop, a blade as long as her hand sprang from the side of the barrel. "And number seven, never runs out of ammo."

Dava watched the gun slide back into its holster and noted that Seven-Pack's belt was well stocked with cartridges. She definitely approved of the blade, but was glad to see the shooter wasn't going to run short on ammo. They would need every bullet.

"Next up." Thompson reached up to thump the chest of a tall and lanky baby-faced man. "This is Half-Shot. Younger brother of Professor One-Shot."

"Half-Shot." Dava snorted. "Z'at mean you're half as good?"

The boy slowly unslung a long and expensive-looking rifle from his back and hefted its barrel across the front of his chest. "Raymond's specialty was sniping. Headshots, when he could get them. Vital organs when he couldn't. One bullet, one kill." He raised the gun an inch. "Fuck those old-fashioned bullets. These motherfuckers cut through everything. One shot, at *least* two kills."

Dava reached out and touched the gun, felt the heat coming through the casing even while it was powered down.

Her eyes flicked up to meet his. "Sorry about your brother. He was a good capo. He didn't deserve to get shot by some piece-of-shit Mister."

Half-Shot's eyes narrowed, and she could see his pupils jitter. Like they wanted to shoot glares elsewhere, but he was keeping them in check. "Yeah, well. It was a lucky shot."

"Uh. Sorry about that."

Dava turned to see Lucky Jerk behind her, tipping sheepishly from side to side. The Poligart story was coming back to her. Lucky had once been a Mister. Press-ganged into their crew, if she were to believe his story. In any case, he'd found himself as one of the few left alive. Thompson would have liquidated him, except that he could fly a ship and she needed a pilot.

Half-Shot grunted. "Was he shooting at you?"

"Well, yeah," Lucky said.

"Then what's done is done," he said. Dava looked at him for a long moment to try to decide whether what was done really was done. The burn of her stare stirred him to speak again. "Tommy-Gun brung him on. I ain't gonna cross her."

"Good. There's few of us here and we need to be solid." Against the far wall, there leaned a massive figure with ghost-white skin. "Who's the big guy?"

"That's Polar Gary."

"What, like a polar bear?" Lucky said with a knowing nod. "All big and white."

"A polar bear?" Thompson flared at him, causing him to flinch. "No one has seen a fucking polar bear in four hundred years, asshole. We call him Polar Gary because he's bipolar. So don't piss him off."

"Sorry, Tommy." Lucky straightened up to give a nod in

the direction of the big man. "Sorry, Polar Gary."

"Whatever." Gary's deep voice was more vibration than sound.

Dava could hear Lucky whispering to Thompson, "Does he med? Why not just get gene therapy?"

Thompson's reply was low and weighty. "When he was a domer, yeah, he was medicating. He came to us to get away from that pacification bullshit."

The word *pacification* jolted Dava with déjà-vu. A teenager from Earth, orphaned, forced to live in the domes. Always getting into trouble. Always troubled, always troubling. They'd put her on a special diet, which she'd seen at first as straight discipline, another form of forced conformity. When she caught herself staring blissfully at the fake clouds in the sky, she realized they'd been drugging her food. The confrontation with her guardians that followed was muddy in her mind; most memories from that time were hard to solidify.

Pacify her.

"So." Thompson's voice jarred her back to the present. "That makes five grunts: me, you, Seven-Pack, Half-Shot, Polar Gary. And Lucky, if we need a pilot."

Dava looked around at them. It was a small outfit, but that was good. She didn't know all of them well. She had no choice but to trust them, but that seemed easier at this point. Was it desperation? Or was it that they'd be easier to leave behind if she cared less for them?

Whatever it was, it didn't matter. There was a job to do, and though she hadn't gotten any order, she knew it needed to be done.

"I assume we need a pilot," Thompson prodded.

"We need several."

CHAPTER 7

"Get ready for the next hop." The pilot, Ayliff, was losing enthusiasm quickly. "Ninety seconds."

Granny sighed and checked her straps. "Better get in the back, kid," she said to Jax with a nod.

McManus pouted in his nearby chair, already strapped in. "Let's get it over with."

Jax tugged on his tether, pulling himself back toward the harness at the rear of the cabin. They'd unstrapped him at the end of the ten-day drag between systems, but decided they didn't want him to have free run of the ship, so he was bound by a long, thick cord to a locked fastener along the back wall. This allowed him some limited movement; not that he was any good at zero-G locomotion. In that sense, the tether was not only to keep him from escaping, it kept him from drifting into something important.

He wrapped the harness belts around his legs and then his abdomen. He made sure to get the mask on nice and tight before pulling the upper straps over his head and shoulders. It was strange how quickly the action had become routine, had become ritual. They'd explained it once to him, then told him if he did it wrong he would die. He'd asked how, but they'd given no details, leaving him to imagine terrible things himself: crushing asphyxiation, organs being pulled out through his throat, exsanguination via explosive depressurization. A myriad of bloody images in his head, he decided not to forget the instructions, and managed the four times after that.

"Thirty seconds."

He tried not to hold his breath, but it was almost impossible. It was a terrible shock, jumping to Xarp speed for a time, then dropping back out, only to jump again. He had no idea how long each leg was, but he guessed they could be measured in hours.

At first he didn't understand why they were Xarp-jumping after an already extensive Xarp trip from Eridani. After a few of these hops, he remembered that first Xarp experience, when he and Runstom absconded in a Space Waste dropship. Runstom had been jumping, changing trajectory, then jumping again; several times, to throw off their pursuers. Yet who were McManus and his crew pursued by? No one, as far as Jax knew.

He thought about all this in the stretches of nothing during each jump. Eventually it came to him: they weren't bouncing because they were shaking off a tail, they were bouncing because they didn't know where they were going. In between each hop, the crew would sit around grumpily, taking the downtime to suck food from tubes and use the vacuum-powered lavatory. McManus would periodically punch unenthusiastically at one of the consoles in the corner.

A communication unit of some kind. Jax figured the cop

was getting coordinates for the next hop. Wherever they were headed, someone was sufficiently paranoid to keep it well hidden. And that paranoid someone was X.

They came out of the last Xarp and they all slowly picked at their straps.

Jax had been trying to gauge how loyal McManus's crew was. It was hard to tell. They seemed to take every order, and though they complained a lot, they never disobeyed. Maybe they weren't smart enough to be suspicious, or maybe they just didn't care.

While poking around the system during the interstellar trek, he'd found a way to send Ayliff and Granny a message, but it hadn't panned out. He must have found an unused part of the operating system, something that was long ago deprecated. So in between every short jump, he debated on whether or not to express his fears. Fears he thought the crew should share, if they weren't so blatantly ignorant. They couldn't know anything about X; they were too by-the-book in their operations to be part of that ring of corruption. Jax suspected that the pilot and the gunner were only along for the mission because they thought it was official, and they were told not to question. With each jump, they grew more restless. Was it time to play his hand, to blurt out all the information he knew about X? Would they listen, or would they ignore him? And what would McManus do to him if he involved the others? Would he simply drag Jax out of the cabin and stow him in another part of the ship?

These questions burbled to the top of his muddy mind whenever they came out of Xarp. It was just a matter of making something come out of his mouth. Easier thought than said.

Granny was the first to exercise her voice. "How many more of these damn jumps do we have to make, Sarge?"

"We're close," McManus said quietly.

"X keeps himself well hidden," Jax said. His brain was still mush, and he didn't have a plan, but he needed to say something.

"Shut the fuck up, Jackson," McManus shot, fire in his eyes.

"What does he mean?" Granny said, scrunching her face at Jax. "Who or what is X?"

Jax tried to stare as sharply at McManus as the cop stared at him, but he felt his will sapping. McManus had long ago shut off the part of his brain that was open to reason – no, that wasn't it exactly; he'd shut off the part of his brain that was open to options. He was like a train on a track and was not going anywhere it didn't want him to go.

"Contact!" Ayliff shouted, breaking the silence.

The world jolted and Jax was slammed in the guts by the straps still half harnessing his body. The ship lurched and twisted, all of them gasping and cursing.

"What is it?" McManus blurted.

With a series of grunts, the pilot recovered enough to respond. "We're hacked. Remote control."

"God dammit, McManus," Granny shouted. "What the hell did you get us into?"

"Just calm down," he spat back.

"X." She pointed at Jax. "You said X. Who is X? I've heard of him. I know I have. What kind of shit did you get us into?"

"Tell them," Jax gasped through another lurch. "Tell them who he is. He's going to kill us, dammit! He's going to kill us!"

"Shut up, Jackson! Shut the fuck up!"

"Ayliff, reboot it," Granny shouted. "Break the connection. Break the goddamn connection!"

"Sarge?" was all the pilot could manage.

"Just fucking relax," McManus said. He was half strapped to his console, and half reaching out with a hand as if to calm the room. "Just trust—"

He was cut off with a wheeze when the ship pivoted and began accelerating.

"Alright, fuck this," Ayliff said. "Granny, reboot sequence. It takes two consoles to do it."

"Hit it," she said.

And the lights went out for the space of a silent breath.

Then came back on, only red instead of white. The hum of electronics came too, normally background noise, now seeming louder as they powered back up.

"It's coming up now," Ayliff said. "I'm going to try to kill the remote access virtual ports before they try to reconnect."

"Wait, what is this?" Granny said. "Ayliff, are you seeing this? What's OS MOTD mean?"

Ayliff's head cocked side to side in thought. "Um. Operating system. Uh. Message? Of ... of the day?"

Jax felt his breath catch in his throat and lodge there like a lump of rock. He glanced at McManus, whose eyes were glued to the communications console in front of him. Reading.

This is Jackson. I've done no harm to the system, I only overwrote the OS MOTD.

The man we're going to see is known to most as X. His real name is Mark Xavier Phonson. He is – or was, I don't know any more – a cop with ModPol. He is a master manipulator and has used his skills to extort others for power and money, and where necessary, to end lives.

Sergeant McManus is under orders to bring me to X. Maybe he thinks he's just doing his job, but this operation is far outside the normal operating parameters of ModPol. X doesn't want me arrested, he wants me gone. He wants me disappeared. And he's very good at covering his tracks. So it's not a stretch to think that he'll want this whole ship to disappear.

What you do next is up to you. All I'm asking is that you be officers of justice when you do it.

There was a metallic scraping sound, and Jax realized after a cold second that McManus had drawn a weapon.

"No one touch anything," he said quietly.

Granny pushed herself away from her console and drifted to the center of the cabin. "That's enough, Jared," she spat. "Enough of this bullshit. You're not shooting anyone, you bastard. Kyl, shut down the remote access before they get a lock on us."

"Ayliff, don't touch anything," McManus said louder. His gun couldn't decide whether to point at Granny or the pilot.

"Just do it, Kyl," she said. "This ends now. Jared McManus, you put that weapon away or I'm relieving you of duty."

He blinked and the gun went slack for just a moment. "You … you don't know what we're dealing with."

"Enlighten me."

"Just let him pull us in," McManus said, the gun still

up, but less threatening. "We turn over Jackson, and then we're on our way."

There was a silence that followed, and Jax began to panic. "No, you won't be on your way," he said. "He'll have no more use for you. You'll be loose ends. Pilot, how many jumps did you make to get here?"

"Uh, five."

"This is what I'm talking about," Jax said, looking from Granny to McManus. "Where the hell are we? His secret fortress or something? No one hides this well and then lets people come and go freely."

After another stretch of silence, Ayliff piped up. "I disabled all the remote ports."

"Good," Granny said. "I have a sudden urge to phone home. Can you take us to the nearest ModPol comm beacon?"

"Yeah." He was looking over his shoulder at Granny, then at McManus, as though giving the sergeant an opportunity to protest. When he didn't, Ayliff continued. "We'll be on our way just as soon as the drives come back online."

"And the contact?"

"Still out there. We're moving right with it. I think when they took control of the patroller, they set us along the same trajectory."

Jax looked at Granny and McManus, who both frowned. It was too late.

A clang erupted from somewhere below them.

"What was that?" Granny said.

"We're being boarded," McManus said, flexing his fingers around his gun.

* * *

The interstellar patroller was well divided into lots of small sections. It was designed to be able to take hull damage without affecting the entire ship. It was also kind of a damn maze.

McManus looked at his arm-pad again. Boxes, a dozen or so, all interconnected. He punched the three-dimensional view, causing a small holoprojection to rise from the pad's screen. He'd left Ayliff and Granny in the control cabin, and had dragged Jackson to the tube room. There was no time to shove him into a tube, so he'd bound him to a door handle and left him there.

Now he needed to get to the cube flashing red in his projection: a small cargo bay near the rear-bottom of the ship. As he pulled himself through another hatchway and into the long corridor that ran through the middle from fore to aft, he tried to inspect the map. The cargo room had openings on three sides. The more he studied the map, the more he realized there were no natural choke points anywhere; every room connected to at least two or three other rooms or corridors. With a sour grunt he realized it had probably been designed that way so that if something went bad in one room, you could still get around it and get to other important parts of the ship.

He whipped across the handholds, down the corridor, punching the release on the hatch at the end. Down into the next room. This section was a small cluster of adjacent cargo holds. He checked his map and spun open the door that opened back in the direction of the ship's fore.

And he had to shield his eyes from the bright sparks coming from the floor. He cursed himself for not grabbing a helmet – at least then he could extend a visor. But it didn't matter. Within seconds, his mind resolved the flash he'd seen: they were cutting through the hull.

This could be his choke point. He could wait for the cutting to stop, position himself behind a crate, and blast anyone that poked their head through the hole. For a second, his brilliant mind came up with the thought of just covering the hole with crates from around the room. As the scenario played out in his head, the bulky containers were brushed aside with little force in the absence of gravity.

The other scenario playing in his mind showed him the cutting finishing, the circle of metal floating up, followed by canisters of gas, smoke, whatever. Hell, maybe something flammable. As a choke point it was too obvious, and McManus had no real protection against any of those attacks. The red on his map began flashing more quickly. He needed to get out or he'd be the one choking.

He went through the door on the other side. As it sealed behind him, he frantically looked for a way to lock it. He pawed through the doorpad interface until he found the lock controls. They were faded in color. Disabled. He punched the icon anyway.

LOCK CONTROL REQUIRES COMMAND OVERRIDE.

"Command override?" He smacked the door with the flat of his hand. "I'm the goddamn commander of this ship!"

VOICE COMMAND INTERFACE ACTIVATED. INSUFFICIENT PRIVILEGES.

"What the fuck," he mumbled. Then he stabbed at his armpad. "Ayliff. Ayliff, are you there?"

"Yeah, Sarge," came the reply through the pad's speaker.

"I need you to lock this door." He scanned the surface, then noticed the doorpad's interface had a number at the bottom. "Door number F, one, six, six."

"F, one, six?"

"Six, six."

"F, six, six?"

"No, goddamn it," McManus shouted. A crunching sound came from the room on the other side of the door. He tried to breathe. "F, one, six, six."

"Got it," Ayliff said. The lock icon flashed on the doorpad.

"Okay, good." McManus was already on the move, heading for the door to his right, on the starboard side of the room. "Can you figure out what door is directly opposite that one, to the aft?"

"Uh, yeah, sure."

"Lock that one too."

"Okay, Sarge."

McManus muted his armpad. He'd just have to hope that Ayliff figured out what door he was talking about. He went through the door, then turned aft. He picked his way through the small hold and went through the far door.

This put him in the hold directly starboard of the hold they were cutting into. He glanced at his map to verify, then flinched as louder crunching and squeaking sounds came from the door to the port side of the room. He was in the right place alright.

He floated to a stack of crates in the center of the room. They were strapped into place, and he hooked one foot under one of the straps to anchor himself. Then he braced himself with his left hand gripping a handhold on a crate, with his right aiming his weapon around the edge of it, pointing it at the portside door. He watched the holomap hovering above his armpad. He'd been grilled in many ModPol training sessions on the expected behavior of a boarding operation. If the attackers had the means to cut through a hull, any room they cut into was going to lose pressure. If they had any hope of opening doors of other rooms without destroying the whole ship, they'd need to restore that pressure. And generally, if they were bothering to board the thing, they wanted to keep it mostly intact.

The red turned yellow. That meant they'd sealed the hole they created, probably with an attached tube. The ship's life-support system was trying to backfill air into the room. After a few quiet minutes, during which McManus felt he might have a heart attack, the yellow flicked off and the room on the map went back to the standard gray color.

He switched off the map and watched the door. Gun close to the side of the crate, but not exposed to view. His head just poking around enough to see the door slide open. He pulled back and listened. How many were there? In the intense silence that followed, he could pick out the tiny clicks and swishes of movement. He knew that they couldn't come through that doorway more than two at a time.

He pulled his gun and face around the side of the crate. Sure enough, there were two reaching handholds on either side of the door. A third waited behind. They were wearing flexible, but expensive-looking armor and carrying flashers. High-charge pistols that could be used to stun or fry, depending on the business they needed to discuss. He took aim and fired.

The stunner screeched and all three of them jumped, though one of them jumped by the force of electricity coursing through his system. As they raised weapons, he took another shot.

And the gun beeped at him. He slid back just as arcs of light flashed his way. He looked at the stubborn weapon. The charge indicator was blinking a useless red. He'd forgotten to charge the damn thing after zapping Runstom. And he'd used a max-charge on his ex-squadmate, leaving the weapon nearly drained. He realized with a cold sweat that he probably didn't even stun his target with the one shot he managed – the charge was too weak. Strong enough to slow him down for a moment, but that was about it.

Weapons. His brain trying to kick his body into motion. Get to the fore, the weapons cabinet, just off to the side of the main cabin.

He unhooked his foot from the strap. Reached down and smacked the release on the bar that ran through the hooks at the end of the straps. It didn't budge, so he hit it again with the butt of the spent weapon. All the straps on one crate popped.

Grabbing a handle on another crate for leverage, he shoved the loose box in the direction of the armored goons. The flashing of their weapons paused long enough for him to brace a leg against the remaining crate and launch himself at the door he'd come through. It returned to scorch the doorway just as he made it through. The door slid shut behind.

"Ayliff!" he shouted at his arm. "Ayliff, where the fuck are you?"

No response. He was already at the portside door, another one he'd come through originally. He went through it. If he was fast enough, he might be able to lose them in the cargo-hold cluster. Through the next room, then up.

He'd reached the long corridor that ran the length of the ship. The weapons cabinet was in the armory, almost all the way to the main cabin.

He hissed into his armpad. "Ayliff, come in!"

Sweaty handhold to sweaty handhold, he pulled fore. "Ayliff, what the fuck." A tiny voice rattling around the back of his mind said *mute*, and he remembered to turn up the volume of his armpad. "Ayliff, are you there?"

"Yeah, Sarge, I said I'm here. Can you hear me?"

"Lock all the doors in the cargo holds."

"What door number?"

"All of them, Ayliff!" McManus shouted as he pulled with both hands, his empty weapon discarded. "All the cargo hold doors!"

"Too late, pal." The voice behind him came through an external helmet-speaker, giving it an electric coldness. McManus didn't bother to look back.

"Should we toast him or just stun him?" The helmet speaker failed to modulate the volume of this quiet aside, which blared down the hall.

"X says to stun everyone first. I think he wants to toast them later."

McManus kept pulling, cursing the length of the corridor. Cursing his exposure. Cursing himself for not listening to Jackson sooner. Cursing Runstom for using up all the juice in his gun.

Cursing Runstom for any of it; Jackson, X, the whole mess was Runstom's fault.

"Damn it," he muttered as he yanked his body just past the halfway mark of the passage. Maybe he should have listened to Runstom all along.

It was the last thought he had before his body erupted with electric fire and his vision brightened into blankness.

* * *

Jax had tried to hide, but it hadn't taken the goons very long to find him. The pilot and the gunner had managed to lock themselves in the main cabin, but no one seemed to care. They'd restrained Jax with simple plastic cuffs and pulled him down to the cargo holds, through the hole in the hull, down the attached tube, and into their ship. They'd brought him into a room whose function Jax couldn't identify. It was spacious, but there wasn't much in it, other than a panting mound of Sergeant Jared McManus in the exact center. They removed the cuffs, and Jax could see McManus was also unbound.

Phonson – Jax decided to think of him by his real name, to take the sting out of the infamy associated with his mysterious and ominous nickname – had come in shortly after. He strolled in idly, checking a few screens on the walls, nodding to himself without comment. He was helmetless and his bald, red head gleamed in the bright, hot lights of the room.

"What the hell is this?" McManus said, breaking the quiet. Shaking, he got to his feet. Jax was tempted to support him as he struggled against the weak artificial gravity, but that was just reflex. He kept a few paces' distance as McManus mustered anger. "You put a hole in my goddamn ship!"

Phonson spoke without turning to them. "There are days when I feel like I can't trust people." Though low and even, his voice carried as though amplified. "Do you ever have those days?"

McManus braced his hands on his knees, working his way to a half-crouch, half-upright stance. "What the hell are you talking about? I came all the way out here, didn't I? I brought you Jackson, didn't I?"

"Due diligence," Phonson said with a dismissive wave by way of explanation. He checked another screen and then finally turned to face them. "I just need to find out where you stand, and what you know. There may be some light torture. If you survive, then you'll be free to go."

Jax felt his long-empty stomach twist. He reflexively looked around the room for an escape. The door that Phonson had come through seemed unguarded, and it was off to the side, away from the screens he was inspecting. It was too easy, which told Jax it wasn't possible. He felt compelled not to move. He couldn't see anything that told him he was restrained, but he felt it.

"Light torture?" McManus cocked his head. He was working hard to project bravado, but Jax could see the sweat beading along his brow and hear the slight quiver in his voice. "How long is this going to take?"

"Oh don't worry," Phonson said. He came closer, to within a few paces of them. "Your ride won't leave without you. One of my guys left a bomb onboard that will trigger if it gets too far away from us."

Evidently McManus had run out of rebuttals. He paced, his head swiveling. He must have sensed a containment as well, and he was trying to identify the edges of the invisible barrier. With an unexpected quickness, he dropped to a crouch and bolted at Phonson.

He managed a few strides before he collapsed, his momentum causing him to tumble and slide forward. All of his muscles bulged and quivered and an airless sound hissed from his clenched jaw.

"Wow, that thing actually works," Phonson said. Jax couldn't tell if he was joking or genuinely impressed. "I wanted to test it out but I couldn't get any volunteers. None of my guys are quite so stupid."

"What was that?" Jax said. "I mean, I only ask because you seem anxious to brag about it."

Phonson's growing smile wavered and he glared at Jax. "Anti-aggression technology," he said, stuck between pride and mild embarrassment at being a braggart. "It's in the room. Very sophisticated AI. Infrared cameras, they scan every movement, every muscle twitch. Even when we think we're being stealthy, our muscles betray us with micro-movements. This thing picks up all that data and ..." he started, then stalled, his head cocking as he looked for the words. "Calculates intent."

Jax thought about this. "So I can walk around the room as long as I don't try to hurt you?"

"Yeah," Phonson said. He reached out a hand. "When we first met, it wasn't proper, was it? I'm Mark Phonson."

Jax regarded the red-skinned man with trepidation. In some ways, he would have felt safer if he were in an actual cell or if his hands were bound. The blatant lack of restraint was unnerving. He felt a breath suck into his chest and he blew it out and took a step forward. He reached out to take the offered, gloved hand.

Phonson shook, holding it for just a moment. "See? No aggression, no reaction. But if aggression is detected," he said, nodding at the stiffened form of McManus, "then the safeguards kick in."

Finally he let go and Jax felt himself breathe. There was a time on Terroneous when he was helping out an agriculturalist on his plot of land. A farm; that's what he'd called it. They'd been setting up perimeter detection gear – garbage tech that somehow had value on a backwater moon like Terroneous – and it had picked up movement. They watched an animal through the cameras and the feeling it gave Jax was something primal, something that reached into the core of shared memory passed to him through thousands of years of DNA. Something that said, *fear this animal.* It was long, like a tube, its skin slick and shiny. There were many small appendages along its body that twitched and clawed as it coiled and uncoiled through the shrub. The farmer called it a *snake*, and though Jax had heard the word before and knew of its Earth origins, in his world it had meant something utilitarian, something useful. This thing was nothing of the sort. They'd caught a glimpse of an orifice at one end, and it peeled open for only a moment, revealing rows of fibrous tentacles. The farmer had explained that these were used to paralyze prey before consumption.

That same ancestral fear uncoiled inside Jax when he shook Phonson's hand. The man was a predator, and Jax was prey. He wasn't getting out of this place alive. Whatever this place was.

"What exactly is this place?" Jax asked. "A ship?"

"Cool, isn't it?" Phonson said, looking up and around, as though he could see it from the outside. "It's kind of a comet. Or modeled after a comet, I guess. I'd tell you more about it, but ... well ... *you* know."

"What?"

"You'll be dead soon."

"I see," Jax said, using all his energy to tamp down his screaming terror. "There's one thing you could tell me: how will my rescuers find me?"

His face tightened, registering a mild frustration. "You're afraid. But not afraid enough. Ain't gonna be a rescue. This baby moves fast and is very hard to find. And the only people who know about it are very well paid and very well threatened."

McManus uncurled with a groan. Evidently, the effects of the aggression counter-measures were temporary. "I'm going to kill you, you bastard," he mumbled. He turned over and got on all fours, then took another panting break before attempting to stand.

Phonson narrowed his eyes and held them on McManus for a moment, then walked to the screens on the side of the room. "Death threats only make the torture more fun."

CHAPTER 8

The barge had finally arrived at the prison and Runstom was awakened to finish his duty. He felt like shit. The process of flushing the hypersleep out of his system took time and effort. The ingest of nutritious chemicals, the egress of narcotic toxic sludge. His only consolation was the bomb-ball feeds his personal vid-player picked up upon arrival in the Barnard system. Though once he left his quarters he couldn't remember what he'd watched.

The prisoners went through the same cleansing process, only with smaller doses of the good stuff. To keep them compliant during the transfer. As a guard, it was Runstom's duty to wake up faster. After a full morning of intensive recycling, he got the call to move. No one said much of anything. The other guards looked as bad as he felt. The prisoners looked dazed. He and another guard – Werner, by his name tag – paired up to open each cell in their assignment. Run a scan on the prisoner in the cell. Secure the prisoner with bindings. Escort the prisoner to a holding area.

The artificial gravity was active on the barge, pulling only a half G, give or take. Mostly for the benefit of everyone's inner ear as they recovered from the sleep. It would be turned off once it was time to dock and transfer.

One by one, Runstom and Werner worked slowly through their charges. Each inmate was a groggy pool of human. Except one. Moses Down.

Runstom stood in front of the cell. "Hands above your head."

Down stood in the center of the cell and stared. He said nothing.

"Turn around and put your hands above your head," Runstom repeated.

Nothing. Not a twitch. Just a long stare. But not intimidation. Something else.

Runstom sighed and tugged at the uncomfortable uniform. A tickle flickered through the back of his mind. This Moses Down was apparently a prize catch. He was destined for a cell deep within the prison. "You're some kind of boss, right?" There was no response, so Runstom tapped the stunner in its holster at his side. "If you don't cooperate, I have to stun you."

"Have you ever been on the receiving end of one of those stunners?" he finally spoke.

"Yes." Again, he was engaging. He shouldn't have answered. But he wasn't going to back down from this bullshit. He *had* felt the sting of a stunner, and not long ago. That bastard McManus—

The tickle was back. He looked at his chest. *McManus.*

He unlocked the cell. Stepped in. Up to Moses Down. "You called me Mr. Runstom before," he said quietly. "How did you know my name?"

"That's easy, Stanford." Down's deep voice was calm. "I knew Sylvia."

Ice slid down Runstom's spine. So that was it. Down would have been with Space Waste back when his mother was undercover. Runstom knew the Wasters had found her out. Knew that she had to go into witness protection after that. Which was why she was hiding on Epsilon Eridani-3, under an alias. Could Down or anyone else possibly know she was there?

"I don't know what you're talking about." Runstom had to force the words out. He didn't want to let on anything about his mother.

Down grunted and cracked a hint of a smile. "Good. She taught you to be quiet."

"I—"

"I *was* a boss," Down said. "To answer your question. You're lookin' at the top dog, Stanford. Course, now I'm just an inmate. Someone else better step up."

Runstom let out a grunt in an attempt not to be flummoxed by the presence of celebrity. "Had to happen some day," he muttered.

Down laughed shortly, then leaned in and lowered his voice. "I don't want to sound like a cliché or something, Stanford. But there's a storm brewing."

Runstom took a couple of slow breaths through his nose. "What do you mean?" he said evenly.

"ModPol. Mixing, always mixing. Fixing to make something. Always fixing to make something."

"To make what?"

His long hand rolled with his words. "Make something new. Make something work. Make something blow up."

"When does this storm get here?" Runstom asked for lack of anything better to say.

"It already started." Down looked away, as if he could see into the distance. "It's been building for a while now. Lately there's been some big thunder. Like what happened in Eridani."

"What happened in Eridani is that you attacked ModPol and you lost."

Down looked at him again. A mirthless smile. "It was just a raid. Not an attack. But it felt different, didn't it? Do you feel what's happening? Can't put your finger on it, right? So you keep busy. But that something is still there. Growing. Something heavy. Something warm. That's the way the air changes, right before a storm."

"I feel it." Runstom swallowed, his throat feeling dry. "It doesn't feel like a storm."

"No?"

"It feels like war."

The smile dropped away and Down nodded slowly. After a moment of silence, of meeting his eyes, he turned around. "You better bind me, Stanford." His hands went up to his head. "Don't worry. I won't stay bound forever."

* * *

Like a rock in his boot, something else pestered Runstom. Something that needed to be dealt with. An earlier version of himself would have been eager to chase it. To follow the clues. Connect the dots. But he was tired. Not tired, exactly, just out of energy. Out of the kind of energy it took to try to stay above water in an ocean of deceit.

And that's what he was mentally preparing for: a conversation with a liar. Liar, manipulator, murderer. And somehow, however remotely, an ally.

In a place that never had gravity, there was no up or down. The entire thing was a sphere, more or less. The curving hallways were tubes whose round edges had been squared off octagonally. Whatever wall was at his feet was the floor for the moment. The electromagnets all around the sides of the tubes awakened in clusters in response to the proximity of his special gloves and boots. This allowed him to walk without much trouble. He could jog if he wanted to, but that would be trickier. In his younger days he practiced jogging on a zero-grav magnet track back on his ModPol outpost. Would it come back to him if he tried it? The practiced rhythm that was necessary to work with the magnets and not against them. Their pull on a curve, stronger on contact, weaker at a distance. Unlike the pull of gravity, which was consistent through a stride, from top to bottom.

His temporary assignment as prisoner transport guard included a time-limited assignment at the prison, for the purposes of transfer and hand-off. It also gave him access to the local databases. A quick search had turned her up. Mass murder charges for the victims on Barnard-4 – charges that were originally applied to Jax, until Runstom helped prove his innocence by proving her guilt. A litany of other related charges, such as tampering with life-support equipment and operations, development of malicious software, misuse of company property, extortion, and so on. Her sentence was permanent residency at a zero-gravity, zero-connectivity, maximum-security facility. To Runstom's knowledge, this place was the only such prison that met the criteria.

It was designed to be self-contained. Impossible to escape. Even if a resident got outside, there was nowhere to go.

Deep in the outer belt of Barnard space. If they managed to find a ship, navigation through the asteroids was treacherous. Required defenses like the barge had: full coverage, low-latency sensor arrays, paired with microlasers for picking off unavoidable rocks.

It was also designed to be riot-proof. Inmate uniforms were lined with thin strips of lightweight metal, highly magnetic. At any time, the focused electromagnetic modules that pervaded the entire complex could be triggered, targeting specific prisoners or groups of prisoners. The strength of the magnets could be varied, powered up to the point of immobility.

And it was completely cut off. The only transmissions coming and going were heartbeats. Some kind of short, periodic signal that the prison pinged out to a couple of ModPol outposts in the system. Those periodically pinged back, letting the prison know that the rest of the universe still existed. The pings were automatic, but they included a handwritten message at least once a day, just to confirm there was a human alive somewhere and still in charge.

Of course, there were broadcasts out there bouncing around space. News and sports. Some of it made it through the interference generated by the asteroid field, so the denizens of the prison weren't completely cut off.

Was it enough for someone like Jenna Zarconi?

He came to a part of the tube that broke open into a connector. A three-dimensional version of an octagon – he didn't know what it was called. Another tube connected at a ninety-degree angle. He followed it. Metal boots ticking along the magnets. Deeper into the sphere.

The center was reserved for the most dangerous inmates. To hear how some of the administrators talked about them, they were also the most valuable inventory; the fees that the complex collected to keep a prisoner in the center were as much as an entire block of regular inmates. It was as though the outer sections of the prison only existed to make the center seem deeper.

The ambient lighting dimmed as he progressed. He wondered if it would be completely dark by the time he reached her. Before he realized it, he'd passed through three more of the bands of corridors that formed layers around the center of the facility. There was no way to go deeper, so he followed the last ring around. Didn't matter which direction; it was a complete circle, and there was only one hatch that led into the Core.

The Core. That's what they called the cluster of sixteen cells at the center. Designed in such a way that only one was accessible at a time, through some rotation mechanism. Because he'd filed the request earlier in the day, they'd already dialed up Zarconi. No one had asked him why. He suspected most knew that he was the one who arrested her. Back when he was an officer for Justice.

That, plus the fact that Stanford Runstom and Jenna Zarconi were a pair of the few people in the universe to have spent their developmental years on a spacecraft, bringing a green pigmentation to their skin. When he saw her through the window to her cell, he noticed right away that hers was looking better than the last time he'd seen her. Back on Sirius-5, her skin had begun to ashen, the luster fading. Now it was back to its former richness, a deep, almost forest green.

"You don't have to say it," she said. A small and dangerous smile. "I've been adapting to my new environment. My new world, really. Once I saw it like that – once

I got my perspective straight – I was able to change my attitude."

She was a murderer. Cold-blooded. Remorseless. But she'd helped him. Her help may have even saved his life. "I'm glad to see you're well."

"It's funny," she said, pacing lightly behind the window. It wasn't a solid window, but a field of some kind. Probably electromagnetic like everything else. "I sometimes wonder why they go through all this trouble to keep people locked up for life. Why not just kill them? Out the airlock, a one-way trip to the void?"

"You were prosecuted and sentenced," he said. "If we executed people, we'd be no better than murderers."

"Unless they were enemy combatants."

There was no doubt that he struggled with this difference. Especially working for Defense, when he used to work for Justice. He was no longer in the business of upholding the law. He was in the business of something else. Something that was preventative when it worked, and bloody when it didn't.

Sensing his unwillingness to share his thoughts on the matter, Zarconi continued. "Or – since they want to keep us alive – why not put us in sleep pods? You don't even need guards for prisoners that are in stasis."

"Just let you sleep until you die?" he said. Wishing he had not allowed her to drag him into this useless banter. But he would have to let her talk if he were to get any information out of her.

"Yes, I see what you mean," she said. "Pretty much the same as killing us outright." She waved her hand. "Also, we wouldn't suffer the same as we do now. In this waking prison."

"Well," Runstom mumbled. "At least you're not suffering too badly."

Her smile grew and her head dipped. "Stanford. You were worried about me."

He forced a laugh. "I'd never worry about you."

"Yes, I can take care of myself, can't I? They let us out, to mix with the other rings. Part of the humane thing again. Or perhaps part of the suffering – I'm not really sure. In any case, I found it easy to make friends."

These things he also knew, thanks to some of the other staff: Core prisoners were brought out of their cells, but only one at a time. The reason was that it was the humane thing to do. To at least allow them some social interaction. Complete isolation would be the equivalent of torture, and no civilized government could subscribe to ModPol policing services if they tortured anyone, murderers or not.

He'd also learned a little about how she'd made friends: the staff suspected she'd been trading contraband. Which was supposed to be impossible in the sphere. An administrator he talked to had shrugged this off, observing that desperate people will always find a way. When Runstom had balked at this, he was assured the desperation was on the part of her clientele, with so much of the population being addicts of some kind. For Zarconi's part, she was merely amused by the whole business. If she was desperate for anything, it was entertainment.

"You always bring something to the party," he tried, hoping to keep it light enough to get her to open up.

"You know me well." Her face got a little more serious. Thoughtful. "It's a closed economy. It's very interesting. I wonder if anyone studies it. Nothing comes in, nothing goes out. But there are resources. They're just very hard to come by. The study of the allocation of scarce resources – that's economics. Have you ever heard that definition?" Runstom hadn't, but she didn't wait for his answer anyway. "A gifted person can cultivate those resources. Very low supply, and very high demand. And since there is no currency, what's exchanged? Favors. Allegiances. Power."

He considered this. The prison administrators would love to know what it was she was up to. He could try to talk it out of her. But as she said, it was a closed economy. What difference did it make? Whatever action she had going on, it was probably keeping her alive.

"And power means protection," he said. "And other privileges, I'm sure. Stuff I can't imagine."

She smiled again, this time with a wiggle of the head. "You're trying to flatter me. And submit, at the same time. Must be you want something."

He sighed. Never any good at the games, so he might as well be straight. "I need some information."

"Well, I don't collect much of that anymore," she said with a soft sigh. "Unless you want the latest dirt on some of my fellow residents."

"A former acquaintance," he said. "Tim Cazos."

Her face scrunched up. "Timmy Cazos. Good programmer. Uptight shit."

"What can you tell me about him?"

"I won't guess what you already know," she said. "Used to be a software engineer. Got into cryptocurrency fraud. He was damn good at it, too. Good enough to fool most systems, anyhow. And good enough to fool the fools who thought they were getting untraceable payments for unsavory acts."

"Pay-offs then," Runstom said. "Bribes? Jobs?"

"Yeah, anything like that. We only used his hacked cash when we knew it'd never come back on us."

"We."

She rolled her eyes. "Me and Mark and Jorg." She lifted her wrists to the invisible window. "Want to arrest me for conspiracy? I keep trying to spill this stuff and no one will take my statements."

By Mark, she meant Mark Xavier Phonson. Jorg, his brother. Her target when she put into motion the chain of events that led to the asphyxiation of the block of residents on Barnard-4. Her defense had been that she was trying to leave them, to disband the trio of corruption they were entrenched in. That they hadn't taken well to it. Extorted her. Threatened her freedom at every turn.

She'd planned it out well enough. Every step, she'd manipulated X's cronies and other extortion victims. Had one of X's hitmen attack Jorg. Then through an elaborate hack, the dome vacated its air supply, suffocating the fatally-injured Jorg, the hitman, and thirty innocent residents. Because she'd impersonated X every step of the way, used his people, the connected dots all led back to him. Or so she had hoped.

"How did Cazos end up as a mole, working inside Space Waste?"

She grinned. "Be careful, Runstom. I've got nothing better to do with my life sentence than tell long stories."

Runstom didn't know what his next move was. Other than checking in with his director, Victoria Horus. She was in Sirius, so any communication with her would be via d-mail. And the prison had no d-mail system. There was no rush. "I've got time."

"Well then," Zarconi said. "Let me tell you the tale of three greedy goons."

The special uniform Runstom was forced to wear in order to maneuver about the facility had no pockets that would fit his old-fashioned pen and notebook. He listened to the story and quickly forgot the names of the less important cast. The three villains of the piece were dirty cops that were on X's payroll. They toyed with a few side operations of their own, and when X found out, he was not happy. He decided to cut them loose.

Of course, he'd done so with manipulation. He came to the cabal and expressed concern that they weren't being used to their full potential. That there was more money to be made on all sides. A laundering operation. A healthy cut promised.

"Timmy was involved of course," she said. "These three idiots had no idea how to launder cryptocurrency. Mark told them, just do as Cazos says."

She continued in dizzying detail the ins and outs of cryptocurrency fraud, which cruised over Runstom's head like a passing comet. Cazos, who was never a cop, was not privy to all that X was capable of. He unwittingly found himself the target of a sting operation.

"So he's fucked," she said. "He doesn't know that X tipped off the fraud squad. He thinks X is still his friend and cohort, and when X comes to meet him, he explains that he's arranged a deal. Timmy had no choice but to take it."

The deal involved flipping on the aforementioned trio of goons. Cazos had testified. The others were tight-lipped, feeling double-crossed by Cazos. They waited for X to find a way to save them, but he never came through. The three dirty cops went to prison. Runstom had no doubt the rest of their story was painful and short.

"So X gets these three assholes out of his way, which sends a message to any other insiders on his payroll that can read between the lines."

Runstom grunted. "Kind of an elaborate plan."

She smiled broadly, the green of her face creating small triangles around the corners of her mouth. "It was my plan."

He shook his head and frowned. "What about Cazos?"

"He made his deal and was free to go. Placed into witness protection." She waggled her head. "Not without strings, of course. He would remain at the beck and call of ModPol."

"And he was thankful to X," Runstom said with a sigh.

"In his eyes, Mark pulled his ass out of the fire, so yeah." She leaned closer and lowered her voice in mock conspiracy. "I heard they put him on a Space Waste sting." She leaned back and crooked an eyebrow. "Maybe it was the same sting that recently gave this prison a population boost. There goes the neighborhood, right?"

He glared at her, then tried to soften his face. "You said he was a good programmer."

"Oh yeah," she said, relaxing into boredom. "I mean, he used to do it for real. Solid background with COMPLEX and Qubidense. Had a knack for interface design."

This was all meaningless to Runstom. He began to think out loud. "So you heard it was a sting. Cazos was sent in. He probably helped set the trap by hacking the computers somehow."

She laughed. "Hacking the computers – yeah, that's what you'd call it."

"Whatever," he mumbled. He tried to imagine what Cazos had actually done, but the pictures were not forming in his mind. He supposed it had something to do with navigation systems. Or comms. Or the contact computer. "They'd stolen some equipment from the research base on Vulca. Space Waste. It was some ... some kind of *detection* equipment."

"And you and your unit of Defenders ran them off that little moon," she said.

"They still got the equipment," he said. "But it was old. It had recently been replaced. They thought they were grabbing the new stuff, but they got the old stuff."

She drifted lightly, giving the impression of pacing. "So they had a bunch of equipment that probably didn't work. Someone needed to make it look like it worked, in order to set up the sting."

Runstom nodded. Everything was lining up with the conversations he'd had with Jax and Sylvia. "So they sent in Cazos. ModPol sent him in to fake the equipment, to set up the sting." There was still more missing. "Who planned it though? Was X involved?"

"Cazos belongs to Mark as much as he belongs to ModPol," she said. "It's possible that Mark was involved, but I don't know what he would want out of a Space Waste sting. Unless he was trading favors."

Runstom was only half-listening when he snapped his fingers. "And Jax said Basil Roy – Cazos's alias – was new in Space Waste. Which means there was already someone on the inside. Probably still is."

She narrowed her eyes at him. "I'm hearing a lot of past tense when you mention Timmy."

He regarded her for a moment. It wasn't that he didn't think she could bear the brunt of learning that her one-time acquaintance was dead. It was the fact that it had gone unreported. Of all the pieces of information she managed to get her hands on, this was one that would never come to light. Runstom had jettisoned Cazos's body, which would have burned up in the atmosphere of Eridani-3. Complete disintegration. He'd done the wrong thing by not turning it over to the locals, or bringing it with him to the ModPol base. He'd participated in the cover-up of a murder.

This whole business had dragged him farther and farther away from the pursuit of justice. Here he was, chatting it up with a mass murderer. Popping corpses out of the airlocks. Way out of his jurisdiction. Way off course.

And why? He tried to reignite that fire, that passion. That need to know. That need to connect the dots. To uncover the shady dealings of those who sought to abuse their power. Again, why? Justice? It didn't seem like enough anymore. He'd been broken of that idealistic pursuit.

"How's Jack?" she said, breaking his fall.

It jarred him, a necessary reminder. If he couldn't properly pursue justice, he could at least aid his only friend. "Not good," he grunted. He wondered if she felt remorse for fucking up Jax's life so badly. Then realized she probably could not.

She sighed. "At least he has people who care about him."

He nodded, then caught himself. "People?"

"Oh," she said. "You probably missed it while you were out of the system." She chuckled. "Terroneous officials, they sent out some broadcasts. Making a big stink out of the illegal extradition of one of their ex-pats. They really don't like ModPol right now."

He mulled this over. He'd better have a look at these broadcasts. Wondered how much information they were revealing about Jax. "I have to go," he said.

She frowned. Not one of her mock faces, but a genuine sadness darkened over her. "Goodbye, Stanford Runstom."

He'd turned, but paused. His chest felt heavy, despite the

lack of gravity. Turned back to her. "Why are you saying it like that?"

She looked away, then looked back, not meeting his eyes. "My usefulness is thinning. This is probably the last time I'll see you."

It was true, he realized. She'd been helpful, but she was cut off. From her networks, from the world. Any information she had now was history. Whatever happened next, he wasn't going to come back to this place. And she was never going to leave it.

He reached through the field. It dissipated momentarily at the proximity of his marked clothing. She was frozen, floating in the center of the small meeting room, not moving. He touched her hand. Looked at her face. A droplet of water formed at the edge of her eye and peeled away. Drifted between them.

"I know I'm a bad person," she whispered. "I don't know how to care about anyone. And I don't know why I care about you."

He withdrew. He wished she were someone else. But she was who she was. And he left her there to drift in her null-gravity cell.

* * *

There was pain, followed by more pain, followed by relief, but that was just to avoid desensitization before the new pain. Jax had started off by pouring details like a fountain. The kind of pain Jax had known before was limited to the occasional scrape or bump. Of course, there'd been the empty pain of hunger, of being cold and shelterless, of being less than human, that long stretch of blankness before he found his place on Terroneous. In some ways the pain of physical abuse, though immediate, held no candle to the infinite painlessness of inhumanity.

Nonetheless, the torture hurt, and so Jax told Phonson as much as he could, to a point. He told him what happened on Sirius-5, everything about Jenna Zarconi and the clues they'd followed. And then after that, when he'd fled and made his way back to Terroneous. He told him about McManus's failed attempt to capture him there, the "rescue" made by Space Waste. Phonson kept asking for names, like he wanted to know every single person Jax had met in the past year. Jax wanted the pain to stop, but he also knew that when it did, he was no more use to the paranoid man.

McManus had held up a little stronger, but then again, Jax suspected he knew even less. He was another of Phonson's pawns – another one who only knew X, didn't even know the man's real name – and he was being tortured just to add to the fear that Jax was already brimming with. Once in a while, McManus would work up the courage to attempt a sly attack against Phonson, but the anti-aggression sensors always caught him.

"I don't think those aggression safeguards are tuned right," Jax said when the next break came. His face felt puffy and bloated from the beatings it'd taken and his limbs were raw and hot from some kind of electric prod. "They keep letting you hit us."

Phonson allowed himself a small laugh. "Naturally, they know my pattern. The system ignores my movements."

"Naturally," Jax said quietly. "So it's got built-in asshole-detection."

Phonson slapped him across the face with his gloved

hand. The tender, battered nerves around his eye socket faintly wailed. The hand raised again.

"I'm trying to give you everything," Jax said with a flinch. "What the hell do you want?"

"You're not telling me anything about Eridani-3," Phonson said. His hand dropped and he looked away. He began pacing the room.

This much was true: Jax was withholding everything he could about Eridani-3. Would Phonson know anything about Sylvia Rankworth, originally Sylvia Runstom? He couldn't risk it either way. He'd die before he gave up any information about Stanford's mother.

The side effect was that his withholding was probably keeping him alive. Phonson was absolutely certain there was more information to be had, and as long as Jax was tight-lipped about Epsilon Eridani, he had something of value. He might have to leak something to keep it going. Something about Basil Roy and his Space Waste shenanigans – would that be enough to keep Phonson going?

"I never expected a domer to be so resilient," he said, walking over to his screens. "I guess you're no ordinary domer anymore. But I didn't get to this point in my life by relying only on physical threats."

Jax took the momentary pause in the action to try to slow his breathing, to try to quiet the pain. He knew the moment of relief wouldn't last, and that was the point. But he wondered why he wanted to keep going anyway. Why he wanted to draw out the torture, to make it last as long as possible. He was either hoping for rescue or he was punishing himself.

"Ah, here we go," Phonson said. He turned and motioned. "Come on over here, Jack. There's something you'll want to see."

Jax stiffened. "What is it?" he said quietly.

"Just come on," Phonson said with a wave. "It's a video. Some friends of yours. Seeing them might lift your spirits."

He approached cautiously, trying to come at an angle where he wouldn't have to get close to Phonson but could still see the screens. Phonson tapped a few times and a panel opened up and extended, revealing a holovid display. The projection winked to life.

A man stood in front of a podium. He was tall and thin, with beige skin, thick eyebrows and dark bushy hair, and a heavy jacket that almost looked expensive and almost fit him. Lettering hovered below him, reading *Jarvis Wainrite, Terroneous Federated Security Committee*. The holovid zoomed closer to his face, which hung dourly. A face that had seen a long, difficult life and had been hardened by it.

"The FSC has collected all the evidence in this matter," he said in a low, raspy voice. "Statements have been taken and security footage has been examined. The committee has come to the only conclusion possible. That conclusion is that *first*," he said, then paused for effect, pointing up with a single finger. "Modern Policing and Peacekeeping illegally sent personnel onto the surface of Terroneous. This is a violation of the Earth Colony Alliance Accords which explicitly state that any colony that wishes to ban the presence of *any* security, police, or military organization has the right to do so. *All* the recognized governments of Terroneous have gone on record explicitly banning the jurisdiction of ModPol. Their unwelcome presence on our moon constitutes *invasion*."

"Second," he continued, raising another finger. "ModPol *kidnapped* one of our own citizens. Jack Fugere was not only an outstanding citizen, well respected in his local community, his skills and knowledge were instrumental in preventing disaster several months ago during an equipment malfunction experienced by the Terroneous Environmental Observation Board."

There was a long pause then, and Jax almost thought the holovid had ended, given the stillness with which Wainrite stared into the camera. The twitching of his hair in a breeze and the slow drift of gray clouds in the sky behind him were the only indications that the recording was still going.

"Third," he said quietly, three fingers going up. "And let me say, the first two points are enough. But third. Third, we know who Jack Fugere is. Who he used to be. We know that he was wrongfully accused of murder. We know there was evidence that led to the arrest of Jenna Zarconi. And yet *despite* the arrest of the real killer, ModPol *continues* to pursue Mr. Fugere." His voice dropped, becoming guttural. "We know this pursuit to be a vendetta. Jack Fugere is an innocent man, and this corrupt organization only wants him to cover up their own mistakes!"

The camera panned out quickly to reveal a crowd surrounding the stage, which was in the middle of some small town. The small square was surprisingly full of people, their cries and fists rising in unison.

"We demand that ModPol return our citizen," Wainrite shouted above the noise. "We demand the return of Jack Fugere!"

Behind him on the stage was a small retinue of supporters. At a distance, Jax couldn't tell who they were, but something fired through the back of his mind and his breath stuck.

The holovid froze in time, but in space it zoomed closer to the stage, framing a still shot of Jarvis Wainrite behind the podium. It partially flattened and became a panel behind a newscaster sitting at a bright, gold desk.

"This and other statements have been broadcasting from various sources on Terroneous for the past several days," the woman said. She was a domer, a B-fourean like Jax, tall and pale skinned. "Pictured here is Jarvis Wainrite, public relations spokesperson for the Terroneous Federated Security Committee. The FSC is a loose coalition representing security interests of several larger settlements on the moon, including Sunderville, Stockton, Predash, Bensonton, and Nuzwick. The FSC also has support from the Terroneous Environmental Observation Board, and our analysts say that some of the entourage accompanying Mr. Wainrite in this broadcast are members of the TEOB."

The frozen shot zoomed out just enough to show some of the faces standing behind the weathered face of Wainrite. One face caught him, and Jax screamed inside. He locked down every muscle in his limbs, clenched his jaw to prevent his mouth from moving, and tried to do whatever it took not to leak a drop of the emotion that was washing through every cell of his weary body in that moment.

Bright-blue lights penetrated him.

"Sources tell us that it was the TEOB that came to the FSC to request assistance," the reporter continued. "As was revealed in a Terroneous-based documentary earlier this year, the man known as Jack Fugere was pivotal in preventing the mass evacuation of the moon due to malfunctioning magnetic field sensor equipment."

"Jack Fugere," Phonson said with a crooked smile. "I like it, Jackson. It's *almost* creative."

Jax ignored him, his attention locked on the reporter. "ModPol has yet to respond to the demands of the FSC or anyone else, at least officially, and their public relations offices declined to comment. It's difficult to say what will come of this development, as the FSC has no military forces other than the individual defenses of each settlement in the committee. Our analysts say the next course of action will be trade embargos – regulations that would be extremely difficult to enforce on the sparsely populated moon."

"We all know *that* won't work," Phonson said, apparently compelled to provide color commentary. "Terroneous can't survive without trade. They need imports much more than everyone else needs their exports."

Jax barely followed galactic politics, but he knew there was more than a trade embargo threat in the statement. The governments of Terroneous were testing the relationships they had with the rest of the Alliance. They were asking the Alliance to choose between one of its own members and a multi-stellar corporation like ModPol. As much as the domers loved ModPol, it might set a bad precedent if they sided with a corporation over a colony of citizens. To do so could amplify the thought in the back of many people's minds: that dome republics were basically corporations themselves.

"No word yet on whether this will affect the latest Earth Kin Rescue mission," the reporter said. Phonson made a move to switch off the holovid, but paused, apparently interested in hearing the last bit of the story. "Commonly referred to as the 'doomed to domed' program, the next Rescue ark is the first immigration ship destined for Terroneous. Although no single colony on the moon is a voting member of the Earth Colony Alliance, various 'partner members' there have long lobbied to be the new home of Rescued Kin. The frequency of arks leaving Earth has dropped considerably in recent decades, and for reasons that are unclear, the ECA voted to allow what is possibly one of the final batch of Earthlings to emigrate to Terroneous rather than one of the domed colonies."

Jax had heard something about the next ark being destined for Terroneous; it was a popular topic of conversation when he was living there. Most people were excited to welcome some Earthlings, feeling good that the immigrants weren't destined for domes. Those conversations had always made Jax uncomfortable, putting him on a bit of a defensive edge, which was weird – he didn't want to defend dome life, especially not to the hard, resilient residents of Terroneous, but the domes were where he came from. To their eyes, the domes were a place of weakness, of soft lives and consumerism, massive shopping malls masquerading as civilization. And maybe they were to some degree, but that didn't make their residents bad people.

She always understood how he'd felt. She'd lived on Barnard-4 for two years. Gone to the same college he had. They could have passed each other on an avenue – who knows if they had. Their destiny to meet wasn't until many years later, when he went to Terroneous to live out his fugitivity.

Phonson scrubbed the holovid back. In Jax's frozen silence, he begged the universe not to let the video stop on her face.

But the universe wasn't listening.

Phonson looked at Jax long and hard. Then he looked at the holovid. The frozen frame showed Wainrite and the handful of supporters that stood behind him. He waggled a finger at them. "One of these people really cares about you, Jackson."

"I don't know what you're talking about," Jax said weakly.

Phonson looked at him and grinned his crooked grin. He stepped close to the holovid, close enough so that when he began jabbing at it, his pointing finger merged into the three-dimensional image. "Could be this guy. Or this woman. Or this old bag. Or this – I don't even know what this guy is supposed to be." He looked back at Jax. "Doesn't matter. Because I can get to them all. You know my style. When in doubt, slaughter the whole block."

"I thought that was Jenna Zarconi's style," Jax said, unable to resist slinging the barb that was so well set up.

He frowned and jabbed himself in the chest. "It's *my* style. That woman was trying to flatter me by imitation." He paced a slow circle around Jax. "Anyway, I *will* hunt them all down," he said, waving broadly. The only person on the screen he hadn't pointed at directly was Lealina Warpshire. He stopped, standing next to Jax, so that they were facing the holovid together. "That one on the end, she's a pretty young thing," he said. "Nice eyes."

Jax managed to land a single weak punch before the anti-aggression safeguards leveled him.

CHAPTER 9

"I can't believe I'm flying this beast," Lucky Jerk said. "It's ironic that I have to fly this thing. Right? Is that irony?"

"Fuck if I know," Thompson-Gun said. "Just shut up and fly."

Dava and her team were in a black maria. It was the same small, boxy prisoner transport ship that they had encountered at Terroneous, back when they rescued Psycho Jack from a bunch of Pollie chumps. The irony Lucky was on about was that he had taken a fighter and flown circles around the bulky black maria, finding its weak spot and disabling it with a few well-placed shots. Dava didn't know if it was irony that Lucky was now behind the stick of the same ship he once disabled. She didn't really know what irony meant. In any case, she felt a small tingle of happiness in using the ModPol ship in their devious plan. It seemed like something Moses might think of.

After they'd disabled the black maria just off Terroneous and rescued Jack, they'd left the Pollies adrift. The ship had managed to push itself into orbit around the moon, but otherwise it'd been stuck. Evidently, someone had come along and rescued the crew, leaving the ship to be dealt with later. Some scrapper who was either desperate or blessed with massive balls had come along and towed it off. After that, it'd shown up on the market. Naturally, Space Waste had been eager to add it to their collection.

Captain 2-Bit had come through. She had to hand it to the old bastard, he was true to the cause, even in the face of disheartening betrayal. He'd gotten her the location of the zero-G maxi, through a combination of pestering Jensen and creative scouting. It was deep in Barnard space, nestled among the rocks and dust of the outer cloud.

And he'd gotten her the black maria, as well as four of his most reckless pilots.

"Hey," Dava said to no one in particular. "How come you call someone reckless, when you really mean they wreck stuff a lot?"

"Ooh," Lucky said with genuine interest. "That's a good one."

"For fuck's sake," Half-Shot groaned from the back of the cabin. "The total collective education in this entire bloody vessel doesn't surpass primary school."

"Half-Shot, what did we tell you?" Thompson said. "Your brother might have been a smart one, but you only got half his brains, so piss off. You keep it up and I'm gonna stuff you into the hold with Polar Gary and the flyboys."

Dava grinned. There was something about taking control of the situation that was putting her in a good mood. They were on a ModPol ship, a prisoner transport. It was perfect for getting them into the zero-G maxi. The cabin was packed full, between her, Thompson, Lucky, Seven-Pack, and Half-Shot. They had to stick Gary and the pilots in the prisoner hold. 2-Bit always called his pilots flyboys, but that was something to do with his past. Lost sons that he never talked about. In any case, the four flyboys were actually one guy and three women.

"Coming up," Lucky said. "Prepare for deceleration. If you have to take a leak, you shoulda done it by now."

* * *

Docking with the prison was as smooth as it could be. The thing was top-of-the-line tech. From the outside, the structure was a big geodesic ball, although by appearances, there were no outer walls, just crossbars. Beyond those, a confusing mishmash of tubes and blocks, some of which rotated slowly while the rest did not. They'd all held their breath as the dozens of turrets mounted at the intersections of the supports trained on the black maria. Then the ship was locked in by the dock's system and parked automatically.

"How many we got out there?" Dava said, hovering over Lucky's shoulder as he poked at the controls.

"Looks like they trust the docking system," he said, bringing up the views of the external cameras. "Got four guards walking out to greet you. Don't be fooled though, they have grabber boots and gloves. No gravity in this whole place."

"We get a layout?" Dava asked, nodding at the pilot's screens.

Lucky looked back and frowned. "Nothing. The docking station only fed us the stats on the outer perimeter and the docks. Everything else is a big ball of who-the-fuck-knows."

"Here's how we're gonna run this," Dava said, meeting each of their eyes. "I want us to stick together this time. We get caught, we all go down together. I'm going to have to leave you here, Half-Shot, to stay with Lucky and the other pilots."

"Stay here?" Lucky blurted. "But you *just* said we need to stick together this time."

"Someone has to stay with the goddamn ship, numbnuts!" Thompson said, raising an open hand and causing Lucky to flinch.

"Our most valuable things right now are this ship and our five pilots," Dava said, pointing at Lucky. "And we're going to need to find more ships if we hope to get everyone out. So in the meantime, you and the other pilots are going to be safest waiting here." She turned and looked at her gunman. "You got it, Half-Shot?"

His lips twitched a little, then he nodded. "Lots of ammo and a wide-open docking platform. It'll be a cinch." He gave a little shrug. "I'm not great in enclosed spaces anyway."

Dava already guessed that, looking at the length of the tall man's favorite rifle. He would be better at guarding the ship than joining the boarding party. "Okay, good. So going in, it will be me, Tommy, Seven-Pack, and Polar Gary. We're running blind, so we're going to have to take this place apart piece by piece. We'll have Gary strap the weapons crate we brought to his back. Any Wasters we find get their pick outta the crate."

"We should find Johnny Eyeball first," Seven-Pack said. She didn't need to follow up with why. Dava was thinking the same thing: Johnny would tear the place apart with a big fat gun in his hands.

"We probably won't have the luxury of choosing who we find first," Dava said. "But if we get any info at all, Moses is a priority. Johnny would be next, and Freezer too. We might need his hacking skills."

"If he's still alive," Thompson-Gun muttered.

Dava frowned in agreement. She hoped the prison experience had humbled the cocky hacker. It would be better for him if he'd been laying low.

In the silence that followed, everyone instinctively checked their weapons – even Lucky. Dava had made sure everyone left the base with the best armor they could find. Which wasn't necessarily the strongest; she knew in the complete lack of gravity, they needed to be flexible. However, mass was no concern. That meant they all wore dense nanomesh that was completely impractical on the surface of a planet, but perfect for the weightless prison.

They watched the guards take position around the black maria. They were attentive, but only just so. Dava guessed that in a place like this, getting dock duty was the closest thing to vacation. It would be downright banal compared to working the yards or the cells. Usually.

Half-Shot leaned into the screen and studied it for a moment. "I'm going right, aiming left."

Dava nodded. "Good. Tommy, you're on the left side. Me and Seven will follow. Lucky: you're on lights."

It was a good team. Without hesitation they moved. Lucky rigged the inner lights to go completely black. The side hatch peeled open, bending down toward the floor, though without gravity it might as well bend in any direction. Half-Shot nestled into the dark recess of the airlock. The barrel of his rifle was a cold, black lump in the darkness, pointed at the opening. It sought out its aim, to the left of opening, the aft of the ship.

It let out a sharp crack that sounded more like the snap of bone than a gunshot.

"Two down," Half-Shot whispered.

"Go!" Dava shouted.

Lucky hit the outer lights, cranked to full lumens. The docks glared into white brightness. The guard who'd been standing near the fore of the ship had already been stunned by the unexpected shot; now he raised a gloved hand to shield his eyes from the sudden explosion of white.

Tommy plugged him with a short burst. She was braced against the side of the hatch, and after her shot, pulled herself all the way out. Dava knew that damn submachinegun of hers was too much recoil in zero-G. "Wait here," she said.

She slipped up along the side of the ship using the handholds. She felt light. One with her blade. She scrabbled across the flat top of the boxy ship silently. The fourth guard clicked loudly in his grippers, stamping his way around the rear of the ship to investigate the eruption of light and sound coming from the port side. Effortlessly, she yanked against the top of the hull and propelled herself to him. Her blade sank into the side of his neck. She allowed him to slowly turn his head, to screw his eyes back and see her face before she twisted the blade and ended it.

"I'm coming, Moses."

* * *

They unpacked Polar Gary and strapped him up with the weapon chest. It was bulky and awkward, but without gravity, its mass was no burden for the big Sirius-Fiver. When Dava asked him to check his straps, he yawned and ignored her. He just stared into unseen distance. She hoped he would prove useful and not turn into dead weight.

Moving around the dock was tricky, but they'd all been

trained in zero-G. Dava relished it. Yes, it was a disadvantage, but being a disadvantage for everyone equally meant she could turn it into an advantage. The floors and walls were dotted with handholds and they pulled themselves across the open space toward the hatchway that led into the docking control room. As she gripped, tugged, released, and again gripped each handhold, she felt like she was dancing.

She reached the hatchway first. There was a pad next to it and she tapped at the interface. She hoped it would recognize the presence of the ModPol ship in the bay and simply open, but it wanted some kind of access code. Gary's shadow eclipsed her and she glanced back at him, hopeful. He was the one of them who'd done time in ModPol lock-ups, and she needed his guidance.

There was a clink and a squeak and she whipped her head back around to see the hatchway open. A slender, pale-skinned man in a gray jumpsuit lined with bright-silver piping leaned against the door as it opened.

"Hey there," he said. He looked young, and Dava would have mistaken him for a lanky teenager were it not for the odd patches of dark stubble scattered around his face. "What's going on?"

She flicked her blade loose from its sheath on her chest and made a move toward him. Then, with a quickness she didn't expect from the big man, Gary grabbed her forearm with a meaty paw and pulled her back. Her mouth opened to protest, but when she glared at him, his focused intent caused her to falter. His big right hand reached forward and grabbed the extended arm of the gray-suited man. Dava could see Gary hook one foot under a handhold on the floor for purchase before he yanked the man forward, whose face widened in shock.

"Hey! Who—"

Gary let go of Dava and slapped the man with the flat of his open palm. The wide shock twisted into terror, his mouth hanging open soundlessly.

Dava looked from one to the other and crooked an eyebrow. She raised her blade questioningly.

"No," Gary said. "He's an officer."

"So?"

"You," he said, shaking the man by the arm. This officer – Dava now understood the style of the outfit – was wearing magnetic boots and his feet stuck to the floor, but Gary rattled him like a wet noodle. "Who are you?"

His mouth went up and down a few times before he managed to spit it out. "Wa-wa-warden Perzynski," he said.

"Warden," Gary and Dava said simultaneously.

"Assistant Warden!"

She looked at Gary. "I didn't know there was such a thing."

He nodded shortly. "They take shifts in a place like this. No one is supposed to be head warden for too long or they go bad."

She furrowed her brow at his choice of words. "You mean, like corrupt?"

He ignored her question. "Assistant Warden Perzynski will open doors for you," he stated. He tugged on the man's arm a few times, looking down at the boots stuck to the floor.

"Tommy, Seven," Dava said. "Get his boots and gloves off and bind his hands."

Her soldiers went to work quickly while Gary held the assistant warden in place. His protests were halfhearted, resigned to his fate and not compelled to resist. Dava pulled herself into the control room to find a pair of operators gawking at her from the chairs they were strapped to. They too were of B-fourean stock, skinny and pale, a young man and a middle-aged woman.

The look on their faces was all too familiar. "Never seen a black woman in person, have ya?" Dava said.

They glanced at each other and after a few moments of icy silence, the woman spoke up. "We have black people here," she said cautiously, then tipped her head to one side. "Are you here to visit them?"

Dava's eyes narrowed, unsure of where to start facing ignorance on so many different levels. Then she realized that though she didn't know all Earth-borns just because they shared the same skin color, there was a good chance she knew all the ones in the prison. There were a few in Space Waste, especially one in particular, and that's who she precisely came to visit.

"I am," she said with a wicked smile. "I'm here to visit family. Some are black and some are not."

"Oh," the woman said. She looked past Dava, at the restrained assistant warden, then glanced at her screen. Dava could see it was lit up with red warnings; probably indicating the state of the downed guards in the hangar.

"I bet you can tell me where my family members are," Dava said. The ceiling was low enough for the average person to grab the handholds along it. She sheathed her blade and hand-walked herself across the room, coming up behind them. She looked at each of them in turn and fingered the hilt of her knife. "Can you help me find my family?"

"Well." The woman seemed to be contemplating whether to fear for her life or to grasp at what little authority she had. "Is Warden Perzynski going to be okay? Or are you going to hurt him?"

"Fuck Warden Whatever," Dava said, leaning closer. "You need to be worried about us using your insides to decorate this drab control room."

"It really could use some color," Thompson said.

"We can look up all the inmates from here," the younger man quickly sputtered. When the woman cast him an admonishing look, he said, "Hey, Bar, I'm not getting turned inside out for a temp job."

Dava looked from the man to the woman and grinned. "Let's see who you got in here," she said. "Starting with Moses Down."

The woman sighed and turned to the console. She tapped at the interface and frowned. "Moses Down, 45-8387. He's in the Core."

"Can you open his cell from here?"

"What?" she said, turning to Dava. "In the Core? Of course not."

"The Core is the center of the facility," the young man said. "It's only accessible by special permission from a warden, and the shields can't be accessed remotely."

"So you're saying we have to drag Warden Whatshisface all the way to the center of this place to get to Moses," Dava said.

"Hey, Capo," Seven-Pack said from behind her. "I think these boots might fit me."

"She's not Capo anymore," Gary grunted. "'Member?"

"Lock it down, grunt," Thompson warned.

"You don't want to wear those boots," the young operator chimed in.

Dava looked at him and gestured for him to explain, but the other operator interrupted. "That's enough, Kindel!" she whispered.

Dava grabbed the woman by her short, mousey hair, causing her to chirp shortly in alarm. "Listen, lady, you just don't know how deep into the shit factory you are right now." With a single movement, she pulled her blade and sliced through the tuft of hair. She flicked it at the woman's face and it exploded and floated there, partially stuck, partially nowhere to go due to lack of gravity. "When I run out of hair, I start slicing off skin."

Her face bunched up and tears began forming at the corners of her eyes, lifting up and sticking to her skin like tiny, wet welts. She seemed unwilling to protest further, so Dava looked at the other one.

"They don't work like standard mag boots," he said quickly. "Each one is on a unique frequency and the whole place is wired up like a big electromagnet. If you put on those boots, someone can track them and they can activate the triggers in the floors to make them stick at maximum strength. The mags can be used for traction when we want it, or for control when we need it."

"Well, aren't you Mr. Helpful," Dava said. "Before we tie you up, I need to see some maps of this place."

* * *

"Look, I'm not even in Justice," Runstom said. "I'm in Defense. I work in the Marketing department."

"Marketing." The squat, older woman behind the desk that had the words *Modern Policing and Peacekeeping Incarceration Facility Administration* stamped across the front gave him a pucker-faced glance before returning to her console. "What the hell are you even doing here, son?"

"Well, I *thought* I was doing you all a favor by helping

out with the inmate escort mission from Epsilon Eridani," Runstom said, folding his arms in what he hoped was an indignant gesture. The extended stay in zero gravity was causing him to feel puffy all over and it was making him uncomfortable to say the least. "But I *really* need to get back to my duties."

"We all got work to do," the woman muttered.

Runstom squinted at her nametag. "Ms. Olay," he said. His hands went out in a natural movement that would have normally landed them flat on the desk, with him leaning over her. Without the gravity, *leaning* wasn't really a thing and being anchored to the floor by his gripper-boots, his arms simply floated. He was forced to gesture with them instead. "There is a matter. An urgent matter. Someone's life is at stake!"

"Whose life?" Olay said without looking up.

After seeing Jenna, he'd gone straight to the lounge to find a holovid. He'd searched quickly through the history and found the broadcasts she'd been talking about. The people from Terroneous, stirring the pot. He had no idea what effect their message would have. Jax was on his way into the hands of X, perhaps already was. X would likely catch the broadcasts, but what would he do with them? And how would the rest of ModPol react? As yet, no official statements had been released. They couldn't stay quiet for long though. It was bad publicity.

It suddenly occurred to him that this sort of thing probably fell under his responsibility as a public relations officer for ModPol.

"Obviously, I can't discuss that," Runstom said. "Ms. Olay, please. I would hate to have to get my superiors involved."

"Oh really?" She looked up at him. "Because I would *love* to get my superiors involved. I know exactly what they'd say. Somehow, some marketer from Defense conned his way onto a Justice transport and found himself stuck at one of our deep-space facilities. Now he wants to use our valuable time and resources to hitch a ride, like we're a goddamn taxi service." She looked over her shoulder and addressed an invisible supervisor. "Hey boss, which hard-working *Justice* employee should I bump from the transportation schedule so that this important marketer can get home?"

"I'm not going *home*," Runstom said through his teeth.

She turned to face him again. "Look, Mr. Runstom. The spot I gave you is the best I can do. You're just going to have to wait it out."

The spot she had given him was another four weeks out. Four weeks of sitting around – floating around – doing nothing.

Before he could protest further, his armband buzzed. Some kind of facility-wide alert.

Olay must have gotten the same alert on her console. "Well, Mr. Runstom. Maybe your stay here won't be so boring after all."

He stared at his arm and tried to make sense of the alert. A few guards had been killed. A couple of dock operators had been assaulted. A warden – an assistant warden – had been kidnapped. There was nothing that said who was responsible, how many there were, or where they went.

"Space Waste?" he said to himself.

"Maybe," Olay said. "Not smart of them to make a move now when we still have a full complement of guards from the transport here. We're at double ranks."

"Your slow off-site transport pays off." Runstom realized what the alert was going on about: he was to report for emergency duty. It blinked with directions to the nearest guardhouse where he could report in and suit up. "Damn it."

Olay continued her snide commentary but Runstom shut it out as he headed back into the corridor. Tangling with Space Waste – or whomever was crazy enough to break *into* a zero-G maximum-security prison – was not an activity he wanted any part of in that moment. His confidence that Jax was still alive was dropping with each passing hour. He needed to get a ship, and he needed to find Jax. Which meant he needed to find X. He didn't exactly have a solid plan. He had the registration of the interstellar patroller that McManus took Jax aboard. Being a ModPol vessel, it would be tracked if it went anywhere near any of the hundreds of beacons placed throughout the system. Runstom couldn't get to any of those records from the prison; he needed to get to an outpost.

But now he was making his way through the labyrinth of the penitentiary so that he could report for emergency guard duty. Why was he doing it? Was it just to follow the rules put before him? Or was it just because he didn't know what else to do? Given directions, he tended to take them. Of course, that wasn't always true. But in this case, it got him moving at least. Sometimes moving was good for thinking.

Space Waste. If they sent someone to break in, then they were breaking people out. Moses Down could be one of their targets. He thought back to the conversation with the aging criminal. He'd called himself a once-boss. Apparently considered himself retired by being caught. Perhaps he was too important to let go. Had the Wasters realized they'd be facing double ranks? It was going to be bad for both sides.

Runstom didn't really care. He felt bad for the dead guards. They were just trying to do their jobs. And there would be more casualties before it was done. He was getting used to seeing bloodshed coming and not being able to do anything about it. In this case, it was a Justice problem. Justice clearly didn't give a shit about what he thought. He tried to think of a way to take advantage of the situation. Was there a way such an emergency could get him on a ship? It didn't seem likely.

He reached the guardhouse. As the warden on duty barked orders, he wondered what kind of ship the attackers arrived in. If the assault was stopped, maybe he could commandeer it.

And then he was slapping on body armor and checking the charge on a combination stun/laser rifle.

* * *

Dava glanced at her arm again. She had all the prison's maps uploaded to her pad, and it was a damn good thing: the layout of the place made no sense to her. Architecturally, it was built like layers of spheres, but the tracks that ran around and between those spheres created a maze of odd passages. She got the sense from the map that they could be moved, and were probably rotated periodically just to shake things up.

They reached the closest yard, which was labeled *Yard Beta* on the map. The database had only alpha-numeric strings to identify the inmates, so it was no help in telling her where any of the captured Wasters were. The only data she had to go on was the prisoner intake date: all the Wasters came in on the same barge, so she had a long list of numbers whose dates all matched. Those didn't include Johnny Eyeball and Freezer, who'd been picked up after the raid on Vulca several weeks before. She couldn't figure out on what dates they might have been transferred to the maxi, and she knew she needed to move quickly, so she hadn't lingered over the terrified operators for long.

"Here," Dava said as they reached a broad hatch, a door that was spiraled shut. Circling the edges, the words YARD BETA repeated eight or nine times. "Tommy, bring over the warden."

Thompson-Gun pulled herself along the wall, the warden towed along behind her by a cord that attached to a crude pair of zip-cuffs wrapped around his wrists. "Okay, buddy, better open it up."

She gave the cord a final yank that sent him slow-motion-flying toward the lock on the side of the door. With a grunt, he stopped himself by angling a shoulder at the wall as he bumped into it. He looked over at Dava and for a split second she thought she caught a twinkle in his eye. He quickly turned his attention to the panel.

After a few long seconds, the hatch twisted apart with a hiss. Beyond it was a small room, shaped a bit like a tube the same size as the opened hatchway. It extended for a couple of meters where another hatch waited.

"It's kind of like an airlock," the warden said. He nodded at the tube-shaped room. "We have to go in there and then I can open the other door."

"Yeah, we get it," Dava said. She raised a hand and motioned her team to go in.

Once inside, Thompson pulled the warden over to the panel on the opposite wall. He prodded the interface and the door behind them slinked shut. For a cold moment, they floated there in silence.

"Okay, open it up," Thompson said with a yank of the cord. Dava was glad she broke the silence. Without gravity, the round walls of the small room became disorienting quickly.

The warden flinched, then poked some more. "I ... I can't open it," he said. Dava heard the quiver of fear dominate his voice, but there was something underneath. A cockiness?

She braced a toe against a hold on the nearest wall and with a twitch, flung herself toward him. Her blade extended toward his throat, then she turned it so that she stopped her progress by placing the flat of it against his neck. "Open it or I open you."

His eyes went wide, then he blinked them defiantly. "I'm afraid I cannot," he said with a swallow. "You ... you are all under arrest, now."

"Are you kidding me?" Seven-Pack said from her position in front of the hatchway waiting to be opened. "This prick is going to die for this shithouse?"

Dava flipped the blade so that the edge rested against the cloth of the assistant warden's collar. "Come on, buddy. This job ain't worth dyin' for."

"You won't kill me," he said, raising his chin slightly – both an act of defiance and of fear of the knife edge against his throat. "If you do, you'll be stuck in here."

"Sounds like we'll be stuck either way," Dava said. "So we might as well do some zero-gravity experiments with your organs while we wait for this arrest you're promising us."

He looked at her, then the others. "I've already triggered the alarm. The door cannot be opened, even by meEEAAA-UUGHHH!"

Dava grabbed him by the shirt with her left hand while sliding the tip of the blade slowly down the side of his chest, cutting through the fabric and a few millimeters into the flesh beneath, drawing a line of red that started at his collarbone, crossed one breast, and ended at the first rib. There she turned the blade perpendicular and slid it slightly deeper, notching the rib-bone with the tip.

"Okay, okay!" he screamed, tears peeling from his eyes in such a stream that while one end clung to his cheeks, the rest of the liquid drifted like fat, wet strings. "I can use the emergency override!"

She let go and spun him to face the panel. Dark red plasma drew away from him in the same clingy, stringy manner as the tears. Not enough blood to immediately threaten his life, but he shook at the sight of it.

Seven-Pack and Polar Gary aimed their weapons at the hatch as it spun open. The yard yawned before them, a massive globe-like structure a good hundred meters or so in diameter. Dava glanced at the map on her arm. It was one hundred and seventy-eight meters across. There were only two doors into the yard, and the other was on the opposite side. It was a hell of a lotta space with nothing to grab onto.

They were greeted by a face so familiar, it caused Dava to momentarily forget where she was.

"Jerrard," she said.

The Waster's face broke into a wide, open-mouthed smile. "Dava!" He was one of the few black-skinned people that Dava knew, one of the few that was born on Earth and "rescued" as a child, shipped off on a massive transport from Sol to a new home in the domes around Barnard's Star and Sirius. Like her – like most of Earth's children – the transit left him orphaned. Until he'd found a new family in Space Waste.

His arms and legs went wide, forming a human-sized X, topped with an asterisk, a splay of braids coming from the back of his head. His outfit was a gaudy bright neon-green one-piece with a number stamped in red across the chest. She pushed through the hatch and embraced him, the force of her arrival causing them to drift.

The lack of anchor caused her to flinch, and she realized she should have tethered her team together to keep from getting stuck in the open space of the yard. He must have read the worry on her face.

"Look around, Dava," he said. "There's not just a ball of inmates floating in the middle of the yard."

She looked up and over his head. There were dozens of inmates in the yard, but they were clustered into packs, like swarms of lazy insects. She looked down to see more of the same below them. "How do you keep from getting stuck?"

"Air currents." He pointed at an inconspicuous vent in the wall that loomed behind them. It was just to one side of the hatchway, but once she knew what to look for, she saw dozens of them dotting the spherical wall. "Takes some getting used to, but spend enough time in the yard, and you get a sense for the lanes they make."

She took it all in for a few seconds, and though the prospect of invisible streams of air intrigued her, she was quickly overcome with a feeling of exposure. Though the spherical space was probably meant to disorient the inmates by removing any natural sense of direction – some kind of pacifying mindfuck to not know which way was up – when she looked below, she could see the wall almost solidify, and when she looked above, the wall itself appeared transparent.

A web of crisscrossing beams held everything together, but between them the black of space loomed heavily.

"Can you get us back to the hatch?" she said, glancing back at the others.

"Sure."

Jerrard grabbed her by the wrist and twisted them around like a double-ended pendulum. The yard spun sickeningly around her, but then she felt them move with direction, with purpose. They were at the hatch within moments.

There was a brief reunion between Jerrard and the others. "We have thirty-three here," he said. Dava noticed his face had gone puffy, the tell-tale sign of extended zero-gravity exposure. Acid burned in her belly at the thought of her family stuck in that place for so long. "They randomize the yard access so that we never see the same inmates, and we can never plan anything. But we keep The Flow."

For a second, Dava missed the emphasis, but as the words sank in, she remembered. The Flow, another one of Moses's inventions. It was a communication channel, a way of spreading information between Wasters that were spread out across space. Which also meant spread out over time, when it came down to it: any given piece of information quickly went stale. Though that didn't mean it was useless. It just meant it was important to track the freshness of the info as much as the info itself. According to Moses, they were to think of this as a Packet: a piece of info wrapped in a timestamp.

Another concept of The Flow was that Packets were spread whether a Waster thought the info was relevant or not. This info was often itself a code, and it was good that not everyone knew what it meant. As long as it was passed along, it would mean something to the right person eventually.

This meant that the Wasters in their randomized cell blocks and yards would stay tight. If there were thirty-three of them alive and only four yards to be spread between on a daily basis, it wasn't much of a challenge to keep The Flow moving.

"Where's Moses?" she said.

Jerrard reflexively looked at his feet. "Down in the Core," he said, and she realized he was looking toward the center of the entire prison structure.

"How do we get to him?"

"I don't know," he said, his face hanging despite its puffiness. "We only see him once a month. His yard schedule is limited or something."

Polar Gary turned and smacked the crate. "Better get a weapon, Jerry."

Jerrard popped open the crate and dove in, rifling around like a starving animal. "How many are we?" he said, coming away with a bolt-action piece with a retractable blade.

"Not many," Thompson said quietly.

He looked at them and nodded solemnly. "This is it, ain't it?"

"Half-Shot is back at the ship," Dava said. "Along with five fly-boys. So we'll need to jack some boats if we wanna get all thirty-three out."

"Then we should get Freezer," he said.

"You know where he is?"

Together they looked at Dava's map. Freezer and Johnny Eyeball were in the same cellblock, a circumstance that Dava couldn't tell was coincidence or through the insistence of the big psycho. Last time she'd seen them was back on Vulca, and Eyeball was protecting Freezer like some prized piece; that's how they'd gotten caught together. The prize being that Freezer promised Eyeball his allowance of liquor, which was of particular interest to Eyeball since he'd been put on the Diet.

It was bad enough to imagine the torture for Johnny to have his drink taken away when he was a Waster, but as an inmate, the sobriety would be an extended period of pain.

"Okay, we need to get them out first," Dava said. "Frank will be able to help us get everyone else out. We need to protect him above all. And nobody gives him a gun, or else he'll blow his own damn head off."

"The path inward to the cellblock we want is that way, about ninety degrees," Jerrard said, pointing at the opposite end of the yard.

"How many Wasters are in this yard today?"

"Six, including me."

"Can you round 'em up and get them to meet us at the other hatch?"

"Of course." He turned to go, then looked at her sideways. "How are you going to get over there?"

She frowned, looking at her small crew. "We don't know the currents. We're gonna have to follow the wall."

Jerrard regarded her for only a second, then seemed to agree with her assessment. He reached above the doorway and scrambled up the wall before snagging a current and swimming into the void.

"Well," Thompson said, pulling the cord of the bleeding warden tight. "Should we go up or down?"

"Or left or right?" Seven-Pack said with a shrug. "Same distance, no matter which way we follow the wall."

"Come on," Dava said. The way the framework was structured, she could see that out from the sides of the hatch, it made a straight circle. If they followed it in one direction, they'd be guaranteed not to wander. She led them, hand over hand on the holds that speckled the frame.

Just beyond the frame, she began to realize the outer wall was always clear. It was a trick of perspective that when she looked toward the inner part of the prison, it appeared to be more opaque. It was just that there were more walls beyond, representing whatever the next layer was. Cell blocks, as best she could tell. As they went, she could look through the wall and see the corridor they'd come down to reach the yard. It connected to a maze of other corridors that went both outward, to the docks they'd landed at, and inward, disappearing from view.

Toward the center of the yard, she could see Jerrard's sprawling form making its way from cluster to cluster. The currents weren't fast, but they were certainly more direct. The slow path she and the others were making would give him plenty of time to get the word around the yard.

Judging by the angle of her view through the glasslike wall, she guessed they were about halfway across. There was a crackle and a hum, loud and unnerving. Dava couldn't tell where the sudden sound was coming from. Then it spoke.

"Everyone in Yard Beta, your attention." The voice came from nowhere and everywhere at once. "Unauthorized individuals have entered the facility. This yard is now on full lockdown. Proceed to the nearest wall and prepare for magnetic restraints to engage."

"It's in their clothes or something," Polar Gary said sadly. "In the standard-issue uniform. They can glue you to the walls whenever they want."

Dava glanced around. Many of inmates in the yard seemed

to be aware of the maglock restraints and were attempting to dance between currents in order to keep themselves hovering near the spacious center.

"They're just going to change the air to push everyone to one side," the warden said. He'd followed Dava's hopeful gaze out to the crowd avoiding the walls. He looked at her. "Any minute now, all of your friends will be glued to the wall."

She narrowed her eyes at him and he flinched, which was followed by a wince of pain at his still-open wound.

"To the infiltrators," the booming voice came again. "Release Assistant Warden Perzynski immediately and don't move. Securibots will arrive shortly to collect you. Repeat, do not move from your location, or we will be forced to fire upon you."

"Ugh, they never miss a chance to call me *Assistant* Warden," Perzynski said with a small sigh.

"Fire on us," Thompson said, looking around. "From where?"

"Turrets," the warden said. The single word conjured back images of the weapons Dava had seen as they'd approached the spherical prison in the black maria.

"Aren't those facing outward?" Seven-Pack asked on behalf of the rest of the group.

Perzynski smiled, though the pain made it look lopsided. "They have full three-sixty rotation. Which means they can target the yards just as easily as anything else."

"Repeat, release Assistant Warden Perzynski," the speakers bellowed. "You have ten seconds to comply."

"What are they going to do, shoot through the wall?" Thompson said. She tugged the warden closer to her. "I don't think so, will they?"

Dava shared her skepticism. "Come on," she said. "Keep moving."

They began pulling themselves along the wall again when Thompson suddenly cried out. "Ow, what the fuck?"

She twisted at her torso, like she was trying to see the back end of herself. Her arms flapped around in the zero-G, flailing to stop some unseen assailant. A string of obscenities erupted forth. "God damn, motherfuck that burns!"

Dava froze for a moment, a spike of fear at the unknown. Then she pulled herself closer to the wall and got a look at what was happening. A thin beam of red shot through the clear wall and danced around on Thompson's body, drawing a line of smoke as it snaked about. "What the hell is that?"

The warden was being tugged at odd moments thanks to Thompson's gyrations, as though he were only getting the aftershocks of the attack. "It's a focused light beam," he managed through sporadic coughing and yelping. The jostling was causing more blood to pop from his wound in spouts with each hard jerk. "The walls filter out a certain amount of background radiation, but the beams are tuned to a frequency that can penetrate."

Dava suspected there was a reason they hadn't been outright fried: the turrets could get through the thick, clear walls, but not without some loss of intensity. It was probably good for crowd control in the yards, but not good for actually trying to kill someone.

"Gary, grab him," she said. "Hold him in front of you with your back to the wall."

Polar Gary complied with a snakelike strike of one large hand, his torso barely moving. With his other hand, he reached back to steady against the wall, grabbing one of the handholds. As Thompson continued to spasm and yank against the tether, Gary pulled the warden in close to his chest and held him tight.

The beam left Thompson and sought out Gary. He scrunched down his head and pulled in his arms as best he could, shielding himself behind the massive crate strapped to his back.

Dava kicked off the wall and grabbed the warden by a tuft of hair as she began floating past. He yelped, and she pulled in closer, drawing her blade up to his throat once more.

"Do I have to prove my violent tendencies again?" she said.

"No!" He attempted to squirm, but under Gary's grip, there wasn't much room to move.

"Tommy, Seven," Dava said. "You two keep moving. Get to that other hatch."

Without protest, Thompson popped her end of the tether from her belt. The two Wasters began moving as quickly as they could fling themselves along the handholds of the wall. Without the warden or Polar Gary and the crate slowing down their progress, they moved much faster.

Dava grabbed the loose end of the tether and attached it to Gary's belt. "I'm not trying to treat you like a packbot," she said to him. "But I got a plan."

She sheathed her knife and slipped her hands and legs in and around the warden, under Gary's massive grip. She tapped a control at the end of the tether that was attached to Perzynski. The tether went slack, several meters of it spooling into a floating mass of thin cable.

"Okay," Dava said, winding her fingers tightly into the drab uniform of the warden. "Gary. I need you to fling us as hard as you can. Aim at an angle – we need to be able to hit the wall, but we need to get a good distance out. Can you do that?"

His answer was to perform the maneuver without comment. With a sudden shove, he sent Dava and the warden sailing. Despite the impulsive action, the route was direct and smooth, and the wall beyond a bit of curve rushed at her fast. She could make out the laser as it tried to follow their trajectory. It looked as though the turret operator intended to sever the cable, but was having a hard time locking on long enough to burn through it.

With a hard whump, they smacked into the wall. One of her hands lost its grip on her human counterweight and she struggled to maintain her hold, constricting her legs around the tall man's waist. She used the free hand to grab a handhold, and she pulled them closer to the wall.

The tether was connected to Perzynski's belt, so she had to keep her legs wrapped around him high enough to avoid the now-taut tether. She reached both hands past him and threaded each arm through a handhold, hooking at her elbows. This pressed her so hard into his body, she could feel the chest wound seeping wetly into her thin clothes.

She intended to signal to Gary the next move in the maneuver, but the big man seemed to have an intuition that launched him into action. He pulled his legs under and pivoted so that the wall became the floor. And then he jumped.

There was a tug of force against Dava's elbows, but it was not as bad as she expected. Polar Gary coasted through the space, anchored by the tether around Perzynski's waist. The cable pulled him into an arc that smoothed out instantly. Twisting her head, she watched him fly deep into the yard and then disappear from her vision. She whipped her head around to the other side to catch him on his downward path. Somehow he'd managed to rotate so that his legs extended toward the wall. He landed like an animal, the legs touching first, his back and the crate angling forward, so that he pitched over and brought his hands to the wall. He froze for a few seconds, getting the proper grip. The laser found the cable again.

Gary looked up and met Dava's eyes. She unhooked her elbows. He wrapped the cable in his arms and pulled as she pushed off from the wall.

Her arc wasn't nearly as smooth as Gary's was. She felt like she was careening out of control through the air, barely connected to the world by a thin cable and a thin warden. The yard spun around her and she lost her bearing. When the wall came, she wasn't ready for it. She squeaked a cry when her shoulder and thigh slammed hard into the clear surface. She lost control of her limbs just long enough for the warden to slip away from her. In a panic, she scrabbled at the wall but came up emptyhanded.

Perzynski meanwhile had managed to grab one of the handholds. His head was tucked between his arms, and the shudder of his back gave her the impression that he was softly sobbing.

The nearest handhold slowly spiraled in her vision, growing smaller as she drifted away from the wall. She felt a twisting in her stomach, a churning nausea. The thin cable stretched past her, just out of reach. She could see the red glow where the laser was once again trying to sever it.

She turned and looked at the expanse of the yard. Bodies swirled, trying to navigate the changing currents and avoid the walls. It was like watching people trying not to drown. They spun recklessly in her vision and her breath went shallow. Her organs seemed to be sliding down to her feet and back up to her skull. A burning heated her throat, and expanding pressure was building inside her.

She took a look over her shoulder and saw the cable. She reached back toward it, a few meters from her extended fingers. Then she turned her head the opposite way. As directly opposite as she could get it as the dizzying nausea overtook her.

And she vomited.

* * *

A sick feeling of frayed consciousness tormented Dava, making her wonder where she was, when she was. It quickly passed. The cable was firmly in the grip of her right hand. Behind her floated the partially digested chunks of her breakfast, yawning outward in a cone-like shape. The force of the discharge had pushed her close enough to grab the tether.

She turned back to the cable. Hand over hand she quickly pulled along it until she grabbed onto the sobbing Assistant Warden Perzynski. He seemed to have a death grip on the wall. She weakly wrapped her legs around his midsection from behind him and reached out, finding room on the same handholds he was clinging to.

His weight shifted under her slightly and he gave a startled yelp. The cable was swinging. She looked over her shoulder to see Polar Gary in another arc. As he peaked, she swiveled her head around to the other shoulder to watch him land.

Only this time the cable didn't hold. The laser had weakened it, and it stretched thin, the nanofibers splitting apart where they had been burned. It split just as Gary's arc was coming back down and he sailed untethered through the yard.

"Shit!" Dava watched his trajectory. Fortunately, he was well on his way toward the wall and it looked like he would land close to the hatch.

That just left her and their keymaster. She grabbed the cable and reeled in the limp, impotent remainder. Without a connector at the end, she couldn't do much with it except wrap it around her left arm to secure it.

She pulled herself against the wall, planting her feet against it in a squat. She could see the hatch. They were close, maybe a couple of dozen meters.

"Let go," she said. Perzynski didn't move, didn't even breathe. "Hey, fuckerhead. I said let go!"

He didn't respond other than to shake his bowed head. She lifted one leg and kicked him with the point of her foot, right into the ribs where the chest wound ended. He yelped and reached down with his left hand reflexively. The right hand twitched as well, but the instinct to hold on took over and his fingers curled back around it.

Dava repositioned her legs. Left arm still wrapped with the cable, she pulled her blade from its sheath with the right. With a one-two motion, she severed his digits and kicked off the wall.

CHAPTER 10

They found Johnny Eyeball and Freezer in cellblock four. Their cells were side-by-side, two in a great long row, of which there were several above and below. The block was like a grid. At the back of each three-meter-to-a-side cell was a cot with straps; though the way it was fixed to the wall made the back of the cell seem like the floor. It didn't much matter. Dava and her crew were looking in through a mesh screen.

Johnny and Frank were both naked.

To be more precise, Freezer was wearing a pair of gray underpants, his skinny yellow form clinging to one wall near the mesh. Eyeball on the other hand was stark naked, winking furiously and doing some kind of calisthenics, his arms raising up to a clap above his head and back down, his legs spreading apart and coming together, his flaccid penis jouncing with the rhythm of his exercise.

"Dava!" Freezer cried. "Boy, I'm glad to see you! Wait, you're not a prisoner are you?"

"N—"

"No, of course not," he said speedily, words running together. "Lookit, you have a gang with you. And lots of weapons!"

"No guns for you," Thompson said.

"Whatever, Tommy-Gun. That's fine. I don't want a gun. Just get us out of here! Hey, is that a warden? Did you guys kidnap a warden?"

"Not that I don't enjoy the show," Seven-Pack said. "But what are you doing, Johnny?"

"He does that all the time," Freezer said. "It's hard to exercise in this place. They have some stretchy things in the yard, but you have to check them out and there's a timer and everything. It's like they only want you to get the minimum amount of exercise to keep your bones from completely deteriorating. Like if they could, they'd take it all away. But there's something about it being torture. The brittle bones thing, I mean. I think it's torture that you have to exercise at all. But here, if you don't exercise, you get so weak you'd break your ankles just walking in normal gravity."

"For fuck's sake," Polar Gary rumbled. "Does this kid have an off switch?"

Dava looked at them. Frank had always been skinny, but the way his flesh clung to the bones, she knew there had been significant muscle loss, and it had only been a few months. As she watched Johnny's muscles flex with the wing-flapping motion, she could see the desperation in his good eye. The fight against the decay. A fight he was losing. His muscles shrinking, becoming stringy, veins running blue underneath the paling yellow skin.

The rest of the Wasters she'd encountered in the prison had only been there for a couple of weeks. The bodies of

Johnny and Frank were reminders of how long they'd been neglected, how long they'd been left to rot since their capture on the Sirius-5 moon of Vulca. She blamed her bosses. Blamed Jansen for chasing one greedy mission after another. Blamed Moses for being swept up by the underboss's ambition.

"Where are your clothes?" she asked.

"It's an experiment," Freezer said. "When they want to restrain us, they can stick us to the walls. It's all this very complex electromagnetic system that runs through the place. It's got different modes, so that it can do different functions. Like, it can be a light grip for boots, or it can be a strong, body-wide grip to restrain inmates."

"Okay," Dava said, glancing around and wondering how much time they had. She looked back at him, and looked past him to see a neon-green uniform strapped into the cot at the other end of the cell. "So you think they can't stick you to the wall if you don't have the clothes on."

"Exactly," Freezer said with a grin. "The targeting system relies on encoded chips and wires that are stitched somewhere into the fabric. So small you wouldn't be able to see them with the naked eye."

"So you just get naked instead," Thompson said. She'd been delegated the keeper of the warden once again, though the cable was no longer attachable to their belts, so she had to hold it by hand. She yanked his drifting form. "How do we get them out?"

"Uh." The warden's hand was hastily wrapped in cloth that had turned dark, and his chest wound had mostly stopped bleeding. But his eyes lolled, and he blinked to attempt to focus. "You. You can't. Can't open them from here."

"Why didn't anyone tell us that before we got here?" Seven-Pack said, narrowing her eyes at Polar Gary.

The big man didn't respond to the barb. He was looking at something far away, something the rest of them couldn't see. Dava knew the crate he was carrying weighed nothing; yet he was tired. Defeated. She shouldn't have brought him to this place.

"And they won't open unless someone is inside the uniform," Perzynski added. He frowned at the naked forms of Johnny and Frank and tried to muster a semblance of confidence. "This is a *very* secure facility."

"Assistant Warden Denis Perzynski," Freezer said, in a voice deeper than he usually spoke.

The warden flinched and looked up at him, his eyes finding new focus. "What? How do you know my name?"

"I'm like a sponge, Denis. Every bit of info I pick up, I remember. Even the most trivial shit." Freezer pointed at each of the corners of the mesh, making a circle with his finger. "Like here's something: I heard that in the right kind of emergency, these gates pop right off."

Perzynski's mouth opened and closed a few times. Finally, he weakly managed, "I don't know what you mean. I'm just an assistant warden."

"Safety first, right?" Freezer rubbed his fingertip along the surface of the mesh. "They must make you go through all kinds of safety trainings to work here. And I bet even more to get promoted to *assistant* warden, right?"

"I – I guess."

"So it's in there," Freezer said, tapping his temple. "You just have to search your memory. Cellblock safety measures. Something bad enough that the inmates could lose their lives. This is ModPol Justice. It's part of the deal: you take care of the criminal element for the known galaxy, just as long as you promise to be humane and shit like that. In an emergency, you can't just let the inmates die."

Eyeball had finished his wing-spreading exercise and began working on something else. He squatted against one wall, then sprang forth with his legs, in what looked like a horizontal jump across the three meters of space and shot his arms out, flat palms smacking the opposite wall, arms flexing as they bent. Then he repeated the process in reverse, straightening his arms and springing himself backward. Dava watched a few reps of this, watched him use the force of his momentum as a form of resistance.

"Think, Denis," Freezer prodded.

"I don't know," the warden whispered. Then his head lifted suddenly. "Right, the fire suppression system! If there's a fire in the cellblock, all the cells open and vacuum is created. It will suck the inmates out to the main corridor. Then it seals so that the oxygen can be burned off and the fire will die."

"So wait, all the inmates get sucked out of their cells?" Thompson said.

"Well yeah, mostly," Perzynski said, his voice dropping to a barely audible mumble. "Mostly. With acceptable losses."

"Where are the sensors?" Freezer asked.

The warden half-nodded over his shoulder. "In the walls. All up and down and across. But it needs to be a big enough fire to trigger the evac procedure."

"What can we set on fire in this place?" Seven-Pack said.

"We need something fast," Dava said. She looked back at the hatch they had come through. They'd made short work of four guards on the way from the yard to the cellblock. More would be coming. And there had been a promise of securibots, which would not be so easy to dispatch as flesh-and-blood staff.

Thompson yanked the crate open with her free hand. "I think there are some firebombs in here. Seven, take a look."

Seven-Pack holstered her pistol and pulled a rectangular box from the crate. "A whole case of them. There's like a dozen in here."

"Do they have adhesive on them?" Freezer said excitedly. "Is there a remote trigger? You could spread them out around the wall and trick the system into thinking there's a massive fire!"

Seven-Pack peered into the box. "There's sticky stuff on them and a little clicky thingy. Is that what you mean?"

Dava grabbed the box and held it open. "Tommy, Seven, Gary. Each of you grab two of these. Spread out and get them out on the wall." She looked back at the cells opposite the massive, featureless surface. "Try to get them in spots where the cells across from the wall are empty. No need to set fire to any inmates. The more that survive this, the better. Even the ones that aren't Wasters."

Her team went to work. Thompson handed over the warden's cable. Dava kept one eye on Gary as he pulled his way up the wall. He wasn't moving as fast as he could, but at least he was moving. The directive seemed to give him enough purpose to get out of his funk.

"Johnny, how are you holding up?" she said, leaving the others to their work. Watching them wasn't going to make it go any faster.

Eyeball grunted. Coming to the end of his exercise routine, he was stretching out his arms and legs. "I hate this place," he said finally. The first words he'd spoken since she saw him.

"I'm sorry," she said quietly. "I wanted to go back for you."

"Food's terrible, but I'm used to that," he said, not looking at her. "Wasting away in the null grav, but I'm a Waster anyways, so that don't matter."

"Johnny," she said softly. There was a soft ring of fuzz growing around his head. She knew he wouldn't be allowed to shave it himself. When she looked at him and pictured the head without the hair, she remembered that moment. The corridor. The Pollies – no, they weren't Pollies, they were Fenders. The ModPol military types. Too many of them. Overwhelming him while he tried to protect Frank.

"Not much to entertain a man in this place," he droned on, head into his chest. He reached down and slapped his maleness lightly. "Can't get it up. Not that I have any enthusiasm for it, so that don't matter neither."

She looked at Freezer, who shrank with embarrassment. "Takes gravity to make an erection work. Something about the blood flow." He looked down, then back up at her. "I hear lady parts don't work much better here."

"But what keeps me goin', day to day," Eyeball said, lifting his head slightly. "What keeps me going is the knowledge that my friend Frank Reezer is okay. Because someday I'm gonna get out of this place. And Frank too. And we're gonna go back home. And Frank is gonna get his rations. And he's gonna give 'em to me. Four bottles a month."

Dava looked at him. Waiting for something else to spill out of him. That was it though. His speech was over. She looked at Freezer in the next cell.

"That's right, Johnny," he said, talking forward through the mesh, but turning his head to the left as though he could see the other man through the steel wall. "Four big bottles of whiskey every month." He looked at Dava. "When we get home."

"All set," Thompson said, floating over and grabbing the warden's cable. The warden had gone quiet again, his expressions migrating from shock to confusion to pity and always back to fear.

Seven-Pack and Polar Gary came quickly after Thompson.

"Okay." Dava pulled herself close to Perzynski. "Job's almost done, pal. You might actually live through this. So tell me where the vacuum is going to pull everyone."

* * *

"What's wrong with them?"

Runstom was staring up at the walls of the yard that bent all around him. Yard Beta. It was a massive sphere, and there was no real ground. The word *yard* had been borrowed from traditional prisons; the wide-open stretch of space that inmates were free to move about in. Going by that definition, it still matched: it didn't have a ground, but the place was wide open, and the inmates were free to move around. Usually. At the moment, they were stuck to the walls all around him, limbs splayed at odd angles, like splattered bugs.

"Mag-locks have been activated," an older guard grunted at him. He was a B-fourean, lanky and pasty, and his name badge said *Chen*. "It's tuned to their pajamas."

Runstom had gotten a rundown of how the mag system worked. Seeing it in action, it sunk in better. He and the other three guards were stuck to the wall with the grip-boots, and could move almost as well as walking in gravity. The magnetic force tuned to the sunny-green prison-issue uniforms by contrast had been turned to maximum strength.

"So what now?" he asked.

Chen, who was supposed to be in charge, scanned around the yard in silence for a moment. "There," he said eventually, pointing. "A couple still in the middle. We push them to the wall to get them stuck. And look for anyone not wearing green pajamas."

"You mean the infiltrators." Runstom was feeling a need to be blunt and overt. "They will be armed."

"Yeah, I *know*," Chen said.

"Weren't there supposed to be securibots coming?" Runstom had heard the announcement that had been piped into the yard before he and the others arrived. Since he'd been in the facility, he hadn't seen any bots in operation that weren't cleaning something.

"I heard they're running diags on 'em," one of the others said. She looked like a teenager to Runstom. Like most of the guards, she was also a B-fourean.

"Diags?"

"Nostics," she said. "Takes a while."

It took him a moment to put the two halves of the word together. He wanted to probe, find out why the securibots weren't already active. He feared the possible answers: they were too costly to operate, there were too few to risk them, they didn't work reliably. Some combination of those.

"Come on, let's just get the greens and get out of here," Chen said.

They disengaged their boots and pushed off to the middle of the space. The other guards seemed to understand the invisible streams of air currents and were using them to navigate. Runstom had watched a quick holovid training on them, but again, it was a different thing to experience them in person. So while he clumsily made his way to the others, he watched them pursue green-suited inmates and shove them lightly in the direction of the walls. Once they drifted within a handful of meters, the magnetic force kicked in and pulled them the rest of the way.

Runstom caught up just as the last inmate was away. Chen floated and stared into nothing, giving the impression he was listening to his earpiece. He glanced down at his arm for a moment.

"Roger," he said, then dropped his arm and looked at the others. "Orders are to go through the far hatch and secure the next corridor."

Runstom looked across the way at the small round door in the middle of the wall. He absently stretched an arm toward it, as though he might swim his way there. Chen either took pity or didn't want to wait for him to figure out the current system. He grabbed Runstom by the uniform and shoved him in the direction of the hatch.

After he hit the wall, he managed to grab a handhold and re-engage his grip-boots. As he clomped his way to the nearby door, a blurry white blob floated into his vision. He flinched, leaning back so that he could see the object and pluck it out of space.

"What is that?" the young guard said as she waited for him to step through the hatch.

He held it up and frowned. The white surface contrasted with the olive-green skin of his own fingers.

"Better hold onto it," Chen said with a humorless grin. "If you collect enough pieces, we might be able to put him back together again."

Runstom didn't bother to ponder whether this was sarcasm or naive intention. He slipped the wayward digit into a chest pocket and pulled himself through the hatch.

After passing through the short lock tube, they came to the corridor to be secured. It was empty of life, but not of bodies.

"Shit," Chen said softly. His resolve was holding, but he stared at the dangling forms of the four dead guards in silence for a moment. Each was stuck to the floor or the wall by a boot or two, leaving the rest of their bodies to the will of weightlessness. Chen probably knew them all. Runstom wondered if he had considered any of them a friend.

This was the work of Space Waste. They would tear the place apart. The guards had become complacent, even lazy. The job was too easy, thanks to the tech, the zero gravity, and the deep-space location. Maybe these guards were never prepared. Maybe they were ModPol's washouts. Given a job that even a fuck-up could handle. The magnetic fields were their safety net. Runstom wondered how much of a guarantee that tech was. How easily it could be subverted.

He checked the charge on his gun. Still one hundred percent. Was he going to allow himself to walk into a slaughter? Should he die because the architects of the prison never expected a crew of Wasters to break in and run amok? Because the administrators were sold on inexpensive tech? Decided not to spend precious money on properly trained and outfitted personnel?

"Room is secure," Chen said into his headpiece. Runstom couldn't hear the reply. He imagined the vita-sensors and hidden wall cameras told the remote superiors the rest of the story.

"They want us to move on," Chen said. Something in his voice told Runstom it wasn't the type of *move on* he was hoping for. Move on back to your quarters would have been nice. Move on from the deaths of these colleagues would have been acceptable. But the tone said, move on through the corridor. Move on to the next horror.

"This is fucked," the young woman said. "What are we supposed to do?"

"We have to go down to hatch seven and into cellblock four," Chen said gravely. "That's where the infiltrators went."

"And what the hell are we supposed to do when we find the fucking infiltrators?" She waved an arm at a nearby corpse. "Get ourselves killed?"

"Don't talk to me like that. I'm your superior."

"Well what, then, oh great superior?"

The two glared at each other for a moment. "Are there cameras in there?" Runstom said, trying to get a look at the screen on Chen's armband.

"Yes," he said. "I don't have authorization for them. But Command does."

He stopped at that, prompting the woman to stick her arms out after a few seconds of silence. "And?"

Chen swallowed. "They said the hatch is clear inside."

This caused a string of unprofessional obscenities to pour forth from the woman as she stalked around the corridor. Angry pacing wasn't easy to pull off in mag-boots and zero-gravity, but she managed her best. Runstom noticed the fourth of their group hadn't said anything in the thirty minutes or so that they'd been on the mission. His eyes just stared forward, shiny with glaze. He was either scared senseless or stoned. Or both.

"I'll go in first," Runstom said.

"What?" Chen looked at him with narrowed eyes. "Why?"

"There's another one of those airlock doors, right?" Runstom was already stamping down the hall toward hatch seven. "I can go through and tell you if it's clear."

"Hey." The woman stopped her pacing. "Hey, that sounds like a plan. Let the new guy go first!"

Runstom almost stopped to tell her he wasn't a new guy to anything, then just let it go. *Move on.* He reached the hatch and tapped at the side panel.

"Okay," he said as it slid open and he stepped through. The three of them came up behind him, stopping short of the doorway. "Wait here. I'll go through and take a look. I'll call you when I know it's clear."

They nodded at him in silence and he tapped the panel. The door irised closed. He turned and face the other side. He was probably going to get himself killed. Did it matter that he might have saved three lives? Maybe they would be killed anyway. Maybe they would have stood a better chance if the four of them went through together. But he knew it wouldn't matter.

He checked the charge on his rifle. Ninety-nine percent. The damn thing was leaking electrons or something.

With a deep breath, he hefted the gun, then reached out and tapped at the pad. The familiar hiss started and stopped, cut short. The door was immobile. He blinked and reached for the pad again, then the cylindrical room turned red. His ears buzzed with an alarm both in his earpiece and coming from unseen speakers in the small space.

"Warning. Fire detected in cellblock four. Emergency evacuation procedures in effect. Warning. Fire detected in cellblock four. The block will be evacuated and purged."

* * *

A few dozen people lay about the containment chamber coughing and sucking wind. Or at least, they would be lying about if there were any goddamn gravity in this place. Instead, Dava watched them drift awkwardly all around her.

The firebombs had all blown together with the trigger, and the alarms started only seconds later. There had to be cameras, and she wondered if anyone tried to stop the evacuation. If that were the case, automated systems had prevailed. A long side door had split apart, allowing a narrow space through which air began to suck. The mesh doors all swung open and every inmate in the cellblock came through the slit, right after Dava, Thompson-Gun, Seven-Pack, Polar Gary, and Assistant Warden Perzynski.

There were several faces Dava recognized, and it brought a small thrill of victory to her chest. She never thought she'd be so glad to see so many ugly Waster mugs.

"Clothes," Freezer managed to shout, biting back a cough. "Take off your clothes!"

Dava, having been closest to the doors when the charges blew, was suffering the least from the effects of the vacuum. She picked up on Freezer's cries. "Everyone take off your clothes!" She grabbed a nearby inmate by the neon-green jumpsuit. "They're going to activate the mag field any second now! Get these clothes off *now* or your ass is going to be stuck to the wall!"

Most of the room took the hint and began stripping. Voices grew stronger as the command spread through the crowd. A wave of green was displaced by a mix of white, beige, pink, red, brown, and black. If they weren't in the middle of a prisonbreak, Dava thought it might have been some kind of performance art.

"Johnny," she said, going to the big man first. "Get something from the weapon crate. You get first dibs."

Eyeball glanced to one side, his good eye blinking while his bad eye stuck, creating that angry wink she was so glad to see again. His gaze rested on Freezer, and once he'd gauged that his meal ticket hadn't strayed far, looked toward the crate. Polar Gary had unstrapped it from his back and tied it to the wall. Eyeball nodded at it. "I want explosives. And lasers. Projectiles are no good in this place."

"Why not?"

He frowned. "Recoil. Hard to brace yourself." He looked down at his exposed body. "You need muscle to take a good shot."

She wanted to pity him, to feed her guilt. But she needed the real Johnny Eyeball. "There's a flamer."

His head lifted and his good eye brightened. "A flamer?"

"A compact. Nice jetstream on it. Good range."

His grin told her that would do. She followed him to the crate while he fished the flamethrower out, along with some gas bombs. Freezer joined them, showing no interest in anything in the crate, for which she was thankful. The hacker was not exactly competent with a weapon.

"We still have a bunch of people in other cellblocks?" she asked him.

"Yeah, of course," he said. He tapped his head. "I know where everyone is, cuz of The Flow. But there are sixteen cellblocks and four yards. We got Wasters spread out all over."

She figured as much. "And a lot of them will still be in their suits, so if the mag-lock kicks in, they'll be stuck."

Freezer nodded. "I can fix that, if I can get to a security station."

"Good." She put a hand on Eyeball's arm. "You can escort Frank?"

He huffed. "Yes."

"We should take Perzynski," Freezer added, nodding at the warden. The man was shivering now, just floating through the room with his arms around his legs. Thompson held the cable casually, as though he were a balloon on a string.

"Fine," Dava said, motioning for Thompson to bring him over. "You and Johnny go to the nearest security station. Can you find it?" Freezer just tapped his head. She allowed herself a small smile. "Good. And Seven, Gary. Get the other Wasters armed up. Each of you take half and get to the two closest yards. As soon as Freezer breaks the magnets, we need you to grab everyone you can find. Get to a dock."

"You got it, Dava," Seven-Pack said. Gary grunted and nodded.

"Oh, and Seven. Make sure Jerrard is okay." The thought of leaving one of the few Earth-borns behind gave Dava a sick feeling in her gut. It was bad enough he'd helped them in Yard Beta, only to get stuck to the wall when the mags kicked on. She looked at her last mate. "Tommy, you're with me."

Freed of the burden of tugging the warden, Thompson had both hands wrapped around her submachine with the massive drum-like magazine. Either she didn't have the same concerns about recoil that Eyeball had, or more likely, she would rather deal with it than give up her favorite weapon. She certainly managed in the corridors between the yard and the cellblock. "Aye, Capo," she said.

They moved through the masses of disrobed bodies to a hatch on the other side. Dava consulted her map one last time, committing the route to the Core to memory. She looked at the panel next to the hatch, ready to have the warden brought over, but it was in a different state than she'd seen before. It flashed with some kind of emergency warning and a brief message about evacuation. Had the fire temporarily disabled the locks? She tapped at the screen and found the door control. It hissed open at her touch, with no request for identification.

For a moment suspicion washed over her. She couldn't believe someone could be so stupid to create a system inside a prison where the doors became unlocked in the case of a fire. A trap? Then she realized the doors were just a backup method of inmate control. The magnetic locks embedded in the walls and tuned to the clothes of everyone in the station were the primary. And it was likely that while the fire unlocked these doors, they had not unlocked access to any docks. The final and strongest method of control was the fact that the station was in deep space. An escaped prisoner had nowhere to go.

She waved Thomson forward and they passed into the lock room. After a brief cycling of the doors, they were in a new corridor. This one was darker and narrower than the others.

The two of them traveled much faster, alone and with no burdens. They snaked through the corridor and its occasional turns and forks and within fifteen minutes of silent gliding, they reached a circular hall that bent around the Core itself.

Though the hall curved, it was long and there were no corners to use as cover. She suspected there would be guards somewhere, so they floated in silence. Listening.

After a few minutes, she heard a voice and held up her

hand to freeze her anxious mate. She listened. One voice, but speaking, pausing, responding, like a conversation. It came from the leftward curve of the hall.

She used hand signals to silently communicate to Thompson. *I'm going right. Follow at a short distance behind.*

They proceeded around the hall at a careful pace. Dava kept her eyes fixed on the horizon, the inner curve of the wall. She estimated they'd gone about a quarter of the way around. It was hard to tell without any point of reference but the hundreds of handholds on the walls.

She stopped and signaled again. *I'm going on. You go back. Pinch.*

Thompson nodded and flexed her hands around her rifle. Dava held up a hand to hold her and signaled again for her to use the blade attachment.

This caused a moment of silent facial contortion. She knew Thompson hated attaching the bayonet to her rifle. They'd gone this last stretch in silence, and Dava wanted to continue to take advantage of their small team of two and remain invisible. After Thompson had a few seconds to throw a silent fit, she dug the blade out of her uniform and fastened it to the barrel of the submachinegun.

They parted ways. Dava watched as Thompson pulled herself along with one hand, the other aiming the gun that was strapped around her shoulder. Dava turned and eased herself along the curve hand over hand, her own blade clamped between her teeth. She was counting on making faster progress than her mate.

After another minute or so, she let go of any chance of knowing where in the circle she was. Then she saw another hatch on the outer wall. By the map in her head, there had been only two hatches that connected into this hall, and they were directly opposite one another. She'd gone halfway around. She stopped and listened. No voices, no sounds at all.

She kept going. Steadied her breathing, which was not easy with a knife in her mouth. Then she heard the voice again. Just an inquisitive grunt.

She raised her arm and tapped out a message to Thompson. *Turn around and head the other way.* There was a code, a way to add an audible beep to the message using symbols. Freezer had figured it out and for a few days everyone annoyed each other by sending beeping messages to everyone's Messengers. She tapped out the signal several times and sent the message.

A second later, she heard the series of beeps from ahead of her, still a few dozen meters distant.

"What the hell?" The voice was much closer. "Heya, Command? Hey, yeah. We got any personnel down here in the Core right now?"

Dava crept forward, her eyes on that horizon. A tiny bump appeared, perhaps a hand or a weapon. She froze and listened.

"Okay, I'm gonna do a walkaround."

She heard the clicking of gripper boots. The bump disappeared. She grabbed a pair of handles and flung herself through space toward the opposite wall at an angle. Just as she reached the wall, she could see the guard moving along, angling his head to try to peer around the lengthy corner, in the direction he'd heard the beeps. She softly grabbed the wall as it came to her and reoriented herself, this time bracing her feet against the holds. She launched herself forward.

She sailed silently through the air and pulled the knife

from her teeth. She was on a direct course with the guard's back, but lacked the velocity she had hoped for. She had no choice but to let her momentum carry her to her target.

At just a few meters from the lanky, pale-skinned guard, her Messenger beeped.

The guard's head cocked, then turned. With the awkward clicking of grippers, he managed to get his body half turned toward her before her knife reached his throat.

Eyes wide, he batted at her blade with the barrel of his gun. She grabbed at it with her left hand so that she floated to the side when he tried to aim it at her. He pulled frantically, but in the absence of gravity it was easy for her to maintain her grip. She swiped at him with the blade, slicing through his uniform and into his forearm.

His sudden yelp was cut short by a gurgle and a forward lurch. Dava let go and floated off to the side as he teetered forward awkwardly, the gripper boots still fixing his feet to the floor. Thompson rode him, her feet against his ass and her bayonet firmly buried between his shoulder blades. She bent her knees, then straightened them, yanking her weapon free in a fan of crimson plasma. Some of it sprayed into the surrounding walls, some of it gathered into spherical puddles like wayward asteroids.

They looked at each other, both of them scowling fiercely. Neither of them could hold it for long – Dava wasn't sure who cracked first, but soon they were both silently laughing, nearly bursting blood vessels trying to control their hysteria. All Dava could think about was how badly she wanted to tell the story back at the Space Waste base. About how she'd used Freezer's beeping Messenger trick to turn Thompson into guard-bait, only to have the trick reversed on her. All in good fun, considering they both survived.

And as she kicked against the floor with one foot to avoid one of the drifting globules of blood something very, very small twisted deep inside her. They would rejoice in this man's comical demise. An innocent man? No, anyone on a ModPol paycheck was not innocent. She had taken so many lives. What was this one to her? Her reputation was for an intimidating forty kills, but in reality she had stopped counting long before that and had gone far past it.

She needed Moses. These acts, they were murder one by one. But Moses would tell of something much bigger. He wasn't fighting individual guards or cops or soldiers. He was fighting systems. She needed him to remind her of that. She needed one of those speeches, the kind that started soft and grew to a deep, chant-like bellow. The kind that rode strong on undeniable righteousness.

They followed the featureless hall back the way Thompson had come until they found a lone control panel. It was unlike any she'd seen before, such as those accompanying the hatches. She prodded at it, not really understanding what she was looking at in the sea of unlabeled icons.

Thompson flinched, reflexively raising her weapon, causing Dava to flinch. A curved segment of the wall slid away, revealing a short passage of only a few meters. Just beyond, she could see the shimmer of some kind of barrier. Beyond that, a wedge-shaped cell that tapered in three dimensions. The cell was empty.

She looked at the panel interface again, having identified the door control by chance. This hint allowed her to make some further guesses and she found a list of prisoner numbers. The operator at the dock had rattled off Moses's number, but Dava had been too keyed up to think to remember it. There were only two on the screen. She picked one and it started some kind of sequence. The door slid back into place, becoming nothing but a wall once again. The sounds of machinery could be heard just beyond, and within a few minutes, the door reopened.

As the wall slid away she squeezed through the opening before it was even complete. She pulled herself down to the barrier.

Moses drifted near the rear of the cell, his back to her. His form seemed limp, and her heart-rate ramped, a sudden fear that he'd died in this place. Died alone. Had left her.

"Moses?" she whispered. She reached for the barrier and tried to penetrate it, but it resisted her with a soft but firm force, darkening and glittering where she touched it.

His body stretched out to its full length, which seemed even longer in the absence of gravity. He slowly turned, a measured, tumbling rotation on multiple axes. His foot flicked, kicking off the tapered wall near the back of the cell. He drifted up to the barrier. When he braced his progress against it, it flexed toward her in a glittering hand-shaped outdent.

Reflexively, she put her palm against his.

His momentum arrested, he pulled the hand away. The barrier where he had touched it reverted to the soft, barely visible sheen. "Good to see you, Dava."

She wanted to say something, to cry out, to embrace him. Another part of her wanted to gush, to tell him everything, to unleash her fury at Basil Roy's betrayal. To demand he do something about Jansen. To put the man on trial. To find out what he knew. To take charge again. To guide them, to guide her.

But she couldn't say any of that. None of it would come out. He looked the same as always, great and strong and wise, but something in him was broken, something beyond what she could see. She was rescuing him. Expecting him to rescue her in return.

"Thompson," she said without taking her eyes off Moses. "Drop the barrier."

After a few seconds of silence, the reply came. "I don't know how, Dava." There was another panel in the middle of the short passage. Dava looked back and watched Thompson poke at it uselessly. "It wants some biometrics or something."

"Like what?"

"Retinal scan, voiceprint, or fingerprint," Moses said. "They usually don't need them, because they have their identities in their uniforms. But down here in the Core, they have to confirm using one biometric."

Dava started tapping at her Messenger. *Did you find a security station yet?*

The reply from Freezer was almost instant; he was always so quick with interfaces. *Yepper.*

Can you unlock cell 7 in the Core? she tapped.

This time the reply took longer. *No can do. Biometrics on site only. Requires warden clearance.*

She stared at the message in silence, then closed her eyes. She was so close. She would not leave this place without Moses. "What is this barrier made out of?" she asked when she opened her eyes.

"Some kind of nanomaterial," Moses said with an idle prod at the flexible stuff. "Lots of little particles. Probably uses magnetic force like everything else around here."

"Maybe we can track down a warden," Thompson said. "We only need a finger or an eye—"

"Wait!" Dava almost lost control of herself in the null

gravity as she twisted around, rummaging through her pockets. Finally she felt the small, cold slab of meat and pulled it out, holding it up triumphantly: one of Perzynski's fingers.

She passed the digit off to Thompson, who took it with a smile. "Dava, I didn't think you were the trophy type." She turned back to the panel and prodded at it a few times – first with her own fingers, then with the estranged finger when prompted. "Damn, it's not working."

Dava craned to see. "What does it say?"

"Identifying Assistant Warden Perzynski," she read aloud. "Insufficient clearance. Shit."

"He's only an assistant warden," Dava said, thinking out loud. She tapped out a message to Freezer. "Let's see if Frank can get into the personnel database."

"What for?"

"See if we can get this poor bastard a promotion."

Okay, it's done, Freezer sent back after a few minutes. *Under the reason, I put that he's a dynamic go-getter who synergizes and thinks outside the box.*

"Congratulations, Perzynski," Dava said. "You're a full warden now."

Thompson went back to the panel with an ear-to-ear grin. "Yes!"

The barrier split down the middle, at first creating a thin gap that widened with a slinking sound until it was wide enough for Moses to pass through.

Dava didn't wait for him to come out before she crashed into him with a full embrace.

CHAPTER 11

When the alarm finally let up and the hatchway opened, Runstom took one look into the cellblock and pulled the door closed. They were all loose – the entire cellblock. Coming through the hatch on the opposite side. Armed. And naked.

He opened the door back into the corridor he'd left the other guards in. There was no sign of them. As the round hatch began to swing closed, he grabbed it. Fortunately, some safety protocol prevented it from crushing his fingers.

Safety protocols. The fire had released them from their cells. To be evacuated from the area. And the maglocks would have no effect without their clothes.

There was no stopping them now, but he could slow their progress. They were intending to come back through the same locking hatch, but Runstom knew the other door would not open until the one he held was closed. He thought he might be able to wedge something in there, but the only solid object on his person was his blaster. He decided not to part with it. Rifling around his pockets with one free hand, he brushed something stiff. Pulled it out. A severed finger.

He took the chance that the door couldn't tell the finger was already severed and slid it into the opening. Quickly pulled his own fingers free. The door twitched by a millimeter then froze, the long, white finger held between it and the frame. It waited patiently for the owner to remove their extremity from danger.

It would be waiting a long time.

Runstom pulled his way back down the corridor, once again passing the floating remains of the guards that had tried to stop the Wasters. Spherical pools of gore were beginning to collect, with no gravity to spread it. He carefully steered himself around the mess. Liquids tended to get clingy in zero-G and the last thing he wanted at that moment was to carry the blood of the fallen around on his clothes.

He came to an intersection. He didn't want to go back the way he and Chen and the other two came; there was no telling what kind of shape the yard was in. If he could get to one of the outer guard towers, he could get a better picture of the situation. Once he'd thought of it, he realized the others had probably gone up to one of the towers as well.

His map was near useless, but at least it was a map. The nearest towers were above Yard Beta. The towers were not towers in the same sense that the yards were not yards, but close enough to the same functions that the original terms were kept. As he inspected the holo-map, he realized the ringed corridors were shifting. This was a function of the facility he had not seen, except for in the Core. Was it in response to the fire, or to the assault? What was the point? In any case, it meant his ruse to delay the Wasters behind him would be short lived; they would be able to go around and reach any of the yards in time. In fact, they were probably splitting up, sending a contingent into the other cellblocks as well. They would spread like a virus and infect the whole prison within the hour.

He checked his gun again. Ninety-eight percent. He tried not to think of the leaking charge as a countdown timer and moved on. The hatch to his destination should have been blocked to a low-ranking guard such as himself, but the panel flashed brazenly that it was unlocked and safe to use as an evacuation route.

* * *

The guard tower wasn't meant to hold so many, and there were a lot of banged elbows and knees resulting. Chen had managed to get the other two guards safely there, but now the three of them were antsy, feeling useless. Being useless, Runstom realized. There were a few other guards stationed in the tower trying to do their job, which mainly consisted of tracking all the inmates in Yard Beta and the connecting corridors. Through a round cage at one end of the tower, the turret could be seen. Manned by a gunner actively trying to control the chaos in the yard. The sound of the laser was a pale hum, outspoken by the whining actuators that were in constant motion as the beam tracked its targets.

He'd only been there twenty minutes, but the situation was deteriorating. By the chatter on the radio – which was set to loudspeaker mode, so that all in the tower could hear it – the Wasters were advancing all over the place. Some of them had taken over one of the special guardhouses that contained a security terminal. It was just a matter of time before they started making their way to the docks.

Flashes of the first prisoner barge infected his mind. They'd torn it apart. If they made it to the docks, they'd find a way to rip the facility into pieces. It would no longer be a prisonbreak. The words of Moses Down. It would be war. The Wasters had been pushed, and they would push back.

The murmured conversations around the room hushed. Runstom's ears pricked. The radio.

... is Tower Beta Two ... we ... ack ... ZZT *... no! ... hellllpaaaAAAH...*

"Can they get to the turret in that tower?" The young woman from Chen's group. Her voice quivered, her stare fixed on the grate-like portal between them and the turret in their own tower. "Can they fire it?"

Chen looked at one of the guards stationed in the tower. "No," he said with a grunt. "Gotta have the right clearance to pass through the cage. Right?"

The other guard looked at them in silence for a terrifyingly long second. "Riiiight," he said. Before anyone could relax, he added, "But you can't even get to the tower without *some* clearance."

Runstom noticed the man had given himself a discreet shove in the direction of the back of the tower. It registered. If the Wasters had gotten into Tower Beta Two, then they were subverting security. What would stop them from using the turret?

There was a scope attached to one of the walls. Runstom had used it to scan the yard and surrounding corridors for activity. Had scanned with it obsessively for ten or fifteen minutes before the measured advance of the enemy became too exhausting to watch. He looked through it again, this time aiming it at the other tower. Panning to the turret. A large white blob filled his view. When his eyes focused, it became a man. Pale white skin like a domer, but as wide as a Sirius-Fiver and as tall as a B-fourean.

Through the scope, names hovered above any identified person in the view. Names derived from a ModPol database somewhere, correlated by facial recognition and whatever else it needed. It would show stats or other info if Runstom knew how to operate it properly. But he didn't, so it only showed names. Like the figures in the picture had little flags tacked to the backs of their heads. Not all of the infiltrators were identified, but some had been arrested before and were in the system. Eventually, it recognized them. The big Sirius-Fiver's flag said *Gary White*.

Gary White was in the process of beating and extracting the turret's previous operator. Blobs of red plasma floated behind the clear sphere that surrounded the controls of the gun. White swatted them aside. Strapped into the control chair. The barrel fixed to the bottom of the sphere began to rotate.

Runstom jumped back from the scope. Momentarily forgetting the lack of gravity, his *jump* was more of a twisting flinch that sent him into the panic-space of the room where there was nothing to grab onto.

"They got it!" he shouted. "They got the other turret! I think they—"

He was cut off by a shrieking, tearing sound. They all turned to face the grating that led to their own turret control sphere. The scream from within, quickly cut off. The suck of decompression. The room spinning.

Runstom was no longer free-floating, he was being pulled. He grabbed the hand of one of the other guards who was latched to a handhold on the wall. He looked up the length of his arm briefly. It was Chen. He looked down at his feet, the source of the pull. Quickly understanding. White had turned one gun against the other. Blasting a hole through the control sphere.

Air rushed past him and his eyes began to water. There was something moving, just beyond the grate. A round hatch mechanism, twisting shut. Over the sound of the wind he could hear Chen moaning. He gripped Runstom's hand tighter, so tight that it felt like it might squeeze them apart.

Then the iris was closed and the air pressure stabilized. A hiss of replacement air coming through unseen vents. Chen tugged Runstom toward the wall, then released his hand. Runstom caught the nearest handhold.

The screeching sound began again, only slightly muted.

"They're blasting through the door!" one of the other guards shouted. "They're going to smoke the whole tower!"

"We gotta get out of here!" Chen yelled, thrusting himself toward the rear hatch.

Runstom followed, and so did the others, as well as they could. Which wasn't very well. They were all disoriented and banged up. Chen hit the panel and the hatch spun open, revealing the small tube-like lock beyond. They'd have to all cram into it in order to cycle the doors and get out the other side.

Runstom was the third one in. He'd managed to grab a handle on the floor when another blast broke through the tower. Again the rush of air, this time accompanied by the whining bend of metal.

He looked back and the scene of flying debris and bodies was slowly getting smaller. The door was closing, before they ran the cycle. A safety feature, he realized: it was closing due to the sudden drop in air pressure. His stomach was in his throat as he saw three bodies batted around like leaves in the wind, disappearing beyond the wall at the other end of the tower.

The last body was Chen. He was pulling his way across the floor, one handhold at a time. His form disappeared from view as the door's opening shrank.

Runstom remembered the finger – the door would stop if it detected a body part in its path. Leveraging himself with one hand gripping a hold tightly, bracing one foot against the floor, he raised his other foot toward the door. Stretched, as it spiraled inward. It closed around his boot halfway up and stopped.

"Get it back open!" he shouted to the others. "Chen is stilllllAAAAAAHHH!"

His foot, his whole leg blazed with pain. He could hear the crunching of the bones over his own cries. No one had touched anything. The door kept closing.

He pulled frantically, bringing his other hand down to the floor and doubling his grip. Pulled through his own screams. Twisting his foot unnaturally.

Pulled it until it pulled apart and he was flung across the tiny room, smacking into the far wall.

As he slid out of consciousness, the voices of the others echoed distantly through the black.

"What the hell happened? It didn't stop! What about the safety protocols?"

"The decompression! Safety override!"

"Damn, look at his *foot*!"

* * *

"This plan," Moses said, his bare chest heaving. "This plan could have been a little more thought out."

"Most of my plans are just for killing people, not for saving people," Dava muttered, examining the holo map in her armband.

They were pulling their way away from the Core. They needed to get to the docks. Any dock would do, but preferably one with a pilot. Dava and Thompson didn't know the first thing about piloting, but Moses could fly if he had to. She didn't dare ask when the last time he took hold of a flightstick was. It was bad enough to be reminded of his true age by the fact that she made him strip out of his inmate jumpsuit, exposing wrinkled skin speckled by patchy tufts of soft gray fuzz. His muscles still demonstrated strength and flexibility, but there were parts of the aging process that were harder to cover up without the help of clothing. The important part was that he *could* pilot at one time. All they needed to do was get to a dock.

Unfortunately, the map was giving her some trouble.

"This doesn't make any sense," she said. "We came into Dock C, then through Yard Beta. Then Cellblock Four. But they're all scattered now."

"The whole place moves around," Moses said. "It's automated, but as far as we can tell, it's random. The screws probably know the schedule, but to us it's pure chaos."

She tapped out a message to Freezer. *Near the Core, need a safe route to a dock.*

After a few seconds, the response. *Polar Gary got into a turret and is carving shit up. Going to send you around to the other side. Route incoming.*

Her map blinked and she tapped at it, acknowledging

the incoming data. A green line appeared, drawing jaggedly from the Core to Dock A.

Freezer, she tapped. *Get the word out and make sure everyone gets to a dock safely. You and Johnny have to escort the pilots.*

Roger, Capo. Stay alert. I'm hacking security, but it's a tug-o-war. They keep overriding my overrides.

"Okay, let's move," Dava said.

She filled them in as they pulled their way through the twisting corridors. The reconfiguration set Dava on edge. She was used to memorizing the layout of a ship or a structure, designing her own route, building it up in her head, knowing the options and alternatives should it go bad along the way. This place didn't play by her expectations.

But she had Moses. She got here, got in, and got him out. They just needed a ship.

After a series of locks, they reached one of the outer corridors. The curve was much wider and they could see a longer distance before the walls bent away from their view. They were only a few legs from the dock in Freezer's route.

A few minutes of pulling handholds, and four hatches came into view on each side of the hall. Dava checked her map. The connecting corridor to get them to the dock was just a bit farther up. The map showed that the four connecting rooms were small, like utility closets or something. It wasn't explicit about the contents, other than displaying an icon that looked like a three-dimensional asterisk, just a small central dot with a series of lines extending from it. There was another icon that looked like a lightning bolt, the universal symbol for power. Either a generator maintenance panel or some kind of charging station.

Taking the lead, Dava slowed their approach to the four hatches with the palm of her hand. Either prospect might be useful. If it was a power control, she might be able to disable power to the outer defensive turrets, making their getaway much less risky. If it was a charging station, there could be weapons or powered armor inside.

The latter of which they didn't have a need for necessarily. Thompson-Gun had given up her sidearm to Moses, so he and Dava were both packing compact but powerful laser pistols.

Just a few hops from the hatches, the walls turned red. She froze for half a second, then realized the hatches were opening.

"Get back!" she said. "Back, back!"

They hastened back the way they came, but without gravity they were not in any position to sprint. Dava glanced back over her shoulder to see dozens of shapes pouring forth from the pulsing red walls.

She turned back and kept pulling, letting the split-second image resolve in her mind. Spheres, about a meter in diameter. Legs or tentacles protruded from them in all directions, ropelike limbs that were reaching for handholds. Dozens of pairs of eyes turning to face their direction. One eye shining: the protective glass over a camera? The other eye hollow and dark: the barrel of a weapon?

"HALT FORWARD PROGRESS." The machines were speaking simultaneously, working on a hive brain of some kind. "SURRENDER YOUR WEAPONS. SURRENDER NOW."

"Dava, tell me you're packing grenades," Moses said. Her heart sank in remembrance of her strict commandment that she would never carry explosives. Then it jumped when she remembered she decided to violate that particular personal virtue, just this once.

She reached for one side of her belt: anti-personnel. Reached for the other side: electro-magnetic pulse. She yanked one of the EMPs away and tossed it at the chorus of spiderbots that were chanting for their surrender.

The bots were flinging themselves down the corridor at alarming speed using those whipping limbs. The small grenade floated straight until it bopped into a bot in the middle of the pack. There was a bright flash and a ball of crackling white fingers danced across them. Dava felt a tingle as the momentum of their movement brought a couple of them tumbling into her. She spasmed, twisting her body and kicking the cold, limp limbs away from her. When she got her cool back a moment later, she saw the crowd of them – about two dozen in all – were drifting around her like corpses.

She looked back, Moses and Thompson going through the same motions: spastic fear, then a sudden relaxation at the realization that the monster-bots had been fried. She turned back to the hatches. In the few seconds that had passed since the doors opened, they had fled back down the corridor a good thirty meters.

She stared fixedly at those hatches. She didn't know what the range of the EMP was, or whether its effects were permanent or temporary, and if the latter, how long they would last. They needed to move, but she stuck frozen to the spot. Watching those hatches.

"WARNING, HOSTILES DETECTED."

This time the chorus was smaller, but the handful of bots that came out, came out shooting. Anchoring themselves with their limbs, they fired some kind of charged projectiles, orange balls that blazed forth and ripped into the partial shielding created by their stunned brethren.

"Take 'em out!" Dava yelled, whipping her pistol from its holster. She squeezed the trigger and nothing happened. The charge indicator on the back of it was dark. "Shit, my gun is fried!"

"Mine too," Moses said. "Pull back!"

Dava turned and using a foot against a handhold, shoved Moses as hard as she could, sending the old man gliding down the tunnel. Tiny orange explosions burst against the wall around her. She grabbed the handhold and pulled herself into a crouch.

The sound of a wet crunch followed immediately by a gurgling scream. She looked to her left. Thompson-Gun flailed, spinning like a top. Dava could see straight through the fist-sized hole in the left half of her stomach.

Thompson managed to grab the far wall and righted herself. She let go to put both hands on her submachinegun. With a metallic clatter, it ripped bullets down the hall, smashing apart two of the spiderbots. In the same instant, the recoil of the full-auto sent Thompson tumbling down the corridor in Moses's direction, a string of blood and excrement and intestines extending from her form.

Dava, still crouched, kicked off. She brought her hands forward, reaching out with her fingers and straightening her body. As she flew at the curving wall farther down the hall, she quickly grabbed a handhold, brought her knee to her chest, planted her foot against the wall, and kicked off again. This time she caught Moses as she passed him.

She grabbed another handhold as she found Thompson grunting with effort. She was upside-down from Dava's perspective and was messing with the strap of her

Tommy-Gun. Her guts hung half out of her side, like some kind of festive gore-decorative.

"Thompson, we have to go!"

"Fuck! No!" Dava realized she was looping the strap through a handhold. Which meant the gun wasn't going anywhere. Which meant Thompson wasn't going anywhere.

"Tommy, please!" Dava blinked, surprised by the sudden sting in her eyes.

"Get Moses out." Thompson finished her work and hugging the ceiling, aimed her weapon down the hall. Her voice was cold and non-negotiable. "Go, now. I'll take care of these fuckers."

Dava swallowed and went, yanking Moses with her. When she heard the bursts of Thompson's gun, she swallowed harder. When she heard Thompson's shouts of defiance, she swallowed so hard she thought she would break her own throat. When she heard Thompson's cries of pain, she swallowed a massive yellow sun, like the one that hung behind the smog of her youth back on Earth. She swallowed it down and locked it into the deepest parts of her insides that she could find. Farther down than she kept the lives that she took with her own hands. Farther down than she kept the other Wasters she'd seen fall over the years. All the way down to the place where she kept her father.

All the way down to the place where she kept her mother.

CHAPTER 12

A steady chime pinged softly at regular intervals. It quickened with Runstom's heartrate when he opened his eyes and tried to move.

"Relax." A female voice, but lifeless. "You have regained consciousness. Pain blockers have been administered to reduce the trauma of your condition."

"My condition?" he uttered. It was a small medical room of some kind. The source of the voice wasn't immediately obvious. He wasn't strapped down to complete immobility, but he had loose, stretchable bands attached to his limbs that kept him from floating around the space.

"Your condition is stable," the voice said. "Stitch-adhesive has been applied to the damaged area and there is no internal bleeding. Bone regrowth and accelerated cellular repair functions are not available at this time."

"Why not?" Runstom tried to stretch feebly.

"The facility is on maximum alert. You have one message. Would you like to hear it?"

"What? Oh. Yeah, play it."

The room filled with a new voice. "Hey dude, sorry we had to dump you in medical. We got orders to report to Guardhouse Tango. Looks like you managed to save your foot, but it got pretty mangled in the door. The boot's a total loss though."

Runstom looked down at his numb foot. It was wrapped in some kind of hard foam. An emergency field dressing, he realized.

"Anyway, try to get to Tango if you can," the message continued. "They're going to start locking out parts of the prison though, so you might not get through. In which case ... you should uh, evacuate or something?"

"For fuck's sake," Runstom breathed. "Hey," he called out, unsure of how to address the room. "Release these straps."

A minute later he was limping along and glancing at his map. He couldn't use his right leg. Not that he could feel the pain, thanks to the drugs the med-bot had administered. Regardless, he'd lost the mag-boot on that foot. So he made his way like some kind of animal, loping down the passages using his left boot and the grippers in his gloves. Guardhouse Tango was at a spot more than 90 degrees away from his location. Not as far as 180 degrees, but far in any case. The shortest route would take him close to the Core.

Maybe that's why he found himself heading directly for the Core at that moment. Just an easy route to the destination he'd been ordered to report to. Or perhaps the Core, as the center of this zero-gravity facility, had a gravity of a different kind that pulled him toward it.

The lights of the corridors alternated between their normal clean white and a murky yellow every few minutes. Systems were failing. Browning out. Dipping into reserves. The

Wasters couldn't destroy the whole facility, but they were doing significant damage. Runstom was left wondering whether he should care. Whether he should hang around to help pick up the pieces. Or whether his other responsibilities carried more weight. He didn't work for Justice any more, he worked for Defense.

That didn't matter, he realized. His existence, his purpose had been tested many times. But in that moment, it was clear.

So maybe the fact that the place was in a state of chaos was a sign. A calling. Time to leave. Time to finish this business. Time to find Jax. Time to put X away.

Which meant he needed a ship. Inside an inner pocket, a small data module pressed against his ribs. It contained a program for tracking the interstellar patroller that Sylvia managed to mark before it jumped into Xarp. But the signal was a radio wave. Limited by the speed of light. Potentially blocked or obscured by planets, asteroids, any bodies in the system. And Runstom had no idea where to start looking for it.

But he knew someone who did.

Could she be controlled? He wouldn't offer her freedom, of course. He wouldn't offer her anything other than a chance to get X. That would be enough. What he would do with her afterward – turn her back in? – was a problem for later.

That's what it had come down to, he realized as he loped into the final connector that led to the corridor circling the Core. It had come down to shortsighted thinking. Move to the next thing. There was no long-term plan. To make one would only mean to have it fail.

Runstom was never good at long-term planning anyway.

He pulled his body through to the corridor and began to circle around to the entrance of the Core. After a few meters, he saw the gore that hung in the middle of space. It looked like a wide shot of a solar system, with a large red ball in the middle orbited by spheres and chunks of various sizes, some of them strung together like asteroid belts, others free floating like planets. None of it moved other than a slight shimmering at the movement of air that his arrival caused.

Beyond the haze of crimson, there was the form of a body. He looked away. An innocent guard. He knew without looking. He decided to circle around the other direction.

The other end of the corridor remained spotless, and soon he reached the entrance to the Core. He opened the inner passageway and stepped inside. One of the cells was exposed. Empty. He looked at the panel. Moses Down. Of course. The whole reason for the assault. A break-in, break-out. The conversation he had with Down floated into his mind, but he pushed it away. There was no time to contemplate the consequences of his escape. Runstom narrowed his focus to his own purpose.

He tapped at the panel and it reacted to his credentials, the gripper-glove relaying his fingerprints. He called up Jenna Zarconi. Yellow lights flashed. The door just outside the cell slid shut. Machinations emanated from the inner cell globe. Another power dip caused the entire room to drop into shadow for a handful of empty seconds. After a few minutes, the door slid open again.

Zarconi floated in front of the nanogate. "I suspect all is not well."

"How would you know?" he said quietly, still at the panel.

She nodded, looking up at something unseen. "The cells

moved around. By my estimates, they moved to an orientation that brought Moses Down to this access passage. They haven't moved again since."

He thought to ask her how she knew which cell Moses Down had been in – wondered if she knew he was the only other resident of the Core – but stopped himself. She had nothing but time to sort these things out. And she had her contacts. She wasn't always restricted to the Core; she was given limited time in the yards. She would always find a way to learn, to lock up data inside that analytical mind.

"Space Waste," he grunted.

She smiled faintly and spoke with a wistful air of respect. "They broke in just to break him out. Ah, to be so loved."

"X has Jackson," Runstom said. He hoped the directness would shake her, but it had no visible effect on her face. "I think he's going to kill him."

"I expect so," she said, her smile twisting to a narrow snarl. "But not quickly. If Mark took Jack, then he wants to pump him for information first. He will torture him to make sure the information is genuine."

Runstom grimaced. "Torture leads to as much false information as anything real. He'll say whatever he thinks X wants to hear."

"It doesn't matter to Mark," she said grimly. "He wants all of it: the real, the false, everything in between. It all has meaning to someone who thinks in terms of games and manipulations. *What* you lie about and the *way* you lie about it can be more informative than the truth."

"How do I find him, Jenna?" Runstom approached the gate. "Please."

She looked at him. Looked into his eyes. "You can trust me?"

He returned the look. Her face pale in the yellow light. Her brown eyes glinting. Blinking in plea. Not a plea for freedom. He sucked in a breath. "I can trust you."

She exhaled and looked away. "I know where he will be. But you'll have to take me with you. There are ... calculations."

"What does that mean?" He assumed X had a ship, but maybe it was something else. "His location is ... what? You have to do math?"

"Yes," she said. "I need access to a computer with astrophysical data."

"I see." He was expecting this. Expecting she wouldn't just tell him. Or maybe couldn't just tell him. If she was telling the truth, then her information wouldn't be useful to him unless she came along. He knew his way around a navigation computer, but anything more complex than using pre-constructed routes and destinations was beyond his skill. AI could only help so much.

"Let me help you," she said weakly, her voice barely a whisper. She was still not facing him. "Let me make this right."

He watched her silently. Was her plea just for his trust? Was her plea to have one person in the universe care about her? A naive part of him wanted to believe her – that she really wanted a chance to make things right. To prove she felt remorse for her crimes. To rectify the danger she put Jax's life in when she involved an innocent man in her schemes. To counter her injustices by stopping a greater enemy of justice.

He kicked off with his good leg and drifted back to the panel. It didn't matter what she wanted. They were using each other. And Runstom was only looking one step ahead.

The panel refused his command to open the nanogate. It warned him such action was only possible with a warden's authority. How had the Wasters gotten it to open for Down?

He looked back at the cell. He knew the nano-lattice would peel away for him because of his uniform. A safety measure, to ensure a guard could enter if necessary. In case an inmate was trying to hurt themselves. But the opening would form a seal around the suit as he passed through it. There was no way for him to go in and pull her out. The gate would seal around his arms as he passed back through, it would shed anything outside the suit like a reptile shedding skin.

He glanced at her. Decided it would be bad form to tell her to wait. He pulled himself back into the main hallway that ran around the Core. Sucked in a breath, and then loped to the side opposite the way he came through.

The guard's form hung motionless, like he'd fallen asleep on the job. A blob of shiny crimson for a pillow on his backside. Runstom looked at the pale B-fourean's face, the white skin going blueish-gray. He'd been young.

He brought the whole body back. He wasn't sure the suit would be able to pass through without something inside it. He also wanted to delegate the work of extracting the body to someone else. Why not let the sociopath handle the corpse of the recently deceased?

She watched him patiently as he loped back down the passage with the limp guard. Using his left foot and his left hand for locomotion, his right hand for towing. He pushed the body through the nanogate and it passed without issue, the particle screen stripping away the loose collections of plasma when it crawled around the shoulders and across the back. He frowned and wished he had something to brush away the free-floating blood. Beyond it, he could see her silently going to work on the body. No explanation needed between them.

Rather than watch Zarconi extract the dead body of a young guard from the suit and insert her own naked body, Runstom pushed himself back into the main corridor to wait. He examined his limited map, charting a route to the nearest dock.

* * *

Dava's alternate route took her into a long corridor that ran more or less parallel to the one with the spiderbots. It meant she would have to pass by an access passage that led to a guardhouse. Just beyond that was the passage leading to the dock.

Before they entered the corridor, she looked back at Moses, still in the lock-room. His tall form seemed to stretch even longer without gravity and without clothing. He was a tall black tree, perfect posture despite the circumstances.

They had discarded their fried laser pistols, and so their only weapon was Dava's blade. "I need to scout ahead," she said.

He frowned at her, no doubt feeling as inadequate as he could ever feel, floating there without a weapon or even clothes. "Right," he said. He kicked his head back in a nod to the hatch behind him. "This lock won't cycle as long as one door is open. And it won't close if it detects that something is blocking it. Seen a guard once get his foot caught in it. Really thought he was gonna lose it, all for my entertainment. But the door just stopped."

"Okay," Dava said, understanding. If he stayed and

blocked the hatch from spiraling shut, then the other door would never open, giving them temporary relief from the advancing spiderbot sentries.

He drifted forward and planted himself just inside the lock-room, within reaching distance of the hatchway. She nodded and pushed off down the corridor.

Within minutes, she was near the linking passage to Guardhouse Tango. She held for a moment just in front of it. Straining to focus with her ears, ready for any sound at all. There were cameras all over the place, and she knew they'd be too small and too hidden for her to see them and take them out. Her only hopes were that Freezer managed to take down the circuit for the feeds, or that the staff of the place all had their hands full and couldn't keep an eye on every image that was flickering by. If they were going to come after her, this would be the spot.

So she waited. Counted her inhalation-exhalation cycles to one hundred. Listening. Nothing.

Then something. Not from the side passage, but further down the main corridor. The whirr of a hatch opening, the hiss of an air vent balancing the air pressure. Voices.

Dava looked at her map. There was a connector, coming down to the ceiling (from her perspective), not far from where she was. The corridor was close to the edge of the facility, so she could see several dozen meters before the horizon. The connector was closer than that.

She turned to flee, kicking off the wall with both feet. The voices shouted together. Two distinct voices. She heard the hum of a weapon powering up just before it loosed a shot that sparked off the wall just beside her as she flew.

The tacking of their gripper boots rattled through the hall. She managed to keep the distance from shrinking, grabbing the wall and re-launching herself. White bolts narrowly missing her along the way. She flew past the lock where she left Moses. The picture formed in her mind as she blinked on by. The door had spiraled closed, but not completely. Large brown hands formed a circle in the middle of it. Large brown eyes peered through.

She looked back to see the pair of guards gaining on her, running along the ceiling. A man and a woman. They passed Moses and Dava turned to face them. She spread out her arms and legs, forming a wide X.

"I give up!" she shouted. "Please, I surrender!"

This brought them to a clumsy stop, the man stumbling into the woman. "What?" she said as she fought for balance.

"I said I surrender!"

The man began to whisper something but the woman waved him off. "Put up your hands," she shouted at Dava. "I mean, keep your hands up like that. Don't move."

The woman stalked toward her while the other guard kept his gun drawn and pointed forward. Dava couldn't move if she wanted to: she'd released herself from the wall and was floating freely in the middle of the wide corridor. She kept her hands wide as the guard approached.

"Turn around."

Dava twisted her body. "I – I can't." She briefly wondered how long this guard had been stationed here. She didn't seem to get the limits of movement in the absence of gravity.

"Right, okay." She took another cautious step forward. "Just wait there then. Keep the hands and legs spread."

She complied as the woman stamped up to her. The zip of a door pricked up Dava's ears, even though she'd been waiting for it. If the guards noticed, it was already too late. Moses was out of the lock-room, and his long, strong limbs were wrapped around the other guard. He quickly maneuvered his arms, bringing them into a hold around the man's shooting arm, and with an awkward twitch, squeezed a tortured cry out of the guard.

The woman was an arm's length from Dava. She wrenched her body around without detaching her feet, drawing her pistol shakily. Dava brought her right hand down to the knife in its sheath on her chest and reached out with her left hand. With a stretch, she grabbed the woman's collar with two fingers, then twisted it into a fistful of uniform. She pulled herself close as she yanked the knife free, and as the guard cranked her head around to face her, Dava struck.

It was clear that in the course of the events of the last few hours, the guard had lost her helmet. The blade sawed effortlessly through her eye and into her brain and she gasped airlessly, dead before she could scream. Dava yanked the weapon free, the string of red plasma dotted with pink chunks of flesh and brain tissue.

Another pang of guilt as she looked into the remaining eye, wide with fear. Another wasted life. This woman was important to someone. Like Thompson was important to Dava. "God dammit," she spat, not caring if Moses heard her.

What was happening to her? No one was an innocent victim, she made that decision a long time ago. In a universe that could – no, there was no time to go dark. She pried the blaster from dead fingers and shoved the body away.

She looked down the hall to see Moses doing the same. She hadn't seen it happen, but the dark purple-red marks on the man's neck told the story.

"Come on," Dava said tightly after watching Moses stuff the guard into the lock-room's hatchway to prevent it from closing. "The dock is close."

They traveled in silence back the way she had come. Past the silent guardhouse. Past the passage the two unfortunate guards had come through. On to the corridor that led to the dock.

They moved quickly and quietly. Into the last lock-room. When the door spiraled open, they almost blasted Jerrard to dust. Likewise, Jerrard, naked but for a massive pulse rifle, twitched and gasped.

"Shit," he said, then lowered his gun with a laughing sigh. "I am so glad it's you guys."

"I'm glad it's us too," Moses said. "How many are we?"

Jerrard shrugged. "A lot. Everyone's been grouping up and heading to whatever dock they can get to. We got a pilot with us. Plus eight more Wasters."

"Good," Dava said. "It's hot back there. We need to take off. Is the ship prepped?"

"Aye, Capo. Most everyone is loaded in."

She nodded and looked over at Moses. "Ready to go home?"

He grinned at her, and it filled her with warmth. She felt a peace, a completeness that she hadn't felt in a long time. It slammed into the vision of Thompson, torn-open and leaking guts in a trail. She turned away from him and blinked away the stinging feeling. She pulled on a handhold, launching herself in the direction of a transport ship whose entrance was decorated with a pair of naked Wasters.

She sailed through space, the side hatch of the transport growing slowly larger. She felt Moses and Jerrard behind her. Sailing for freedom.

When the alarm came, she was still in space. Halfway to the ship. The piercing electric scream of sentry-bots locking onto a target rattled through her guts.

"HOSTILES IDENTIFIED. SURRENDER WEAPONS IMMEDIATELY."

She turned in space, drawing her laser pistol. She had no clear shot, with the long dark bodies of Moses and Jerrard between her and the bots. They both raised their guns, Moses with his liberated blaster and Jerrard with a pulse rifle. A swarm of the spider-like bots spilling through the hatch. One in the middle with four larger limbs instead of eight thin ones. A massive sphere that barely fit through the three-meter diameter door. In the center was a circle of barrels. Around that, the surface of the sphere read ANTI-PERSONNEL UNIT: STAND CLEAR *OF* PROJECTILE WEAPON.

The air erupted. A mess of sound rushed around her from all sides. The spark of Moses's pistol. The high-pitched report of Jerrard's pulse rifle. The clatter of the smaller bots as they advanced along the walls.

All of it drowning in the crushing waves of the spinning autocannon in the center of the big bot. The pistol trembled in her hands and a cold helplessness pumped from her heart and through her body. When her brain started to work a full three seconds after the shooting began, it demanded to know why she was still alive.

Instinct tugged at her attention. The smaller bots were flanking them. She took aim to her left, frying one that got close enough. Then two more. There were too many, and she was only covering one side. She hazarded a glance back to the right side. The bots there were tacking along, then twitching and bouncing away, one by one. Her ears picked out the coinciding pop. She wasted another second craning her head back to see Half-Shot braced in the open hatchway of the transport.

As she turned back to pick off more bots rising along the right side of the wall, she caught the movement of the big one. It occurred to her that it was missing on purpose; not missing them, but missing the expensive ModPol asset: the transport ship. And now its large tentacle-legs were clanging along the wall above them, slowly pulling it into an inevitable angle. When it achieved enough clearance, when it reached the point where the ship would no longer be in the shot behind them, they would be shredded.

She looked at the ship. Another thirty seconds was all they needed. She turned back to continue firing at the faster spider-bots to keep them from flanking. Jerrard's gun was drilling rounds into the front of the big bot, but the shots were either not penetrating, or penetrating but not hitting anything vital. The surface was dimpled and scorched, but the damned thing kept moving, kept firing in those heartbeat-pulse spins of its autocannon.

And then she heard Half-Shot yelling. She turned and he grabbed her, pulling her into the hatch. She looked back. Jerrard and Moses right behind her. And then both of them dancing with spasms.

Jerrard's leg bloomed red and he spiraled at a shallow angle toward the floor. He had enough of his senses to catch himself and fling himself back toward the ship. But Moses was hit in several places, ricocheting hard against the floor and bouncing up to the ceiling, a vortex of gore twisting through the space behind him.

Dava wanted to scream out in fear and anger, but her body had beat her voice to the reaction. She sprang from the hatchway and grabbed Moses's flailing body around the waist. Her momentum carried them to the wall, where she twisted and kicked off. Noises whipped around her, stinging her ears and her skin. The vertigo of being slapped around in null gravity finally began to catch up to her, clouding the edges of her vision with static. Then the stinging was replaced by pressure and the clouding vision was replaced by darkness. The rattling wave of the autocannon was replaced by the sound of cranking doors and buzzing engines. Weightlessness was replaced by the pull of acceleration.

A distant flash of sharp fire. Like a strike against another part of a shard of her existence, severed and estranged. Then another and another. All of her limbs throbbed with punching pain that crept toward her center, up her back and into her head until there was so much that there was nothing.

* * *

Runstom's map was an absolute necessity. The Space Waste attackers had managed to badly damage several sections of the prison. In addition, the facility had *shifted* several times. It was something it did periodically, on a schedule that seemed random to the inmates, but was known to the staff. It had gone off schedule. Runstom wasn't sure if it was trying to adapt to the spreading damage or trying to quell the activities of the enemy with confusion. He guessed it had been designed with riot control in mind.

In any case, it meant he needed to check the map and adjust his route periodically as corridors spun imperceptibly on their invisible axes. Not that he could find his way through the maze-like structure if it was fixed. Every time they passed through the automatic hatches, his numbed right foot throbbed anxiously.

Jenna Zarconi stuck close to him silently. She had adapted to the lack of gravity during her stay and moved gracefully.

He could feel her peer over his shoulder whenever he checked his map, but she offered no commentary. This was less a matter of trusting him, he realized, and more a matter of showing submission. Considering the source, it was a little forced. How long the feigned obedience would last once they made it out of the facility, he was most uncertain.

They passed into another long, bending corridor and froze at the clattering sound of a pack of securibots. They were maybe half the size of a person, a round center, flailing limbs. A dozen of them. They approached and Runstom could see brown-red stains on some of the claw-like tips of their appendages.

"PLEASE PAUSE FOR IDENTIFICATION." The voice didn't come from one of them, but all of them in unison. Runstom felt the hairs on his skin raise up at the sound.

He and Zarconi held position, each holding a separate handhold on the corridor's wall. The bots crowded around them. Singular mechanical eyes twitched, the lenses dilating like pupils.

"STANFORD RUNSTOM, TEMPORARY GUARD DUTY ASSIGNMENT. THANK YOU, STANFORD. HAVE A GREAT DAY."

He frowned at their clumsy niceties. Some misguided attempt to make crawling death machines appear friendly. Or some programmer with a sense of humor.

Zarconi was surrounded, and he realized it was taking longer than expected. She hovered there in the suit of a much taller person, folded at the wrists and ankles. Her face was bunched up, eyes and mouth closed tight. The identification process was either retinal scan, voiceprint, or fingerprint. He wondered if they would force her to open her eyes or speak, or take her gloves off.

"KAL PORTMANSON IDENTIFIED *BY* SUIT. UNABLE *TO* CONFIRM IDENTIFICATION. CONTACTING COMMAND."

"Shit," Runstom said. "Um, the place is falling apart. Can we just continue on our way? We just need to—"

"WARNING. HOSTILES."

At that, he felt his heart drop into his stomach, which was a weird thing to feel without gravity. The securibots spun into action and he braced himself for the inevitable suppression, whatever form it would take. And then they were gone.

"Um, they left," he said after a few seconds of listening to the metallic tacking disappearing into the distance.

She opened one eye and looked around. "Where'd they go?" she whispered.

"Higher priority orders," he guessed out loud. With the bots out of sight, he checked the charge on his pistol for the umpteenth time. It had dropped to ninety percent. Ten percent loss and he hadn't fired a shot.

Both eyes opened and she peered down the hall. "Thank goodness for greater evils."

Runstom wasn't exactly sure whether Zarconi or Space Waste was the lesser of evils when it came down to it. But he decided not to press the question. "We're almost to the docks. Let's move."

Less than a minute later, they faced the source of the stains on the claws of the securibots. It was a Waster, that much was clear from her outfit, which was mostly leather and bore patches in the image of the outfit's twisting-arrowed logo. Not much else was recognizable. The corpse, surrounded by pockets of blood and gore with nowhere to drain, still held a weapon. It was rifle-sized, with a large, round magazine.

Despite their outdatedness, the Wasters often favored projectile weapons. He considered taking it, given that he was only armed with a leaky stunner/blaster combo rifle. It only took a moment of imagining what it would be like to fire it to realize how uncontrollable it would be in zero-G.

"Take it," Zarconi said. He shot her a look, unnerved by her intrusion on his thoughts. "Unless you want to regret it later."

"It's useless in zero-G."

She looked down the corridor, and he followed her gaze. "Not entirely."

There was a tangle of non-functional securibots bumping lightly against the wall several dozen meters away. Pockmarks dotted their surfaces, and at least one had smoke trailing from the front where the eye once was.

He looked at Zarconi and then the submachinegun. Sensed that she was really telling him if he didn't take it, she would. And he didn't trust her to that extent: that was a fact they both agreed on.

He gingerly reached for the strap that looped around the corpse. Found the release. Pried the lukewarm fingers away from the grips. Pulled the gun loose. Yanked out the drum, confirmed that it was empty. Grabbed a spare from the belt. Slapped it into place. Re-attached the strap and swung the gun over his head.

Then he looked at Zarconi. The bots had been confused because the suit said one thing, and they couldn't verify with their usual means. But while the bots relied on data in the form of retinal scans and fingerprints, any living person would recognize her instantly. First, there was the green skin. There weren't very many people in existence that had it; Runstom and Zarconi shared that mark of their births. And then there was the fact that she was the famous murderer of thirty-two people on Barnard-4.

The chances that they might run into human staff would increase the closer they got to the docks. He should have realized that. He cursed himself for not thinking his plan through.

"We should cover your face," he said.

Her eyes narrowed at him, then her mouth squinched on one side. "I suppose you're right. If we run into any of my fans, we won't have time for me to stop and sign autographs."

He frowned at her inappropriate humor. Looked around helplessly, wishing they had a helmet. Then he looked at the corpse again. "Maybe we can use some strips of cloth. Make like you've been badly injured."

"Wrap my head in bloody leather. Sadly, that's less suspicious than my green skin." She pointed. "There's a knife in that pocket."

Again she was passing an opportunity to arm herself. He almost wished she would just take the blade. Was thankful that she didn't. Was not thankful that he had to take it and cut strips from the clothes of a corpse.

After a few minutes, he had her face sufficiently wrapped. It would have been much harder before they'd buzzed her hair off. Her skin still showed around her eyes and mouth, but the wet gore decorating the leather was distracting enough.

"If we run into any people, don't blink," he said. "Your eyelids will give you away."

"Right," she said quietly. "And if we run into any more bots, close them tight, or my retinas will give me away. Let's hope we don't run into both at the same time."

He sighed, the risks stacking up like unseen weight. They needed to move fast before he changed his mind and left her there. He returned the knife to its original owner. Motioned silently that it was time to move on.

At the next junction, he checked his map again once inside the lock. They were very close to Dock D.

"It may be hot," Zarconi said.

"The dock?"

She nodded. "By the reaction of the local security forces, I'd guess the whole place is in chaos. Which means lots of bad guys on the loose. Which means, bad guys wanting to get out. Not to mention trigger-happy good guys with bad aim."

Which meant everyone had the same idea: get to the closest dock and secure a ship. Runstom fiddled with his comm. "Uh, this is Enforcement Officer Runstom, contacting Dock Delta. Anyone there?"

The reply was quick and shaky. "Enforcement Officer Runstom? I don't have a record of that name. Can you spell it?"

He scowled at his armband, knowing they could see by his transmission signature who it was. Maybe they were testing to see whether he'd been compromised. "R, U, N, S, T, O, M," he said slowly. They were probably verifying by voiceprint. A thought occurred to him. "That's *Temporary* Enforcement Officer Runstom."

"Ooh, *Temporary*." There was a pause, then the young male voice continued. "Okay, Runstom. What's up? We kind of have our hands full here."

"Have you seen any action at your dock?"

"No hostiles, if that's what you mean. But we're prepping ships for evac just in case there's a need."

Runstom nodded, feeling a small amount of relief. "I'm headed to you, along with another officer." He looked at the name badge on the oversized uniform Zarconi was wearing. "With Officer Lancer."

There was a pause, then, "Request denied. All non-critical staff should report to the nearest guardhouse. If there is an evac, we'll let you know."

"Dammit," Runstom muttered to himself. "I can help," he said into the comm. "I'm a certified pilot. Class C."

Another pause, as though some off-line discussion was taking place. "Okay, Temporary Enforcement Officer Runstom. Come on in, you can help with the prep."

When they passed through the hatch and into the dock's control room, Runstom expected them to give him more trouble. But they just waved him on by, directing him to the door at the other end that lead to the dock itself. Gave him the number of a patroller he could check on. They didn't say anything about his companion. Only glanced at her bloody, wrapped head and then looked away. Their pale faces unable to get much paler.

In the dock, he pulled himself along the handholds. The designated patroller was at the other end. A standard ModPol ship. Small, but capable of carrying about eight if the passengers didn't mind close quarters. Fast. It would suit him just fine. He glanced back. Zarconi was not slowed by the headwrap.

"Lancer!"

They looked to their right. A lanky B-fourean was attending to something on the side of another ship, a boxy prisoner transport vessel. Runstom turned away and kept moving, hoping Zarconi would take the hint and follow suit.

"Hey!" Runstom looked again. The B-fourean wasn't a guard, but some kind of technician. He repositioned himself, grabbing a handhold and pulling just a little closer. Still several meters away. "Lancer, I heard you were coming. You still owe me twenty-five from the other night. Don't think that you're getting out of it just because of a riot."

"We don't have time for this," Runstom said. "Get back to work."

"Get back to—" he started. Then he cocked his head. "Lancer, what the fuck happened to you? Your head?"

Runstom looked toward their destination. The small patroller was still several dozen meters away. He turned back to the tech. "He's hurt. He can't talk. Just get back to work, dammit."

But he persisted, grabbing a handhold and drifting closer. "Hey." He grabbed another hold and stopped his progress, his eyes widening. "You're not Lancer."

"Come on," Runstom said to Zarconi. Turned away from the tech and kept moving.

"Where'd you get that gun? That's not regulation." The tech tried to be firm, but Runstom could hear his voice cracking. "Oh shit. It's … it's a coilgun. What the fuck!"

"Relax," Runstom shot back. "I took it from a Waster. I'm an Enforcement Officer. Okay? Enforcement Officer Runstom. I've got orders to prep the patroller down—"

He stopped as his brain finally caught up and registered the word *coilgun*. He didn't know what that meant exactly, but it wasn't a reference to the submachinegun on his back. The tech flinched, his hands going up, his eyes on Zarconi. Her hands rose, a thin, pipelike device between them.

"Jenna, no!" Runstom said. "We're almost out, you don't need to—"

He was interrupted by a blast at the other end of the dock. They all looked back toward the control room. Black smoke billowed in concentric circles where the door should have been. Shouts, of command, of anger, of fear. From out of the black cloud, a figure tumbled, end over end. Wearing a guard uniform. It flew off to one side and slammed into the nose of a large patrol ship, bending with an audible crack that raised the hairs on Runstom's skin.

Another figure ejected from the smoke, this one with purpose. Arms pointing forward, legs stretching behind. A massive, all-muscle man brandishing a bulky laser pistol. Stripped to nothing but bare yellow skin and colorful tattoos. He took aim.

Runstom yanked his blaster loose. "Drop your weapon!" With the gun raised, the charge reading glared at him from the back of the piece. Seventy-six percent and not a shot taken.

The Waster fired, brilliant blue-and-white light screeching forth. The tech had only enough time to turn his head before his body was spun, twisting and burning and screaming. Runstom didn't wait to see the final result. He fired on the Waster.

The blaster hummed in his hand, issuing forth its own jagged mess of blue light that went wide to the right of its target. The charge indicator blinked double-zeroes at him. Having used both hands to aim, he drifted helplessly away from the floor.

"Sonova—"

"Stanford!"

The room lurched as he was pushed from underneath. Another blue flash lit up the air below him. He slammed into the ceiling with a grunt, and the useless blaster tumbled from his hands. Zarconi's body cascaded into his, and then they rebounded. Once again suspended, drifting, not close enough to ceiling, wall, or floor to grab anything.

The Waster's flight had taken him all the way to the transport the tech had been working on. With a thud, he managed to grab a handle on the side of it. He shook his gun and yelled something incomprehensible at it.

Runstom recognized the model: an older military laser pistol. Devastatingly effective, especially in a zero-gravity situation like this, but it generated a great deal of heat and could not be fired in rapid succession. At that moment, tiny mechanisms inside the bulk of it were rearranging heat sinks, prepping it for another shot.

He could hear the ready-ding across the several meters of distance between them. The Waster grinned and leveled it at him. Instinctively, Runstom had pulled the submachinegun from his back. Squeezed the trigger.

The blue light missed him, only because his own gun recoiled. It kicked upward with each bullet, and simultaneously kicked back. In the space of a short breath, five or six rounds had given him the sensation of falling backwards. With a short shriek, Zarconi had gripped him tightly.

They were still drifting, though moving at an angle. Given a few more seconds they would reach the floor. Or they would be fried by laserfire. He looked back. Any ship would do, but the patroller at the rear of the dock already had his ident loaded into it by the control room. No overrides necessary.

The Waster shook his gun and cursed. A streak of red across one shoulder. At least Runstom had clipped him. He could try again, but didn't know where the recoil would send him. Other figures emerged from the dissipating cloud at the innermost side of the dock.

Looking back and forth over his shoulder, he lined up the gun opposite the patroller. Braced it with one hand over the top to keep the upward kick under control.

"Hold on!"

He felt Zarconi's grip tighten. Squeezed the trigger. Short bursts. The patroller behind growing in size at every glance over his shoulder. Until it was on top of them.

They slammed into the side of it and Runstom felt himself rebound. He twisted and flailed, grabbing only air. Then his body jerked to a stop. Zarconi had him by the strap of the submachinegun, her other hand gripping a handle near the fuel access port.

He tried to shout, but only a cough came out. She pulled him close, and his body pressed against hers. For a second, met her eyes. All that was visible behind the stained leather wraps. She blinked, showing him her green eyelids.

Then she released the strap. He grabbed the nearest handle and pulled himself to the top, to the cabin access hatch. It slid open immediately at the touch of his encoded gloves. Another explosion. He didn't look to see it. Could feel the heat. Close enough. He dropped into the cabin. Zarconi right behind him. Closed the hatch. Strapped into the pilot console.

"I'm putting the co-pilot console into emergency mode," he said. "Won't have access to everything, but it won't check your authorization."

"Okay," she said, sliding her form into the space beside him.

"Get the dock to move us to a launch tube." He tapped furiously, kicking the engines into an emergency pre-start warm up.

He glanced at the monitors around him. The outer

cameras showed the chaos they had escaped. The chaos that would be upon them in another thirty seconds. He flipped off the cameras and concentrated on encouraging the progress meters as they calmly ticked off percentages of readiness.

* * *

The distant pain that had ferried Dava out of consciousness greeted her when she returned. There was a dullness, an evenness to it. Like ice that had melted back into liquid, free to spread through the form of its container.

She couldn't move. Well, she could twitch. With effort, she could turn her head. Through panicked thrashing, she discovered her arms could only move at her shoulder, her legs could only bend at her hips.

"Whoa, Capo." Half-Shot, appearing through a haze like some summoned demon. "We got you all splinted for a reason. *Lights.*"

The world turned piercing white and Dava flinched. The room quickly coalesced in her vision and nausea washed over her. She closed her eyes tight. "Where are we?"

"Out. On our way home." She felt Half-Shot's touch. Checking on her, then fading away. "We're still on the transport. It's got a pretty fancy med bay, lucky for you. Unlucky is that it's only got Warp, no Xarp. So it's gonna take us a while to get back to base. But that's more good luck for you, because you need the rest."

She opened her eyes the minimum needed to see his face. "The others?"

"Four ships altogether," he said with a blurry half-smile that quickly flattened. "When Johnny Eyeball and Freezer showed up with a bunch of our Wasters, we grabbed the pilots and split up. Not everyone got out of course. Waster headcount is thirty-six."

Strange that it comforted her. And hurt her. Those saved and those lost – they all affected her. She felt an urge to know names and faces. "You got a list?"

"Yeah." There was a long pause and she tried to focus on his face. "Dava … Moses."

She sat upright, which would probably have been painful for her had there been any gravity to fight her. Of the names she desired, Moses hadn't come to mind. As though her default state of acceptance was one where Moses was always okay. Then it all came back.

She was wearing projectile-resistant armor. Nice and thin stuff, not great against anything explosive or too hot, but plenty good at deadening bullets with its responsive fibers. The impact from the autocannon had still done plenty of damage. She couldn't tell with the opaque tubes covering her arms, legs, and torso, but she could guess. Bad bruising, broken bones, and probably a few lacerations from where the big gun had managed to penetrate.

But Moses and Jerrard had no such protection. They weren't even clothed. The way their bodies twisted in the rain of bullets. Bile rose in her throat.

"Into this, into this!" Half-Shot jammed a plastic jug to her face, forcing its soft opening around her mouth. Not much came up, but at least she hadn't booted all over the med bay. Vomit in zero-G would not improve her mood.

"Where is he?" she gasped when she was able to.

He looked at her grimly, but she saw resignation cross his face. Like he wanted to force her to rest, but changed his mind. The thought drained all warmth from her chest.

If he was letting her see Moses now, did that mean there wasn't time to wait?

Half-Shot tapped at the loose straps and pulled her away from her bed. Dava was again thankful that there was no gravity pushing against her battered body, but the stiff tubes meant she was more or less invalid, forced to rely on him to get her around. He navigated her through a central spherical connecting passway. The bay was segmented into small chambers, about eight of them, with doors in the center. They went from hers to another.

Moses was in similar wrappings. Where she could see his skin, it was gray ash. She coughed at the sight.

Half-Shot pulled her to the bed. "The tubes have all kinds of repair robotics in them."

Now she could see that there were readouts drifting around the tubes. She realized that her own tubes also had the dancing markings, but not nearly as much as those wrapped around Moses. Graph lines, numbers, progress indicators, and cautions decorated him like some bizarre, poor-taste art display.

"Dava." The deep voice rumbled through her like thunder.

She glanced at Half-Shot, who showed a rare moment of surprise. Like he hadn't expected Moses to be able to speak, to even be awake. He looked back at her silently, then attached a nearby strap to a hook on her waist to keep her from free-floating. He pressed a comm into her hand and gently pulled her thumb over the button at the bottom of it. She couldn't even see it because of her limited mobility, but she could at least press the button. Half-Shot nodded to her and drifted away.

She was quiet until she heard the opening and closing of the hatch. "Moses. I'm sorry."

He coughed in short, rasping breaths. Laughter, she realized. "Sorry as shit," he said. "Nothing to be sorry for. You got us out."

"You can make it," she said softly. To herself, more than to him.

"Bah, the bots are doin' all they can," he said. His eyes were closed. "But they ain't magic."

She twisted her body, and with painful effort, managed to grip his bedside with her free hand. She walked her fingers up the edge until she felt his. Then she listened to his breathing. Deep and steady.

"What are you going to do when you get home?" she said.

"What am I gonna do?" More of the laughing cough. "You mean who's gonna spacewalk?"

She tightened her grip on his hand. "That fucker Basil Roy, he was behind the ambush. And I know Jansen—"

"Forget all that, Dava." His voice found new strength, and hers died in her throat.

"Why?" she said weakly.

"It doesn't matter. I been running around this galaxy for decades. There's *always* some motherfucker tryin' to game me."

She let it all bubble up and out. "Moses, wake up! These motherfuckers *did* game you! They fucked us bad! Half of Space Waste was in prison for fuck's sake! People died!"

"Ain't what I'm talkin' 'bout," he said firmly. His eyes pried open to meet her stare, though she could tell it pained him. "You got to think bigger, Dava. I always told you that."

"I don't know what you mean," she said, her voice cracking.

He closed his eyes again. "What's most important to you?"

She swallowed. "You are."

"Bigger, Dava. Who am I?"

"I don't—"

"Who am I? Who am I to you? What am I to you?"

A question she never knew the answer to. Friend. Mentor. Father. But not her father, because she had a father. And a mother. "Family," she whispered.

"What about Tommy?" he said, opening his eyes again.

She looked down. "Please don't."

"What about goddamn Tommy-Gun, Dava?"

She coughed down on a sob. Friend. Soldier. Supporter. Sister. "Family."

"Johnny," he fired, voice growing louder. "Dan. 2-Bit. Barney. Seven-Pack. Lucky. Jerrard. All the rest of the glorious bastards you risked your goddamn life to break out of that prison! What about them, Dava?"

"Family!" she yelled. If she could move her arms she would have beat it into his face. "They're my goddamn family."

"Finally broke you," he whispered, eyes closing. "I knew you had it. Got what I could never get to."

"What do you mean?" she said quietly.

"You love the bastards," he grunted. "But it wasn't easy, was it? Not because they're all bastards, but because you didn't want to hurt when you lost them."

"You don't love them?"

A long sigh came out of him, causing a shimmer among the readouts along the tube around his chest. "I tried. But I also tried not to. There is a universe where Space Waste can be a family. But it wasn't the one I was living in."

The past tense grew the hole in her stomach. "Moses, don't you think they love you?"

"Doesn't matter." His face scrunched up, eyes still closed. "I didn't build this for love. I built it to break shit."

"But you built it."

"I built it to kill, Dava. I built a machine of death and destruction. I built it because the human race had gone backwards. Consumerism, conformity. Work, shop, work, shop. We don't fit. They're breeding us out. It's a quiet war, Dava. And I built a loud-ass war machine to fight it."

She nodded along with his words. The memories she held, the reasons she joined. Waking up after a long stasis trekking from Earth. Waking to find that they'd jettisoned her mother and father. Sickness. Not welcome in the new world. And then they forced her to live in those domes. A black girl among pale-while ghouls. The children, such bastards. She was a disease to them, rejected by their immune-system reaction.

So the day the tall, strong, deep man whose skin was darker even than hers came along and winked at her, she knew she'd leave with him. Not yet old enough to be free, but he'd freed her anyway.

"We keep up the fight," she said. Her words sounded lame. She didn't have his fire, his courage; only his anger. His bloodlust. "I'll kill them. All."

He hissed, something between a sigh and a laugh. "I don't doubt you could. But see, I been thinking lately. For years now. Been thinking about this war I been fighting."

"You have to keep fighting," she tried.

His bunching face dismissed her. "No, Dava, just shut up for a goddamn minute and let an old man speak his last words."

"Moses!"

"Dammit, Dava!" The eyes came open again and she lost her breath. Everything inside her was sucking away, like her insides were nothing more than the vacuum of space. She froze in his stare. Finally, his face relaxed slightly. "I said I been thinking. Thinking that the reason I ain't yet won this war has to do with strategy. I mean, tactics, we got them in spades. We can strike smart. We can breach. We can steal. We can destroy.

"But these are all tiny victories. These are like fixes for a junky. That's what I am now, Dava. I'm a junky, looking for the next kill-fix. I thought Rando Jansen was gonna help me get into a real strategy. Something long term."

"He's rotten," Dava managed through a weak whisper.

Moses grunted. "Probably so. But anyways, don't matter. Ain't a war that can be won this way. The way to win is to make a family. To make a home."

"We have a home. We're going home."

He laughed in earnest. "Girl, I know you ain't had a real home, maybe in all your life. But that collection of shit flying through space is just a base of operations. It ain't no home."

"But it's ours," she said into her chest.

"Aye, that it is," he said. "It's been good to us. But lemme ask you something: you understand this war of mine, right? What if we actually won?"

"I – I don't know."

"See what I mean? What does it even mean to win at what we're doing?" He paused, but only for effect. She wouldn't have an answer and he knew it. "So I started thinking what's the best-case scenario here? What would make us happy?"

She tried to speak but could not. She had moments of happiness. Back at the base, in the bar with her buds. But they were people she kept trying to push away, to keep at a distance. Not true happiness. It wasn't allowed, not by the rules she lived by. And before, well there'd never been happiness. The domes were pure depression. She had to go all the way back to the days on Earth. Before she understood what kind of shit lives they were living, crammed into filthy shelters. Before she knew that food and water were more than just different brown liquids varying only in thickness. The happiest moment was the day her mother cried so hard Dava thought she was dying. The day Dava learned that it was even possible to cry from joy. The day they learned they were getting tickets on the Doomed-to-Domed ship.

"A new home," she said. The words were hers, but she didn't know she'd spoken them. She only heard them after the fact, long after they'd left her mouth.

"A real home," Moses whispered. His fingers tightened around hers. "Space Waste needs a real home. That's how we win this goddamn war."

They rested in silence. Her floating there with her stiff limbs, him strapped to a bed. The poor-taste art crawling up and down his body. They were silent, lightly flexing each other's fingers. Assurance that the other was still there.

His eyes opened. "Dava, there's something else."

"What?" she said, getting close to his weakening voice. "What is it?"

"The green guy." The vacuum back in her stomach. Thinking he's fading away in that moment. Not making sense. Until the next words. "The green cop."

She cocked her head. "From the barge, and Sirius-5? The one who stole our dropship? Busted up some ring of corrupt cops?" She remembered following the broadcasts of some of the aftermath after that day on Sirius-5. Developing both respect and contempt for the idealist justice-seeker who'd spent months poked, prodded, and praised by the media.

"Yes." Moses coughed lightly, and she drew closer to keep him from overstraining his voice. "I met him at the prison."

"Really?"

"Dava, watch out for him," he said. He took a breath, pulling deep for the strength for a story. "My brother, Bishop. You never met him. Did you know I had a brother?"

"No," she said quietly. It pained her that she didn't.

"Bishop, a beautiful man. A Romeo. Fell in love with his own Juliet."

"Who are you talking about?"

He sighed through a smile, the closest he could come to the wheezing laughter he'd managed before. "Romeo and Juliet? Dammit, girl, this is what I'm talking about. You need a proper home, where people read, and put on plays and shit like that."

She sighed through her nose in frustration. Moses had a habit of slipping into fiction, a practice she never understood. What was the point of wasting time with things that had no basis in reality? It was all a bunch of made-up shit. "Moses, what about Bishop? The green cop?"

"Right, right. The cop, his name is Stanford. I think he's my nephew. I think he's my brother's boy. Bishop's boy. I don't know if Bishop even knew. I didn't know. But I could see Bishop when I looked in his face, Dava."

"God damn," she whispered.

His hand tightened around hers. "He deserves to know that. The cop, I mean. Stanford. And I shoulda told him.

But I didn't. I thought I would be there for a while, and I wanted to think about how to tell him. So you got to, Dava."

"To what?" she said. "Tell that cop? That he's your nephew?"

Moses swallowed. "I don't think he knows. His mother would never have told him. Tell me you'll tell him. Tell me, Dava."

"Okay, Moses," she said. "I'll tell him."

This seemed to ease him, because his tightened face relaxed. His eyes closed, and a sigh parted from his lips. "That's my Dava. Assassin with a heart of gold."

She shook her head at him. It was like him to say these things that she didn't understand sometimes. Gold – just a color to her – was a kind of slang he'd always used to mean something good. Something he liked. Something rare and special.

"You are gold too," she said, unsure if it meant to him what she wanted it to.

The faint smile that appeared on his softening face told her it meant something. She stayed with him in the silence that followed. If time passed, she could not measure it. She just touched his hand, felt the warmth of his fingers. Fought back the growing emptiness inside. Fought until the animations on the surface of his bandages went as still as his fingers.

Then she stopped and the emptiness consumed her from the inside out.

CHAPTER 13

Phonson was gone for a long time. He'd shut down all the screens, locked out access. There was nothing in the room that relayed the passage of time. More than a few hours. A day, maybe. More than a day. Jax didn't like the way McManus stared at him. Was this another test? Or just torture by silence and hunger? He hoped the aggression monitors were still working, in case McManus tried to eat him.

They hadn't spoken. They had nothing to say, taking turns at being the outlet for Phonson's paranoia and frustration. McManus had brought them here, into this mess. Jax couldn't care less if one corrupt cop killed another.

No, that wasn't right. Phonson was the evil one here. McManus was just … stupid wasn't the word. A poor decision-maker?

There was a flicker from one of the consoles. Jax groaned. How many times this had happened, he'd lost count. It was probably once an hour. If he'd counted, he'd know how much time had passed, measured by *something*. But he wasn't counting.

The flicker gave way to a holoprojection. There was no audio, only the three-dimensional video. The same scene that had played over and over: the broadcast news story with the spokesperson for the Terroneous Federated Security Committee, members of the Terroneous Environmental Observation Board standing behind.

Lealina Warpshire, director of the TEOB, in the background when the view zoomed out. As much as he tried to turn away from the images, he always turned back to find her eyes. Blue, across time and space. Looking. Searching. Searching for him.

The video stopped and the room soaked with shadow.

"I'd like to say this is all your fault," McManus croaked after a while. Those were his first words after several hours of silence.

Jax looked up. His eyes had re-adjusted, using the faint ambient light that made the room a kind of gray instead of merely black. Presumably, Phonson wanted them to be able to see one another, perhaps in the hope that they might turn against each other.

"You brought us here," Jax said flatly. The will to argue had run dry.

McManus sighed. "Yeah, I did. I did." This was merely a whisper. Then he stood and spoke aloud. "This is more of his 'light torture'. He's trying to starve us."

"He *is* starving us," Jax said with a glare.

The cop nodded heavily, the lines of his muscled neck throbbing with the effort. "Yeah, I'm getting pretty goddamn hungry. Anything would taste good right now, even those damn ModPol emergency rations. Never been this hungry in my life."

Jax suppressed his response, which would have been a

simple, *I have.* At his best estimate, his longest stretch was three days without food – without *any* food. And then half a protein bar, followed by another stretch of nothing. He thought about the phrase *anything would taste good.* Had that half a protein bar tasted like a banquet after three days of nothing solid in his mouth? It hadn't tasted like anything. Weeks of scraps, of whatever he could get. He'd been as empty as his stomach. He'd become less than human. Tasting food was a human thing. Consuming calories was a function of the mechanical thing he'd been forced to become.

So the hunger wasn't bothering him like it should. It was hollowing him. Food had no use for a shell.

"I guess …" McManus started, his voice turning up, then going quiet.

They sat in the gray shadowlight for a long time. The silent broadcast came and went. Bright-blue eyes came and went.

"I guess I should have listened to you." As if a second-long pause had occurred since he'd last spoken, when it'd been almost an hour.

Jax said nothing, didn't even look at him.

"I should've listened to Runstom, too," he went on. "I just always … I didn't hate him. I just didn't like being told what to do. And he always knew what to do. I guess I hated … I hated that he was a better cop than me." His voice got softer. "I wish I could tell him that."

Jax's face bunched up. "Well maybe you can issue an apology in the afterlife," he rasped. His throat had gone so dry, it hurt to speak; but he did anyway. "Of course he's a better cop than you. My stark white ass is a better cop than you."

"I should've listened to my brother," he said, as though

he hadn't heard Jax at all. "When I still had the chance."

Minutes of silence ticked on and the anxiety of an impending replay of the broadcast ate at Jax's empty stomach. "Okay," he said finally. "Tell me about your brother."

"Jeffy," he said. "My big brother Jeffy. Always used to say, there are too many ways to die in this universe. Why be a cop and increase those odds?"

"And what does Jeffy do?"

"Jeffy's dead." His voice gave and he coughed life back into it with a series of hacks. "Died in the cold vacuum of space. Shipyard construction, in orbit around B-3. A simple hull-patch job. Dunno what actually happened, because they just called it an *equipment malfunction*."

Jax let an appropriate amount of silence pass before he said quietly, "Why *did* you become a cop?"

McManus grunted. "Cuz Jeffy told me not to."

Bright white fire burned the night into oblivion. Jax reflexively covered his eyes, and the multicolored stains floated in his shaded vision.

"Well, well!" Phonson's voice boomed with an impossible strength and vigor. The voice of a man who was well fed and well rested. "Seems like you two lovers are getting along just fine. Just fine. Which is funny, since one of you dragged the other one here in cuffs."

"I'm just giving him a break because he didn't have the balls to kill me himself," Jax said with the best voice he could muster. He creased his eyes open into slits so he could see Phonson standing in the middle of the room.

"Ooh, shots fired!" Phonson said with a clap of his hands. "Wanna know something? I only sent this loser out after you because I thought for sure you were already dead."

"In Epsilon Eridani?" Jax asked, then wished he hadn't engaged.

"That's right." Phonson took a few steps toward him. "Big attack there. Space Waste walked right into it. Stupid fuckers. A well-crafted slaughter."

Jax gritted his teeth. He had no love for Space Waste, but he suddenly realized the gangbangers were more human than this *snake*. "You knew? About the ambush?"

He grinned. "Let's just say I know someone who knows someone who knew." He pointed at Jax. "And I knew you'd be there. Your corpse at the scene would have cleaned all this up nicely."

Jax failed to see how his death in Eridani could clean up anything, but suspected that Phonson really meant it would have muddied things further. The wrongfully accused fugitive, proven innocent of murder, turning out to be a Space Waste raider after all. The added confusion was something X would relish. The snake hid well in the muck.

"How do you know all this shit?" McManus blurted. Jax almost felt sorry for him. He'd never accuse the cop of being naive, but he knew so little about the extent of Phonson's network.

Phonson tipped his head back, philosopher air blowing over him. "You see, Jared – everyone has intentions. Energies. Ambitions. Needs. Whatevers. They point their energies in very obvious directions. Sometimes they can't get there without some help. Me, I'm a helper. I see where they're trying to get to, and I help them jump the gap."

"A conductor," Jax said. He was too hollowed out to activate the filter that kept him from speaking thoughts aloud.

X cocked his head at this. "No, I don't think so. I'm no

director – I'm not telling anyone what to do. I'm just helping them fuck each other over."

"No," Jax said. "A *conductor*. A material thing – something that takes, like, electricity – or heat – and transfers it from one place to another."

"You don't tell anyone what to do," McManus said, talking over him. "Then what's the point?"

Phonson turned from Jax and advanced on McManus with a smile. "The point is I'm in the middle of it all."

He went on for a bit and Jax lost the sound of his voice. Consciousness was a tenuous thing. He thought about conductors. They needed insulation. He realized that X had lots of insulation, and that's why he'd managed to survive as long as he had. Everything he did, all of his actions were through others. He was always a few steps removed. A good conductor.

But no longer. Out here he was raw and exposed. The distance this fortress afforded him was also an exposure.

"—man inside," Phonson was saying.

"Jansen."

He turned to face Jax, his confident grin turned down. After a second of controlled silence, he flattened his mouth. "So you know."

"I was just guessing," Jax said, allowing a grin to accompany his wisp of a voice. "But now I know."

Phonson's eyes narrowed, then looked around in that classic paranoia motion. "Whatever." He kicked his head back and clapped sardonically.

"Why is it that no one at Space Waste suspects Jansen is a mole?" Jax wondered aloud. "How has he gotten away with it?"

Phonson shrugged. "More wins than losses," he said.

"Eridani was a slaughter, but up until that point he led them to some pretty good hauls. Built up their morale."

"Until Eridani."

"Right, until Eridani," Phonson said coolly. "And there they lost their top man."

Jax thought about it for a moment. "Moses Down, you mean?" he said. "He's dead?"

"Arrested, along with about thirty others. In a zero-grav lockup. Might as well be dead."

Again Jax felt an unnatural pity for the Wasters. "And that leaves Jansen in full control. To do whatever he wants with them."

"Like what?" McManus blurted, catching up to the conversation. "What will he do with them?"

Phonson was apparently done with the topic, because he ignored the question and strode over to one of the wall consoles. After a few minutes, he finally spoke. "I'm going to be honest," he said, not facing them. "I don't have any good contacts on Eridani-3. It's too isolated and ModPol in general doesn't have much influence there yet." He turned to Jax. "But I know you and Stanford Runstom were up to something there. And I want to know what."

He stood in silence, waiting. Jax sat on the floor and looked at him. After a moment, the door opened. One of Phonson's goons – a pink-skinned woman with dark-red hair cropped just millimeters from her skull – came through carrying a small, plastic container. She peeled the lid off the top as the door slid closed behind her.

McManus reacted immediately to the smell. He scrambled to his feet and took a big step toward the woman, then froze, remembering the aggression-suppression system. He raised his hands innocently and took a tenuous step forward.

Jax shut it out. He detached his senses from his body. There was nothing in this place, this mobile torture chamber, that he would recognize, that he would dignify. Not food, not even the smell of food. The base part of his human nature wanted survival above everything and begged him to reach for the food, so he detached that too. How broken had he become to achieve such detachment so easily?

"What's for dinner, Carr?" Phonson said.

"Kibu breast," she said. "Sautéed with vegetables and a wild-fungus gravy."

"Mmm." He made a show of rubbing his stomach and licking his lips. "Wholesome food from Terroneous."

If Jax hadn't been so tired, he might have rolled his eyes. There was no way the food was anything other than reconstituted garbage. There would be no real food in a station like this.

"What do you want?" McManus said anxiously, evidently ready to give up the universe for a bite of food.

"I want Mr. Jackson to tell me exactly what happened while he was on Eridani-3," Phonson said evenly. Then his face brightened and he gestured around the room. "Oh, I forgot to mention. This anti-aggression system – it's extremely well tuned. It only stops you two from attacking me and my crew."

Jax's detached mind was forced back into reality when McManus tackled him.

* * *

"He calls it *Comet X*. It's not very imaginative, but then again, neither is he."

Runstom watched Zarconi tapping at the navigation

console as she talked. "His hideout is a comet?" he asked.

"No, it's a space station," she said calmly. "Its original name was something like Herb."

"Herb."

"Highly Elliptical Research Base, I think," she said. "H, E, R, B. It was originally commissioned for this eccentric researcher who wanted an easy way to grab a ride from Barnard planetary space that would sling out to deep space, to the outer reaches of the system."

"Why wouldn't he just use a ship?"

She shook her head. "This was well over a century ago. Warp was costly, and Xarp hadn't been perfected. The comet-station didn't need any thrusters. It just needed to be towed into position, and then shot into a trajectory that would hook it around Barnard's Star at the right angle and velocity to catch orbit."

Runstom went back to preparing his status report, only half-listening to the stuff he didn't understand. "So how did X get hold of this thing?"

"The original researcher passed and the institution was gutted. All their equipment was auctioned off to pay their debts. The station changed hands many times. I have no idea how Mark came to be its keeper. Some trade, of course. Probably hadn't intended to keep it, but once he had it, he became enamored with it."

Runstom looked up. "Really?"

"Yeah, he was always quite proud of it," she said with a far-off grin. "Sometimes he talked about retiring to it. Turning it into some kind of hotel. For people with too much money, looking for a taste of old space."

"You know how to find it?"

"It's a ridiculous idea," she said in a retort to herself.

"The orbit of that thing is almost thirty years. You have to take another ship out to it. It goes so deep, there's nothing out there. What would be the point?"

Runstom thought about the cruise ship, the *Royal Starways* superliner. He could only guess that *Comet X* did not have the same amenities. Then again, he wouldn't be surprised if there were some rich jackasses out there that were willing to pay for *less* amenities. For some kind of thrill. For bragging rights, for the story to tell. "No point," he said, just to agree with her. After a moment of thought, he added, "Unless you were hiding from something."

"I can get us close," she said, finally answering his earlier question. "He took me there. Twice. Once when we were together, and then again later when he was trying to win me back. He thought the place was some kind of … *aphrodisiac.*"

Runstom looked up at her. Her face wore an up-crooked brow and a smirk. There were times when his mind would rewind his memories all the way back to that day on Sirius-5, in that bar where he first met her. To that time when he didn't know what she was. She was just a beautiful woman then, smart and funny and understanding. When he rewound to that time and looked at her now, a kind of hole opened in his gut. A feeling he never felt around anyone else. It wasn't *love*, he knew that. It was the torture of never even having the chance to love her. Of the universe lining up someone like that, giving him a taste of what he didn't know he was looking for, only to twist it black and terrible.

He looked away but she must have caught his grimace. "I'm sorry, maybe that was too much information," she said, not really knowing the source of his disgust. "Fortunately, he made me navigate both times. I remember the coordinates and the dates. I can use those two points in time to plot a course for *Comet X*. Taking into account the effect of the star's gravity, of course."

"You remember all that?" he said, skeptical.

She tapped her head. "Mind for numbers. That's what made me such a good engineer."

"Right," he said. He'd almost forgotten she was an engineer; but then again, that was how she was able to plan and execute the sabotage of a life-support system, killing thirty-two people on Barnard-4.

Runstom scrawled a pen across a pad, letting it digitize and clarify the details of his report to his superiors at ModPol Defense. "When you get the location figured out, we need to plot a course that will take us close to a ModPol relay," he said. "It's best if I check in so no one comes looking for me."

"Would they come looking for you?" she asked. When he glared at her, her face dropped in regret. "I mean, I should hope they would," she said in a small voice.

He glowered and then turned back to his console. Paused. Looked at her again. "You said you can get us close."

She swallowed. "Yes. I can only estimate the location."

"We'll be able to detect it if we get close?"

"If we get close enough." She shrugged at him. "Like I said, it has no thrusters, so there's no drive signature to lock onto. There's a heat trail, of course, but that's not so easy to find. If it's making any transmissions, we'll be able to pick up the radio waves. But Mark is very careful about that kind of—"

"Radio waves," he said, snapping up straight. He began padding around his chest pockets, finding his notebook. He flipped it open. Found the spot where he'd taped the thin device that Sylvia had given him. "How about a homing beacon?"

He tried to explain the purpose of the device, but once they got it hooked into one of the consoles, she understood it better than he could have. "The signal this is set up to receive is going to travel a lot farther than a heat signature," she said. "The radio waves don't travel well through all the debris of space – not to mention they are limited by the speed of light. But once we get close enough, we'll be able to pick it up, no problem. The pings are atomically timestamped, so we should know how far away we are when we receive them by the differential with the ship's atomic clock."

"Uh, right," Runstom said. "The tracker is attached to the patroller that McManus was flying. We just have to hope that he's still at the comet."

They looked at each other in silent thought. A shared expression that gave Runstom the impression that they were thinking along the same lines. If McManus brought Jax to the comet, what were the chances X would let any of them live? McManus's usefulness had to be limited. And X didn't seem like the type to care for loose ends. Especially when they were in a deep-space hideout with no witnesses. Runstom only hoped the bastard hadn't simply blown up McManus's ship.

"Well, I hope so too," she said finally. "You're lucky someone on Eridani-3 was willing to help you," she added, stepping over her words carefully.

Once again he felt himself straining to trust this psychopath. A force within, wanting, needing badly to trust her. This force in conflict with his core, repulsed by her actions, her capabilities.

"You know what kind of man he is," Runstom said. "What will he do to Jackson?"

"Kill him," she blurted thoughtlessly, then caught herself. Tried a casual wave of the hand. "Not right away though. He'll want to pump him for information."

"Torture?"

She paused. Not to steel herself for the reply, because she had no need. The pause was to give Runstom a chance to steel himself. "Yes," she said plainly. "Torture."

He sighed, squeezing his eyes tight. "Motherfucker," he whispered.

"I hope we can save your friend's life."

He felt her fingertips on his arm and opened his eyes. "There's something else, Jenna." He waved at the port holding the tracker device. "Sylvia Rankworth gave that to me."

She cocked her head. "Sylvia ... who?"

"An alias," he said. "For Sylvia Runstom. My mother."

Zarconi blinked. He'd learned not to expect emotion from her. "She's in hiding," she said with a nod. "Witness protection? Does anyone know?"

"No one."

"Except your friend," she said. "Except Jack."

He took a long, slow breath. "I want to believe he won't tell X."

She shook her head. "Mark will break him."

* * *

When they passed a ModPol relay, Runstom had found a message waiting for him. His next orders were to return to Ipo, Terroneous's sister moon around Barnard-5. To finish the job there, which he'd been pulled away from to make the long trek out to Epsilon Eridani. There was a ModPol Onsite Rapid Defense Unit at Ipo still in trial status. Trying to convince the mining operation there to invest in defense services. He was to go there and help close the deal. It was a message from Victoria Horus herself, ModPol Defense's Director of Marketing; though she referred to herself as "Big Vicky", always insisting on the casual moniker. She'd been pleased with the report he sent from EE-3. A great victory, she'd called it, and a safe future in which a brave new world could prosper.

He'd frowned at the language. He understood the need for market-speak in messages to the public, but it seemed inappropriate when used between boss and employee. Did she truly believe it? Was she allowing her words to reflect her belief? Or was it just a fancier form of deceit?

Victoria Horus had known. Runstom only just realized. His boss had known about the ambush and sent her favorite public relations officer into the fray. So that he could relay the message to the new colonists of the region: the galaxy is a dangerous place, but ModPol will be there to protect you.

He could have been killed or seriously injured. He'd been given no warning. Wasn't even armed. Maybe he wasn't her favorite public relations officer. Maybe she wouldn't have missed him if he hadn't made it back.

He'd replied. Acknowledged that he'd head straight for Ipo. Gave his report of events that transpired at the prison. He knew this would interest her, but only mildly. Ammunition for when Defense wanted to take jabs at Justice.

These thoughts were running around Runstom's head as they traveled at maximum speed for the coordinates that Zarconi had come up with. He was strapped into an acceleration pod. Waiting for the nav computer to announce their arrival. Trying to figure out what his role in everything was. Trying to figure out to what extent he was being used.

Red lights flashed and a series of chimes sounded. His muscles tensed as the ship decelerated rapidly. Held his breath, both voluntarily and involuntarily. And then the pod released him.

After several minutes of mostly unsuccessful recuperation, he forced himself to float to the bridge. To the ship's main console.

"In the Core," Zarconi said when he arrived. She stopped talking and proceeded through some breathing exercises. For a moment he suspected she had already recovered from the faster-than-light jaunt, but then he realized she had not. Her presence in the bridge was born of a stronger drive.

"The Core in the prison?" he said quietly, practicing his own breathing exercise and squinting against the vertigo.

"In the Core, when the cell is rotated away from the entrance," she continued. "It opens up. There are no handles on the walls. No straps. Just a smooth sphere. A good fifteen meters in diameter."

Runstom tried to picture it. He didn't know why she was describing it to him. The details she was trying to impress. Nothing to hold on to, no reference points. A prisoner could generate movement by kicking off the wall, but eventually they would fall asleep. When they woke up, how often were they floating, out of reach of the wall? How often had she hung there, unable to move simply because of the lack of gravity?

"Sensory deprivation," he said. "Bone loss. Muscle loss."

"Meals were slow-release caplets. Lasted a full day. Some days, the arrival of the caplet was the only thing that broke twenty hours of nothing." Zarconi coughed, re-engaging her breathing. He realized he was gripping the edge of the console, not yet strapped in, but terrified to let go. She went on, answering the questions in his head. "It's not technically torture, they said. Because they let me into the yard for three hours every couple of days."

"But when you got back into any kind of gravity ..." he started.

"Back?" She shook her head, staring at the blackness of space stretching across the viewport. "The Core is a permanent residence. Lifers only."

They worked in silence for a while. She got the tracker initiated. Runstom was thankful for that. Despite the help that Sylvia had given him, he wasn't sure he could make use of it on his own. He couldn't help but suspect that the coordinates Zarconi had come up with were a ruse. Had she laid some trap long ago? What waited for him in the depths of space around Barnard's Star?

"I think we got something," she said. He froze, listening silently for a confirmation. The console bleeped at him. "There."

"Is it the right signal?" he said.

"Most definitely," she said. "Your mother signed it with a hash, hidden among the noise. Very clever."

Runstom tensed at those words. Zarconi hadn't asked anything about Sylvia since he'd mentioned her hours ago. Hadn't asked who or where she was. What she did. How he felt about her. Nothing. She'd been surprised when he revealed it, but no curiosity followed that surprise.

Another beep interrupted his thoughts.

"Take this course," she said, transferring data from her console to his. "I'm going to turn off the audio alarm now that we're locked into it. I'll send you adjustments as we get more pings, but right now this course is the best guess at general direction."

"How far is it?"

"Not far," she said quietly.

After twenty minutes of silent tracking, the knot in his stomach needed release. He needed something to kill the quiet. "If they only let you out of the Core a few hours every couple of days, how did you manage to trade contraband?"

She huffed a small laugh. "Don't you want to know what the *contraband* was first?"

He looked at her. The grin crooking up one side of her mouth. "Drugs," he said.

The other side of her mouth joined the grin. "So sure, are we, Detective Runstom?"

"Don't call me that."

"How do you know I wasn't selling my body?"

He shook his head. "I spent several years of puberty in and out of gravity," he said. He left it at that, not anxious to talk about the inhibitive effects of zero-G on arousal.

Her smile scrunched up and she looked away from him. "You're right, of course. I got hold of a recipe, before I was transferred. In the facility, they have all these soft utensils, for eating with. They don't want people sharpening them into shivs, so the material is this special compound that is hard long enough to use them for eating, but degrades quickly afterward. When it's exposed to certain acids, the compound's molecular structure breaks down. An ammonia wash will pull it back together in a mildly toxic form. Boiling it will cause the toxins to release as a gas, which can be inhaled for an intoxicating effect."

Runstom grimaced. "Is it safe to breathe?"

She shrugged. "Less safe than most alcohol is to drink, but only just so."

"How did you do all those steps?"

"Delegation," Zarconi said. "The acids for the first part can be found in the stomach. So first, someone has to ingest pieces of utensils, wait about an hour, then induce vomiting."

"God damn," he said.

"The ammonia comes from cleaning compounds, that certain privileged prisoners get access to."

"Privileged?"

"Yeah, the ones who are lucky enough to get custodial jobs." She waved a hand dismissively. "The boiling comes from the high-pressure ovens in the kitchen. Used to reconstitute preserved foodstuffs. There's a valve that releases the pressure, and they trap the gas in that with half-filled water bulbs."

"That all seems like a lot of work."

"Don't underestimate the determination of people with nothing to do and nothing to drink," she said. "The measurements of everything have to be just right. I had to manage the recipe and the labor."

Runstom decided he didn't need to know any more about it. "How close are we?"

When she failed to respond right away, he turned back to look at her. Her wistful gaze fell to nothing visible. "They'll miss me, I bet."

"I'm sure." He didn't hide his bitter tone, not that she would pick it up anyway.

She looked at him with a hint of a smile. "But there are more important things to do anyway, aren't there?"

"Yes," he said firmly.

Her eyes drew deep into him, and her voice took on a

tone he'd not heard from her before. "The woods are lovely, dark, and deep, but I have promises to keep." Her voice was a strong whisper, the words moving with a rhythm. "And miles to go before I sleep."

"Miles?" he said quietly before he realized she was not done.

"And miles to go before I sleep."

After a few moments of silence, he spoke, avoiding her eyes. "Well, um."

"That's the end of it. I could recite the whole poem from the beginning." She leaned forward and tapped her head. "I've got tons of that crap stored up here. Some people find it meaningful. I never cared for it, but it seems to have an effect. Would you like to hear more?"

He cringed. Poetry as a means of manipulation. In that database of a brain of hers, there were cross-references to results, experiments to test the effect of lines of verse on the emotional state of those she was interacting with. She thought those words would mean something to him. Not because she understood how he felt. Because she categorized how people reacted.

So what was it? Runstom wasn't much for poetry himself. It was usually over his head. Double-meanings, metaphors. The best he could do was that the words sounded nice together. *Miles*, an outdated measurement of distance. But had it been *And kilometers to go before I sleep*, it would not be the same at all.

"No," he said. Felt shame for being stuck on the unit of measurement, unable to grasp anything deeper. "How close are we?"

"Ah, you're right," she said, her gaze falling to her console. "We're picking her up now."

Runstom sat up straight. He caught himself swallowing nerves. "Close enough for radio contact?"

"I think so," she said. "Not just the tracker your mom gave us. I'm getting residual heat and radiation. Two distinct sources. Looks like the ModPol ship is still attached to Comet X."

"Try to get visual, when you can." He knew they were moving too fast for even the computer-aided scope to track the targets. "This thing has pretty good brakes. I'm going to maintain speed until we get closer."

"Okay, boss."

Runstom frowned when she said that. More submission. Not to be trusted.

He hesitated above the comm controls. Protocol would dictate that he contact the other ModPol patroller. The big question was: how deep in was McManus? Runstom had a hard time believing the sergeant was loyal to someone as low as X. McManus was always an arrogant ass, and had a particular disliking of Runstom, and yet. He was still a cop, inside and out, wasn't he?

Runstom downshifted to subwarp. Zarconi fed her data to his console. They drew closer. Another monitor winked to life, displaying the scope. They were like toys on the screen. The comet-styled base station, about eight times the size of the interstellar patroller attached to the side. Shifted blue as they grew in size.

"Hold on," he said. Unnecessary, as they were both strapped tightly to their station chairs.

As they drew close, the computer's calculations of the comet's position and trajectory became increasingly accurate. He tapped out the commands for an emergency brake and approach. Told the ship to try to match the comet as best it could, within certain parameters. A gamble between accuracy and safety.

He executed the commands and closed his eyes. He probably should have warned Zarconi to do the same. He knew she would anyway, reflexively. The sudden change in speed and the accompanying shudder it produced was nothing the human eye wanted any part of.

After what felt like several minutes of being ripped apart by gravitational forces and being bombarded by blaring alarms, the ship's shaking calmed to a mild jostling. Runstom opened his eyes. As the klaxons quieted, another lower-volume sound revealed itself with a patient persistence. The comm. An incoming connection.

He looked at the console, rubbing the blur from his vision. It was from the interstellar patroller. He accepted.

"Holy shit, I can't believe you found us!"

"This is Stanford Runstom, ModPol Defense. Please ident—"

"Yeah, yeah, this is Pilot Officer Kyl Ayliff. ModPol Patroller F-7-L."

Runstom tried to control his breathing. "Ayliff, where is McManus? Where is Jackson?"

"Hey, appreciate the concern," the reply came back sourly. "Your buddies were dragged into that station. Meanwhile, these assholes apparently planted a bomb in one of our holds that I can't get to because the fuckers ripped a hole in my hull and I can't get that room pressurized."

Runstom's brain wanted to go in two directions. "What kind of bomb? Wouldn't they put the station in danger?"

"They *said* it won't go off unless we manage to detach and get too far from their signal."

An insurance bomb. Runstom had read about them. One

was used in a robbery a few decades back. It would have a timer that counted down, probably only a few seconds maximum. But a constant remote signal was sent to it, telling it to reset. Limited to the speed of light. They could get a good distance, but at around a million kilometers, the time cost was more than three seconds. In these far reaches, a million kilometers might as well be one kilometer.

"Okay," Runstom said. Because he didn't know what else to say, he added, "It's going to be okay."

There wasn't an immediate response, which was good. He needed to think. With a few taps, he found that the local network had been automatically established between the ModPol ships. He pulled up the schematic of the big patroller. There were several holds, linked together. Ideal for isolating cargo or suspects, as needed. Also served as a safety mechanism, in that if one hold was compromised, that damage too was isolated. With the breach, there was no way to pressurize the hold in question. But an adjacent hold could be depressurized.

"Okay, Officer Ayliff," Runstom said into the comm. "Who's with you there on the ship?"

"Just me and Granny."

Runstom wondered if he'd heard the other name right, but decided not to waste time questioning it. "Just two of you then. If one of you could get into a suit, you could go down to one of these other holds, like this one, number sixteen. Then you can depressurize that hold and you should be able to get into the breached hold. If you can—"

"Wait, what are you looking at?"

"Um, I have your ship's schematic—"

"You're on the network? Shit, no! Shut it down! Shut down the mesh network! Quick, before he hacks you!"

Runstom stiffened, then looked at Zarconi. "What is he talking about?"

Her face was stone. "Mark probably used an exploit in the mesh network to take remote control over their ship."

"How do we stop it?"

She tapped her console a few times. "We don't. We let him think he's got us."

Runstom's stomach tightened. "And then what?"

"We go in," she said quietly. "I know a backdoor."

He thought about it for a second. What had she left behind when she was last at this place? "A backdoor through the network?"

The stone-face cracked with an unnerving half-grin. "More literal than that."

* * *

Jax groaned and tried to roll over, but only got as far as tipping onto his left side.

"Get up." McManus's voice had an otherworldly tone to it. "Get up and start talking."

Jax managed to get to his hands and knees. He wheezed, and his lungs felt like they were breathing in shards of glass. If the gravity had been a full G, he might not even be alive. McManus had been throwing him around the room for what felt like an eternity.

"I have been talking," he managed through clenched teeth. In reality the beating had probably only lasted five or ten minutes. "There isn't anything else to tell."

"I will beat you until shit comes out of your ears." He had that calm tone, a matter-of-fact cop tone, just stating the facts, no matter how terrible those facts were.

"God *damn,* this is good fun." Phonson took another small bite from the roast kibu. He turned to the woman who'd brought it. "Carr, are we recording this?"

She looked at one corner of the room. "Yeah, I guess. The security cameras are on."

"Oh, no, that's not good enough," he said through a mouthful of half-chewed meat. "Get up to the control room and turn on the high-rez three-D recorders. I want to savor the moment when this asshole cracks."

She shrugged and walked away. Jax turned to Phonson. "I'm telling the truth about Eridani. I gave you everything, the complete story."

"Why was Stanford Runstom on EE-3?" Phonson asked for the millionth time.

Jax sighed, then coughed as pain lanced through his guts. He was fairly certain McManus had dealt him a broken rib or two. Then again, he'd never had a rib broken – or any bone broken – so what would he know about how that felt?

"He works for the marketing department." The same answer he'd been giving the whole time. "Of ModPol Defense. And he was on EE-3 to meet with some administrators of the new colony there."

Phonson rose from his seat, still holding his meal in one hand. "And *who* did he meet with?"

"*Whom*," Jax said.

"Sergeant," Phonson said with mock exasperation. "Tell our friend here to answer that question."

McManus strode to Jax, yanking him to his feet and spinning him around to face away. From behind, he wrapped one arm around Jax's neck and squeezed. "Answer the question, Jackson."

Jax tried to speak but no air passed through his throat.

He pulled uselessly at McManus's wiry, rock-hard forearm. Finally, it relaxed enough for him to pull a panicked suck of air into his lungs. "I don't know their names," he rasped. "I was in hiding the whole time."

"Let's try just one name," Phonson said, stepping close to him. "I bet ol' Stanley Runstom mentioned at least *one name*."

Jax felt like he was sandwiched between the two bad cops. He tried to think of happier thoughts, of the views of the Terroneous landscape, of all the non-violent fixing he did while he was there, of Lealina Warpshire and the time they'd spent together. These thoughts fled as quickly as they appeared, chased out by the alarms in his brain that he was suffocating, that his windpipe was being crushed.

"Sylvia." The mere whisper scorched fire through his throat. A new hole inside him tore open, one that far eclipsed the emptiness of hunger.

Phonson leaned in so close that Jax could feel the heat of his breath, and suspected he would be able to smell the food still in his mouth, if his airway had not been cut off. "What? Sylvia? Did he say Sylvia?"

McManus's grip came free all at once. "He can't hear you, Jackson. Maybe you should get *closer*."

His vision blurred and it was only afterward that Jax realized what had happened, his brain replaying the situation back for him slowly enough for him to grok it. McManus shoved him, hard, in the back, an act of aggression against him, which was allowed. The result of that action was that Jax collided with Phonson, both of them tumbling over one another across the room, unhindered by the fractional gravity, coming to rest only when they slammed into the far wall.

While they lay there stunned, McManus calmly strode up to them. He reached a hand down to lift Jax to his feet, disentangling him from Phonson. He didn't spare any more energy making sure Jax could stay standing, but instead bent down to offer the same help to Phonson, who was face down and getting to his hands and knees.

McManus's hands passively passed around the other man's chest. They hooked under his armpits, as though to lift him up. Then with a snap, they went beyond, under the arms and up to the head, the fingers lacing together behind the neck.

The friendly gesture was finally deemed aggressive by the system, and both men howled in unison as McManus's wiry muscles went taut. It took a fraction of a second for Jax to realize that the nervous-system lock bound both men.

McManus's plan all along, then: beat Jax silly until he could make his move.

Phonson's howling rose in pitch. He struggled uselessly against the frozen-meat bonds. "Carr, goddammit! Can you hear me?"

It wouldn't take long for someone to glance at the output of the cameras in the room. Jax shoved aside the pain and exhaustion in his battered body and the drag of the weight in his guilt-sodden head, getting his ass to the nearest console. He tapped through the top menus of the system. He figured on having only seconds, and he let his hands and eyes and mind work independently, searching for anything familiar enough to make a difference.

What he found was the life-support system. The controls were nearly identical to the systems he operated back on Barnard-4. Back when his life was boring, when he had a career as a button-pushing robot.

"Uh, boss?" The woman Carr's voice came on over a speaker. "There's another ship here. A ModPol patroller. She just joined the local Mesh."

"Snag it," Phonson gasped, desperately trying to twist out of McManus's ropey arms. "And get someone down here!"

On the screen before Jax, there was a schematic of the station. All the rooms were connected via narrow corridors of various lengths. He could see the vital stats that the system was tracking, every living creature in the whole station. The station had a crew of nine, including Phonson. They clustered into rooms; the corridors were too small to hang around in.

He tapped out a command: an emergency atmosphere purge on all corridors. The system began the process of verifying they were all empty, locking them down, and sucking the air out of them. A timer appeared. It would take seventeen minutes for the atmosphere to be purged and then replenished, before the safety mechanisms would allow the corridors to be used again. Seventeen minutes to figure out what to do next.

CHAPTER 14

Runstom waved his hands at his useless console. "Well, we're locked out."

"Good," Zarconi said. She began unstrapping herself.

"I suppose this means you have a plan," he said warily.

"We go outside," she said.

He unstrapped. He didn't like her running the situation. But this was her element. Runstom knew very little about X, and even less about his remote hideout.

He led her to the equipment locker of the patroller. There were four extravehicular mobility suits, each equipped with a set of tools, including nanoglue guns and enclosure-laser-cutters, designed to work in the vacuum of space. Though the patroller's navigation and piloting systems had been compromised, the rest of the ship's internal systems were functioning just fine. He ran the minimum diagnostic profile against two of the suits, as it was the only way to get the damn thing to let go of them.

Before he got into his suit, he opened the armory locker. Took out two freshly charged stun pistols. Strapped on a chest holster for one and tucked the other in the waist of his pants. The ship's database had last been synced with the prison, so it still considered him a guard on temporary assignment. It encoded the pistols with his prints.

Runstom could have overridden the safety feature, which would allow Zarconi to carry one. She might have had the plan, but he was still in control.

He sighed at himself for the delusion.

They got into their suits and exited the adjacent maintenance airlock. Runstom wondered if the station would detect them in their EMUs, but decided it didn't matter. He and Zarconi needed to move quickly.

They used the handholds around the surface of the patroller to get closer. The hacked piloting system was already bringing it in line with the station, lining it up on the opposite side from McManus's larger interstellar patroller. Runstom got a good look at so-called *Comet X*. It was oblong, with clusters of polygonal panels shaping the corners. In the center, there was a bulge like a fat welt. This rotating cylinder was the bulk of the station. That would be the part that had some fraction of gravity. A bank of six massive thrusters sat aft. Dozens of small stabilizing thrusters protruded from various panels along the sides of the front and rear non-rotating sections. It wasn't easy to turn any space-faring vessel, but he guessed that it took this thing thousands of kilometers to turn a single degree. Based on Zarconi's explanation, he knew none of the thrusters – main or other – had been used in decades. It was locked into a comet's orbit.

Next was the leap. From the patroller to the side of the station. He'd attached the two EMUs by a nanofiber cable. Zarconi, despite her confidence in her plan, had very little extravehicular activity experience. When Runstom was a ModPol officer, there was little to do at the outpost but read and practice things. Piloting, target shooting, EVA walking. Whatever he could do to keep from going soft from inactivity.

He put out a hand. They had opted for radio silence. He pointed at her, and then put out his hand flat, to indicate that she stay. He pointed at himself and made an arc with his hand, then pointed at the base. Then he tugged lightly at the cable drifting between them.

She gave him a thumbs-up. This was going to be dangerous, and he didn't want to trust her. Lives were at stake, and that wasn't something she was capable of caring about. He had to remind himself of that. But she was good at self-preservation.

He crouched, bending his knees as much as the suit would let him. Not much. Enough to point his head in the direction of the station. He fired the thrusters.

The surface of the station wobbled toward him. It'd been quite some time since he'd done a spacewalk. A year, perhaps. Still, it came right back to him. Large handholds came into view and he turned toward the closest one. Seconds, then he was there. Gripping the handhold.

He looked back. The cable curved wildly. Zarconi was in mid-flight. She hadn't waited. Stupid. Runstom was stupid because he should have known.

It was clear she was losing control. Was she capable of panic? Even an animal can panic. He could see by the wild firing of her thrusts that she was losing control. The line was going taut. He wrapped an arm around the bar, hooking it at his elbow and grabbing the wrist with his other hand. The jar of her flight would have yanked his arm from its socket had the suit not been so solid.

He waited to see if she would calm down and lay off the thrust. After a moment, she resigned. He began the slow process of pulling her in by the cable.

The shielded helmets wouldn't let him see her face, nor her his. Runstom wanted Zarconi to see how pissed he was that she putting them in danger. But he was thankful for not being able to see the stone-face looking back. The face that was all too determined.

Seconds after she reached the wall and grabbed the bar, she was gesturing. To the aft. He waved for her to lead. It felt safer if he could keep an eye on her.

They made their way more quickly than he wanted to. Zarconi was not accustomed to the suit, not accustomed to working along the outside of a ship. But accustomed to traversing handholds. Accustomed to zero-G. And not just from her prison stay, he had to remind himself. Her green skin meant she'd been born and raised in the depths of space. Like him. Spending their developmental years calling a spaceship home.

A small hatch greeted them at the edge as a panel bent down toward the dormant thrusters. She faced it. Froze for a moment. Then found what she was looking for: a small impression which slid down and away when she punched it with the base of her fist. She gripped the thick handle within. Pulled it out, her other hand braced against the side of the hull. Twisted it.

Four yellow lights flashed around the corners of the square door. The door shifted, one edge of it moving back slightly. She pushed on it and it swung the rest of the way.

They pulled themselves into the small airlock. Runstom closed it and Zarconi went through another procedure with a lever on the inside to lock it. More angry yellow lights.

Seconds later, they changed to a faint blue. A panel along one side lit up green.

She reached up and removed her helmet. He followed suit when she didn't immediately choke.

Runstom looked around the small airlock. "Cameras?" he whispered.

"Likely," Zarconi said. She pulled herself to the inner hatch. It came open easily. "This maintenance hatch can't be locked. But once they see us, it will be harder to go further in."

Runstom thought of the flashing yellow lights. "Was probably an alarm to let them know the maintenance hatch was used. Let's assume they see us."

She nodded and pulled herself through the opening. He followed.

The next room was a good deal larger than the airlock. Sporadic equipment clung to the walls. It was severely understocked, and Runstom sensed that the sparsity made the room feel bigger than it was. Zarconi closed the hatch behind them. Floated to the opposite end of the room. Without following her, Runstom could see the arresting red of the panel at the door.

"They locked us out," he said. "We can cut through."

"It's not them, it's some kind of system lockout." She examined the small screen, prodding it for more details. "The pressure in the next corridor is all wacky."

He frowned. "So cutting through would be dangerous."

She turned to him. "I know another route. We just have to hope that whatever issue the station is having isn't widespread."

The words *issue the station is having* gave Runstom a sinking feeling. It was capped by a small amount of hope.

If someone was making the tech in the station misbehave, that someone could be Jax. Which meant he was alive and kicking. It was a desperate thought, but he allowed it. The whole thing was desperation.

She floated to the side of the room and gestured at some empty straps. "We need to leave the suits here. They're too big."

"Too big for what?"

She ignored him and strapped herself to the wall. Proceeded to wiggle out of her suit. With another frown, he went to the wall to do the same. Once he was out of the EMU, his sole consolation was that he could now reach his pistols.

By the time Runstom was out, Zarconi had detached the laser torch from her suit. She kicked off and latched onto the ceiling. Near the center, she found some panel that Runstom wouldn't have noticed. She raised the shield on the cutter to cover her eyes and he looked away. Listened to the fizz. Smelled the melt of metal. Seconds later, it was quiet.

She lightly shoved aside the panel and it drifted away. "Electrical conduits and gas lines," she said. "They all run through these access tubes."

He drifted up to meet her. Tightening his breath against the stink of charred metal, he poked his head through the breach. The tube was very dark and very small.

"Those channels aren't necessarily pressurized to match the ship," she said, tugging him back down. She pointed at the other wall. "There are some snug-suits over there. Made for internal maintenance work."

The snug-suits were well named. Flexible enough to move easily, but rugged and airtight. A small air tank ran down the middle of the back.

Zarconi lifted the accompanying helmet to her head and Runstom stopped her. "Once we go up there, we're going back to silence. Where are we going?"

"We need to get to the control room," she said. "It's on this side, close to engineering, and it's the best place to collect data."

"Collect data." By which she meant, find out how many hands were on the base. How many souls would get in their way.

She nodded shortly and put her helmet on. Before he sealed his suit, he pulled the pistol from his waist and latched it to a loop on the outside of the snug-suit. Then he got his helmet on and followed her into the narrow channel above.

The tightness of the tube. The quiet sounds of their progress coming at him through tiny speakers in the helmet. The view through the visor of the helmet, enhancing the visibility in the absence of light with eerie blue-green shapes. All of it adding to the caved-in feeling. He supposed Zarconi wasn't claustrophobic; or if she was, she had learned to cope with it in her time locked deep in the center of the zero-G prison.

As always, she was eager and they moved quickly. They took a left turn, and then another back to the right, and then finally a turn downward. All of these directions were relative without gravity. It was even harder to keep track with tunnel vision.

She held up a hand to stop their progress. Traced a rectangle along one side of the tube. Detached the laser torch from a hook on her hip. She watched him in silence for a moment, until he realized she was waiting. He readied his stun pistol and took aim.

Zarconi began cutting, and Runstom knew it was going

to draw their attention. How could it not? But what would they do, that was the question. And how many were in there?

After several long minutes, she stopped. She'd made cuts in a square, but left just enough metal in place to keep the piece from coming loose.

They paused. In the silence, Runstom's suit increased the speaker volume. Voices from below became clear, muffled at first then filtered.

"Who's up there?"

"It must be someone trying to fix the corridors."

"Mackie, is that you up there?"

There were two distinct voices, one male, one female. Runstom flexed the grip on his gun. He positioned himself opposite the cut and braced himself against the tube, using his free hand to hold a bundle of cables. Nodded to Zarconi.

She leaned back and away, stretching her arm out to make the final cut. The piece drifted slowly, and at first it still obstructed his view.

"Hello?" The male voice. "Mackie, everything okay?"

A full minute of silence. Then a hand brushed aside the square of metal. A man hovered, squinting up into the darkness. He wore no armor, but instead was dressed in some kind of exercise suit.

"Mackie?" he whispered. Looking directly at Runstom's form in the darkness.

Runstom took aim and blue light crackled from the pistol. The man shook and went limp. Runstom let go of the cabling and pulled himself through the narrow opening, leading with his outstretched gun.

Halfway through, his hip hitched on the jagged edge of the opening. With his free hand he tried to push off against the ceiling of the room, but he didn't have the leverage. He waved the pistol around, seeing nothing but banks of monitors and controls. He twisted around as far as he could. Someone grabbed his arm.

The large woman wrenched his arm into a hold and Runstom yelled out with the pain. If it weren't for the reinforced strength of the snug-suit, he was sure she would have broken a bone. She pulled his fingers from the pistol one by one. He could feel Zarconi's fingers at his waist, working to free the snag.

Just as the woman pulled away the pistol, Zarconi got him loose. She grabbed him by the crotch and shoved him through the hole. He flailed, causing the woman in the control room to flinch and swing wildly away from him. His reflexes braced for an incoming stun, but when his brain caught up, he spotted the pistol drifting peacefully away from them.

Zarconi pulled herself through, and the three of them formed a triangle. Neither Runstom nor the woman were holding anything. Adrift.

She brought her wrist to her mouth. "All hands! We've got intruders in the control room!"

Zarconi curled her body in on itself, one hand firmly around the edge of the hole she'd made. "Mira, please." A mirthless smile. "*Intruders*. Far too formal for an old friend stopping by."

The woman named Mira raised her wrist again. "Boss, you should know. It's—"

She was cut off when Zarconi sprang at her. Collision, then the momentum carried them to the floor. Runstom saw the tool in Zarconi's hand. Coming down around the back of the other woman. She howled with pain and fear.

"Jenna, no!" He twisted desperately, the small amount of momentum from the previous struggle causing him to drift by millimeters toward the surface of the ceiling. "Don't kill her! Stop!"

After a few seconds, Zarconi turned back to him. A globe of gray goo oozed from the tool in her hand.

"Nanoglue," she said. "Did you think I was using the laser torch?"

He looked past her to see the panicking Mira flailing her arms and legs. Pinned by her back to the floor. Zarconi turned back and aimed the glue gun at the wrist-pad.

She grinned to herself and looked up again. Kicked off and glided into him, sliding one hand around his waist. In any other situation, the move would have been intimate. Her momentum carried them to the ceiling. Then she kicked off again, this time aiming for the console bank.

* * *

Phonson forced out a strained half-grunt, half-howl. Jax felt a cold rock forming in his stomach as he watched the man produce a thin blade from a fold of his clothing, struggling against McManus's petrified arms. He drew it upward and slid it up into flesh and muscle, severing enough fibers to cause one arm to flap loose. The spray of blood looked like water against the crimson skin of Phonson's face.

As he shook himself loose, he roared, flinging the weakened limbs away. With a flash, he jabbed the blade into McManus's stomach, yanked it back out, then kicked him away. In the low gravity, the cop's body soared into the far wall, a trail of dark plasma in its wake.

Phonson turned on Jax. "What did you do?" His voice was commanding but low. The scrunched, blood-sodden face, heaving chest, and dripping blade were enough to make up for lack of volume.

Jax swallowed. "I ran a purge on all the corridors." He tried to straighten himself up. "You're not getting any reinforcements until it finishes."

"Reinforcements." Half his mouth smiled. "I'm going to skin you alive, you piece-of-shit domer."

The plan, such as it was, didn't involve Phonson having a knife. Jax took a step back. He was drained, he knew that. He couldn't fight the ex-cop, and he had no weapon. His only choice was to run, and he'd effectively locked the only exit.

"There's more," he said without thinking. "I – I figured I was going to ... going to die here."

Phonson had taken a step toward him, but at this he stopped and lifted his head slightly. "You are."

"So I sabotaged the life-support system."

He pointed with the wet, maroon tip of the knife. "How so?"

"I assume you remember that I am – I was – a life-support operator back on Barnard-4."

Phonson's eyes narrowed. "Yes."

"Right, of course you do," Jax said, trying to take on a relaxed tone. "Being that it was your contacts that Jenna Zarconi abused to hack my system. You know, to murder all those people."

He pointed the blade again, not at Jax this time, but at the console behind him. "What did you do?"

Jax threw up his hands. "I can't *tell* you, unless you're going to let me live."

Phonson's knife-hand dropped slightly, though Jax didn't get the sense that it meant he was suddenly safe. "So what, you think—"

"Boss, you there?" The unseen speaker interrupted him and caused him to glance upward. "We got a problem."

"What problem?" he said. "Where's Carr?"

After a moment, the speaker came back. "We lost contact with the control room."

Phonson looked at Jax, who put his hands out defensively. "I didn't do that."

"Abberis, what's going on with life support?" he asked the ceiling.

Jax tried to breathe slowly as they waited for the reply. Other than the corridor purge, he'd done nothing. The trick was to make them believe he'd done something that they couldn't yet detect.

"All corridors will be accessible in seven minutes," the voice of Abberis reported back.

"See," Jax said, pointing up. "They can't detect the little bomb I left in the system."

Phonson scowled, white ridges forming across his red forehead. He closed his eyes and appeared to suck in a deep breath, then opened them, tipped his head back, and exhaled. After blinking a few times, he looked at Jax. The blade disappeared back into the invisible folds from whence it came. His hands came together, one clasped over the other. "Fine, Jackson," he said quietly. "You're smart. We all know that. And you've got nothing to lose, right?" His hands unfolded and he pointed. "Wrong. We both know you have something back on Terroneous."

The confidence he'd mustered drained away, bringing back the weariness in his muscles, the emptiness in his stomach. "No," he said, meant as a counter, a denial, but instead it came out as a plea.

"You're nobody, Jackson." Phonson began a slow pace, not coming any closer to Jax, but making a back-and-forth circle that made him feel hunted. "You're not my problem. I could snuff you out right now and no one in the universe would care. Those hillfolk on Terroneous can bitch and moan all they want at ModPol, but they can't touch *me*."

"So what do you want?" Jax said weakly.

"Runstom," he growled. The pacing stopped and he stepped closer. "I want you to tell me about Epsilon Eridani-3. We got so close, thanks to your dying friend over there." He gestured, and Jax felt cold at the sight of the crimson lake slowly growing around the twitching McManus. "There was a name," Phonson continued quietly. "Sylvia."

"What will you do if I tell you?" Jax's voice sounded like it came from some other person, some other place.

Phonson drew a wicked smile. "What I always do. Move people around. Make deals, bargains. Keep the *peace*." He waved a finger. "And you, Jackson, you don't have to worry about shit. You go on your way. Unmarked. Free."

For a moment Jax wondered if Phonson believed his own words. Was this the main goal of his manipulations? To make some deals, come out ahead when he could but otherwise keep things peaceful whenever possible? He probably wasn't a killer at heart. The dead were a lot harder to keep in the pocket to be called upon later.

All of that could be true, but it was a seduction to think that Phonson would prefer not to kill. Jax knew when it came down to it, there were only a few ways to truly silence people.

"You're running out of time," Jax said. "Another ModPol ship is here."

Phonson tried to laugh but his heart wasn't in it. "You think they're here to rescue you?" he snarled. "Don't count on it. You're nobody."

Deep in the emptiness that pervaded his body, a fire sparked to life. "We're all nobody. Specks of dust to the universe." He spoke the next words as the thought occurred to him. "Isn't this station supposed to be hard to find?"

"It's *very* hard to find," Phonson bragged.

"So if another ship came out here, then it must be someone that knows the location." Jax remembered how McManus's ship gave up its controls, some kind of remote hack across the ModPol mesh network. "And it's not someone you were expecting, because you told your people to 'snag it'. To take control of it. One of your loyal friends turned on you."

"Sergeant McManus is *dying*," Phonson shouted with a broad gesture to the groaning form behind him. "And you're next, Jackson."

Jax allowed himself a smile. "I hope not before we find out who infiltrated your ship and took over your control room."

The blade appeared again and Phonson took a few lunging steps forward. Jax flinched and stepped back, bumping into a wall console.

The hidden speaker system hummed to life. "Whose woods these are, I think I know."

Phonson stopped, his threatening advance deflating as his eyes turned up. "No," he whispered. He looked at Jax. "Well, we're all fucked now."

"His house is in the village though."

"Oh come on," Phonson said. "Enough with the poetry, Jenna! What the fuck do you want?"

"He will not see me stopping here to watch his woods fill up with snow."

"God damn it." He stalked toward the consoles. "Get the hell out of the way, Jackson."

Jax obliged, circling along the perimeter of the room. The poetry recital continued, but he couldn't make out the words as Phonson attempted to smother it with a ranting stream of insults. On the other side, he bent down to look at McManus. The suppression-system effect had worn off, but he was in bad shape. Groaning softly, he held his stomach with the hand of his good arm.

"I don't know what to do," Jax said in a low voice as he knelt down next to the bloody mess of a cop.

"There's nothing you can do," he said, grimacing as the words came out. "It hurts like hell, but I'm still alive. For now."

But not forever, Jax knew. In the distance, Phonson's insults to Jenna Zarconi mixed with an argument he was having with his own console. Something about locks and the locations of his crew members. Jax knew the console in this slapdash brig had no real control; it was by the fortune of oversight that the emergency controls over the life-support system were accessible.

"You'll make it," Jax said to McManus. "We just have to get you to Medical."

"Sorry about kicking your ass," he mumbled.

Jax nodded. "You were just trying to get a jump on him. And it worked." After a moment, he added, "I'm sorry I said my ass was a better cop than you."

McManus almost laughed, then groaned, eyelids pinched

in pain. Jax felt an awkward mixture of pity and pleasure. He still thought they wouldn't be in this situation if McManus hadn't been such a shitty person and a worse cop. But the truth was, Phonson would have just used someone else.

"But I have promises to keep," the voice above was saying. "And miles to go before I sleep."

A series of clicks and beeps drew their attention to the only door in the room. The door slid away.

"And miles to go before I sleep," Jenna Zarconi said as she stepped through.

"Jax, are you okay?" Runstom edged into the room from behind her.

"Oh fuck me," Phonson said. He pointed up. "That was a recording? I thought you were taunting me from the control room! That's just low, Jenna."

Zarconi and Runstom stepped fully into the room and Phonson reacted by bolting across it. Jax tried to straighten back up quickly, but lost his balance trying not to trip over McManus or slip in his blood. Phonson managed to grab him by the wrist. With little effort, he pulled Jax's weakened body to a position in front of him. He looped an arm around Jax's neck and brought the small blade around to rest heavy and cold against his chest.

"Let him go," Runstom said. He was bracing a hand against the wall, favoring one leg in the light gravity. Whenever it touched the floor as he moved, he winced and shifted his weight back to the other foot.

"Be careful, Stan," Jax said. "I think he's after you. More than me."

"It's true, I don't mind if I have to kill Jackson." Jax could feel Phonson's hot breath on the back of his neck as he spoke. "But I don't want to kill you, Stanford Runstom."

"He wants to own you," Zarconi said. She sounded bored.

"He knew about the ambush in Eridani," Jax said. He felt Phonson's grip tighten, but the reaction was restrained, so Jax tested it further. "He confirmed that it's Rando Jansen on the inside. Jansen is the mole in Space Waste."

"Doesn't it feel better to know?" Phonson said. "That's what I love about what I do. I know every little bit of who's fucking with who. Shit, half the time I'm helping them fuck each other over. But we're at a new level of cooperation right now in ModPol. And that's thanks to a balance."

"This might go on for a while," Zarconi said.

"Just let go of Jackson," Runstom said.

"Single-minded," the voice in Jax's ear went on, the blade taking respite from pointing at his chest to momentarily point across the room. "That's why you fit in so well with Defense. Defense is a single-minded organization. More. That's all they think about. More. More sales, bigger contracts.

"Justice, on the other hand, has been actually trying to control the criminal threat in our little corner of the galaxy. We've been putting people inside Space Waste for years. But it's hard to make traction. Once you're on the inside, it's just a matter of time before you're made. Or you're converted. But now, we got Jansen. We finally have some control over the most dangerous criminal outfit in the known universe.

"And so along comes Defense. To Defense, this is another weapon. Space Waste is a gun to be aimed. A threat that furthers their agenda. Space Waste is like an ion storm or a solar flare – they strike without warning. That shit is why high-tech hull shielding makes money. This is the same thing: Space Waste attacks are why Defense makes money. Sometimes you just have to remind people of that threat."

"So they use the man on the inside to tell the Wasters who to attack," Runstom said. He was carrying a pistol of some kind, but it hung low in his hand, the other hand unable to stray far from the wall. Jax hoped the weapon was of the non-lethal variety, in case Runstom had to take a wild shot.

"That stunner won't do you any good, Public Relations Officer Runstom," Phonson taunted. "Didn't the lovely psycho tell you about my special anti-aggression defense system?"

Zarconi half-turned to Runstom. "It's an electromagnetic matrix," she said, tipping her head as if to nod at the invisible energy in the air. "Some tech that was being tested for lock-ups. Ultimately deemed too dangerous and controversial to use. This small-minded man found himself in possession of one of the prototypes, supposed to have been recycled."

"I'm not small-minded," Phonson growled in a measured voice.

She rolled her eyes. "I had to install it for him. Otherwise he would have fried everyone in his little playhouse."

"Anti-aggression?" Runstom said.

"It's tuned to exclude the vitastats of the crew." She pointed. "So it won't stop him from slicing open Jackson there. But if you try to draw down on him right now, you'll get a nasty shock."

"Hurts like fuck," McManus murmured before lapsing back into his soft, painful groaning.

"If I try to draw on him," Runstom said. He lifted the gun, barrel still pointed down, and motioned it toward Zarconi. "I could give it to you, couldn't I?"

She smiled at him in a way that made Jax extremely

uncomfortable, even after dozens of hours of torture, starvation, and the more recent position he was in. "Smart, Stan. You're right: I am protected from the system as one of the crew."

"I removed you," Phonson said quickly. Even without seeing his face, Jax could hear the desperation in his voice.

"Maybe," she said, one finger lingering on the grip of the proffered pistol. "And maybe when I set it up, I made sure I was always hardcoded in there."

Phonson sucked in the air behind Jax's ear, his next reply taking some effort to think out. "Okay, right," he said finally. "But I bet your ex-cop buddy encoded that pistol. It will only work with his fingerprint."

As stone-faced as Runstom tried to remain, even Jax could tell it was true. He felt relieved in that moment; Runstom had been desperate enough to recruit Zarconi's help, but at least he hadn't trusted her completely. He'd taken measures. Not that it helped so much in the current situation.

She pulled her finger back and brought the hand harmlessly to her hip. Runstom drew the gun away from her. "I'm sorry, Jenna."

"It's okay, Stanford," she said gently without looking at him. Her eyes were affixed to Phonson. "I didn't expect you to trust me that far. And I actually owe *you* an apology. For taking my own measures."

A small, dull cylinder appeared in her hand. It flashed, and Jax staggered.

* * *

"She shot me! She fucking shot me!"

Runstom ignored X's panicked tirade. He didn't much

care that Zarconi had shot him in cold blood. He cared a lot more that she almost hit Jax.

He looked down at the spent coilgun in her hand. He'd seen her pull it out during their escape from the prison. In the chaos, some part of him had blocked that from his memory. She'd been armed the whole time.

"Okay, you psycho," Jax said. He'd picked up the knife that X had dropped. Waved it in Zarconi's direction. "How about you drop that gun before someone else gets shot."

She smirked mirthlessly and tossed the spent weapon aside. "It only had one shot. And it only had one target. Were you afraid I'd waste it?"

"Stan," he said. "McManus needs medical attention."

Runstom could read the cross of anger and concern on Jax's face. It felt good to have someone sane in the room. Even if McManus was a terrible piece of shit, letting him die while they watched was not something either of them was willing to do.

"Where's the med bay, Jenna?"

"You don't want to stick around here, Stanford." She walked sideways, circling X. The red-skinned ex-cop watched her warily, on his knees, hand at his side where she'd put a hole in his ribcage. "Mark and I are staying," she said.

"We should arrest you both," Runstom said weakly. It was hard to put any feeling behind the empty threat.

"Of course you should," she said. "But you can't. The anti-aggression system won't let you take either of us by force."

"What do you expect me to do?"

She took her eyes off X for a moment to gaze at Runstom. "You did it. You helped me, and I helped you. We're rare, Stanford. We share the mark of outcasts. And we helped each other." She paused, her eyes dropping slightly. "I hate to say this, Stan, but we don't need each other anymore."

A churn passed through Runstom's stomach. He didn't want to be kin to Zarconi, but there was a certain truth to her words. There was no denying the rarity of their green-tinged skin bound them in some way. And yet, his reasons for bringing her along were not of some kind of twisted tribalism. He used her. It was only appropriate to find she was using him as well. His goal was to get Jax. Hers was to get X.

She could have used the coilgun on Runstom. Taken control of the ship. Gone her own way, whether it led to X or not. She could have had her freedom. But she didn't. In her mind, they had worked together. As friends, maybe.

"Jax," he said. "Let's get McManus out of here."

He hobbled to the slumped form that Jax hovered over. Then he locked eyes with the B-fourean.

"I hope this is the last time I have to thank you like this," Jax said.

Runstom felt his face betray a smile, despite the levity. "ModPol isn't after you." He nodded at the pacified X. "Only he was."

"Good," Jax said. "Because I'm pretty sure he was after you more than me."

He looked at his friend in silence, his smile fading. "Jax," he said.

"I tried to hold out," Jax said, his face dropping. "I tried so hard."

"It's okay," he said quickly. Whatever Jax had given up could wait for later. "It doesn't matter now."

Jax looked at Zarconi, his face tightening. "No, I suppose it doesn't."

She watched them with a calm patience as they hoisted the groaning McManus upright and slowly carried him from the room. Jax was beaten and weakened and Runstom's foot couldn't allow weight, but the gravity was only about a quarter G, so they managed. Either X had resigned to his fate, or he intended to sweet-talk Zarconi once they were gone. Runstom knew there was no possibility of changing her mind. A very small part of him wanted to stay to watch X fail to plead for his life. But suddenly, with Jax safe, there were more important problems in the universe waiting for attention.

"You won't see me again," she said as they drew close to the door. He looked back at her. A normal human being might be subject to a tearful parting. Regret. But he saw nothing of the sort on her face. Another kind of pain rippled there. "You understand, don't you Stan?" she asked softly.

"Good," Runstom said, growing colder. "I'm done with your games." He briefly looked down at the glowering face of X. "Both of you. And I've got—"

"Miles to go before you sleep."

He looked at her for the last time. Tried again to rewind everything back to the day he'd met her. If she hadn't been who she was, and he hadn't been who he was, what would that day have been like? A man walks into a bar. A woman's voice teases him about the green tint of his skin. He flares up, only to see she's even greener than he. She buys his next round. They talk about their mothers and fathers, about what they know and what they don't. She is lovely, dark and deep, and her eyes gleam with intelligence and mischief. He lets down a life-long guard.

A stupid dream. Runstom swallowed away the bliss-stained drama. Turned from her, dragging the sack-of-shit cop through the hatch, before the idiot bled out completely. Hesitated before the door closed her off forever.

A final look back.

And miles to go before I sleep.

CHAPTER 15

No one came to greet them when they got home. The ship Dava was on docked a few hours after the first couple of arrivals.

Half-Shot helped her bring in Moses's body. She knew he wouldn't have wanted her to take the trouble; the old man would have preferred to drift where he passed. But she wasn't ready to let go of him. Not until he was home.

Once there, they brought him in and Half-Shot went off in search of a shower. She thought about telling him to turn down the gravity in the center while he was at it. She drifted through the dock, but once she got further she knew it would be painful to feel the weight of her broken body.

Truth was, the fancy ModPol med bay had done a pretty good job. Her broken ribs were mended, any loose shrapnel had been extracted, and her lacerations were finely sealed. The bruising was left for her body to heal naturally. It hurt.

She stared at Moses's face, the rest of his body wrapped tightly in black plastic. Eyes closed. Somehow he'd managed to die with a goddamn smile. A frozen, unbreakable bliss.

Dava wanted to hit things, but her body wanted to sleep. She secured Moses in a cold-storage unit in the dock – they could have a ceremony later – and pulled herself through the hatch. The deeper in she went, the more she regretted bringing him here. Even coming back here. The halls were joylessly silent. Normally someone was on music duty, but the speakers spoke only a fine hiss of quiet static. Even the familiar scent of humans living in an enclosed space had faded into a stale, lifeless scent of memories passed.

It was no longer home.

She reached the hub and began the climb up to her quarters. As the gravity increased, it magnified her weariness. She slumped down the hall. Slowed to brush a hand against Thompson's door, then fell to one knee. She panted, and squeezed her eyes tight, grit her teeth. The tears came anyway, all at once in a short fury and then were gone. In seconds, she was empty. She stood and reached her door.

Was it ever home?

She sank into the bed and slept.

* * *

A few hours of sleep seemed to make the pain of healing worse, but she soon realized it just meant the drugs had worn off. Grimacing as she fought gravity to get out of her bunk, she decided the pharmacy would be her first destination. Then to the bar, where she could get a drink that was as caffeinated as it was alcoholic.

Only when she got to the rec level, the bars were all closed up. A couple of the lounges were open, but empty. Finally she came to a large one where about two dozen Wasters had gathered.

"Dava." Lucky Jerk approached her and held up a can. "You want this? I just opened it. The vendamatics are the only way to get grub around here."

"The shift schedule," she started, then decided she didn't even know what to ask. She took the can and slurped the sugary liquid.

"RJ and 2-Bit left a skeleton crew behind." Lucky turned to the small crowd and scanned for a moment, then spotted someone. "Toom-Toom, come 'ere a sec!"

A tall, athletic olive-skinned young man barely out of his teens strode to them. "Capo Dava," he said with a nod. "Good to have you back home, sir."

"Toom-Toom is 2-Bit's favorite cadet," Lucky said. That was why Dava recognized the young man: she's seen him with the captain. She gave Lucky a short nod and he turned back to the kid. "Tell the capo about the mission."

"They took the *Longhorn* to Barnard-5," Toom-Toom said, his eyes squinting serious as he recalled the details. "Loaded up with what fighters we had left after the Eridani mission. Took everyone he could. Left behind only enough of us to keep this place humming."

"That's not a large force," she said. After losing a couple dozen lives at Eridani, and a couple dozen more arrested. Then again, what force did he need?

"More new guys showed up," Toom-Toom said, interrupting her thoughts. "From that new alliance Boss Jansen made."

"The fucking Misters," Lucky Jerk said. Dava never had occasion to see true anger on the pilot's face except when the subject of the Misters came up. "I still can't believe RJ made a deal with the fucking Misters."

It was low, Dava agreed, but maybe worse than that, it

was desperate. Or maybe it was opportunistic. Two gangs, one stronger but currently weakened, and their rival, a poorly-led upstart. Jansen could play them together or against each other as he needed to fill his agenda. Whatever that was.

"What did he offer the Misters?" she said.

"Control of trade on Terroneous," Toom-Toom said. By *trade*, meaning the buying and selling of anything off-market, which for the Misters was mostly drugs. The market they tried to break into on their own, only to be disrupted by Space Waste. A disruption that Dava herself had a fairly large part in when she and a small team had smoked them out of their nest on the moon.

"You said they went to Barnard-5," she said. "To go after the Doomed ark?"

"Yep. Boss Jansen said it was critical to replenish our ranks, and the Earthlings would join us."

"How does he know?"

"Pressgang tactics," Lucky muttered. "That's how I ended up in the Misters back in the day. Ain't no way to raise a crew."

"No," Dava said. Space Waste was a criminal organization, a gang, all that was true. But it was also a family. Moses Down recruited, but never forced.

"Boss Jansen says they'll be vulnerable," Toom-Toom continued. "That they won't have jobs or money – except Earth money, which ain't no good – and they'll be homeless on Terroneous. Boss Jansen says—"

"Stop calling him that," Dava said.

Toom-Toom's face hung. He glanced at Lucky, who gave him a short nod. He continued in a quieter voice. "I'm sorry, Capo," he said. "It's just that – well, RJ is in charge, cuz of Moses getting arrested. And now Moses …"

"Toom-Toom, get the capo something to eat," Lucky said gently.

"Aye." Toom-Toom turned to leave, then paused and looked back. "Before I forget, Captain 2-Bit had a message for you, Capo Dava. He said to tell you he would be on the *Longhorn's* bridge, right there a'side RJ. He said to tell you he's there for Space Waste, just like always, from training to mission."

After this cryptic message, the young cadet strode off. "Not very bright, but not bad to look at," Dava said as he left. She looked at Lucky. "I think we can trust 2-Bit, but I don't get that message."

"From training to mission," Lucky said. After a moment of thought, he looked at her. "In training exercises, we always used an extra channel for anyone that was playing the other side. You know, so we could practice against each other. The other channel was encrypted with a different code so you couldn't hear each other."

"Could 2-Bit pick up this channel on the *Longhorn*?"

"Of course," Lucky said. "He'd have to decrypt it, but he's got all the keys."

"Any chance Jansen would pick it up?"

Lucky tilted his head in thought. "RJ never took part in trainings. Around Barnard-5 you're going to have lots of encrypted chatter on different frequencies. One more is just noise in the soup."

After a moment of quiet, she nodded in the direction of Toom-Toom. "He's really 2-Bit's favorite?"

Lucky's face dropped a little, and at first Dava took it to be envy. Then she realized it was a different kind of sadness. "His mother was one of the original Wasters. Rei Toomi. No father. Rei was already pregnant when she came to Space

Waste. Everyone says 2-Bit had a thing for her, but she didn't for him. She was lost in a raid when Toom-Toom was a couple years old. 2-Bit took care of him after that."

"I've seen him around." Dava knew 2-Bit saw himself as a father to all his pilots, so she hadn't picked up on a favorite. But 2-Bit had no children himself. It made sense to her that he would care extra for this orphaned boy of a woman he loved.

"Yep, since he learned to fly about two years ago, he's gone on every run with the Captain."

"Every run except this one," Dava said, realizing the significance as she said it. Which meant two things: that 2-Bit needed to leave this message for her, and picked the pilot he trusted the most to leave it with. And that he saw this as a bad mission, one that he did not expect to come back from. The risk was too great to bring along his favorite flyboy. To bring along the closest thing to his own son.

She took inventory of the room. She needed someone to talk to, someone she could trust. Someone who knew what to do. Lucky Jerk. Half-Shot. Seven-Pack. Johnny Eyeball. Freezer. People she trusted, but couldn't talk to. They'd listen, but they wouldn't lead.

They'd lost a few coming out of the prison. Polar Gary wouldn't leave the turret he'd commandeered and forced ModPol to take the whole thing out with a guided rocket. Thompson she saw shredded before her eyes. Jerrard and Moses cut to pieces mere meters before the safety of the getaway ship. A few others that didn't make it out. Adding to the losses from Eridani.

And of those that Jansen left behind, who was there? The older warriors, damaged and bitter. The young and inexperienced. Only enough hands to keep the lights on.

"Spread the word, Lucky," she said. "We're having a ceremony at the docks. One hour. I want everyone there."

* * *

As they gathered, she gave some time to ensure everyone was there. She saw Freezer and Johnny Eyeball and approached them.

"Still waiting on that payment, Johnny?" she said.

He grunted, and gave her his trademark angry wink, the effect of one damaged eye unable to close. "Lost the taste for it."

Freezer cleared his throat and leaned in to Dava. "He's been sober too long."

"There wasn't anything on the inside?"

The skinny hacker shrugged. "Homebrew drugs, but not alcohol. He only likes alcohol. And now, nothing."

She gave Eyeball a sideways glance. "What's wrong with him?"

"I woke up," Eyeball grunted.

The three words landed hard. "Freezer," she said, though she had her eyes on Eyeball. "Get me a headcount."

With a nod, he went off to circle the room. She and Eyeball stared at each other. He was one of her oldest mates; even fooled around a few times, though never got serious. She trusted him, but as she looked into his eyes, she could see something missing. Alcohol was an escape for him. He treated it like a purpose. Now he had none.

"Are you still with me?" she asked softly.

He looked away, then looked back. "Depends, I guess."

She nodded. It was the only answer she was looking for. She wanted to have to earn his hand. She didn't want to order anyone to come with her. She wanted them to volunteer.

She walked to the front where Half-Shot had pulled Moses back out of cold storage. His wraps were connected to a thin cable to keep him from drifting. She looked out across the dock. Wasters gripped poles and handholds all around the prep space. Conversing in low murmurs. Watching her.

Freezer floated to her. "Forty-two," he said. "That's every soul on the station. They're all here."

She held up a hand and waited for the murmuring to die down. "This is the body of Moses Down. We send it adrift today, not just to say goodbye to the man we loved and trusted, but to say goodbye to all the brothers and sisters whose bodies didn't make it back."

She let a moment of silence pass before she continued. "Moses Down saved my life," she said. "Did he save your life?"

The lot of them whooped in agreement, dying quickly back into silence.

"We owed him for that." Dava looked down at his body, the smile still on his face. "Owed. And we paid. We were loyal to the end of his days."

She turned back to them and locked eyes with as many as she could. "The Space Waste that saved us," she started, then pointed at the body. "*His* Space Waste ... is no more."

This generated a tense murmur, and she raised a hand to still it. "Moses had a purpose. And that purpose was to carve a place in this universe for the outcast. That purpose was to give the so-called perfect world a black eye. To remind them that though they tried to forget us, we're still here.

"And we did that," she said with a shout, and was

answered by a short cheer of agreement. "Goddamn if we didn't. But now we have to ask ourselves what Space Waste is for without him."

She paused again, to gather her busy thoughts and to make sure she had their attention. "Jansen," she said. "Is a traitor."

This caused no small commotion and Dava raised her hand again. "I'm not asking you to believe me, because I don't have the proof. But even if he wasn't. Look at what he's doing. Making a deal with the Misters, those pissants."

She paused to let the jeers pass. "And worse, going after an ark." She let a breath pass before continuing. "Innocent refugees from Earth. *I* was a refugee from Earth, and I came to Space Waste." She pointed at herself and raised her voice. "But it was my fucking choice! Jansen doesn't want to give these people a choice. He wants to pressgang them. To threaten. To exploit. Not to save! To en*slave*!"

An uncomfortable tension spread through the space. She left it to fester, to churn on its own. Some of the mumblings turned into shouting.

It was hard to make out where the emotions lay, until Johnny Eyeball's voice boomed above all. "Fuck Jansen."

Dava felt something open inside as the crowd shouted in agreement. She kept her face hard, but a new kind of joy was born in that moment. One of purpose.

"Tonight we say goodbye to Moses," she shouted, taking back control. They quieted and waited for her to continue. She looked down at him one more time. "And we say goodbye to his Space Waste."

Another moment of silence passed and when she was sure there was no disagreement, she continued. "I'm going after Jansen. I'm going to stop that bastard from hurting innocent people." She pointed out at them. "And you, my friends, my family; I'm taking you with me."

A murmur of agreement. She waited a few tense seconds to see if anyone might drift away, but all eyes remained on her. "We don't go under Moses Down," she said, putting a hand on the cold chest of the man she once would follow to the end of the universe. "We go under his shadow."

After a pause, Freezer spoke up. "The Shadowdown." He looked around, then to Dava. "We need a new name, right?"

"The Shadowdown," she repeated. To remember him, but to be something new. She had to admit, it had a ring to it. "Alright, motherfuckers. The Shadowdown be coming."

CHAPTER 16

Throwing a fit was one of Jax's all-time favorite pastimes, but he was having a severely difficult time of it in the gravityless hold of the ModPol patroller.

"Stan, please!"

Runstom was ignoring him. He'd already declared that he wasn't going to argue. Still, it burned Jax that there was no further discussion. Runstom busied himself with the preparation of a long flight with a few extra passengers in the cramped ship.

He was in the process of locking down a coffin-shaped receptacle. Jax floated to him and grabbed him by the forearm. "Stan! You can't take me to ModPol!"

The green-skinned man's arm tensed, causing Jax to reflexively release his grip. "I told you," Runstom said. "We're not going to a ModPol outpost. We're going to Ipo."

"To see your boss?" Jax said. "Aren't they ModPol?"

Runstom sighed and turned with a weary face. "Jax. I can't just drop you off somewhere. We're in a ModPol patroller. Believe it or not, I can't go where I please. If I try to land at a Terroneous shuttleport, there are all kinds of protocols. ModPol doesn't have any jurisdiction there."

"So?" Jax could feel his face burning. "Just land in the middle of the desert! That's how McManus got me. He didn't follow any fucking protocols."

Runstom took a measured breath. "McManus's stunt got the whole moon on high alert. If we try to land without permission, we're likely to get shot."

"You can tell them you're bringing me," Jax tried, thinking back to the news transmission Phonson had tortured him with. "They'll let you land if they know I'm with you."

Runstom stared at him quietly, then nodded briefly, then shook his head. "I can't risk it. We have to go to Ipo." He put a hand out and caught Jax, who had been slowly drifting away, and pulled him back in close. "It's Ipo. It's another moon of B-5. You can catch a civilian shuttle – they run between the moons all the time."

Jax looked away, letting himself go limp. He was tired. Strung out. Beaten down, physically and mentally. "A shuttle," he said quietly.

Runstom shook his arm lightly so that he would look up. "I'll do what I can, Jax. If I can, I'll get you there myself. Give you a ride from Ipo to Terroneous."

"If you can."

"Yes, if I can." Runstom let go with a small sigh. "I'm still bound by the rules. But trust me. I have more wiggle room than you think."

"Okay," Jax said. He reminded himself that his friend risked everything to come out to that hurtling death comet and rescue him from torture, and likely worse. He couldn't imagine anyone risking so much as Runstom had. And on top of that, to patiently wait out Jax's selfish tantrum. Jax allowed himself a half a smile. “Thanks, Stan. For everything.”

Runstom smiled back, then looked away. His drifting foot touched the floor, causing a small twitch.

“What did you do to your leg?”

Runstom frowned, and Jax read a distant anger on his face. Perhaps a frustration, not at Jax for asking, but at himself for this newly acquired weakness. “It got caught in a door,” he said.

Jax swallowed. “You mean … is it … was it … crushed by a door?”

“It’s not so bad when there’s no gravity,” he said. It was a weak attempt at humor, which just made Jax feel bad for him.

“I’m sorry, Stan.”

Runstom waved it off and nodded at the coffin-bed. “This one is for McManus. But there’s another one on the other side that you’re going into.”

Jax looked at it and felt himself flinch. “What, really? Can’t I ride in the bridge?”

“No. First of all, the control center of this patroller only seats three. Me and the pilot and the gunner from McManus’s ship.”

As if on cue, Ayliff and Granny floated into the bay. They were in their suits still, mainly for the microjets that made maneuvering in zero gravity easier. Even with Phonson under the watchful eye of that psycho woman, and the rest of his crew on lockdown throughout the comet-base, Runstom couldn’t be sure the threat of the bomb on McManus’s interstellar patroller was negated. He didn’t want to leave it behind either, of course. So Ayliff had set it up with a pre-programmed flight plan. Soon the ghost ship would set itself on a course for the nearest ModPol outpost. Maybe it would make it, maybe not. In any case, the pilot and the gunner had suited up and ferried what supplies they could from the larger ship to Runstom's smaller planet-hopper.

The last of their load was McManus himself, barely kept alive by an emergency kit they had onboard. Runstom pushed away from the wall, pulling Jax with him, to the opposite side. They watched as Granny and Ayliff maneuvered their sergeant into position on the bed. McManus was out cold from the kit's sedation, and they proceeded to strap him in.

"Second," Runstom said, tapping at some buttons on the wall. Jax slid to one side slightly as another coffin-bed began to unfold from out of nowhere. "You're beat to shit. Not much better off than McManus over there. And I know this doesn't look comfortable," he said, tapping at the stiff plastic form. "But it's functional. It's going to feed you and accelerate cell repair. And get you the sleep you need."

The words were like a drug, flushing through Jax's entire system with a wash of exhaustion. There was only so much fighting he could do before his body just collapsed and left him hanging adrift in the null grav. A massive yawn rose up and hijacked his body. "Yeah, I guess you're right."

Runstom continued to fiddle with the bed, which was looking less like an uninviting plastic coffin and more like a plush cloud of cushiony happiness. "Besides, I need you back at one hundred percent," he said.

Jax cocked a suspicious eyebrow. "Why is that?"

"We're not done." He held out a steadying hand. "I'll make sure you get to Terroneous, as soon as possible. I promise. But I still need your help."

As much as Jax wanted to disappear from the galaxy

altogether, the debt he owed to his friend was something he could not ignore. "This whole mess with Basil Roy."

"Tim Cazos."

"Right." Runstom had mentioned Roy's true identity, with a promise to fill in more details during the trip. "Whatever his name is. And I suppose whatever connection he had with Jansen."

Runstom nodded, glancing over his shoulder. "We'll talk more later," he said in a low voice. "After you get some rest."

* * *

Runstom wasn't much for fashion or decoration, but even he could tell that the furnishings in the temporary office were out of place. Most things on Ipo were made out of mudbrick and metal alloys. The small moon was little more than a single metropolitan dome surrounded by dozens of ore refineries, those in turn surrounded by docks, both on-ground and anchored above. For the Defense Services Trial, ModPol had been given open access to all docks, so he'd landed at the nearest. Then it was a tram ride that passed several refinery stops until arriving in Ipolopolis. The locals called it Shinerock City when they were feeling generous. Rocktown when less so.

"A missed opportunity," Jax had quipped during the rail ride in. "Should've called it Ipolopi – then it would be a palindrome."

It was some kind of earworm, a useless, stupid thought that Runstom couldn't get out of his head. He tried to distract himself by examining the out-of-place furniture. All of it, plastic with wood highlights. High-end fashion, imported from Terroneous. That was an assumption, he realized. Or was it a deduction? No plant life grew on Ipo. Nor was there any material production that wasn't metallic or mineral. Trees were fairly abundant on Terroneous. Plastic manufacturing was prevalent there. A deduction then. Based on observation. Bright-red plastic, molded into curving seats and tables, rimmed by marbled wood strips.

He sighed, closing his eyes to the sights of the room. They could not distract him from recent events. The facts. That he'd fled the scene of a terrible attack on a ModPol institution. That he'd facilitated the escape of a convicted murderer. That he'd failed to bring this same murderer back. That he instead allowed her to serve out some twisted vigilante justice. Her victim deserved what was coming to him. And clearly was immune to the proper kind of justice. So it was the only option.

He hated that option. Hated it because he couldn't disagree with it. Hated it because there was a time when he believed in something better.

He opened his eyes and scowled at the room once more. The decoration was the work of Victoria Horus, Director of Market Strategy Management for ModPol's Defense division and his direct supervisor. He'd come to understand that she spared nothing when it came to the appearances of her department. Despite the fact that he needed to rush to get there to make up for time lost on his excursion to Comet X – which included a stop on the way back to put McManus on an emergency shuttle to ModPol Outpost Gamma – Runstom had taken a detour to a shopping center to pick up clothes. It was better to be late and well-dressed than timely and wearing the tattered uniform of a penitentiary officer or one of the spare monochromatic jumpsuits stashed in the recesses of the patroller's meager storage bay. He'd left an entire wardrobe on the OrbitBurner, as the prisoner transport barge had allowed him only a single bag.

Thankfully a young sales clerk was all too delighted to dress him up in what she swore were the latest fashions. A spotted gray shirt. Brown slacks and jacket, but not a drab brown; more vibrant in a way he couldn't put his finger on. She'd insisted that it was the pairing with his "lovely olive skin" that made the outfit work so well. He was relieved to find that his line of company credit was still alive and fiercely kicking in the face of the minor extravagance.

The clerk had also noted the location of a nearby barber. The hint was not lost on Runstom, and so he'd dallied another hour for a shave and a cut.

"Stanford!"

He turned to Victoria Horus arriving only a few minutes late for the appointment he'd secured as soon as he'd landed. "Ms. Horus," he said with a nod.

She beamed at him with a genuine smile. "I told you to call me Big Vicky, like everyone else!" She reached out to shake his hand in a single, warm, up-and-down motion. She leaned back. "You look absolutely *fantastic*, Stanford."

He detected pride in her compliment. The tiny cluster of braincells that was catching onto the ways of marketing and sales struggled to take over. "You look well too." After a hesitation, he glanced around the office. "Did you decorate this office?"

Again he was rewarded with a genuine, prideful smile. "I certainly did," she said with a knowing nod.

"It's quite," Runstom started, then faltered. He scanned his brain for words that rarely came into his vocabulary. "Striking."

She jabbed at him with a playful poke. "Thank you! I really love it. It's very authentic," she said as she shuffled past him, heading to a chair on the other side of a red plastic and deep brown wood table that he realized functioned as her desk.

"Authentic?" he said, then wished he hadn't. He hadn't wanted to challenge her, he was actually lost on her meaning.

"Well, not for Ipo, of course," she said with a dismissive wave. "No one on Ipo wants to *be* on Ipo. They all want to be on Terroneous."

"I see," Runstom said. He debated on whether to overtly agree with her, or whether to wait and let her dispense further insights. But he was tired. Weary. And this hastily fashionable office was a few light-years from her real office on Sirius-5. "What are you—"

"Oh, I forgot," she said. Her face crinkled with concern. "How is your foot?"

Runstom winced, though he couldn't feel the pain any more. The Onsite Rapid Defense Unit stationed on Ipo had a medic who gave him some kind of field dressing. An implant that regulated pain suppressant to the local area. And a special boot to keep what was left from moving around. "It's fine."

"I heard you'll need surgery."

"Yes." He'd been trying not to think about it. "To replace parts of it."

She frowned sympathetically. "We'll make sure you get some paid time off for that. And for vacation, not just for surgery. You'll have earned some time off."

Her tone told him this time off wasn't coming immediately. That there were other things to deal with first.

"So," he said, looking at his hands, then back at her. "What brings you to Ipo, uh, Vicky?"

She dropped into the chair with a satisfied sigh. "God I love the gravity here." After situating a few items on the surface of her desk, she looked at him again. "You're doing a fantastic job, Stanford," she said. "I want you to know I'm not here to check up on you."

"Uh." There were too many questions in his head. Hadn't been room to wonder if his boss was checking up on him. But the question was planted. "You asked me about my foot, but you didn't ask me about the riot."

She smirked. "Or why you were even at that prison," she said. She waved and smiled. "I'm not much for micro-management, Stanford. I like it when my people take initiative. It's true: I expected you to stay on EE-3 until the next interstellar flight back to Barnard. But I figure someone like you has some contacts in Justice. It's only natural to find ways to keep those intact. Networking is a big part of your job."

Runstom stared at her silently, waiting for a reprimand that would never come. He forced a smile. "I thought it would be a shorter trip. I wasn't expecting to get caught in a riot."

She laughed, loud and short. "I'm just glad you made it out in one piece. And you made it here."

He had a hard time keeping the smile going. "Yeah. Here."

"There are a number of pieces moving in an organization like ours, Stanford." She leaned forward and motioned for him to sit. "This part of the galaxy is *critically important* to the success of ModPol."

"Terroneous," he said by way of acknowledgement as he sat down. The tiny mining colonies of Ipo had value as potential customers, but more value in the proximity to their neighbor-moon. It was Horus's strategy: if ModPol Defense impressed Ipo, it would improve future talks with governments on Terroneous. And Terroneous was a major prize. Fractured into many disparate city-states. Many individual contracts to negotiate.

She watched him for a moment, as though waiting to see if he had more to add. He didn't. "What's your opinion of ModPol as an organization, overall?" she asked.

Runstom blinked, surprised by the question. "It's necessary." When put on the spot, he found himself falling back to long-ingrained values. "Modern societies shouldn't have to manage judicial and defensive services themselves." Listening to himself, he thought he sounded like an advertisement.

"Yes, of course," she said. "But from the inside, Stanford: how well does the ModPol operate, would you say?"

He shifted uncomfortably in the plastic-wood chair. "Fair." He lifted his chest. "There are pockets of corruption. And trust issues. But overall, it's ... effective."

She nodded slowly. "Yes. That's good. Very honest." She paused, then pointed at him. "Now you've worked in both Justice and Defense. How do you feel the two arms work together?"

He frowned. "It's not a secret that they don't cooperate." His voice trailed off as he remembered X's rant. About how Justice established a mole inside Space Waste, and how they allowed Defense to leverage the insider. "But I think that's just an impression."

She smiled widely. "A common misperception?"

He chewed on that. "Yeah."

"The truth is, these two halves of the whole have very different agendas and goals. We are united by one vision, but our paths differ." She let that sink in, then continued. "And that's okay. But we *do* work together. Our cooperation is just not as visible as our friction."

Again, X was in his head. He didn't know what to say. He wanted to probe, to find out if what the ex-cop was ranting about was true. Then there was a chime and Horus touched a screen on her desk.

She stood and looked at the door. Reflexively, Runstom followed suit.

The door slid away and a tall, broad-shouldered, beige-skinned man stepped in. Runstom recognized him right away, though he'd never met him in person. Francois Newman, the chief operating officer of Modern Policing and Peacekeeping. The low gravity of Ipo did not hide his telltale limp, reportedly a war injury that never completely healed. His hair was completely white, in contrast to the salt-and-pepper images Runstom was used to seeing attached to company-wide operations reports.

It was well known that Newman had served in the military; back when the colonies still had their own militaries. Not much of what happened in those days made it into official recorded history. Even in his mid-sixties, Runstom thought the man's stature was impressive. As he stepped forward, he blotted out the lamp in the corner, shrouding the room in shadow. Beneath the solid, charcoal-grey suit of fine cloth, taut muscles revealed themselves when he stretched out his large hand.

"Stanford Runstom?" he said. "I'm Franco Newman. It's a pleasure to meet you."

After a long second, Runstom broke from his paralysis. Took the proffered hand and relished the strength behind the grip. "The pleasure is mine, sir."

Newman crooked half a smile. "I like it when a subordinate calls me 'sir'. But today, I want you to call me Franco."

Runstom nodded, opening then closing his mouth. Under the gaze of the man's hard blue eyes, he felt uneasy. The invitation to use his first name wasn't like Horus's insistence on friendly familiarity. For some reason with Newman, it felt like the familiarity of collusion.

He bent with a small grunt and sat in the other chair that faced Horus's desk. She sat as well, with a look at Runstom to tell him to do the same. She and Newman hadn't even greeted each other. Which told Runstom this wasn't the first meeting they'd had today.

"Are you familiar with *The Art of War*?" Newman said as Runstom sat. Runstom wasn't, but before he could answer, Newman went on. "It's a very old book written by a great Chinese general named Sun Tzu. From the fifth century BCE – but it got popular again in the twentieth century. Not just in military circles, but with business strategists. They saw an allegory between battlefields and markets."

"I'll make sure to send you a copy," Horus cut in.

Newman waved a hand. "Don't feel pressure to read it, Stan. It's required reading for all executives – among other things," he said with a knowing glance at Horus. She returned it with a sheepish smile, but before she could say anything, he went on. "In fact it's not even the most important piece of literature on our list. But it's relevant to our discussion.

"See, *The Art of War*, a lot of it is about how to play to your strengths, and how to adapt to your weaknesses. How to leverage advantages, how to avoid disadvantages. *Deception* is a common theme. Fighting a battle is much more than the actual clashing of swords or exchange of laserfire."

He leaned into the corner of his chair, drawing slightly closer to Runstom. "For example. One tactic can be summed up as, 'When you are weak, appear strong. When you are strong, appear weak.'"

He paused, as though expecting a reaction. Runstom cleared his throat. "I think I understand, sir. Mr. Newman."

"Franco."

"Franco."

Newman regarded him with apparent patience, then cracked a smile. He pointed at Runstom. "You employed this tactic on Vulca, Stan."

Runstom felt his head pull back in a reflexive retreat. "I—" he started, then swallowed. Vulca. Largest moon of Sirius-5. Site of Vulca City. Site of the Vulca Research Park. Runstom there in his role in public relations. A ModPol Onsite Rapid Defense Unit had also been stationed there. A *trial* unit. Very small, but it was a small property. Still, it had been valuable enough for Space Waste to attack. Specifically, they'd gone after the observatory, well outside of town. Apparently to steal equipment.

He tried to replay Newman's words in his head, but they slipped away. "Tell me about what happened that day," Newman said.

Runstom frowned. "Space Waste attacked. A sneak attack. They hit a power station and the observatory."

"The power station," the COO interrupted. "Why did they strike there first?"

Runstom shook his head. "We thought they were going after the city."

"Don't say *we*, Stan. It was the unit's leadership that believed that Space Waste was threatening the city and the people within." He pointed at Runstom again. "You knew there was more to it than that. This is another page from *The Art of War*. Space Waste was manipulating their enemy by threatening that which they hold most dear: the lives of their potential customers. The ORDU became preoccupied and the city went on lockdown."

Runstom had rolled the events of that day around his mind over and over. Always feeling that he never quite fully understood. Whose plan was what. Space Waste's erratic attack. The cloaked intelligence the unit had received; the intel Runstom was not privy to. The intel that seemed to hurt more than help. The commander of the unit, Captain Lucy J. Oliver, how she seemed to be as clueless as he. Together they had shared a quiet distrust of the shadowy motivations behind the orders they were compelled to follow.

There was more to it than Runstom knew – would ever know. The *art* behind the attack and its defense.

"What did you do?" Newman prompted.

Runstom drew a breath. "Only a couple of Defenders were left when the rest went on patrol. Not enough to take to the observatory and repel the Wasters." He hesitated; publicly, he'd been praised for his actions on Vulca. His superiors were happy with the result. But he'd been waiting for someone to come down on him for the unauthorized actions he'd taken. Newman and Horus looked at him, both exuding patience. "So I went into town. Rounded up whoever I could." He made a fumbling gesture with his hand, trying to coax the words out. "There were people there who were willing to … protect themselves. Protect the observatory."

Newman smiled. "Protect their friends and family," he said, nodding. "Compared to the Space Waste force, was your little posse stronger? Or weaker?"

"Weaker." Runstom's guts drained away as he answered.

"When you are weak, appear strong."

Runstom thought back to that day on Vulca. He'd only managed to secure a dozen or so vehicles, but he made sure to spread them out. And what few weapons the Defenders had, he'd distributed, favoring the loudest and brightest munitions. "We made a lot of noise. Kicked up a lot of dust."

"And you ran off the Wasters," Horus said. "A brilliant tactic." She looked at Newman as she said this, perhaps hopeful that he would back up her praise.

"I put innocent lives in danger," Runstom said coldly.

"You *saved* innocent lives." Newman locked his gaze with Runstom and held it for a moment.

Runstom nodded slowly. "Yes."

"In fact," the older man said, breaking the gaze to glare at Horus, "we're lucky that we landed the account in the end."

The office fell into silence, under a spell cast by the chief operating officer. Horus was frozen, wanting to speak but unable to. Runstom could feel the words just inside her throat, unable to escape. He knew this because his throat was locked in the same way. There would be no more speaking until the three of them understood the unspoken.

Runstom suddenly wished he had read the war book Newman had spoken of. As though within the ancient texts, insights would be revealed. All the plans and machinations of ModPol would come to light. Instead, he had only what little Newman had said. Using advantages, avoiding disadvantages. Deception. Knowing what the enemy holds dear.

And that these strategies went for the market as well as the battlefield. On Vulca, the enemy on the battlefield was

Space Waste. So who was the enemy in the market? ModPol was trying to sell defense services. They had no competition. He scolded himself. Of course they had competition: the status quo. Local defense.

He'd saved lives that day. The unspoken was that some of those lives were not meant to be saved. In that market, the enemy was the customer. The Wasters were never going to attack Vulca City directly, but if he hadn't run them out of the observatory, it was likely they would have taken lives there. More than they had. And with the small Onsite Rapid Defense Unit – the "trial" force – defending the power station, the *enemy* – the people of Vulca – would see that they were weak, that ModPol was strong, and that the galaxy was a damned dangerous place.

The intel. Had ModPol known that the attack was coming? Had the orders to send the ORDU on patrol been designed to provide the perfect balance of threat, bloodshed, and defense?

Runstom felt like he wanted to crawl out of his own skin. He wasn't supposed to do anything that day. He was supposed to get locked down like the rest of the town. To quake with fear along with the residents. To mourn their losses. And then to sell them on defense services, so that something so terrible would never happen again.

"No one blames you for what you did, Stan," Newman said. In an instant, he released the tension in the room with a smile. "You were underestimated. *The Art of War* teaches us that the general who advances without courting fame and retreats without fearing disgrace, whose only thought is to protect his people and do service for his organization, is a *jewel of the kingdom.*"

Runstom felt his flesh rise at the praise. A mixture of

pride and disgust flooded his nerves with electricity. "That's ... I ... I don't know what to say."

"Of course, we always knew you were an asset, Stan," Horus said. "I have to admit, part of the reason we made you a public relations officer was because we didn't know how to use your talents here." She laughed with a small bounce. "We didn't even really know what those talents were! We just knew we needed to get you out there."

"When you are weak, appear strong," Runstom said aloud, this new earworm stuck in his head. "And when you are strong, appear weak?" He looked up at Newman.

The chief operating officer nodded. "You're thinking about Eridani."

The ModPol transport ship had Xarped into Eridani. Appeared poorly defended. An irresistible plunder for Space Waste. Yet ... a trap. A battalion of Defenders hiding in the storage bays. A squadron of fighters hiding among a field of asteroids. A major blow to the Wasters, so many of them captured and sent to the zero-G prison. And a victory for the market, newly born on EE-3.

"How did you get the Wasters to take the bait?" Runstom heard the words coming out of his own mouth. Detached.

"An insider, naturally," Newman said. As though espionage and misinformation were just pieces on the board, as ordinary as any soldier or weapon. He glanced at Horus.

"Now, Stan." She stiffened as she talked. Another rare moment of uncertainty for the woman who preferred to be called Big Vicky. "I just have to remind you that anything said in this office is of the highest confidentiality." She glanced at Newman, then back at Stanford. "The *highest*. This information doesn't leave this room."

Runstom wanted to laugh, but instead held his breath.

After a moment, he blew it out in mock seriousness that he hoped was well covered. "Yes, Vicky. Understood."

"His name is Tim Cazos," Newman said. Again Runstom held his breath, but this time to keep from gasping or shouting. "He was implanted inside Space Waste in the guise of a 'hacker'." The chief operating officer actually employed air quotes around the last word.

"Tim Cazos," Runstom repeated robotically. "As a hacker."

"Cazos lead the Wasters to the spot of the ambush." Newman paused, as though to let that information sink in. Then he added, "It's thanks to Cazos that we were able to capture so many. Including their leader, Moses Down."

Runstom wanted to steady himself against the plastic and wood table, but feared if he moved even a millimeter he might vomit. "Lead them?"

Newman nodded. "As you know, the detection equipment that the Wasters managed to steal from Vulca was the outdated stuff they were getting ready to toss. They didn't realize it, because their sole tech expert was apprehended during the raid. So when we implanted Cazos, we had him fake an interface that would mock out the use of the old equipment."

"Highest confidentiality," Horus repeated.

"Of course," Runstom said with a nod, his mouth on autopilot. He thought he should try to look surprised at the revelations pouring forth from his superiors, but he couldn't remember what surprise was supposed to look like.

"We're getting ready for another move," Newman said. "With Cazos."

Runstom practically chomped down on his tongue. A move. *With Cazos*. The name of the corpse that he'd found in the cold storage on his OrbitBurner. The same corpse that Runstom had ejected outside of EE-3, the corpse that evaporated into dust as it dropped through the planet's atmosphere. Was it some kind of test? Were they even aware that Cazos was dead? Did they want to see if he knew? Or did they even care?

"We want you to be ready," Horus said.

Runstom swallowed. Another move. "I'll be ready." He looked from one to the other. "You can't give me any more information," he guessed.

Newman smiled and stood. "Thanks for your time today, Stan." He nodded at Horus. At the door, he turned to Runstom. "Your mother would be proud."

Runstom flinched, but Newman was already out the door. He turned to Horus. The Sirius-Fiver was already at her pad, tapping something out. "I have your next assignment, Stan."

He took a breath. She had changed the subject without warning. His next *PR* assignment. Not this business with the secret spy whom she may or may not know to be long dead. That would wait. "Okay," he said.

"You came into port with Jack Jackson," she said. Her voice was stern, but she spread her mouth into a wide smile. "I don't want to know."

"Know what?"

"Exactly." She waved a hand. "ModPol Justice. Those fuckers can't do a damn thing right. He was on the run. Someone tries to pick him up. Not officially, of course. I figure those jackasses thought they could cover up their mistakes if they made him disappear. Unfortunately for them, Jackson made friends on Terroneous."

"Vicky," Runstom started.

Again she waved. "Like I said: I don't want to know. Wherever he was, however you found him – maybe you always knew, who cares? Point is, he's here now. He's with you, and he's safe. We want to keep it that way, right?"

"I want him to be safe."

"And he wants to go live with his friends on Terroneous." She leaned on her elbows, spreading the fingers of both hands upward. "This is perfect, Stan. We need an in with the FSC."

"Uh, the eff ...?"

"The Federated Security Committee. It's the closest thing that passes for a central body on Terroneous."

Runstom had a vague recollection of this committee from the broadcasts that he'd seen. "They were demanding Jackson's return."

"Exactly," Horus said with a smile. She pointed at him. "And you're going to return him. Because you – and by you, I mean we, and by we, I mean ModPol Defense – *rescued* him."

"ModPol Defense."

She flapped one of her large hands. "I know, I know, it should just be all of ModPol. But trust me, Justice has few friends on Terroneous. We need to get a foothold with Defense there first. If we can earn their trust, then we can start working on Justice. But Defense is a planet-wide service. Moon-wide service. Whatever. Justice has to go state to state, township to township. None of the local governments are unified. The FSC is the closest they have to a global alliance."

"So, Jackson ... you want me to ... present him?"

"That's right," she said. "We've made arrangements for an important meeting. We haven't informed them yet of what it's about, but we will soon. We'll want them to get as much media coverage as they can. Remember, Stan: you are a public relations officer." She smiled in a way that was probably meant to be disarming, but only made Runstom more nervous. "And you're good at it. Just be yourself."

Runstom shifted in his chair. It didn't seem right, to use the whole mess for publicity. He just wanted to get Jax back to his people. To his home. To his life.

"And like I said." Horus turned both her palms up. "I don't want to know."

And that was it. Runstom sat back in his chair. The offer was before him. His boss would look past the complications of Jax's recovery – which Runstom didn't want to enumerate, even in his head – so long as they used his return for a little PR boost.

He forced a smile to match hers. "Of course, Vicky. I look forward to meeting the FSC."

* * *

Jax thought he might be the happiest he'd ever felt in his life. The couches in the shuttle were the most comfortable he'd ever sunken into. The gravity was dialed up just enough to keep him from flying around. And he was going home.

He beamed at Runstom, the only other occupant of the passenger bay. "Thank you, Stan," he said for about the thousandth time.

Runstom smiled back. "Of course."

The shuttle wasn't civilian, but instead a special non-military vessel that apparently belonged to the marketing department of ModPol Defense. Runstom had explained that this was best for approaching Terroneous, and that the vessel had even been inspected by a third party on Ipo. It was enough to satisfy the Federated Security Committee, not only in terms of being non-threatening, but as a method of arriving at a meeting with them.

"So, Stan – this meeting with the FSC." Jax had limited dealings with them during the magnetic sensor catastrophe only months earlier. They seemed like an uptight bunch. After all, they were a committee with no funding and no power and tons of responsibility. He wanted to probe without probing. "Are you nervous?"

Runstom looked at him like he hadn't considered the possibility of being nervous until it was presented, and then it was all he could think about. "I'm glad to be bringing you back," he said. His previous smile vanished so thoroughly, Jax wondered if he'd imagined it. "But there's a lot more at stake now."

Jax allowed his own smile to die off momentarily. He suspected there was more to this generous shuttle ride than getting him home. "I guess ModPol is still trying to get their hooks – er, I mean services – into Terroneous."

Runstom nodded. "Sorry that we're using your return as an in," he said after a moment of hesitation.

Jax waved it off. "No, no, I get it. I don't care at all really. I'm just so glad it's all over. Turning this into publicity means they're making it official that ModPol doesn't have an interest in me."

"Yeah, that's true."

Well, it was mostly true, Jax knew. This was a gesture instigated by Runstom's current department, Defense. As far as Terroneous – and the rest of the galaxy – was concerned, it would represent the will of the entire ModPol organization. However, there were probably still a number of hurt feelings in Runstom's old department, Justice. But with the public display of Jax's return to Terroneous, the angsty cops would have to get over it. From Runstom's description of what happened at the zero-G prison, it sounded like they had bigger things to worry about.

"How is this whole public relations job working for you?" Jax asked with genuine interest. He'd been curious ever since Runstom got transferred.

The ex-cop's face wrinkled slightly. "It's not really my thing. But they keep telling me I'm doing a good job. I guess ..." he started, then stared off into space.

"Guess what?"

"Oh," he said. "I guess they think people think I'm honest."

"You *are* honest, Stan." Jax laughed. "Like the most honest person I know."

This caused Runstom's face to darken into a glare, a mix of anger and pain. "It's not an honest job."

Jax felt goosebumps rise on his skin despite the perfectly regulated temperature of the high-tech passenger bay. He cleared his throat and lowered his voice. "Stan. You can always talk to me, you know." There were so many things only between the two of them. He knew Runstom knew that.

Runstom blew out a sigh. "Yeah, I know." He went quiet and Jax waited, seeing him collect his thoughts together. Finally, he leaned in closer. "I don't know exactly what's going to happen."

This caused Jax to flush with electric fear. "*Something* is going to happen?" He looked around, then back at Runstom. "On Terroneous?" he whispered.

"I don't know," Runstom said. "What I know is that my bosses – they told me about Tim Cazos."

"Basil Roy," Jax said to himself. He grimaced at the thought of the cold body of the Space Waste programmer, the horrific gash across his throat. "Wait, they told you what about him?"

"That he was a mole," he said. "*Is* a mole, according to them. Though to be honest, Jenna told me a lot more about Cazos than anyone else."

"So they think he's still alive," Jax whispered. He suddenly felt very paranoid about having this discussion on a ModPol shuttle, even if it was non-military.

"I don't know if they think that or not." Runstom's words made Jax believe the man had gotten better at taking nothing at face value. "They want me to think he's alive. That he's still operating under cover with Space Waste."

Jax frowned. "Why?" A second of silence passed, and he knew Runstom wouldn't answer what he didn't know. "What else is there?"

Runstom looked to one side, seeing something invisible, thinking. "Well," he said. "Ipo is a low-value customer. ModPol is obviously only interested because of the proximity to Terroneous. That's the high-value customer."

"Also doesn't really seem like anyone would attack Ipo, does it?" Jax said. "I'm sure there's valuable stuff there, like mined metals and whatnot. But what good is it unless you have a factory to sell it to?"

Runstom nodded. "You noticed how much firepower is hanging around the ports. The one we went into and the other port we flew out of."

"Yeah, both were full of those soldiers. Defenders?"

"Yes. Officially, it's only what they call a trial unit."

Jax huffed. "Some trial."

"Much bigger than the trial unit I saw at Vulca," Runstom

said. "They're claiming that numbers are doubled right now because of a massive shift rollover. But even doubled." He looked off again, then looked back at Jax. "There's a goddamn army there."

The conversations Jax was forced to have with Phonson ate at the edges of his mind. He'd been blocking them out, pushing aside the terror and the pain so that he could face his future with *some* kind of hope. So that he could face Lealina without breaking down into a blubbering mess.

"All that stuff Phonson was talking about," Jax said softly. "About Defense and Justice working together. About Jansen. How Jansen is in control of Space Waste now."

Runstom looked ill, his face pale. "Yeah," he said wearily. The revelation wasn't coming to him, it had been with him. He was only just accepting it in that moment. "I should have questioned them about that. My boss. My boss's boss. They gave me a taste of trust by telling me about Cazos. But it's ..." he trailed off, shaking his head.

"Stale data," Jax said.

He looked up. "Yes," Runstom said, cracking a mirthless smile. "Stale data. But it's still a message."

"Right." Jax turned it over in his head. They wanted Runstom to know that they had an insider. If they wanted him to know, it was because they wanted him to be ready. But ready for what? "Would they use Space Waste to attack Ipo?"

"It's possible," Runstom said. "If they've had this Jansen inside, they must have used him to encourage the attack on Vulca. An attack on Ipo would probably scare people on Terroneous. And if ModPol repelled the attack ..."

"Then it's like free advertising," Jax said. "Well, not really free, but ... you know what I mean."

"Yes."

Jax was about to open his mouth to ask more questions when the cabin was peppered with soft flashing lights. An evenly-toned robotic voice told them to secure their restraints. They were on their final approach to the orbital dock. They had arrived at Terroneous.

Jax was home.

CHAPTER 17

The Wasters had hastily gutted the ModPol ships taken from the zero-G prison. *No, not Wasters*, Dava reminded herself. They were no longer Space Waste.

Their entire fleet was seven ships. Two black marias, prisoner tubes yanked out and replaced by jury-rigged harnesses and weapon racks. A personnel transport that needed some modifications. A cargo transport that they loaded up with a few hands plus their largest guns, including a heavy shell-throwing beast with a hover-base under it; which Dava couldn't see a use for except in a ground engagement, but Johnny Eyeball insisted on bringing it anyway. And finally, three fighter ships, two of which were abandoned Space Waste fighters – repurposed, heavily customized military tech – and one ModPol patroller that was small and light enough to maneuver well, on which one of the weapons experts dialed up the laser modulators well past the safe levels that were standard for ModPol.

Three fighters weren't enough to take on the *Longhorn* with its defensive batteries keeping anyone from getting close and a handful of fighters docked in its combat bays, but they were *something* to protect the four transports. Still, Dava didn't have much of a plan. She talked to a number of her people, and no one had anything intelligent to contribute. Strategies ranged from "ramming speed" to "flying circles around them until they run out of ammo". Her personal preference would be to use the fighters to distract long enough to breach-and-board with a couple of the transports. She was certain that if she could step foot on the *Longhorn*, she could murder her way to Jansen.

As it was, their best and only real hope was Captain 2-Bit.

This was the reason for sitting so far back. They were within striking distance if they went full-throttle on all warp engines, but not close enough to be identified. If detected, the *Longhorn* crew would only see them as just a bunch of random ships. In the space between Barnard-5 and Barnard-7, they wouldn't be anything to worry about.

Though if Jansen had any tactical sense, he'd order his crew to take a closer look at *anyone* coming within a light-hour of his command ship. The best way to do that would be to send a pair of fighters out if anyone got too close. But Jansen wasn't military. Dava could guess that from the missions she'd seen him take part in. He was a sneaky bastard, and smart as hell, but he didn't know shit about real war. He'd be leaning on 2-Bit for tactics. And she knew 2-Bit was going to be less help than normal.

All forty-two that watched Moses jettison from the dock at the Space Waste base were onboard one of the seven ships. How many loyalists did Jansen have? How many Misters had he recruited? According to Toom-Toom, the loyalists numbered less than two dozen. The Misters however were harder to pin down. There'd been about ten of them that showed up to board the *Longhorn*, but everyone knew there were more of them out there, scattered around the system, hiding in the corners.

They'd reached a point inside a light-hour away. Dava had Lucky try the rogue training channel.

"Message sent," Lucky said. "If he responds right away, it'll be ... one-hundred and twelve minutes for the round trip. Give or take."

So they waited. The initial message was only a greeting. Something safe, something to let 2-Bit know they were out there. She knew he was risking his life. She knew he was willing to do what it took to stop Jansen. But he couldn't do it alone. And he had to know he was doing it for *something*.

They were in one of the black marias. Dava would have preferred to sit in a Space Waste ship, as it would increase her chances of getting closer, but they only had the two old fighters. Of course, Lucky Jerk would have preferred a fighter too, but she'd brought him long because she wanted her best pilot with her. And just for the hell of it, she brought the young Toom-Toom to be his co-pilot.

Maybe it was better this way. She would have to face Jansen straight on. United together with her crew.

"Captain 2-Bit's reply is coming through," Lucky said, breaking a long silence.

"Play it," she said.

The recording came through as a robotic voice. He must have typed it out rather than risk speaking out loud.

Hey everyone. 2-Bit here. Backchannel working beautifully. So glad to hear you're out there. Don't have a lot of friends here. My boys will follow my orders, but they'll follow RJ's too. Waiting for your call. Squadron Whiskey out.

"Now what?" Toom-Toom said after the uncomfortable silence that followed.

"We have to tell him everything," Dava said. "About Moses. About Basil Roy. About Jansen."

She had already drafted a message in the waiting hours and minutes since they sent the first greeting. She had laid it all out. Wanted 2-Bit to have all the information. And then she wanted to know what he could do.

"It came through clean?" she said to Lucky as she re-read his message, then re-read her planned response.

"Yeah, the encryption is good," the pilot said. His voice had a question in it.

"We have to be sure, Lucky."

He turned suddenly to face her. "Wait, wait. He said 'Squadron Whiskey'."

"What does that mean?"

"Yeah!" Toom-Toom broke in. "In training, Whiskey is for the good guys. For Waster."

"And the rogue team is Squadron Romeo," Lucky said.

She rolled the names around in her head. "So we used the Romeo channel and encryption," she said. "But he signed it Whiskey."

They both nodded silently at her. It was suddenly clear what it meant: 2-Bit was compromised. What wasn't clear was how. The message wasn't his voice, so there was no way to verify he even wrote it. But the mention of Squadron Whiskey wasn't something that Jansen would say. Only 2-Bit and his pilots would use those words. That left the other possibility: that 2-Bit wrote the message, but knew it was being read. Which meant he was playing along, but left them a clue so they would know it wasn't a secure channel.

She looked at her message. How badly she wanted to let him know that Moses was lost. That Space Waste was lost. But she had to assume the message would be read.

The words came out of her before she could thoroughly think it through. "Send this," she said, flashing the message over to Lucky.

Captain 2-Bit: we lost Moses. We want to rejoin the ranks, but are afraid RJ will fire on us. Dava feels a duty to be there to greet the Earth kin. Can you convince RJ to let us board?

Lucky sent it without question. "What's next, Boss?"

There was no way Jansen would let them dock with the *Longhorn*. Her request was only made to force some kind of response. "Do you have the projected trajectory of the ark?"

"Of course. It's all over the public traffic channels. Right now, they're in the first stage of deceleration around B-7. Then there's a planned trajectory to head for B-5 at subwarp."

"I want to get closer to the *Longhorn*, but I want to approach between it and the ark."

"Well that's no problem," Lucky said, pulling up a map. "The *Longhorn* is already well past B-7, on a course for B-5. We're not far from B-7 now."

"Can't we just intercept the ark now?"

Lucky shook his head. "Nah, these old arks – they don't have the grav-manifolders that modern ships have. It's dangerous to get near them until they slow down the long way. Even when they get down to subwarp; sure, we could match their speed, but then what? Trying to board at that speed is suicide. Even the smallest speck of space dust is like a nuclear-powered bullet."

She frowned at the map. "So what's his plan?" she thought aloud.

"Well, the ark is going to orbit B-5," Toom-Toom said. She looked at him and he shrugged. "Like Lucky said, it's all in the public traffic channels. I guess they wanted to let people know because it's such an old ship, and they don't want anyone interfering with it."

"Okay," she said. "It's supposed to hit B-5's orbit. Then what will it do?"

"A few passes of B-5, then it peels off to orbit Terroneous. Eventually, it will match orbit with one of the orbital docks."

Dava could remember it. That moment some fifteen years ago. Was it more? She'd stopped counting. The sleep-sickness was terrible. Pain through her whole body as the nervous system woke up. Nausea that seemed to run through her bones, and nothing in the stomach to evacuate, no matter how hard it tried. Calling out for her mother and father despite how her throat felt like a fire had raged through it.

And then they told her: her parents had been ejected. They'd brought old-world sickness with them, and they were not fit for the new world. They'd have died anyway – that's what she was told. She'd gone to sleep rescued, awakened an orphan.

If the last ark was decelerating, then in that moment the sleep tubes were cycling. By the time the vessel reached the orbital dock at Terroneous, everyone would be awake. They probably wouldn't be able to dock – Dava remembered that. The Earth ship's tech was incompatible with colonial tech. So they'd have to hold orbit and ferry the passengers back and forth in shuttles.

Is that where Jansen would strike? Try to intercept the ferries? The Terroneous orbital docks had minimal defensive capabilities; and even so, they wouldn't risk using them if innocent lives could be caught in the crossfire. But he wouldn't be able to get to them all that way. There would only be a few ferries in flight at a time. He'd be able to grab one, then the rest would flee. No, the only attack that made sense was to board the ark directly. But the only flight-worthy raiders that Space Waste had were lost in the Eridani mission. Dava's team had done a full inventory and checked the logs at the base, and the only ships that left were the *Longhorn* and half a dozen fightercraft. The fighters could board the ark; there wouldn't be much in terms of security forces on board. They wouldn't be able to grab more than a few people, as the fighters had very little hold space. They could hijack the whole vessel, but then what? The thing would have exhausted its main tanks making the six-light-year trek from Earth.

Dava sighed in frustration. She needed more information from 2-Bit. She felt helpless, but she needed to give him another chance to respond.

* * *

Lealina met Jax at the orbital dock and they embraced for a very long time, eventually interrupted by Runstom.

"We need to catch the elevator to the surface." He pointed to the signs, which indicated a direction along with a countdown timer to the next drop.

"Okay," Jax said, pulling away from her warmth and gazing into bright-blue eyes. She had a smell, something floral and grassy, a thing he hadn't realized until it was missing. He drew a slow breath, then finally nodded to Runstom.

They hooked themselves to the conveyance system that pulled them through the microgravity toward the elevators. There they caught the last car in the stack. Though they almost missed it, the bonus was that they had the space all to themselves for the hour-long drop.

"I saw you on holovid," Jax said after they had strapped in and the stack began its descent.

"You did?" Lealina smiled sheepishly. "Did I look okay?"

Jax laughed. "Of course."

"What in the galaxy are you wearing?" she said, looking him up and down.

"Ah, um." Jax looked down at the lime-green shirt and sky-blue pants he'd put on that morning. "It was the only thing in my size."

"That's my fault," Runstom put in. "I made him go shopping with me on Ipo. Trust me, the other clothes he had on were ..." he said, trailing off.

"Uh, let's say they were 'less presentable'," Jax said. He hadn't owned his own clothes in quite some time. He forced a smile at Lealina. "First order of business is to take me shopping, I guess."

"Nothing would please me more," she said. The return smile she gave him lifted his stomach into his throat and he blinked to keep his eyes from watering. "Unfortunately, we don't really have time for that. Our friends at ModPol convinced the FSC to put on a little show for your return."

"You mean I'm going to be on holovid like this?"

"I'm sorry," Runstom said.

Lealina gave a small hand-wave, her movement limited by the harness. "It's no trouble, really. I'm just so glad you brought him back." She looked at Runstom a little longer. "He's told me a lot about you, you know."

Jax could see Runstom's olive-green face flush. "Only the most embarrassing stories," he said, reddening his friend's face even more.

Lealina and Jax both laughed, which coaxed a smile out of Runstom. "I'm sure," he said.

"Anyway," she said. "We're all booked up for the next couple of days. Aside from the return of The Fixer, it's Ark Week."

He'd almost forgotten about the nickname he'd earned while on Terroneous. Hearing that again made him suddenly realize how special it was. *The Fixer.* The people there really liked him, welcomed him, respected him.

"Ark Week?" Runstom said, breaking Jax's sentimental train of thought. "Oh. The Earth Kin Rescue?"

She put on a bit of a serious face, creasing in places around her mouth that made Jax want to break out of his harness and kiss her. "Obviously, it's a big deal around here."

Jax and Runstom glanced at each other. Of course, it would be a big deal, but it had been a while since either of them had a chance to pay attention to galactic current affairs. It was the last scheduled ark to come from Earth. Maybe there would be another, but as far as anyone could guess, it was likely there wouldn't. And Terroneous had lobbied with the Earth Colony Alliance to be the landing point. It would be the first time an ark wasn't destined for one of the primary domed planets: Barnard-3, Barnard-4, and Sirius-5.

"Some people are saying the ECA only gave us this one because the domes are full enough these days," Lealina went on. She looked pointedly at Jax. "But you know, there's plenty of room still. They're always expanding the domes. On B-4 they don't even cover a tenth of the planet."

"So it's not for lack of space," Runstom said. Jax could hear the unspoken questions in the back of the man's throat. The latent detective inside, probing.

She looked at them sideways, lowering her voice. "Other people say it's because the domes don't want to be sullied. The passing generations have made them comfortable with their ways of life. They don't want to disrupt that."

"They don't want outsiders," Runstom said in a tone that said he spoke from experience, as an outsider wherever he went.

As the representative domer present, Jax squirmed in his harness. "So, Ark Week," he said to Lealina. "What are you – what are we doing?"

She brightened at the question. "As director of the TEOB, I'm on one of the welcoming committees." She smiled intensely. "And you're joining me, since you're a local celebrity. Which means in two days we'll be riding this thing right back up."

"The ark is going to dock at the orbital?"

"Not exactly," she said. "The Earth tech is too old to interface with our stuff. They're currently decelerating around B-7. Then they'll come into orbit around B-5, then hop into an orbit around Terroneous. After half a day of adjustments, they'll match orbit with the dock. Then emergency shuttles will ferry the Earthlings from the ark to the dock."

"Sounds dangerous," Jax said quietly.

"Nothing to do with Terroneous is easy," she said evenly, a light smile playing on her lips.

He nodded and flashed a smile back at her, but he couldn't hold it. Runstom's words were still floating around in his head. The domers really didn't care much for outsiders. It was something he didn't want to admit, but knew it was true. Not everyone was close-minded or isolationist – it wasn't the domer way to take a strong position one way or another – no, it was much more subtle. The air filled with uncomfortable attitudes whenever such topics came up: immigration, expanding trade policies, exchange programs. No one would ever outright oppose these things, but they would leverage bureaucracy and indecision to slow down the progress of unsettling initiatives.

That had been the world he'd come from. The world he'd grown up in, been educated in, been socialized in. But it wasn't the world he lived in any more. For months, he'd been increasingly calling Terroneous home. Only in the moment that his old world was being criticized did he realize how much he agreed. He realized how thankful he was that Terroneous was very much the opposite: the people were welcoming, inclusive, accepting. A lot of Terroneans were not originally from Terroneous. The diversity of backgrounds surely had an effect on the levels of tolerance and acceptance.

Having run for so long, Jax wondered if now that he was safe and home, he could allow himself these questions. To finally have something to believe in that wasn't just blind fear and survival instinct.

He looked up into those bright blues. Here was someone who believed in making a better life for people on a planet that wasn't as forgiving as a dome, but its people were amazing. It would be a wonderful home for the battered souls that managed to escape the ruin of Earth. He decided in that moment he would unconditionally follow her, and join in that purpose: to help make Terroneous a home for *anyone* in need of one.

* * *

We're on a course to intercept and we can't brake to let you board. But you should stay close to Terroneous. We may need you when it goes down.

The encrypted message came minutes after a message directly from Jansen on the main channel. Which was along the lines of: don't interfere; but keep a distance and be ready in case ModPol shows up.

2-Bit wasn't giving Dava much to go on. Or he was, and she wasn't seeing it. She replayed the scenarios in her head. If Jansen's plan was to board the ark, then it was going to be in a way she couldn't see as possible. Cutting into it and ferrying people over to the *Longhorn* would be too long a process. They'd attract the attention of ModPol in no time.

One thing nagged her: the Misters. They were still the unknown element. If only ten of them went aboard the *Longhorn*, then where were the rest?

"Lucky, tell me about the Misters," she said. "How many are there?"

The pilot's face scrunched up. "In the whole gang? Hard to say, really. The Misters use a tree-like hierarchy in their orders. Everyone has one direct boss and one backup boss. And each boss might have a bunch of reports under them. And those reports might also be bosses, with other guys reporting to them. If your boss gets killed or arrested or goes missing or whatever, you report to your backup boss, and they make sure you get a replacement boss. Or your backup boss might become your direct boss, and then they find you a replacement backup."

"Sounds cellular," she muttered. "But convoluted and ridiculous." Every once in a while someone would try to talk Moses into setting up cells within Space Waste. Operators that didn't know each other; and whom no one knew. Moses had always been staunchly against that kind of structure. Sure, they were thieves and murderers, but they were also a collective of sorts. He never liked the idea that his family could be fragmented for the sake of secrecy. It defeated the purpose of creating Space Waste.

"It gets worse," Lucky said with a frown. "The only way to move up the ranks in the Misters is to recruit people that you can boss around. If you grow your reports to a large enough size, then at some point you're required to split your reports and make some of them bosses, and move some guys under them."

"It sounds like one of those things," Toom-Toom said, trying to form a shape by turning one hand upside-down and spreading his fingers. "Like with the triangle. Like a triangle ... something?"

"A pyramid scheme," Lucky said with a solemn nod. "Believe me, that's exactly what it is. That's why the press-ganging. It's one way to grow your reports and move up the ranks."

Dava could see the conversation eating at the pilot. She knew he'd been press-ganged into working for the Misters in the past. It was one of the early confrontations between Space Waste and the newly formed gang that brought Lucky Jerk into their family. "How about their movements?" she said. "Communication?"

"Communication only flows up and then back down –

not cross-ways. You never talk to another Mister unless that Mister is your boss. See, there aren't rankings like in a military – or even in Space Waste. There is only the tree. And no one even knows what the tree looks like. If you're a boss, you only know what branches are below you. Only ones who really know the whole thing are the original Misters. And honestly, no one knows who they are."

Again, the convoluted clandestine cell organization. "Sounds easy to manipulate."

Lucky shrugged. "Supposedly, that's what the backups are for. Most branches have autonomy, but for major movements, attacks, whatevers, the word has to come from higher up. So if your boss gives you an order to meet for a hit, you verify the hit with your backup boss."

"Hey, why are they the *Misters*?" Toom-Toom said with a cock of his head. "Are there really no women in the whole gang?" The look on his face almost read as fear, and Dava suspected the pretty-faced young man had come to expect there to always be women around to wink at him; the thought of otherwise clearly didn't sit well with him.

Instead of answering Toom-Toom directly, Lucky looked at Dava. "Would *you* join a gang of all men?"

Dava ignored him. The homogenous make-up of the Misters was not what she cared about. The cell structure meant that there could be any number of them out there, waiting to join the fray. They were completely unpredictable.

She read 2-Bit's message again, stopping over each word to try and decipher any hidden meaning.

We're on a course to intercept and we can't break away from it to let you board.

This was likely word-for-word from Jansen. 2-Bit was

smart enough to start the message with something that would show his loyalty.

But you should stay close to Terroneous.

As best as Dava could read this, it was a warning. To stay close meant to stay ready. Though oddly, it didn't say to stay close to the *Longhorn* or to the ark. To specify Terroneous was deliberate.

We may need you when it goes down.

Was she crazy? Could she really trust 2-Bit? She knew she could trust his loyalty to Moses, but Moses was gone. And if 2-Bit was on her side, could she trust his ability to pick his words, to send her a message within a message? There was no doubt he was a solid leader. He earned the highest respect from all his pilots. And he knew strategy when it came to space combat. But what did he know of deception, deceit? He didn't grow up hiding like she had.

"When it goes down," she said to herself.

"You think it's going down?" Toom-Toom said suddenly.

"What, the *Longhorn*?" Lucky said. "Or the ark?"

Dava felt herself shudder. "Tooms. Bring up the nav map. I want to see the *Longhorn* and the ark and their trajectories. And I want to see the orbital dock. And Terroneous."

All three of them stared at the holo-projection Toom-Toom brought up. The *Longhorn* was on a course to intercept the ark well before it reached the meager defenses around the orbital dock. Under Moses, 2-Bit never would have plotted such a straight course; it telegraphed your move to your enemy. You might as well send them a d-mail announcing your arrival. Dava didn't have to be a pilot to know that, but evidently it was beyond Jansen.

The fact that 2-Bit had willingly taken the straight line told her he wanted someone to know where exactly in space the *Longhorn* was going to intercept the ark. She hoped it meant that he wanted *her* to know.

If they were planning on forcing the ark down onto the independent moon, they could breach it without any fear of ModPol. No jurisdiction. The local forces were too meager and slow – and conservative – to confront Space Waste.

"Project ahead with current courses," Dava said. "To the point where the *Longhorn* is close enough to use her plasma cannons on the ark."

"A good gunner can hit a non-combatant from hundreds of kilometers off," Lucky said.

Dava considered this. The ark wasn't made for combat and wouldn't have anything in the way of maneuverability. It would have sweeper lasers for any space rocks that came close enough to damage it, but the range on those was minimal. And lasers made for deflecting asteroids weren't going to do shit to plasma blasts. If Jansen wanted to waste the ark for whatever unknown reason, he could plot a firing solution from a massive distance and sit back to watch the target helplessly eat fiery death.

"What if they wanted to damage it?" she said. "Lucky, what would you do to make that ark take an emergency landing?"

"Force it to crash-land on Terroneous?" he said. "I don't think that thing would survive."

"It would," she said. She'd looked at the specs that were picked up by the public traffic scanners. The model of the ark wasn't any different than the one that she arrived on more than a decade ago. It was the last ark model the Earthlings made. A limited number of them were built before the program was halted nearly a century ago. They were all designed to handle an emergency landing on-planet, but once the colonies established orbital docks, the risk was no longer necessary.

"Well," Lucky said, clucking his tongue thoughtfully against his teeth. "I guess you'd want to knock them off course. Make them afraid they won't get to the orbital. Basically, you just want to hit them hard enough to knock them into Terroneous's gravity well. Hard enough so they can't get back out. I guess you might take out their thruster – that would make it impossible to get back into orbit once gravity takes hold."

"Life support," Toom-Toom said quietly.

"What?" Dava leaned forward. "What'd you say?"

He looked at her with a dark frown. "It's what I would hit. If I wanted someone to make an emergency landing. Terroneous has a stable atmosphere."

"It would be their only hope," Dava realized aloud. Put the fear of losing life support into a ship, and the crew would have no choice but to crash into the nearby moon with the atmo.

"No," Lucky said. "That won't do it. They're all in stasis pods. They're barely sipping O2."

Dava looked at the map again. "Right about now, they're coming out. It takes several hours for that old stasis tech to bring them back into consciousness, and then a good twelve hours before they're walking around without injuring themselves."

Her memories from that age had faded quite a bit, but she could remember the torture. It was during this terrible nauseous and painful experience of recovery that they had informed her that her parents had been jettisoned along with the diseases they'd carried. She didn't remember much, but what she did remember was an endless cycle of death and pain and blackness as she fought for consciousness over and over again, only to discover each time she came to that reality was worse than the darkness.

Toom-Toom was right, she knew. It was the best way for Jansen to welcome the new arrivals: while they were disoriented, send them groping for the nearest stretch of land. They wouldn't land anywhere near any population centers, not wanting to endanger their new hosts. Which would make them vulnerable. And then what? Dropships from the *Longhorn* to hit the landing site faster than emergency crews on Terroneous could get to it?

No, they didn't have enough, she realized. Even disoriented, some of the Earthlings would resist if they felt forced. Press-ganging only worked if you had a gang to press with.

And that was it. The Misters. That was their role in all this. There weren't many Misters on the *Longhorn* because they were on Terroneous. Right now, individual cells were getting orders. On the move. Ready to converge on whatever landing spot the ark was forced to make for.

"Tooms. Call everyone," she said. "Make for low orbit around Terroneous. When the ark goes down, we go down with it."

CHAPTER 18

They were on the rail when the word of the attack came in.

Only hours ago, they'd reached the bottom of the elevator. Runstom was increasingly feeling like an uncomfortable extra, getting in the way of Jax catching up with the director of TEOB. He hadn't realized the extent of the relationship. Maybe Jax hadn't realized it either, and only then, in her presence once again, felt overwhelmed with emotion. Runstom was happy for them, but not interested in seeing the emotions play out.

For that reason, he'd been in the dining car drinking lukewarm coffee when it came over the holovid hanging from the corner. Everyone stopped moving. The images were distorted. Telescopic images from the orbital. Still several hundred kilometers out. Another ship, one the newscasters were unable to identify. Taking pot shots at the ark. Distress calls coming in. Too far out for the dock's defenses. Too risky to send help, with the attacking ship still within range.

He had an encrypted communications package on his WrappiMate, but the range on it was mediocre. He needed to amplify his signal if he were to reach Ipo. The rail had a transmission car, but all the pods were full by the time he got there. Worse, there was a line.

Jax and Lealina were both pale-faced when Runstom returned to the passenger car. Well, Jax was always pale-faced, but in any case, it was clear they'd heard the news. Lealina was tapping away at a pad. Jax sat close to her, his lanky hands flexing nervously.

"It must be Jansen," he said when he saw Runstom approach.

Runstom nodded and sat down. "I need to call my boss at Ipo," he said. "Transmission pods are all full and there's a line."

Jax blinked. "ModPol is already at Ipo," he said quickly. "They can move in, right? They can rescue the ark."

An emptiness grew inside Runstom. "They don't have jurisdiction on Terroneous."

"But the space above Terroneous?"

"A gray area," Runstom said. But gray was close enough for something like this. ModPol would rush to the rescue. The meeting with Victoria Horus and Francois Newman ran through his mind. Their inside information. They knew this attack was coming. They knew ModPol would be close enough to help.

They could have sent the info to Terroneous. Warned them of the impending attack. And then what? The FSC wouldn't have accepted their help. Instead, they'd be forced to cobble together a defense fleet of some kind. Runstom started to understand the role of deception in all of this. ModPol could help Terroneous. But Terroneous didn't want that help. Instead, by letting things play out and standing by, ModPol could still fulfill their mission. They could protect people that need it. At that moment in time, it was too late for anything else.

"But you're right," Runstom said. "ModPol can move in."

Lealina looked up from her pad. "The FSC can't agree to a response," she whispered. Pain twisted her face and droplets formed at the corners of her eyes. "Those people are going to die."

"I need to talk to my boss," Runstom said.

"Come on." She stood up and yanked Runstom by the elbow. "I'll get you a pod."

Back at the transmission car, Lealina waved her TEOB credentials and pushed through the growing line. She yanked a young man out of the first pod, flashed her creds, and shoved Runstom inside. The pod door closed off the ensuing argument.

The silence inside the milky-white bubble was unnerving. But it told Runstom his conversation would be completely contained. The makers of the pods had their customers' privacy at the top of mind.

He disconnected the worn and scratched rectangular pad that was still there from the previous occupant and connected the thin cable to the only port in his WrappiMate. His screen winked icon-laden graphics at him, letting him know an external, extended-range antenna had been installed and was being integrated. Everything went green after a few seconds. He opened the comms app.

"Horus – I mean, Victoria. Vicky. Hi, it's Officer Runstom. I mean Public Relations – I mean, it's Stanford. I'm on a rail on the surface of Terroneous. About an hour from a city called Nuzwick. I just got word of the attack." He paused, then concluded with, "Please advise."

He didn't bother to edit the message before it went out. He had no idea whether she would answer right away. Ipo was close enough that the delay could be measured in seconds, but with the attack, she could be occupied.

A minute later, the reply came in. "Stan, thank you for calling in. We're already scrambling the MPD fighters here on Ipo. By the time you get to town, we'll be halfway to the ark."

The icon indicated Horus was still connected. Despite the delay, she wanted to treat it like any other audio call.

"Won't we be violating the no-fly zone around Terroneous?"

"Yes, technically we will. But there is no time to negotiate. We're taking out the Space Waste command ship to protect the ark. We'll ask forgiveness for the no-fly violation after the fact."

As he suspected then. "Command ship?" he said. "The same carrier that was at Eridani?"

"Yes, that's right," she said unevenly. The delay gave the impression of hesitation. "Despite our successful rout of the Wasters at Eridani, the command ship was able to Xarp back to Barnard." There was another short pause, and then her voice continued. "Listen, Stanford. This ain't over yet. A bunch of the members of the FSC will all be in Nuzwick for the homecoming of your friend Jackson. Timing on this is critical. Chasing the Wasters out of Terroneous space is one thing, but we can't put boots on the ground without their permission."

"Why do we need boots on the ground?"

"Now what I need you to do," she started, then stopped. His delayed question interrupted her. "I told you, this ain't over, Stan. I need you to work your magic. Be real with them. Remember, you're good at this because everyone trusts you. Because you tell the truth. They can see it. So you tell them. Tell them what will happen if the Wasters get to that ark before we do. Tell them how important the lives of those Earthlings are – not just to Terroneous, but to ModPol as well. You tell them about how your father was an Earthling."

Runstom's heart stopped moving. "What did you say? My father?"

The delay was excruciatingly long. For decades, he'd wasted no spare thought on the man who had impregnated his mother. And then, only in the past couple of weeks, it had come up. More than once.

"I'm sorry, Stanford," Horus said finally. "I spoke out of turn. I can't talk any more right now. Just remember; troop carriers are going to follow the fighters. If we need those troops to drop to Terroneous for any reason, we need the FSC's permission. I need you to get that permission. This whole operation depends upon it. Am I making myself clear?"

It was the first time Runstom had heard Horus's voice in a tone other than the usual chummy, assuring, encouraging one. It had grown hard. The comms app indicated that the conversation had ended. If he replied to her, she'd receive the message, but she would not hear it right away.

He felt his head grow heavy, pulling against his neck. His father, an Earthling? Sylvia had never said anything of the sort. Never said anything at all. She never lied about it. Just said nothing.

A pounding noise from behind snapped his head back up. He stood and exited the pod.

* * *

The ceremony was already canceled by the time they reached Nuzwick. Lealina had taken the lead as soon as they'd stepped from the train. Swept along in her wake, Runstom and Jax pushed through the crowded streets of the small town. A cold rain had hissed down, muting the meager streetlights that were trying to beat back the dark shadow of the colossus, Barnard-5. Before long, Runstom found himself in the conference room temporarily commandeered by the Terroneous Federated Security Committee. Each of the four present committee members was flanked by a number of staff. Each had taken over a corner of the room, clusters of busybodies jabbing at hastily mounted wall-pads or relaying messages via video, voice, and text to unseen recipients.

Lealina paused upon sweeping into the room. Her entrance got a moment's glance from the occupants, but only barely so. Runstom followed her gaze to an older man he recognized from the broadcast that had demanded the return of Jax.

"Jarvis," Lealina said.

He turned and stepped forward as they approached his corner. He glanced back at the collection of chaos behind him, six people talking at once, and stepped forward further to meet them in the center.

"Lealina." He took her hand. "I'm sorry about the ceremony."

She waved it off with her free hand. "Another time."

"And here's Jack Fugere in the flesh," he said. He released her hand to take Jax's in a firm shake. "I wasn't sure whether to believe that ModPol released you, son."

Jax shook the hand rigorously. "Thank you, sir. For everything."

"Jax, Stanford," Lealina said. "This is Jarvis Wainrite. He's the deputy mayor in Nuzwick, and the head spokesperson for the FSC."

Wainrite nodded at Jax, then turned to shake Runstom's hand cautiously. The grip much weaker than he'd just observed. "Nice to meet you, Stanford."

An old feeling crawled across Runstom's skin. The feeling of being a source of discomfort. The bizarre skin. The unwanted cop. Even if he wasn't a cop anymore. "Nice to meet you," he returned, almost adding *Mr. Wainrite*. Victoria Horus's influence was worming its way through his mind. "Jarvis."

"I should say," he said. "The pleasure is mine. Not every day an old moonbilly like me gets to meet Stanford Runstom."

In the gap Runstom's stunned silence left, Lealina jumped back in. "Jarvis, what the hell is going on? Can we protect the ark?"

He sighed, his face bunching and exaggerating its wrinkles. "The bastards hit it before it got anywhere near our planetary defenses. And you know when I say planetary defenses, I mean the pebbleguns that protect the orbitals."

"What about the fleet?" she said.

Those words surprised Runstom, knowing there was no such thing. Wainrite shook his head. "They're volunteers, all of them. Getting them to sign up to protect the planet is one thing, but getting them to risk their livelihoods – and their lives – to defend the ark is something entirely different. Most of them are terrified of Space Waste."

"So that's it?" she said, her voice growing strained. Jax's face contorted as he made a motion to comfort her, then froze when she jabbed a finger at Wainrite. "You're telling me we're just going to let those people die?"

"Of course not, Lealina," he snapped in a hushed voice. "We're considering all of our options."

She blinked, lips tightening. "Why are they doing this?"

"Recruitment," Runstom said. The three of them stared at him wide-eyed.

"How do you know that?" Wainrite said.

Jax huffed. "Actually, that makes complete sense. They're always looking for new members. Seems like fresh meat from Earth would be ideal ..." He trailed off under their glares, then put his hands up. "Sorry, I didn't mean to be so crude. It's just a phrase I heard when I was ... well ... forced to join them."

"You joined Space Waste?" Wainrite breathed.

"They were the ones that rescued him from ModPol," Lealina said, quick to defend. Jax had given her the full story on the train. In fact, he'd given her far more details than Runstom would have preferred. He could only conclude the B-fourean truly trusted this woman.

"I was forced," Jax repeated.

"Like the Earthlings will be," Runstom said.

"So if they're trying to recruit them, why shoot them?" Wainrite said.

"I don't know," Runstom said. The words of his boss still in his head. *Boots on the ground.* "ModPol is moving in on them now."

"ModPol," Wainrite muttered with disdain.

"ModPol Defense," Runstom said, hoping that meant something. "There were fighterships stationed at Ipo."

"I heard about the trial contract there." Wainrite nodded upward, as though they could see the sky through the building. "But they've got no right to invade Terroneous space."

Runstom nodded. “Of course not. They won’t need to cross very far to engage the Wasters.”

“Sir!” They turned to a particularly insistent aide bounding up behind Wainrite. “Mr. Wainrite, sir. The ark radioed in. Their life support is damaged.”

“Life support,” he said. “Can they get to the orbital?”

“I don’t think so, sir,” the aide said, waving a pad whose screen was decorated with vectors. “The Wasters are between the ark and the dock. The ark has been forced off course.”

“But they’re close, right?” Lealina said. “If their life support is failing, can they land on Terroneous?”

The aide looked at each of them and then at her pad. Her mouth opened and closed.

“Give it to me,” Wainrite said, yanking away the pad. “These old arks are made to handle crash-landings. If they can come down to the surface, we can send an emergency crew.”

“If they land clean, they can just pop the seals open,” Lealina said, her voice brightening. “They don’t need life support here!”

If they land. Boots on the ground. Runstom wasn’t sure how Horus knew it would happen this way. But so it was. If they were landing on the surface, then Space Waste planned it that way. Which meant they were going to follow.

Wainrite pointed the pad at his aide. “Can we get them a message?”

The young woman shrugged. “Sure, they’ve been in communication with our traffic towers.”

“Unencrypted,” he mumbled.

She shrank a bit. “I’m afraid so, sir. It’s our only channel to them.”

“We need to find a place to tell them to land,” Lealina

said. "Close enough that we can get to them with a rescue team. But not close to any population centers."

"Right, right," Wainrite said, poking at the pad. "I'm thinking the Low Desert."

"We're a week into the night cycle," Lealina said. "The temperature in the desert is going to be cold. Dangerously cold."

"It'll have to do," Wainrite said.

Runstom grabbed him by the arm. "Listen, Jarvis. Right behind those MPD fighters are a handful of troop carriers. The FSC needs to authorize them to land on Terroneous."

His head jerked up and his eyes widened. "Absolutely not! Those Fender scum are not stepping a single boot on our sovereign moon."

Runstom threw a palm to the sky. "You think this isn't part of the Wasters' plans? If the ark comes to the Terroneous surface, the Wasters will follow. And they don't care about any goddamn jurisdiction."

Wainrite's face bunched and reddened. "So that's it, huh? That's the ModPol plan? Rush to our rescue and look like goddamn heroes? Well we don't *need* you. We have our own forces."

"Your forces are volunteers," Runstom said evenly. "They'll get slaughtered – if you can even get them to show up."

"Jarvis," Lealina said, pulling him from out of Runstom's face with a gentle tug of his arm. "The people on that ark need us to keep our cool. We need to work together."

He looked at her, breathing heavily through his nose. Then back at Runstom. "We're not making any deals. This isn't a contract."

"We don't need a contract," Runstom said. "Just permission."

"Fine," he finally managed. He waved the pad. "We tell the ark to land in the Low Desert. And the Fenders can drop there. But that's it. They don't leave the fucking desert. And we have no fucking contract."

Runstom took a slow breath. It was all Horus had really asked him to do, though he imagined she wanted him to leverage for more. Did it matter? The ModPol Defenders were the best chance at protecting the Earthlings.

"No contract," he said. "And they don't leave the desert."

* * *

Once when he was a child, Jax's parents had taken him to see a play about the birth of the colonies. He was too young to understand the nuances, but old enough to get the gist. The old world was in trouble: it was overcrowded, food distribution was challenging, and the seas were rising. People were getting sick a lot more than was normal, from a variety of factors. Prolonged exposure in the damaged atmosphere was bad for the lungs, skin, and even eyes. People just stopped going outside, and instead they suffered from viral infections so easily spread in the crowded, closed-in spaces.

And yet, in other parts of the play, men and women stood together uncrowded, entangled in energetic discussion about the future of the human race. These characters were costumed to easily identify their roles. Suits, which were grey pants and a grey jacket over a white shirt and a long red necktie, represented the politicians. The scientists and doctors wore white coats that hung below the knees, every one of them carrying thin squares of wood with flaps of paper attached to them, some kind of old notebook. The third type of costume paired blue pants with short-sleeved shirts of various colors, decorated with logos Jax couldn't quite make out.

Later it had to be explained to Jax that this third group represented the heads of the tech industry. Which qualities best served these unique leaders was the subject of much debate between his father and his mother. His father, the software engineer, praised their pragmatism and their high standards. His mother admired their risk-taking and their willingness to dive in and get their hands dirty when the work needed to be done – even when that meant bending the rules and eschewing the will of the world's governments. According to the play, these five – three men and two women – used their resources in a sort of half-competition, half-cooperation to advance spaceflight far beyond the capabilities of government-funded organizations. Orbital docks, research colonies on Sol-4 (the Earthlings called it "Mars"), and asteroid mining contributed to a cycle of advancement. All of this technology was driven by ever-improving software powered by greater levels of artificial intelligence. There had been a fear in those days that AI would somehow become conscious. Jax had a hard time imagining how such an irrational belief had become commonplace; but then again, it wasn't the first nor the last thing humans would get wrong.

What followed in the next act of the play was the first spaceship carrying humans to leave the solar system. With access to superfuels found in some asteroids, the most enterprising industrialists pushed rocket acceleration to greater limits. In the late twenty-second century, the first mission to an extrasolar star was conducted: the ship made it to Alpha Centauri in just under two decades.

While life on Earth plunged into crowded poverty, a

land-grab was launching into the stars. Alliances were formed, broken, and constantly renegotiated between corporations, while the weakening governments retracted their reach. The first arcologies began appearing on Earth at that time as well: the massive self-contained structures that were the prototypes for domes like the kind Jax grew up in on Barnard-4. Only the wealthiest could afford to live in them, seeking them out to escape the hordes of sick and starving.

Dozens of colonies had been constructed in those early days of the mid-twenty-third century. Only those in the systems of Sirius and Barnard's Star survived. More than survived: they thrived. More and more Earthlings fled the dying old world. They left behind the masses, and the most stubborn of the upper class, still clinging to their plush arcologies in the present day.

The final message of the play had seemed to be "good riddance" to those that wanted to stay on Earth. The colonies were for the brave and the forward-thinking. The separation effectively created a natural step in evolution for human civilization. The governments that were established were hyper-local. The corporations ensured everyone was employed well enough to meet minimum basic needs, establishing what Jax would later hear described as some kind of socialism through capitalism. The entire third act had been concerned with the struggles and successes of the first colonies, particularly the two that survived.

What the play hadn't gone on to demonstrate was how quickly the old world was forgotten. It had reflected Jax's history education as a child: everything was about the early struggles and subsequent triumphs of the colonies. No one had an interest in the dying planet of generations past. And so he remembered the initial shock that he and everyone around him had felt upon hearing about the Earth Kin Rescue missions – more popularly known as the "doomed to domed" missions.

Thinking back on it, Jax realized he had never really understood the motivation for those missions. They had always been somewhat controversial, in an embarrassingly isolationist way. In the past year, he'd gotten out of the domes on Barnard-4, seen more of the galaxy, and maybe that was why he was starting to understand it. The overcrowding of Earth was measured in billions, and the populations of the colonies were a fraction, measured in the hundreds of thousands. The resource the colonies had always been short on was people. The same resource that Earth always had too much of.

So there was a practical reason, one easy to put on paper. Jax had understood that much; it was the justification he'd always heard. It was the people, the Earthlings, that he'd never really connected with. The play from his youth told him they were living in poverty, but he didn't really get what that meant. What it felt like. And that was the difference threatening to swamp his mind with more recent memories. He *did* know what it felt like. The way hunger goes from mild discomfort, to nagging pain, to hollowness, and then at a point a couple of days in just disappears. How much of a relief, and yet how terrifying it is to suddenly realize the body isn't working right any more. Signals are blocked out as the slow death creeps through the veins, and the body begins devouring whatever it can find from the inside out. In that moment, even the fear fades as the shell of shrinking flesh empties of the human within.

Hundreds of thousands like that on Earth. Millions. Probably billions, depending on how wide his definition of hunger went. And only a couple of thousand that could get on an ark. Throw themselves light-years across the dangers of interstellar space in a desperate bid for ... something ... anything. Anything would be better than the dragging vacuum of starvation.

Even being recruited by Space Waste would be a better life for them. But Jax had his opinions on being forced to commit criminal acts just to stay alive.

He felt helpless in the moment. Lealina and the other members of the FSC were working, frenzied, debating between themselves and making calls out to their home districts, coordinating efforts. Runstom had gone off to report back in, to let ModPol Defense know they had clearance to land in the Low Desert. And so Jax stood there, trying to follow the dozens of simultaneous conversations in the room and failing.

He zeroed in on Lealina's voice, rising in frustration. He went over to listen to her argument with Jarvis Wainrite.

"Jarvis, please!" she said, her hands tightened into reddening balls. "I have to be there! I want to help!"

"I'm sorry," Wainrite said. "I'd like to be there too, but it's too dangerous. We just can't afford to lose you. And we can't fly out there because all kinds of debris could be falling out of the sky anyway. We have a limited number of vehicles that can get through the desert."

"Damn it," she said. "What if I enlist in the militia?"

"Lealina," he started.

"It's important to us," Jax said, interjecting into the conversation.

Wainrite shot him a glance. "It's important to all of us. But I'm only sending *trained* militia and emergency personnel out there." He threw his hands up in a half-shrug, half-wave.

"Besides, ModPol is going to rain down and rescue our asses."

Jax frowned. "You'll forgive me if my faith in ModPol isn't what it used to be," he said in a low voice. He knew it made no difference to Wainrite, who was just as distrusting of ModPol as Jax.

Lealina continued to plead her case as Wainrite moved away to dispense orders. Jax looked around the walls of the space and saw an empty net-phone. He walked up to it and pulled up the directory. *Granderson, David.* He dialed.

He was going on a hunch. Granderson was the filmmaker that had blown Jax's cover. Not that Jax had been doing such a great job at staying hidden. But it was Granderson that created the documentary around the magnetic flux sensor crisis; the crisis during which Jax met Lealina and helped the Terroneous Environmental Observation Board fix the bugged sensors and avoid an unnecessary evacuation of the moon. Despite what Jax had thought were clear agreements, Granderson had used his name and face on holovid. It was a matter of days before Jared McManus had shown up to arrest him, shortly after which he was stolen by Dava and her crew who'd seen the same holovid.

The call connected after a couple of minutes of pinging. "Hello? Who the hell is this?"

"David. This is Jax – Jack Fugere."

"Holy shit, Jack? What the hell are you doing calling me on a Terroneous public net-phone?"

Jax watched Lealina from a distance, being ignored by Wainrite. "Where are you, David?"

"Well, I'm in goddamn Nuzwick because I got word of your big homecoming," he said. "I was hoping to revise the film, maybe get another shot at it? It's a much bigger story now."

Jax wanted to rip into the man for even suggesting such a thing, then took a breath. ModPol had let him come back to Terroneous. He was no longer a fugitive. He tried to see it Granderson's way: there *was* a good story in it, one that Terroneans would love.

"So you're still in Nuzwick?"

A huff came through the earpiece. "Yeah. Trying to get into this FSC conference. People are demanding to know what's happening with the ark. The news networks are saying it's dipping into our gravity. Sounds like they may be trying to land. All the people in the know are in this one room and I just want a few shots, maybe a quick soundbite or two. This is history, happening right now!"

Lealina had given up on Wainrite. She stood in the middle of the room, shoulders slumping and head drooping.

"I got something better," Jax said. "You still have that landrover?"

CHAPTER 19

Dava's dropship led the way, crashing through the desert night. Lucky Jerk whooped with glee while everyone else gripped their restraints and gritted their teeth. All the way down was a crescendo, a growing rush of atmosphere and ever-increasing shuddering and smothering heat. Just when she thought her insides had been shaken into a puree and her eyes had melted in their sockets, the landing retros blazed and her ass slammed into her guts. Seconds later, a jarring blackness crushed her head downward.

Adrenaline brought her back from the abyss of unconsciousness. She could move once again, and her voice still worked through the wheezing of her recovering lungs.

"Report," she managed.

There was no immediate answer, and she glanced over at Toom-Toom. The young man's head lolled.

"We're here!" Lucky said through a cough. "Everyone is still alive, according to the vita-stat monitors."

"Tooms," Dava said. "Wake up, kid. He's okay?"

Lucky looked back. "He's breathing. Just give him a

minute." He glanced at Dava with an enormous grin. "I never dropped one of these before. Damn, that was a rush."

Dava nodded back, unable to hide her own smile. "First time for me too," she said. The shielding had gone up on all the viewports and the entire cabin was dark, save a few indicator lights. She poked at an unresponsive console. "What's the status of the rest? And where's the ark?"

"One sec. The landing caused a power-cycle." Screens winked to life around her, scrolling green text against black backgrounds. "Here we go."

After a minute, Lucky started to pull up visuals on the area. Toom-Toom groaned, reaching for his head. Dava looked at one of the screens. Black sky, without a single star, loomed behind a massive structure whose metal edges glowed red. An arc of flattened, blown sand circled it, dotted all around with hot fragments.

"That's her," Lucky said. "Looks pretty bad."

"Looks worse that it is," she said, trying to convince herself as much as anyone else. "It's built a lot like this dropship. A one-way trip to the surface. The edges will be a mess, but the cargo should be safe."

"Got a report here from Captain 2-Bit," Toom-Toom said, suddenly alert. "Says ModPol showed up. Jansen gave him the order to pull the *Longhorn* back."

Dava shook her head. "So they aren't sending any drop ships," she muttered to herself. "Where's the rest of Shadowdown?"

"Controlled descents in progress. The black marias we took from ModPol are the only ships that can actually land on the surface without crashing. The rest are coming through atmo until they can eject."

Dava had ordered them all into a one-way mission. "Everyone?"

Toom-Toom looked at her with a tilt of his head. "Of course, Boss."

She looked away, feeling relief and at the same time shame for doubting any of their loyalty. She looked at the ark, which according to the readout was about two hundred meters from their location. "Try to raise the first maria. See if they have visual yet."

Lucky tapped for a few seconds. "Okay, got 'em. They too busy for chatting, but I got a feed from their scopes. Check it out."

Dava was out of her straps, almost reluctant to leave their safety at first, then feeling a wave of freedom wash over her after shedding them. She came up behind Lucky to look at his screens.

"Pull back. I want the area all around the ark. A couple of kilometers." He complied. The scope enhanced the image as best it could with thermal detection and low-light filters, but under the shadow of the gas giant, the desert was utterly black.

Then dots appeared, like stars in the darkening of dusk, only red from their heat. At first just one, then two, then ten, then dozens. They formed a semicircle around the edges of the view.

"Zoom in on one of them," Dava said. She jabbed at the screen. "That cluster there."

The screen rushed at them, pulling the ground closer and the dots grew, forming squares, then resolving into vehicles. Trucks or jeeps of some kind. Broad and glinting from their headlights.

"Locals?" Toom-Toom said as he appeared over Lucky's other shoulder.

"No," the pilot said dourly. "Misters."

The cells had been activated. They must have been hiding all over the goddamn moon. She took the control and zoomed back out. So many more than she thought possible. Their network had been growing quietly, cell by cell.

Lucky looked back at her. "Orders, Boss?"

The question was for Dava, but it made her wonder what her enemy's orders were. First order would be to take prisoners, alive. Corpses could not be press-ganged. But that also meant some *would* die. Threats made real by example.

If Moses were running the mission, the lives of the Earthlings would be treated like the most valuable materials in the universe. For one, he'd been an Earthling himself, but for another, as ruthless as he was, he'd never taken a civilian life unless given no other choice. Dava feared the Misters might not be so careful. They were following orders, and were probably promised compensation for each soul they brought in.

She looked at the overhead view. The semi-circle was closing. Tactically, it would be better to come at them from behind their advance, splitting their line. But that would mean pressing them toward the ark itself. They couldn't know what Shadowdown was or their motives, but they could guess quickly enough, and when pushed, they would start treating the Earthlings as hostages.

"Tell the first maria to put down right there." She pointed to a spot just in front of the long side of the ark that faced the closing semi-circle. "Get everyone else to try to land as close as possible. It's better if they land on the other side of the ark, then press around it and meet at the maria."

"Got it."

"What about us?" Toom-Toom said.

Dava stood. "Check on everyone in the back. Tell them to pop their punch-pills. We're going to secure the landing area."

* * *

Dava's squad was nine. She'd spread her capos among the other ships, which left her with Lucky, Toom-Toom, and six tough, but less-experienced grunts. Still, the grunts had all been in the breach-and-board of the ModPol transport in Eridani. Which meant they'd all been captured and taken into the zero-G prison. Which meant they'd fought their way back out of the prison with the rest who made it out. That was a lot of hard lessons learned in a very short time.

They had no room for a vehicle in the dropship, so they had to pound through the cold, dark sand on foot. They were closer to the ark than the approaching Misters, but the Misters had wheels.

"Move your goddamn asses!" she screamed at the shrouded desert.

Her own punch-pill had rushed through her veins. It was a last-resort drug, one that Moses used early in his career, then tapered it off due to detrimental effects on the hearts of frequent users. It wasn't an addictive drug; in fact most people were repulsed after their first few drops. Crammed with chemical stimulants and concentrated sugar for a sustained burn, with a pinch of an empathy-inhibitor that ramped aggression.

They fury-stomped over the sand like it had insulted the mothers that had abandoned them.

The cold night swung hotter as they neared the hull of the steaming ark. It was a massive ship, its side rising above the sand several times Dava's height. Some unknown percentage of it had plunged below the surface. They approached it near the rear thrusters, the rest of it stretching away, four or five times long as it was tall. Its form blurred in the heated, shimmering air that stung her nostrils with the dour musk of melted metal.

She stopped for no more than sixty seconds to make sure her team was with her. Then she pressed them on. She wanted to reach the middle-point along the long side of the vessel. There were several access points to the inside, but they couldn't defend them all.

Engines revved and as they jogged, she saw the source of the sound. Three trucks bounded over the dunes, heading directly for them.

"Get low," she said. It was likely the Misters didn't expect anyone to greet them. "Weapons ready. Wait until they get close."

She saw one of the grunts reach for a grenade on the strap across his chest. She held out a hand, shaking her head silently. With the magnets in them, the grenades were likely to hit the front of a vehicle and then stick. It would be a nice surprise, but those things were made for pushing through the sand and were protected front-wise by thick, metal scoops.

She gestured with a flat hand. *Patience.*

The vehicles pulled closer, their glaring lights gleaming off the surface of the ark's hull just a few meters from where Dava's squad crouched in the darkness. She heard doors yawning open. Boots hitting the soft sand.

She pointed at three to follow her, gestured at the rest to stay. The punch-pills made them quake with anxiety. They would have to hold it until she was ready.

She took her three out and around, creeping outward to a point off to the side of the trucks, about thirty meters away. Without the glare of the headlights, she could easily see them. Twelve in all. They moved stiffly, an indication of the durable but cheap armor they'd been supplied. Their guns were more diverse, a hodge-podge of whatever weapons could be scrounged up.

Most of them began a cautious stalk toward the ark. Three stayed behind with the trucks. She crept up to the closest as she watched them. She could hear the equipment of her grunts clinking behind her. Fortunately, the rumble of the massive gas-powered engines blanketed their stealthlessness.

With a glance back at them, she unsheathed her knife and nodded. The three grunts looked at each other, and two took out their own blades: one held a jagged-looking dagger and the other a heavy machete. The third flashed the prideful grin of a wannabe boss's pet, lifting the barrel of his rifle slightly to show off a bayonet that gleamed as though it had never been used.

Dava drew her blade in front of her neck. She had no idea how well-trained these three were, but she hoped they would do the job as quickly as possible.

She moved along the rear of the trucks, peeling off two grunts at the first gap – where one driver stood looking toward the ark – and taking the third with her to the next gap. Two drivers awaited them. She nodded at the boy with the bayonet and sprang forward.

Her blade found the gap between the armor and the helmet like it was returning home. Her victim gurgled, then hissed momentarily before falling away.

A yelp caused her to turn to the other. The grunt had

jammed his bayonet into the driver's back. He must have used enough force to penetrate the armor, but had missed the spine. The driver flailed, trying to aim his pistol behind but unable to pull away from the blade.

The grunt began cursing, trying to push the blade further in but only succeeding in pushing the man, who cried out again. Dava ducked the flailing gun and tried to plan a move to the throat, but just then the grunt's punch-pill got the better of him. He yelled out and pulled the trigger.

The armor might have been thick enough to provide protection at a distance, but at close range, the burst from the automatic rifle shredded his insides and sent chunks of red popping out the front.

The advancing group was halfway to the ark when they spun around at the sound of gunfire. Dava's mind rose above them to see the scene. Nine Misters stood between the ark and their trucks. Facing blinding headlights. Dava and three grunts could see them as plain as day. From the other side, five of her squad could see the Misters as stark silhouettes in the headlights.

"Take them down!" she screamed into both her comm and the night.

Her laser pistol blazed through the black. A split second later, it was followed by the eruption of every kind of gunfire. Lasers, projectiles, semi- and fully-automatic, burning and explosive ordnance. Less than a minute and it was over. The nine Misters were a crumpled pile of moaning.

She looked at the grunt. "Bayonet Boy," she said, unwittingly forever branding him with his new name in that moment. She pointed her gun out at the mound of bodies, some of which were still moving. "Practice your throat-cutting."

While he went to work finishing them off, she directed the other two to each take a truck. She took the third. They turned the vehicles around and lined them up. It wasn't much, but the three heavy scoops now formed a short wall behind which the black maria could set down.

"Dava!" Lucky yelled as she hopped out of the truck. "Get back! The maria is here!"

She looked up to see the retros around the bottom of the fat cube of a ship. In the distance beyond, headlights grew all along the horizon. She felt herself grin with an empty anger.

This was just getting started.

* * *

"We're too late!" Lealina slapped the dashboard of the rover. "We're too late!"

Jax leaned forward from his place in the rear. The massive form of Barnard-5 cast the entire desert in shadow, but here it was lit with orange fire and white electricity.

"We need to wait for the Defenders," Runstom said from beside him. He was scrolling through his arm-pad. "They're closing in. ETA is two hours, thirty-two minutes."

"If they aren't here yet, then who's fighting?" Jax said.

"Gotta be militia," Granderson said.

Lealina shook her head. "FSC ordered them to convene at the north edge of the Low Desert." She looked from the window to her handheld pad and back. "They haven't sent anyone in yet."

Jax looked at Runstom, the green skin of his face creased in deep thought. "What is it, Stan? Who's out there?"

He drew in a breath. "I think," he started, then paused. Finally, he said, "I think it's Space Waste."

"Fighting against who?" Granderson said, turning back from the driver's seat to look at them.

"Space Waste," Jax said quietly. Faces flooded into his mind: Moses Down, Rando Jansen, Dava, Basil Roy.

"You mean, it's Space Waste against Space Waste. In-fighting."

Granderson whistled in appreciation, then turned back to the front and flipped a thin screen down from the ceiling, covering the middle portion of the windshield. He poked at some controls and the screen winked to life. A video image appeared, mirroring the scene beyond. With more working of the controls, the image panned and zoomed.

"What is this?" Lealina asked.

"Roof-mounted camera," he said. "Only 2-D, unfortunately, but it's got a massive zoom on it. And tons of filters. You guys don't mind if I get some footage while I'm here, do you? I mean, Space Waste on Space Waste!"

With those words, the screen went from dark and grainy to bright and clear. It was like looking through a window at a sun-lit day. Heavy-looking wheeled vehicles jounced through the sand, their headlights blazing as they streamed toward a massive structure in the middle of the desert. Granderson panned over to this structure; the ark, undoubtedly. On one side of it was a boxy ship that Jax recognized as the same kind he'd been dragged into by McManus. Several figures were using this as cover and firing at the approaching vehicles. Both sides were trying to blind each other with bright lights. The view panned to the top of the transport for a moment, and Jax could see a massive gun on some kind of tripod, probably recently mounted to the hull. The barrel erupted with a stream of flashing light, illuminating the muscled figure behind the weapon.

"I think that might be Johnny Eyeball," Jax said absently.

"Hey, do you *know* these guys, Jack?" Granderson said.

"This roof-camera," Runstom interrupted. "What does it look like?"

As soon as the question was asked, Jax could picture the camera in his mind. He'd seen Granderson operate it on several occasions. It was protected by a round shell, like a dome, when not in use. When the camera was active, an opening in the dome appeared. For long-range shots, the lens housing extended, a cylinder that protruded from the dome.

"A gun!" Jax said before Granderson could answer. "Close it back up! It looks like a g—"

There was a pop and the screen flickered. The image was replaced by the words INPUT LOST.

"Heads down!" Runstom shouted.

Jax reflexively followed the order, then popped his head back up to look at Lealina. Both she and Granderson were bent over, hands clasped above their heads. Jax snapped his head back down and listened to his own panicked breathing.

For a long moment, nothing happened. Then the inside of the rover was lit by a bright light.

A speaker crackled to life. "Open the doors slowly. If you're just civilians, you have nothing to fear."

"Should we do what they say?" Granderson said. "I think we should do what they say."

"I don't trust them," Runstom growled.

Jax lifted his head just enough to see the light pattern on the ceiling. It was coming through the windows on the left side of the vehicle, where he was. He managed a glance at Lealina. Her head was still down, and her body was visibly shaking.

"I'm going out," he said. Before anyone could argue, he added quickly, "If those are Wasters out there, there's a chance they'll know me."

He popped the door and creaked it open, ignoring the hushed protests from the others. If they didn't know him, then he would have to hope they were telling the truth about not hurting civilians.

He stuck his hands out first. "Don't shoot! We're not armed."

"Come on out of there," the speaker said.

He looked back at the others. Lealina's eyes blazed with terror, her mouth frozen open. He took a deep breath, then slowly slid out of the vehicle.

He saw a truck a few dozen meters away. It was positioned parallel to the rover, but that was all Jax could make out as some kind of mounted light shone down from the top, flooding his vision.

"Who are you?"

"I'm Jack." He paused, wondering whether to try to identify himself as Psycho Jack. "Do any of you know a Jack by any chance?"

Even though the speaker was silent, Jax could hear the mumbles of a confused conversation.

"Keep your hands up," the speaker said. "We're going to inspect your vehicle."

Jax raised his hands higher and waited an eternity before two figures emerged from the rear of the truck. They stalked cautiously toward him, each pointing a handgun in his direction. The air was frigid and the night rang with the distant popping of gunfire, only partially drowned out by the sound of the truck's gas engine. Jax felt his whole body shake.

About halfway between the vehicles, they stopped. "What the hell is on top of your car?" one of them said.

"It's just a camera," Jax said quickly.

"A camera." He lowered his gun by a centimeter and cocked his head, looking up at the roof of the rover.

"Ohh," the other one said, gun dropping even further. "I've seen this thing before. It's just a holovid truck. Like a portable recording thingy."

"Really?" the first one said. He tensed back up and refocused his gun on Jax. "Prove it."

Jax's mouth opened and closed a few times. "Um, well, I'd love to. But it's broken."

"Broken?"

"Yeah ... because you ... shot it."

Both of their guns came down. "We shot it?" the first said.

They looked at each other. A crack supplanted all background noise, and the two figures tossed to the left like plastic bags jostled by a gust of wind. In the cold spotlight, the sand welled red around their twitching bodies.

Jax dropped to the ground and rolled under the rover. More shots fired, these even closer. Screams rang out from the direction of the truck. Then a fast silence.

His brain had two seconds of calm thought and he remembered Lealina. He rolled back out from under the rover and began to stand, but only made it to a crouch before he froze at the click of a gun.

"You're Psycho Jack."

He picked his head up at the sound of the woman's voice. Her skin's crimson tone was that of a Poligartian and she was vaguely familiar to him. So many faces had swam by in his short time at the Space Waste base. "I am," he said quietly.

"Seven-Pack," she said. She tilted a massive revolver downward and slid a couple of bullets in. Dark blood oozed from the jagged blade that was attached to the barrel.

The dreamlike time as a Waster came back to him in pieces. "Right," he said, slowly straightening to a stand. "You're a fan of beer."

"Yep." She finished reloading and slapped the chamber back into place. "What the hell are you doing out here, Psycho Jack? You ain't Mister Jack now are ya?"

"Mister Jack?" he said dumbly. More bits of the dream surfaced to remind him about some rival gang called the Misters. "Oh, no. Definitely not."

She held her gun to her chest, neither pointing it at him, nor holstering it. "You following RJ?"

"Jansen," Jax said carefully. *In-fighting*. Of course, if there was in-fighting, it would be those loyal to Jansen and then some other group. Which side was this Seven-Pack on? He had no good guess. If only he'd spent more time socializing while he was a Waster – such a thought made him nauseous with fear. "Dava brought me in," he said, with what felt like his safest gamble.

"So you're loyal to Dava," she said evenly.

Jax blew out a breath. "Yes?"

She watched him for a second, then cracked a smile. "I know you're Psycho and all, but maybe you better turn this thing around and get the fuck outta here before you and your friends get minced. Half-Shot says he's sorry he shot your camera."

He flinched at her choice of words, trying hard not to imagine what a human being looked like *minced*. A flash of bravado pushed him forward.

"We're here to help."

Her jaw slid as though she were chewing on the statement. "Help who?"

"The Earthlings," he said, trying to firm up his shaking voice. "Has anyone been in contact with them? Their life support was badly damaged."

She glanced over her shoulder as an explosion rocked a distant truck. "I don't think so. They aren't responding to any open channels. We've been busy trying to hold off the Misters."

"Did Space Waste really split?"

"Hold on," she said, listening to her earpiece. "Yeah. Yeah, it's Psycho Jack. He says the Earthlings lost life support. Okay. Okay, Boss." She looked at him. "I can get two of you to the ark."

She flinched, looking behind Jax. He turned to see the driver's door of the rover pop open and Lealina climbing over Granderson.

"I'm going with you," she said. "You and I are the only people qualified to figure out what's wrong with the system."

He completely disagreed that either of them was qualified to interact with Earth-based tech – especially on that scale – but then he realized that Granderson and Runstom were even less qualified.

"Okay." Jax reached for her and took her by the hand. He looked past her at Granderson, then at Runstom as he came out of the back of the rover. "We're going to go."

Runstom put up a hand. "Go. It would be better for me to wait for the Defenders." He stepped forward and handed Jax a small device. "Just keep me up on what's happening. And Jax," he said, fixing him with his eyes. "Keep me up on who's who. It's getting hard to tell."

Jax knew exactly what he meant. The Wasters had shot

down the ark, and yet they were here defending it against some rival gang. And then there was Seven-Pack's inquiry into his loyalty to Dava.

"Yes," Seven-Pack said, and it took Jax a second to realize she was answering his earlier question. "RJ is running Space Waste and he's got the Misters on his side. Dava wants to protect the Earthlings."

"Okay," Jax said tentatively as he tried to process that information. He looked over the device Runstom had handed him; it was simple, just a voice-only transmitter, and very sleek and silver with small markings on it that told Jax it was custom-made for ModPol. He lifted it up and nodded at Runstom. "I'll call, Stan."

Then he looked at Granderson and opened his mouth to show gratitude, but the other man just waved. "I'm gonna see how bad the damage is," he said, nodding to the camera mounted to the roof of his rover. "I got some replacement lenses with me. And if that don't work, I still got my handhelds and my drones."

Jax nodded. Granderson was determined to come away with some footage, and Jax wasn't compelled to stop him. He'd given them a ride out to the site; what he did now was his own concern. And any spare thought burned Jax's mind as wasted time, time that should've been spent getting to the Earthlings in danger.

He turned to Lealina and Seven-Pack. "Let's go."

* * *

Seven-Pack and a tall man with a long rifle named Half-Shot each had small all-terrain vehicles. They'd been on scouting patrol when they'd shot out Granderson's camera and then subsequently saved Jax's ass from some Misters. Within minutes, the two ATVs brought Jax and Lealina right up to the side of the ark, and then into the safety of the boxy transport's shadow, which was lightning-strike strobe-lit from the gun mounted on top.

Seven-Pack led them through the rear door of the transport, and Jax's memories hounded him. If it wasn't the exact same ship that he'd been taken aboard when McManus tracked him down, it was at least the exact same model. He felt his breath growing short as they passed through it.

Dava was sitting in the small bridge, along with a pilot Jax had met before – his nametag reminding Jax the name was *Lucky Jerk* – and another Waster that Jax had seen before in passing. The two young men were operating the consoles with Dava passing between them, looking over their shoulders and periodically speaking into her headset.

"Psycho Jack," she said when she noticed him. A crooked smile dented her cheek. "You have a way of turning up."

"Hi, Dava." He looked around the cabin sheepishly. "Thanks for not killing me the last time."

Her smile grew for a moment, then disappeared into the press of the present. "Seven-Pack told me you can fix the life support on the ark."

Jax swallowed. "Well, I hope I can—"

She stepped up to him, drawing close enough that he could feel the heat of her breath on his cheeks. He wanted to reach behind and blindly seek out Lealina's hand, but he found he couldn't move. "Do you know where I'm from?" Dava said.

"Yes," he said in a whisper. *Earth,* his mind said, but he couldn't get the word out, preoccupied with the glinting blade strapped to Dava's chest.

"Those are my people, Jax." He'd forgotten that he'd asked her to call him that, but as soon as he heard it, a relief came over him. She wasn't threatening him, she needed him.

"We can do it," Lealina said. "We'll make sure they're safe. This is their home now."

Dava's face seemed to relax on first hearing Lealina's voice, then bunched up at the end in a kind of sad anger. She backed away and looked back at one of the consoles.

"Freezer is almost in, at this door, number five," she said. "Take him in with you – he's a better hacker than you are."

Jax almost felt hurt, then remembered he never called himself a hacker – that was always their term. "Okay." He glanced at Lealina, then back at Dava. "Thank you."

"I want those people safe," she said. She turned and faced them again, her face dark and her teeth rigid. "*My* people. I would go with you, but there's no one to murder inside the ark. So I'm going to stay out here and murder anyone else that thinks they're getting in."

Jax's eyes fell to the blade and bounced back to her face. His flesh rose at the sincerity of her promise.

"Why are the Wasters doing this?" Lealina said. Jax trembled at her brazen question. He wished he could pull her aside and relate some of the things that Dava was capable of, as a way to inform her that this was not a woman anyone should endeavor to spend long amounts of time with in enclosed spaces.

"The *Wasters* are recruiting," Dava said, unperturbed by the challenge. Her voice turned cold and matter-of-fact. "Those idiots in the trucks out there are cells of Misters. Rando Jansen made them some kind of deal, an alliance. He's out there in the *Longhorn*. He shot down the ark so the Misters could rush it."

"For ... recruiting?" Lealina said.

"That's why the Wasters and the Misters are here," Dava said. Her voice lowered. "We're here to stop them."

"We're Shadowdown," Lucky Jerk said brightly. Everyone looked at him and he shrugged. "It's still catching on."

Jax finally put it together that Dava was leading this Shadowdown group, while Jansen was leading the rest of Space Waste. Which left a question. "Moses Down?" he said, the quiver in his voice betraying his fear of the answer.

The two men glanced at Dava and then refocused on their consoles. She looked at Jax, her eyes seeing something light-years distant, then snapping back to the present.

She nodded once. "Gone."

A moment later, Jax and Lealina were rushed back out of the bridge by an unseen force, one that told them they were in the way while a commander was managing a battle. They were ejected from the terrible enclosure of the prisoner transport and onto the cold sand, into the dark night.

"Door Five!" Lealina shouted over the bursts of gunfire above. She pointed at the hull of the ark.

They jogged through the sand toward the door a few dozen meters away. A wiry figure in a long black coat was bent before an open panel while another much wider figure looked on.

"Freezer?" Jax said as they approached.

The wide one whipped around to point the yawning black barrel of a massive weapon at Jax, whose hands shot up into the air.

"The fuck is this domie doin' here?"

Freezer turned, then stood and put his hand on the gun to encourage the other man to lower it, somewhat unsuccessfully. "It's okay, Wide-Mouth. This is Psycho Jack. You never heard of Psycho Jack?"

The weapon lowered as the big man's face broadened with recognition. "Oh, yeah, Psycho Jack."

"Jax," Lealina whispered. "Why do people keep—"

"I'll tell you later," he whispered back. Then louder, he said, "Did you get the door open?"

Freezer spun back to the door and slapped the panel shut. The door slid open and he presented it with open hands, like he'd performed some kind of magic trick. The door began to shudder and froze about half-way up.

His hands went down to his hips. "Well, we can get in at least." He looked at Jax. "Missed your chance to pop this baby open."

Jax decided not to admit that actual hacking wasn't in his repertoire. He gestured at the door. "Let's go. We need to find out what's wrong with the life support."

"Wait out here, Wide Mouth," Freezer said, then scooped up a small brown bag and ducked through the door.

Jax and Lealina gingerly stepped past the big man. Jax had to get on his hands and knees to get under the half-open portal.

When he stood back up, Freezer was gesturing in the thin corridor that was dimly lit by red emergency lighting. "I didn't want him to get stuck," he whispered, nodding at the door. "Just trying to spare his feelings. He's self-conscious about his size."

"Didn't you call him 'Wide Mouth'?" Lealina said.

Freezer's head tipped to one side. "That's his name." He looked at Jax, then pointed his bag at him. "Where's your kit?"

Jax stared at his own empty hands. "Um, I don't have one."

Freezer frowned, then wiped away the expression with a

shrug. “Come on, we should start with the control room. Supposed to be at the front.”

They jogged down the corridor, which ran straight along past a few other hatches. Freezer spoke up as they went. “There wasn’t a code on that door,” he said. “It was locked, but not by a person. The system had it on lockdown. Some kind of safety thing.”

“How did you get it open?” Jax said.

“Had to bypass the circuit, make it think the signal was coming through clean.”

“Control,” Lealina said, and they looked ahead at the labeled door at the end of the passage.

As they approached, the door slid open with an electric swish.

Inside the control room were several black monitors mounted to walls full of switches and lights. The room was awash in yellow light, much brighter than the red they’d just come from. There were several mounted chairs at various consoles, and two very startled Earthlings.

The man and the woman both stood, nearly falling over their own chairs. They stretched almost as tall as Jax, but despite their joint efforts to rise to full height, they both swayed and dipped, grabbing equipment around them to stay upright.

“Who da hell are you?” the woman said.

Jax felt stunned for a moment. His mind was trying to process several things at once, thanks to a seed planted by Dava. She’d called the Earthlings “her people”, and that hadn’t registered with Jax. Looking at this man and this woman, whose skin was so dark, he hadn’t seen anything like it since Moses. There had been just a few other black-skinned members of Space Waste when Jax was there; but not many. And if Dava had lost Moses, then that was one less in her life.

Why this mattered was another thread vying for attention in his mind, and he couldn't help but remember what it was like to live on Barnard-4. Everyone, literally everyone other than the occasional tourist or exchange student was tall, thin, and had blank white skin, just like he did. It was something he never thought about – never – until he'd left that planet. Until he'd left those domes and was forced to visit other parts of the galaxy, to see the variety of humanity spread throughout it, he hadn't appreciated what it meant to have a *people*; even if it was a people he was done with. He never intended to go back to Barnard-4, but it would always be there, there was no doubt about that. Those people would always be there, domes full of people that wouldn't look at Jax twice.

Lealina pushed past his stunned state and stepped into the control room. "We're here to help. My name is Lealina Warpshire. We got a message that said your life support is failing. And we haven't had any communication since then."

The two Earthlings looked at each other, and after a pause, both slumped in relief. "I'm Isella," the woman said. "Dis is Amar."

"Everythin' is broken," Amar said with a feeble wave of his hand. Their accents were strange, with letters like "g" and "r" frequently missing from their speech. "Da attack damaged owah life support. We thought it was best to land on the surface, because it already sustains life. But da landin' was bad for us."

"Took out our comms," Isella said. "Took out a buncha sensahs."

"Me and Isella were woken first. But in the attack, the process locked."

"So everyone else?" Lealina said, her voice trailing off.

"Still alive," Isella said. "But half-woke. And we can't get them out."

"They're all sealed up," Amar said. "They got oxygen to them now, but it's real low. If we don't get them out ..." he said, his voice cracking.

"Let's take a look," Lealina said, reaching back to grab Jax's hand and tug him toward the Earthlings.

Isella slumped back into a chair. "Here," she said, motioning to the chair next to her. "I'll bring up the messages."

"Messages?" Jax said as Lealina shoved him into the chair.

The screen before him was a mess of cartoonish icons and free-floating squares of scrolling text. Each of these boxes had a title at the top. He took a breath and tried to focus on each.

LIFE SUPPORT MONITOR
WARN – *Life support alert: pod oxygen supply at 8%*
WARN – *Life support alert: pod oxygen supply at 7%*
WARN – *Life support alert: pod oxygen supply at 6%*

INTERNAL ENVIRONMENT CONTROL
INFO – *Attempting to vent internal environment to external environment.*
ERROR – *External Environment Clearance exception raised: an internal communications error occurred.*
WARN – *Exception raised while attempting to unlock vent control.*
INFO – *Life support alert re-enqueued.*

INFO – *AI subsystem exiting.*
INFO – *Life support alert message received from queue.*
INFO – *AI subsystem attempting to resolve alert.*
INFO – *Attempting to vent internal environment to external environment.*
ERROR – *External Environment Clearance exception raised: an internal communications error occurred.*

EXTERNAL ENVIRONMENT SUBSYSTEM
ERROR – *unable to read external sensor F3*
ERROR – *unable to read external sensor F4*
ERROR – *unable to read external sensor F9*
ERROR – *unable to read external sensor S3*
ERROR – *unable to read external sensor A3*
ERROR – *unable to read external sensor A6*
ERROR – *unable to read external sensor P1*
ERROR – *unable to read external sensor P3*
ERROR – *unable to read external sensor P8*
ERROR – *unable to read external sensor P9*
ERROR – *unable to read external sensor T3*
ERROR – *unable to read external sensor F3*
ERROR – *unable to read external sensor F4*

"What are all these sensors?"

With a few taps from Isella, another window sprang to life. "They're listed here," she said. "It's pretty much anything related to human safety: gas mixes and levels, temperature, radiation levels, levels of known toxins."

"Oh, I get it," Freezer said from over his shoulder. "F is fore, S is starboard, A is aft, and P is port, T is top." He cocked his head. "Must be they don't bother with bottom when you're going to crash land on that side."

"This one," Jax said, pointing at the box labeled *Internal Environment Control*. "It's looping."

"Yep," Freezer said, leaning close enough to make Jax flinch and angle slightly to one side. "It's a halting problem."

"A halting problem," Jax said slowly.

"Damn thing keeps trying to correct the alert, but it's not handling this clearance exception from the other subsystem. That kicks the alert back into the queue and starts the process all over again." He leaned back. "Can we run this venting thing manually?"

Lealina leaned into Jax. "Exception?"

"Programmer lingo for 'error'," Jax whispered.

"We tried that," Amar said at Freezer's question. "All we can do is trigger the venting process. We still hit the same clearance exception."

"Maybe the sensors are just out of whack," Lealina said. "Can you reset the system somehow?"

"Turn the whole thing off and then back on again," Isella said. "Yeah, we tried that too. Twice."

"Three times if you count when it rebooted after the crash landing," Amar said.

"Hang on," Freezer said, once again leaning far over Jax's shoulder. He stabbed at the box labeled External Environment Subsystem. "Notice a pattern here, Jack?"

Jax squinted at the box. The errors repeated "unable to read external sensor" over and over, scrolling up the screen whenever a new one appeared, a rate of a few every second. The words blended together and he focused on the identifiers of the sensors. "The threes," he said finally. "F3, S3, A3, P3, T3."

"Radiation," Isella said. "The threes are for radiation levels."

"They have the same sensors on every side of the ship?" Lealina said.

"Right, of course," Jax said nodding. "For redundancy. The chances that a crash landing would take out all five are probably pretty low."

"The attack took some of them out," Isella said sourly. Jax glanced to his right and caught her eye. She was biting her tongue; he could see that. She wanted badly to demand who attacked the unarmed ark and why, but she was putting the problem of saving lives before anything else. Her composure was likely one of the reasons she was the first to be awoken.

Jax looked back at the looping messages in the control system, the "halting problem" as Freezer had called it. "Fucking engineers," he muttered. He'd seen this kind of thing before. "They had five-way redundancy. This error was never expected to get hit, so they called it an *internal error*. The system is throwing up its hands and saying, 'I'm stuck, try again.'"

"Fuck it," Freezer said. "We just need to call the venting code directly. This whole process is just a wrapper, doing some validation against the sensor subsystem. We need to bypass that and go straight to the raw function."

"How do we do that?" Jax said. Freezer was already over his head and the speed at which he talked made Jax's lungs feel tight.

"It's probably a reserved function," he said. "We just have to write up a quick module to access it."

"You can do that?" Amar said.

"Sure. You know the programming environment? COMPLEX? Or Qubidense? Or K-LANG? Probably COMPLEX."

COMPutational LEXicon was the only of those that Jax knew anything about, since it was the programming language he had to use in his job as a life-support operator back on Barnard-4. It felt like an entire lifetime had passed since then.

Freezer leaned in to the point where Jax thought he might be making a move to dislodge him from the chair and take over. Jax put a hand up. "Hold up, Freezer. This ship is from Earth," he said. "Those languages were all invented in the domes."

"Shit, you're right," he said in a rare moment of slowed-down speech. "No one uses Earth tech anymore."

Jax knew the last statement was an excuse, a justification for the sudden ignorance that had crashed down upon Freezer. The kid was a master hacker of all things in the modern galaxy, but had no opportunity – or reason – to learn anything about old-world technology.

"I just wish I could see the logic behind this sequence," Freezer said. "There have to be some data ports into this system somewhere. If I could connect my rig, I might be able to get a look at the code. Even if I can't reverse-compile it, I might be able to get *something* out of the bytecode."

"There is a physical maintenance port," Amar said. "We have cables."

"Good, let's try it," Freezer said.

"Any cable they have isn't going to fit your kit," Jax said.

"I have a signal modulator." He dug a small black box out of his bag. "I can cut any cable and stick the wires in here and then figure out what level of voltage to use and what kind of signal to send on each wire."

He gave Jax a look, as though waiting for his permission.

It was a strange moment when Jax realized this cocky young hacker was deferring to his judgement. "Good idea," Jax said. "Worth a shot, at least."

Freezer's face brightened slightly, and he turned to wave Amir into action. The two of them went off to another part of the cabin to rummage around in storage cabinets.

Jax went back to the screen in front of him. "Is there a way to see all the sensors in one place?" He didn't like the partial story they were getting from the log messages.

"Yeah," Isella said.

She reached over him and tapped at the screen, flicking through icons until another box opened. This one showed a simple table, each row representing a sensor, its current state and its recent history represented by a tiny trendline. She scrolled up and down the list.

Jax noticed one of the columns showed placement, internal versus external. "Can we filter to just see internal?"

She tapped and applied the filter. "See, all the internal sensors are fine."

"Safe on the inside, unknown on the outside," Lealina said. "It doesn't surprise me the system is keeping the tubes from opening."

"But it's not safe inside," Jax said. "The O2 is dropping."

"If it goes low enough, I think the stasis process kicks back in," Isella said. "That will make a little oxygen last a long time."

"Better to put them back to sleep than let them go outside and be cooked by radiation," Lealina said with a nod. She had grown cold and matter-of-fact, and Jax recognized the focus he'd seen in her in past crises. For some reason, her calm made him more anxious.

Freezer and Amar rushed back to the space just on the

other side of the console. They busied themselves with popping panels and connecting up Freezer's device.

"If I can get into the bytecode, maybe I can see the logic behind the sequence," he said, mostly to himself as he tapped at the small interfaces of his rig.

The statement struck Jax as repetitious, but it was this repetition that made Jax understand a little more. The sequence Freezer was talking about was to initiate the tube opening, to check the sensors, and then to continue the tube opening. If they could somehow get the sensor check to pass, or skip it altogether, then all would be okay.

"I'm in!" Freezer said. His excitement drained away almost immediately. "Ugh, what a mess this code is. I wish I knew what the programmers were thinking. There's probably all kinds of docs back on Earth."

Jax stared at the screen, then turned to Isella. "Help!"

Her head slid back on her neck. "What's wrong wichu?"

"Documentation," he said. "Help text. A manual. A user guide. Is there anything like that on here?"

"Oh," she said. Again she reached over, this time pulling up a box labeled *Ark System Guide* that displayed a table of contents and a search box.

Jax took over. He searched for anything to do with the stasis system and the sensor subsystem. There was a lot of basic explanations of these systems and their general maintenance and operation. There wasn't much in the way of troubleshooting ("try to restart unresponsive subsystems") or emergency procedures. Then he typed in the exact message from the log: *Attempting to vent internal environment to external environment.*

The page that came up was sparse on explanation, but displayed a flow chart. "Look!" Jax said. "If there is an *internal* sensor with a critical warning, then it skips the *external* sensor check. That means the unexpected error doesn't get raised, and it goes straight to opening the tubes."

He took a moment to revel in the discovery, but felt weightless as he realized he didn't know what to do with it. The rest of them hushed with the same feeling of knowing this was important, but unable to capitalize.

"Radiation," Lealina said, her quiet voice a gunshot through the stillness. "We need to flip the radiation. If it's too great inside, then the broken sensors on the outside don't matter."

"Great," Freezer said. He looked around aimlessly. "So you just need to find a massive source of radiation, and point it at a sensor. They're probably all over this ship."

"The primary thruster core," Amar said.

"Jettisoned," Isella said quickly. "As soon as we entered Barnard space." She looked around at the hanging faces. "It's a one-way trip."

Amar frowned, then brightened. "The whole place runs electricity on a nuclear power plant."

"Ooh, we cause a *meltdown*," Freezer said with a bit too much enthusiasm.

Amar came around the console to come close to Isella. Their brown eyes locked. "Would that work?"

She sighed. "So many damn safety protocols. Maybe. It won't be easy."

"If we don't convince the ark's systems that there's a massive amount of radiation onboard," Lealina said, stepping in between them, "then everyone still in stasis is going to asphyxiate."

The word sent electricity through Jax. At first, he felt paralyzed, stunned. All those people in a subdome on

Barnard-4. Their deaths weren't on his hands, but they had been on his watch. Their atmosphere sucked away. The same way his mother Irene Jackson had died, oxygen slowly pulling away.

He stood. "We have to try. Whatever it takes."

CHAPTER 20

Lee "2-Bit" Tubennetal had never thought about retirement. It wasn't love of the job. He knew that. He *did* love his job, but that's just not what kept him from thinking about retirement.

It was the flyboys. An outdated term of his that everyone endured because they knew to him it meant both boys and girls. There were a lot of things about old 2-Bit that people endured. His list of bad habits, annoying quirks, and outdated quips went for miles. That was another one; they kept telling him no one knew how far a "mile" was any more.

But they put up with him, because they loved him. They loved him because he loved them. It stung his eyes to think about it. And most of the time he didn't. But now he had to. Because those times when he didn't, it was a given. Now it was no longer a given.

It's only when love is tested that it matters.

He walked around the bridge of the *Longhorn* and looked at each of his people. Young men and women at their stations. Down in the deck level, more young men and women were suiting up. Prepping hastily-repaired fighters.

He looked at the contact maps. The Fenders were moving fast. They had better ships. His flyboys were better, 2-Bit didn't doubt that. But his ships were breaking down. And his pilots were outnumbered four to one.

He was sending them to their deaths. His beloved children. They trusted his orders unconditionally.

Boss Rando Jansen had disappeared since the ark began its descent. After they'd ripped a hole through its critical systems. Jansen was a ghost, but was still issuing orders, holed up somewhere. 2-Bit laughed shortly at the thought: RJ was probably in one of the escape capsules. Just in case. 2-Bit had seen so many men and women come and go in Space Waste. He got to know the look of the ones that have escape on their mind. RJ tamped it down in the beginning, but was losing control. Too long waiting for escape, and now too close to tasting it. Whatever it was he was doing, he must have been close to finishing. Wherever he'd come from. Whomever he really was.

"Captain, all pilots ready for launch," Ensign Moh said from his console at the side of the bridge.

"Aye," 2-Bit said.

After a pause, Moh said, "Orders, Captain?"

Jansen gave orders, but there was a chain of command. And 2-Bit had done his duty, passed the orders on. He didn't know what would happen if he didn't. He'd never not. Would his people listen to him? Or would Jansen have him spaced while they silently watched?

It's only when love is tested that it matters.

The orders were to hold off the Fenders. It was bad odds. 2-Bit loved a good fair fight, and even loved a challenge.

But this was suicide. No, it was homicide. If he sent his flyboys out there, they'd be slaughtered. He might as well go down to the deck and put a bullet in every brain.

He shook his head. He had to think. To reason it out. He'd been hoping for Dava to take care of all this. He was a father-figure to his crew, but he was no goddamn leader. Dava, despite her stubbornness, ate and breathed every word that had come out of Moses's mouth. She would be an even better leader than the old Earth man was.

But Dava had her hands full. She was down there on the surface, defending the ark from the Misters that Jansen had made a deal with. 2-Bit took a breath. *We shoot down the ark. Misters close in and grab the Earthlings. We all escape.*

The part that didn't fit was RJ's plan for the Earthlings: how was the escape supposed to work? The Misters were on the ground, and had no ships down there. The *Longhorn* only had fighters on board, nothing that could land and bring hundreds of people back up. And even still – ModPol was here to ruin it all.

This bad plan came down to Jansen. The fucker knew ModPol would show up. Probably even told them when and where. But why? And what about the Earthlings?

"Captain?" Moh said quietly.

2-Bit's face crunched together. "Hold, Ensign," he muttered.

Expendable. His pilots. The Earthlings. Whatever Jansen and ModPol were up to, these people were expendable. There was no other reason to send the ark crashing to the surface. Those people would be dead before the end of the day. Just a bunch of old-world people. Casualties. Just numbers.

Numbers for whom or what, 2-Bit couldn't reason. He

knew he had no head for accounting, just a heart for people. And if Jansen was using him and his crew for this shit, it was ending right then and there.

"Ensign, give me the comm," he said. "Set it to all-call."

"Okay, Captain. Go ahead."

"Crew of the *Longhorn*," he said. His voice echoed all around him. Every beautiful eyeball on the bridge screwed his way.

It's only when love is tested that it matters.

"You've always done as I've asked." He felt a tear on his cheek. "And I'm forever grateful. Today, I gotta ask you the hardest thing I've ever asked. I'm askin' you to stand by me."

He paused to swallow down the emotion that he was feeling. Wide eyes met his own. They were fixed on him. Inside, he smiled.

"I'm relieving Rando Jansen from duty. I have reason to believe he's – he's unfit for command." He wiped the sudden sweat from his brow. "We're pulling the *Longhorn* back. Do not engage ModPol. I repeat: do not engage."

The weight of his body grew, and despite the fractional artificial gravity, he felt himself pulled down into his chair.

"One last thing," he said. "If anyone sees Jansen: stun the hell out of the motherfucker."

* * *

"Half-Shot got clipped," Toom-Toom said. He turned to Dava, his young face going pale. "Got it in the hand."

"Shit," she whispered. Her best shot with a rifle, out of the fight. That made eleven of her people critically injured. "Get him back here."

She stood, looking at the makeshift map on the large screen in the center of the bridge. They had used the images taken when the black maria was approaching and landing to plot out the desert and the ark within. Since then, they'd used coordinated communications from the Shadowdowners in the field to try to track what points they held and the movements of the Misters.

The Misters were all over the goddamn place. They weren't well coordinated, which made them unpredictable. A discernible strategy of any kind would have been easier to defend against. As it was, they alternated between taking pot shots from a distance, to sending lightning strike teams into weak spots, to swarming at various locations of the ark itself. Dava's people were burning themselves out trying to position for defense, especially anywhere away from the makeshift camp that the black maria served as.

The black maria had been the most well-stocked vehicle, so Downers had to continuously make their way back to it for restocking of ammo and power. There had been two offensive spikes from the Misters directly against the maria, but they were easily turned back by the quad-barrel, plasma-powered, 30mm autocannon that Johnny Eyeball had bolted to the top of the transport. This had meant the Misters were more likely to come at the ark from other angles. They had too many vehicles and were too mobile.

"How many confirmed takedowns do we have?" Dava said.

"Twenty-three," Toom-Toom said after a moment to count. He looked up at her. "I think that means we're winning."

"Only as long as we don't run out of supplies," Lucky said.

"Right," Dava said with a sigh. She didn't say it aloud, but in a fight like this, she knew the first to go were often the weakest. Which meant they'd culled their enemy down to the most dangerous.

"Dava," Lucky said. "They've been trying to pick away at us, but we're holding. Be ready for them to do something desperate."

The muted rumbling of the autocannon had been going in spurts for the better part of an hour. They all looked up at the ceiling as it became a steady, unbroken churn of anger. Were they making another go at the black maria?

"Johnny," she said into the open comms, knowing he wouldn't respond. "You're supposed to report back with their movements, dammit!"

"Boss," came another voice over the comm. "They're coming at me! Trying to get to Door Five!"

"That's Wide Mouth," Toom-Toom said.

Dava was already out the door. She sprinted through the narrow passages of the transport, nearly colliding with Half-Shot on her way out, his right hand wrapped in a field bandage that oozed red.

"I need your good hand," she said, grabbing him by the arm. "Seven!" she called, seeing Half-Shot's escort heading back to an ATV. "Come on, you're with us!"

The three of them jogged to the side of the ark and followed it toward the fore of the massive, still-smoking ship. From the center where the maria was planted, Door Five was halfway to the front of the ark. It had been one of the few hatches undamaged enough for Freezer to make any progress with. As they moved, she glanced back to see Eyeball firing away at a line of trucks on the opposite end.

This may have been the only half-coordinated move of

the night for the Misters. It appeared they were distracting the big gun on one side so they could send others at the ark. Their scouts must have spotted the opening and someone had cobbled together a plan.

Dava found Wide Mouth crouched against the hull where a slight buckling of metal provided a thin but critical amount of coverage. He was firing his fat shotgun, failing to hit a trio of Misters crouched near Door Five that were covering each other by firing back. They must have overwhelmed the big man and sent him falling back looking for cover.

Half-Shot dropped to the ground with his rifle. A pair of legs sprang out before the barrel touched the sand. He slid behind the propped gun and looked down the sights, his unbandaged hand taking the grip. A breath later, it popped to life. Five or six shots and the bodies of the Misters were twisting away at awkward angles.

Wild shots rang out from further away. Shooters up on the dune just beyond the ark. They weren't in a position to hit a damn thing, but she and her people couldn't take much of a shot back. Dava decided they needed to make a move for the door and get inside. The narrow opening would make it hard to effectively dash over and duck through while under fire, but if they could get in, it would be a much easier position to defend from.

The sun came out.

Or so it seemed for a moment. A swath of sand about thirty meters across lit up all around Door Five from a massive spotlight that rose above the dune. Reflexively, they all ducked down; but they were far enough back to not get caught in the beam. It panned around, but didn't stray far from the side of the ark.

So much for her plan to move at the door. Without the

cover of the dark – which was limited as it was, given the likelihood that the Misters had a few nightscopes – it was suicide.

"Everyone, hold your fire," she said in a low voice. She wanted to stop and listen. What was their plan?

The potshots raining down on them slowed.

"Maybe they're short on nightscopes," Seven-Pack whispered.

It was a possibility. The tech was not cheap, especially on a backwater moon like Terroneous. It would explain the spotlight; they were using it to better see their target. What made the least sense was their actual intentions. It seemed like they wanted to board the ark, but with Shadowdown still holding positions around the vessel, what hope would a handful of Misters have by getting inside? Would they take nearly a thousand people hostage?

"It's only a single gun now," Half-Shot said. Dava listened and realized what he meant. Each potshot sounded just like the last. The others in the group were on the move and had left one behind to continue the blind cover fire.

She looked down at Half-Shot and his sniper rifle. "Wide Mouth, can you help him prop this up so he can get a shot at that spotlight?"

"Sure, Boss. Not sure how Halfie's gonna be able to see it."

"I've got filters on my scope," Half-Shot said. "I'll hit it."

"Good," Dava said. "But wait for my signal. No voice – I'll beep you. Seven, you're with me."

She and Seven-Pack crab-walked into the darkness. They made a wide arc around the circle of light. She heard the clink of equipment and froze, putting a hand against Seven-Pack's arm to still her.

The hush of whispers. Clicking of guns, checking ammo. The brightness of the light made it impossible to see even silhouettes. She looked the other way, staring into the darkness, forcing her eyes to dilate. She held her breath.

Seven-Pack tapped her on the elbow and she looked back, closing one eye and narrowing the other to a slit. Four figures stepped into the circle of light. One of them immediately bent down to the narrow half-opening of the door. Seven-Pack's outstretched revolver tracked him.

Dava signaled Half-Shot.

The beep from his pad was as audible as a gunshot in the cold night, and all four Misters flinched, looking in the direction of the source. A second later, a true gunshot rang through the night and the world went dark.

"Light 'em up," she said softly.

While Seven-Pack unloaded blindly, Dava sprinted further along their arc, counting her soldier's shots. One, two, three. She pulled her heat goggles over her eyes. Four, Five. Unsheathed her blade and stepped toward the four glowing blobs.

Six. The last of Seven-Pack's rounds. Dava leapt forward.

The one near the door was completely prone, two bright-red wounds glowing hot. The other three showed outstretched arms, hands glowing from hot weapons blazing blindly between the source of the continued beeping and the source of the high-powered revolver that had hit them from the side. One of the three was down on one knee, and she suspected he'd taken a hit.

Dava went for the two standing. Slipped up to one and pulled the goggles from her eyes and down around her neck. Her dark-adjusted sight was better at finding the pale flesh of throats than the heat-vision was.

The target was erratic, but her blade found home with a soft plunge that was shortly followed by a sticking resistance. The scream told her she'd missed the windpipe. The Mister had managed to unwittingly twist away at the right moment, which caused her blade to slide into the underside of his chin and catch on his jaw.

It was an older blade, one she'd kept around for nostalgia; what it lacked in mechanicals or poisons, it made up for in length and sharpness. She twisted to dislodge it from the bone and thrusted with a step forward. The scream turned to a gurgle and then abruptly stopped as the blade bit deep into the brain.

As the weight of the body pulled at Dava's hand, she tried to twist the dagger free, but it was too far in. She let go, sensing another coming at her.

She raised an arm to block an incoming blow from a short club, hoping to deflect it to her left so she could lock the attacker's arm with her right. White fire blazed when the club hit her – *stun* club, she learned the hard way – and she staggered backwards, slipping on the sand and onto her back.

The form loomed above her, club raised high. Reflexively, she wanted to grab a handful of sand to throw in his face, but in the dark she caught the glint of goggles protecting his eyes.

Dava's hand found the laser pistol holstered to her leg. As the club came down, she fired into those glinting goggles and the night lit up with the terrible smell of scorched face.

She rose as the body fell. She stood above it as the head smoldered dimly crimson like the dying coals of a campfire. She could see now the Mister by the door was still and dead. The other was on both knees, tilted slightly to favor one thigh that oozed from a bullet wound. He tossed his gun and raised his hands.

She stepped over his burning companion and leveled the gun at his head. "You're dead weight."

"I surrender!" he said unnecessarily. "Please. I didn't want to be a part of this stupid gang. They forced me in!"

Dava hesitated. And hesitation begat hesitation: she wondered why she didn't just end him. There was a time when she would have without question. It wasn't pity – she could still kill those she pitied. In fact, almost all of her victims were pitiable at their end.

"Your flesh is more valuable as reptile food," she said, refocusing her aim. "I'm going to feed you to the desert."

"V-value!" he stuttered. "Information!"

Her gun fell by millimeters. "Ten seconds."

"They're going to blow up the ark!" he blurted. "They don't want the Earthlings at all! L-look!" he said, pointing at the pack lying next to the Mister dead at the door. "The pack is all minis!"

She frowned at him. "Why?"

"I don't know," he said, fear wavering his voice. "We don't know the whole plan, just our orders."

Cell structure. Dava circled the quivering man slowly until she was close to the large bag. She bent at her knees, leveling the gun at him while reaching for the flap with her other hand. She glanced for only a second. Explosives, that was for sure. They could have been breach charges, but they were too large and glinted from metallic casing, rather than the dull matte of putty. Mini-nukes, if this Mister was telling the truth. A few to be placed around the inside of the ark, then remotely detonated. Just one was enough.

"Why?" she said again, knowing there was no answer. She believed him when he said he didn't know.

Dava stood and looked out at the dark edges of the dunes around the ark. This had been an attack of opportunity. A scout had seen the half-open door. The information went up the chain, an order came back down: get some nukes inside. If the mission failed, they would find another way to destroy it.

"Freezer," she said into her comm. "Talk to me. What's going on inside?"

A few seconds passed. "Hey, Boss," Freezer said. He sounded distracted. "There's a couple of Earth operators in here, but everyone else is still locked into their tubes. Their system went into some kind of emergency protocol and we can't get the tubes open."

"You can't get them out?" she said. A flash of memory; trying to crawl out of the cold stasis tube, near-blind and numb and lost. Her breath grew shallow. "What does that mean? They're still alive, right?"

Again, it took Freezer a few seconds to reply. "Yeah, yes. For now. We need to get them out. We've got a plan, but ..."

She waited for more, but got nothing. "Goddamn it, Frank, what's the plan? Tell me the short version."

"We need to trick some sensors," he said quickly. She could hear arguing in the background whenever he transmitted. "We need a burst of radiation. We're going to try to get it from the main power plant, but we ... we can't figure out how ... how to make it leak to the right place."

She looked down at the bag. "Frank. Listen."

"Yes, Boss."

"I'm coming in. I'm bringing a mini-nuke."

A frantic pause. "Well shit, Boss. We'll meet you in the corridor."

Dava leaned down and dug one of the cylinders out of the bag. "You stupid fucks are lucky you didn't blow yourselves up."

"We were supposed to place them and get back out," the Mister said weakly. "They're remote detonated."

Which meant they could be detonated at any moment. The black maria was made for transporting prisoners and any dangerous equipment they might be carrying. Fortunately, there was a special evidence locker wrapped in a faraday cage: no radio signal could get in or out.

"Seven," she said, seeing the outline of the gunslinger approaching. "Get your lights on. And keep your gun on this asshole."

A flick and hum, and a band of ambient light appeared around Seven-Pack's waist. "Got it, Boss."

"Wide Mouth, get your ass over here!" Dava yelled. Then she turned to Seven. "Have Wide-Mouth haul these to the black maria, immediately. Tell him they have to go into the evidence lockup. You hear me?" she said, feeling her voice quiver. "We can't have them remotely detonated. He needs to get them into the faraday cage as fast as he can."

In the low light, Seven-Pack's face looked pale. "Shit. Okay, Boss."

"You go with him and take this piece of shit with you." She paused, seeing the question written on the other woman's face. So many deaths already. Once it didn't bother her. So why now? She shook her head. "He stays alive. For now."

She held the heavy cylinder against her chest with one arm and ducked through the half-open door. Red lights coated the corridor in crimson. Freezer came jogging at her, followed by Jax and his Terronean companion. Behind them was a tall Earth man. The sight of him stopped her heart. He was gaunt with deep-brown skin, almost identical to her own.

"Freezer," she said. "Tell me you got a faraday cage in your kit."

He stutter-stepped as his quick-thinking mind put it all together and tried to tell him to run far away from the nuke that could blow at any second. Fortunately, the logical part of his brain came back just as quickly, and he restarted his run.

He spilled the contents of his pack onto the floor. "Quick, get it in here. The whole bag is lined."

"I don't understand," Jax said. "This is a nuclear bomb? Where did it come from?"

"The situation has changed," Dava said. She couldn't take her eyes off the Earthling as she talked. "We thought the Misters were just trying to take control of the ark. But now they're trying to destroy it."

"They want to kill us?" the Earth man said. She wanted to learn his name, but it would have to wait.

"I'm afraid so," she said softly.

"Why bring bombs in?" Jax said. "Why not just hit the ark with nukes from a distance?" Before Dava could even process the question, his eyes widened. "Because they wanted to make it look like an accident!"

"Lucky for us," Freezer said, tapping the bag with his foot. "This little can of radiation is exactly what we need right now."

"I need to take this to the life-support hub," Jax said, reaching for the pack. "It's the best place to trigger the radiation sensors."

Dava stepped in front of him. "How are you going to get it open, Psycho Jack? You telling me you know all about portable nuclear weapons now?"

He blinked at her, mouth opening and closing. "I'll figure it out," he said, trying to sound determined. "Freezer can walk me through it."

"He can walk *me* through it," Dava said, picking up the bag.

"Um," Freezer said quietly. "Walk through what now?"

They all jumped at the sudden shrieking sound from the door. Dava turned to see the door sliding up another half-meter, a pair of massive hands wrapped around the bottom of it.

Johnny Eyeball ducked through and straightened up. "Give it to me," he rumbled.

"Johnny!" Freezer said, pointing. "He's the explosives expert."

Dava couldn't argue with that. "Johnny, you really know how to pop this thing open?"

"Yes."

"You're going to get a huge dose of radiation," she said.

His face creased and his good eye winked. "I've had worse."

"We got anti-rad treatments in prison," Freezer said quickly. "That shit is still in his system."

Dava frowned. There was no time to argue. Unless someone tricked the radiation sensors, a thousand Earthlings were minutes away from suffocating in their sleep tubes. She handed the bag over. "Be careful," she said softly.

"Take this," Freezer said, handing Eyeball a multitool. "It's my favorite, so don't break it."

Eyeball grunted as he accepted both items. He nodded at the Earthling. "Big man. You're the guide in these parts?"

"Amar," the man said. "Come on, let's go."

Eyeball and the Earthling jogged off. Dava could feel Freezer looking at her. She looked back, into pained eyes. She sighed. "Frank, you stupid shit." Torn between wanting to help his best buddy and completely rational fear of a nuclear weapon. "I order you to go with them."

He flinched, then nodded. "Yes, Boss!"

As Freezer ran off to catch up to Eyeball and the Earthling, the Terronean woman grabbed Jax by the arm. "If this works, we need to make sure everyone can get out of their tubes."

Dava saw the touch, the connection between them, and remembered why she knew the woman's face: she'd been in the holovid flick with Jax. The documentary that revealed Jax's location, causing ModPol scumbags to come looking for him. That had been when Dava and her team made their move, both rescuing and kidnapping him. Press-ganging him into service for her own paranoid purposes: to have another hacker on the team to keep Basil Roy in check. The paranoia turned out to be justified; but seeing these two together in the flesh, she suddenly questioned whether any of the rest was justified.

"An accident," Dava said quietly, then turned to Jax. "You said that's why they were bringing the nukes in. To blow the ark from the inside."

She watched his pale throat bob as he swallowed. "I think ... I think they need casualties."

"What do you mean," she said, hearing her voice strain with anger. She grabbed him by the shirt and pulled him close. "*Who* needs casualties?"

He swallowed again and his eyes widened; he'd always been afraid of her. But his face quickly furrowed in anger. It wasn't directed at her, she realized as he looked into the distance. She let him go.

"ModPol," he said.

CHAPTER 21

Runstom's foot throbbed in the cold sand. He couldn't tell if the distant fighting was dying down or coiling back for a burst of action. A final climactic engagement. The defending group – led by the vicious assassin named Dava – appeared to have the upper hand, despite being outnumbered. The attackers were gaining no purchase, haphazardly rushing in and pulling back. Their ranks fractionalized on each effort.

What Runstom struggled with was whether or not it mattered. ModPol had routed the Space Waste command ship. Defender dropships were inbound. Whoever was left standing when they arrived wasn't going to be standing for long. The Defenders would cut through the battle-weary with little resistance.

"If you're looking for something to pass the time, I could use a hand."

He turned to look at the vid-maker. David Granderson. The man responsible for exposing Jax. Later helped to hide him. Runstom had finally heard the full story while he and Jax were on EE-3.

Granderson was trying to juggle equipment, simultaneously trying to capture parts of the battle with his handheld camera and remotely control the roof-mounted camera.

"I don't know how to work any of that stuff," Runstom muttered and looked away.

"Well, how about an interview then?" Granderson tried. "Tell the galaxy what you think of this conflict?"

Runstom sighed and looked at his WrappiMate. A message from MPD Command. "If you want something to film, aim your camera over there." He pointed off to the left. "Defenders are dropping."

"Really?" Granderson fumbled with his equipment excitedly. "Never seen nothin' like that! Nobody around here has."

Neither had Runstom, unless he counted the time he and Jax crashed an out-of-control dropship on the opposite side of this very moon. He didn't remember much from the experience. Other than being surprised to be alive.

There was a beep from his comm. The detachable communicator he'd given Jax.

"Runstom here," he said.

"Stan!" Jax sounded panicked, and it spiked Runstom's heart rate. "I think we figured out how to get the Earthlings out of the stasis chambers."

He'd filled in Runstom earlier on the issue with the locked tubes. The technical details had gone over his head. Unfortunately, the situation had meant Jax had been light on details from the battle.

"Good."

"Good, yeah, but something's not good," Jax said. "The Misters – that's the other guys who are fighting with Shadowdown – they had a plan to bring mini-nukes inside the ark."

Runstom took a breath. Processed. Shadowdown was what Dava was calling her new gang – Jax had also let him know this before. Ex-Wasters. And the attackers were new recruits for the Wasters. Taking orders from Rando Jansen. The man undercover. ModPol's man.

"Mini-nukes?" he said. "Inside?"

"Yes! Stan, I think they wanted to blow it up."

"From the inside?" Runstom chewed it over for a moment. "Made to look like an accident."

"It wouldn't make sense for Space Waste to kill the Earthlings outright," Jax said. "But someone wants them dead."

"Someone," Runstom said. "You mean – are you saying you think ModPol wants the Earthlings dead?"

"It's the only thing that makes sense."

"It doesn't make sense."

Or did it? If the Earthlings all died during the conflict – a conflict between two warring gangs – then the security of Terroneous would be thrown into question. The Defenders would show up in time to clean up the mess. Not before nearly a thousand innocent lives were lost. It would send a singular message: if ModPol had been here sooner, those Earthlings would be alive.

"Dava thinks she's secured the nukes," Jax said. "But they might have more."

Runstom thought about it. Decided that play was dead. It was a gambit that would have solidified the deal. But it didn't matter. Just the threat of the nukes was enough. That was all that would come of it. The key moves were well timed. They would not stop.

"Holy," Granderson breathed. "Shit."

Fat red streaks cut through the sky like slow knife wounds. Dropships.

"Jax," Runstom said, raising his voice over the distant noise. "Where is Dava now?"

"She just went back out of the ark."

"You need to let me talk to her."

"Stan, I'm not sure—"

"Jax, goddammit!" Runstom shouted at his comm. "You *have* to let me talk to Dava."

"Okay, okay!"

There was a pause. The silence was occupied by Granderson's cooing over the sight of the dropships and the shuddering noises they made as they battered through the atmosphere.

"Stanford Runstom." The voice was cold, but Runstom thought he could hear a hint of a smile in the words.

"Dava, I know you don't have a good reason to trust me."

"No, I don't. But I trust some people close to you. And I'm going to trust you right now if you tell me why ModPol wants to see our people dead."

Our people. He didn't get what she meant by that.

"You can't win this," he said. "Defenders are dropping. They're going to sweep through your attackers. And then they're going to bury you in this desert."

There was a pause, then, "What the hell are we supposed to do?"

Runstom swallowed. "Lay down your arms."

"Fuck you."

When she didn't immediately cut the connection, he continued. "I'll call them off. But if you fire on them, they'll have every excuse to raze your people to the ground."

"And what of *our* people?"

He frowned at the comm. Then looked out at the dropships. Whatever it was she was talking about would have to wait. "You listen to me, *assassin*," he said, his tongue sour with the acid. "Do whatever the fuck you want. That's what you Wasters do. I have a job out here. I'm going to do everything I can to stop these Defenders from stomping you into dust. But if you give them a reason to, there will be no stopping them."

"And then what?" she said. "They arrest us? Throw us back in prison?"

"No one is getting arrested," he said. "ModPol Justice has no jurisdiction on Terroneous. ModPol Defense is here on a special mission to protect this moon. If there's no threat, their mission is done."

No response. She was thinking it over. Fine. He'd said his piece. How much could he back up his promise?

"Mr. Granderson," he said. "Pack it up. We're heading for those dropships."

* * *

Dava dropped the communicator to the ground. Jax flinched, wanting to reach for it, but not daring to approach.

Amar's voice came over the ship's intercom system. "We're in place."

"Okay," Isella's voice responded, also over the intercom. "I'm monitoring the sensors. How is this going to work?"

"I have a munitions expert here with me," Amar said. "He's going to expose the nuclear material in this weapon. We'll point it right where the sensors are." There was a pause, then he added. "And we pray."

"Okay." Isella's voice was tired. "And if it works?"

"Then we seal the room and get the hell out of here."

In the red corridor, Jax looked from Dava to Lealina.

The overheard conversations were apparently over: first the one between Dava and Runstom, then the one between Amar and Isella.

"We should go," Jax said to Lealina.

But she didn't look at him. She stepped toward Dava. "Why are you here?"

Dava's eyes slowly lifted to meet Lealina's. "Why are you?" she said distantly.

"We all want these innocent people to be safe."

Dava nodded. "That sonova bitch wants me to tell my crew to lay down arms." She looked at Jax. "Your friend thinks the Fenders won't slaughter us if we stop fighting. I'm not so convinced."

"He can stop them," Jax said, though he wasn't sure he believed it.

"Even if he does," she said, waving an arm and looking around. "Then what? We just walk away?"

"No," Lealina said. "No, you don't just walk away. You ride with us. Transports are coming. I want you to escort the Earthlings to the nearest city."

"And who the fuck are you?"

Lealina's eyes narrowed and she straightened her back, which only made her look smaller in a room with a lanky B-fourean and an athletic Earthling. Still, she thrust her chest up with pride. "I'm the director of the TEOB. And I'm a member of the Terroneous Federated Security Committee."

Dava actually laughed. "You think your little committee wants anything to do with scum like us?"

"You protected the Earthlings, Dava," Jax said. He stepped forward to unite with Lealina. "You may have saved their lives."

"That's good enough for me," Lealina said. "And trust me. If I go back to the FSC and tell them we have protection from – what is it?" she said under her breath, looking at Jax briefly.

"Shadowdown," he whispered. Dava arched an eyebrow, as though unsure of whether to be amused at their behavior.

"I tell the FSC we have protection from Shadowdown," Lealina said loudly. "And we *don't* need ModPol. Do you know how the committee is going to respond to that?"

Before Dava could respond with something along the lines of not knowing what the fuck some stupid committee on a backwater moon would think, Jax intervened. "I do. They're going to love it."

"Exactly," Lealina said. "We'll get you instated as Terroneous Militia."

Dava's face contorted as the realization set in: that someone else believed in her. That someone wasn't trying to chase her away, or trying to run from her. Jax didn't truly *know* Dava, but he knew her well enough to know she needed a family. And a family needed a home.

"The Earthlings are going to make a home here," he said. "Probably the last people we'll ever see come over from the old world. But there's almost a thousand of them here."

As if on cue, the intercom buzzed to life with Isella's voice. "It's working! The rads are spiking. The tubes are unlocking!"

Lealina and Dava both looked at Jax. Lealina's face brightened with victory; it was a face he'd seen when they worked together before. Dava's face looked closer to cracking. It was a mix of relief and joy and pain.

"We're sealing up the room now," Amar said. "We'll be back in just a minute."

Lealina threw her arms around Jax. "They're going to be okay!"

Jax returned the embrace, but looked past her at Dava. "They're going to be okay," he echoed.

Dava's face completed its confused cycle of emotions, ending in a twist into hard determination. "Shadowdown," she said suddenly and loudly into her comm. "Everyone listen up. Defend Door Five on the ark. Fall back from all other positions." She took a massive breath, her chest heaving. "Fenders are coming. Do *not* engage them. I repeat: do *not* engage the Fenders."

She lowered her hand and glared at Jax and Lealina. "You motherfuckers better be right. If those Fenders come in here guns blazing, I'm making a white flag out of your pale-ass skin."

* * *

On the way to the landing zone, Runstom had the dispatcher at MPD Command get a message to the ground forces. That he was coming in a wheeled rover. That it had a camera dome on top; not artillery. That he would flash his lights on approach so they would know it was him.

They barreled up to the rear side of the dropships, Granderson flashing the headlights nervously. There were five ships in all, and they formed a line that curved away from the battlezone. This allowed them to assemble from behind the protective hulls of the ships. Runstom and Granderson made a long arc in order to approach from the rear side.

The signaling-by-headlight seemed to work, because they weren't immediately disintegrated on approach. The unit had already established makeshift watch duties and a bulky-armored Defender waved them to a stop.

"Stanford Runstom," he said, transmitting an ident burst from his WrappiMate when the guard pointed at his arm.

"Clear," the guard said. The voice came through a speaker on the front of the helmet. "Public relations, eh? This is a big moment for you, Mr. Runstom. Too soon for congratulations?"

"Yes," Runstom said. "Can you send me the unit roster please?"

Runstom couldn't see the Defender's face due to the complete coverage of the helmet. He couldn't even tell if it was a man or a woman. Whoever it was gave a pause at his request, then shrugged. Runstom's WrappiMate beeped with the incoming data.

He scrolled through the list. Focused on officers. He knew none of them. Except one. Scrolled back. Yes. Major L. J. Oliver. Second-in-command. Captain Oliver had earned a promotion since he'd last seen her. Back on Vulca, moon to Sirius-5, where she'd led a trial unit of onsite Defenders.

He wasn't sure if she would be glad to see him.

The data had included the ident of the sender, the guard whose faceless helmet glared at him. "Defender Polin," Runstom said. "I need to speak with Major Oliver. It's extremely urgent."

Polin remained immobile for a moment, then shrugged, or at least came as close to shrugging as one could in such armor. "I'll give her the message, but she's busy with mission prep."

"Just tell her it's Stanford Runstom. Tell her she'll remember me from Vulca."

The Defender strolled back to their post. Runstom hoped that meant they had transmitted the message.

He looked out at the space created by the small arc of the five dropships. Men and women were in various stages of gearing up and collecting into formation. He guessed there were at least sixty Defenders, not including their commanders.

An unarmored figure approached.

"Is that Oliver?" Granderson said in a hushed voice. "I was expecting someone less ... female."

"*Lucy* Oliver," Runstom said. He was also trying not to be distracted by the finely cut form.

"Well," she said, presenting a broad smile as she came up to Runstom's side of the rover. "Stan Runstom. Good to see you again. How's Public Relations? Brought a camera to get some MPD footage?"

Runstom cleared his throat. "Um. Yes. It's good to see you too, Major." She was only wearing a light jacket and instead of a helmet, wore a head-wrap comm device. "Congratulations on the promotion."

"Thank you. It came right after we last saw each other."

"And how's the arm?"

She raised it. Flexed it. Said nothing. Runstom thought it looked just fine.

He glanced over his shoulder at Granderson, then turned back to the door of the rover. Cracked it open and slid out onto the sand. Bounced once on his bad foot with a grimace.

"You're nursing a war-wound of your own," she said, lowering her voice to match their sudden proximity.

He shook his head and waved at the foot dismissively. "Major." He pointed to her headset. Tipped his head in question.

Her smile shrunk away. Met his eyes. Removed the headset. "You got something to tell me, Stan?" she said softly.

"Listen, Major—"

"If we're going off the record," she said firmly, "you have to call me Lucy."

Words caught in his throat. Her eyes snared his. He swallowed sandy air and continued. "Lucy. On Vulca. Remember how ... *off* it was? You got the orders to do an unplanned scouting run that morning. The same morning that—"

"That Space Waste attacked." Her lips pursed. "Yes, I remember. And I remember we were victorious."

"Right." When things don't make sense, but they work anyway. Had she stopped questioning when she got a promotion? Or felt no other action than compliance was possible?

"How's the search for home?" she said.

The sudden change of subject threw him. He traveled back to the last moment he'd seen her. This had been the subject they shared. No ground to go to. Lost, forever.

"Same as yours," he said. A bold assumption, he knew.

She nodded. "So it is," she said softly. "Stan? What the fuck are we doing in this desert on this independent moon?"

He took a deep breath. "It's Vulca all over again, Lucy. An orchestrated event. Designed to provide MPD with an opportunity."

"An opportunity to be the hero," she said. "To save the day."

"To land a contract."

Now it was her turn for a deep breath. "Well." She nodded at the distant popping noise of gunfire. It had been on the decline for the past hour, but was still ever-present. A shot or two. An answer. "There's a threat. Innocent people are in danger."

Runstom grunted. "It's how they got put in danger that bothers me."

A small explosion briefly lit the heavy night. For a singular flash, he could see her face. "I have to go, Stan." She shifted, then paused. "What do you need?"

He stepped closer to her. "What's the plan? The battle plan? Never mind, it doesn't matter."

"Yeah, no kidding," she said. "It's going to be a one-sided fight."

"It's a three-sided fight, Lucy."

"Three? The Wasters—"

"They've split. There's a contingent that's defending the ark from the rest of them." He paused, unsure of how to differentiate the forces. There were no uniforms.

"Defending the ark," she said, eyes narrowing.

"Defending the Earthlings," he said.

"Interesting."

He read the bemusement on her face, felt it himself. It wasn't like Wasters to protect lives. But somehow he believed it. These were Earth lives, and Dava was an Earthling.

"When you get to the ark, those defending forces … they're going to lay down arms."

Oliver huffed. "When squads of Defenders are coming at them, they're going to drop their weapons?"

"It's the only way out of this," he said. "Lucy – all I'm asking is that your people be on the lookout. Not everyone here is an enemy."

"Alright, Stan," she said, looking him in the eyes. There was a pause, only the space of a breath, but enough time for something to pass between them. She quirked a smile. "Since you asked nicely. I'll make sure we don't kill anyone that's not trying to kill us."

She reached out and grabbed his hand. Gave it a single pump. Then pulled away and replaced her headset.

"See you when it's over," he said. Allowing himself this tiny moment of connection.

She nodded. "When it's over."

* * *

Dava sprinted into the cabin of the maria. "Someone tell me those nukes are secure."

"Secure, Boss." Wide-Mouth was looming near the door, unsure of what to do with himself as Lucky and Toom-Toom busied themselves with the monitors all around them. "That evidence locker is as tight as it gets. Multiple layers of cages. No signal getting through that."

"Good." She wanted to breathe relief, but it wasn't over yet. She stood over Lucky Jerk. "What'd I miss?"

"Dava," he said, just noticing her there. "Everything is in pieces. I would kill for some sat-imagery right now. From the intel coming back from the Downers out there, this is the best picture we got."

He pulled up the crude 2-D map that consisted of shapes and lines and numbers. From inside the maria, the entire battle had to be viewed this way: reports from the soldiers – both feeds from some helmet cams and manual reports – were their only data sources.

The green shapes were Shadowdown, and the red were the Misters. Dava pointed at the purple shapes that had appeared along the bottom of the screen. "Defenders?"

Lucky looked back at her. "How'd you know?" He turned back to the screen, not waiting for her answer. "They're pushing straight through the middle, splitting the Misters in half."

"That's good," she said. The Defenders had lit up the

shadows with penetrating wide-spectrum lights beaming forth from the tops of their dropships. A column of sunshine through the middle of the dark desert.

"They're coming directly at us," he added.

"That's less good," Wide-Mouth commented from the back of the room.

"It also means we're getting more pressure here and here," Lucky said, pointing to the opposite ends of the large blue rectangle that represented the ark.

On cue, Half-Shot burst into the room. "Fore-side of the ark!" he spat. One hand against his side, red oozing through his jacket. "They're coming down from the top of that dune again."

"They have a squad pinned down up there," Toom-Toom confirmed, one hand to his ear.

"Where's Seven?" Dava said.

Half-Shot gestured by lifting his rifle with his other hand. "She went up."

"Pop your scope," she said, then turned to point at Wide-Mouth. "Get up to the autocannon on the roof. Keep them from advancing on the aft-side of the ark. Do not fire on the Fenders."

"Um, okay," Wide-Mouth said.

"Wide-Mouth, listen to me," she said, stepping toward him as Half-Shot detached the scope from his rifle and handed it to her. "If you fire at the Fenders, they'll bury us. Don't even point that gun at anyone in purple armor."

"Okay, Boss. I got it."

Sixty seconds later, Dava caught up to Seven-Pack climbing the slope of the massive dune that rose up at the front-end of the ark. As she tapped the other woman and they nodded a silent greeting, she turned to face outward.

The path of sunlight that drove away the shadow. Silhouettes of marching Fenders. Guided rockets periodically leaping forth and spiraling toward the vehicles that turned to face them, incinerating the hapless Misters within.

She turned away. She had no love for the bastards. But did she want them slaughtered? Did she want anyone slaughtered? This was war. She definitely had not wanted war. She just wanted to protect the Earth kin.

Seven-Pack poked her and she looked up. Over the ridge. A trio of Shadowdown grunts crouched against the mangled carcass of a large truck, turned onto one side. She recognized one of them as Bayonet Boy. A fourth body lay motionless just outside of cover. They were down in what looked like a pit in the sand. From off to Dava's left, shots peppered down on them.

Through her borrowed scope, she could see five figures there, alternating their shots. They weren't in proper cover or anything, they were just pressing an advantage of numbers. It almost seemed like they were toying with the trapped grunts.

"Watch my back," she said to Seven-Pack.

She approached the Misters silently. Considered murdering them outright. There were five of them, but she was willing to bet they wouldn't handle the sudden chaos created by a blade-wielding assassin at close range.

Another explosion thundered from the direction of the approaching Fenders, momentarily muting the bursts from the distant but constant autocannon atop the black maria. There would be enough death before the day was done.

"I was going to kill you." The five of them spasmed at the sound of her voice, as though she'd electrocuted them. "But I thought I might give you the choice. Seeing as how you probably didn't have a choice in coming here to begin with."

"It's Dava," one of them whispered. Then he lowered his gun and spoke up. "I give up!"

While the rest were frozen, one of them growled. "Fuck you, assassin!" His gun rose up and with a crack, his head snapped back in a spray of blood.

"Anyone else?" Dava said as Seven-Pack stepped forward, smoke coiling from the barrel of her massive revolver.

The rest lowered their guns, glancing at each other to see who would be the first to drop their only defenses into the cold sand. The three Shadowdown grunts came out from hiding and signaled that they were okay.

"ModPol is coming," Dava said to the Misters. "If you want to live, best lose the guns and keep the hands up."

She left them, their confused whispers fading into the night, and she took her people back down the slope toward the ark. The sound of finely-tuned pulse rifles signaled the closing advance of the Defenders. Their bursts precise, coordinated. A piercing, rhythmic drumming that forced the pace of a battlefield previously driven by more chaotic demons.

Dava signaled to the rest of the Shadowdowners to retreat back to the black maria, instructing them to stow their most prized weapons. To carry the rest – the ineffective, the damaged, the just plain mediocre weapons – with them to the entrance to the ark at Door Five.

She left Lucky Jerk and Toom-Toom to stay locked in the black maria with the weapons. She wanted to have them launch, along with the other black maria on the opposite side of the ark, to take their only working ships away from the Defenders in case things went badly. But even launching the black marias could be misinterpreted as an aggressive act by any overzealous asshole with a hard-on for laying waste to the desert.

Her people deposited their most disposable weapons into a pile just outside Door Five. She had someone set up a portable lamp to rain sunlight in a glaring circle all around the pile. Then she put every last Shadowdowner on nurse duty, to aid the waking ark.

All that was left was someone to present their laid-down arms.

"I know you're looking at this pile of weapons and thinking this is your big chance," she said.

The captured Mister's yellow skin looked pale in the light of the lamp. His wide eyes looked at the guns surrounding him like they were a swarm of poisonous reptiles. "Um."

"Of course, they aren't all loaded. So you'd have to take your chance with them. And of course, if you take any of them up, your choices are to come at my people, inside the ark. Or," she said, pointing a blade out at the desert made darker by the local light source. "You take on a horde of Fenders."

He raised his hands, and she wasn't sure if it was voluntary or reflex. "What – what do you want me to do?"

"I want you to deliver a message, Mister – what is it?"

"Brook."

"Mister Brook—"

"No," he said, a small firmness emerging through the fear. "Just Brook."

She cracked a smile: the defection was complete. "Brook. When the Fenders get here, you tell them we've laid down arms. We have no fight with them. We're only here to protect the Earthlings," she said, with a nod toward the ark. "And with the threat of violence gone, they can turn around and go home. The rest of this is Terroneous business."

"Um, okay."

"Say it just like that. You can remember all that, Brook?"

"Y-yeah, of course."

"Good." She looked him up and down, pausing for a moment. "If they don't kill you, you can come inside and help."

He looked at her, seemingly unsure of whether or not to curse her or thank her. "Won't they try to arrest us?" he said when he found his voice again.

She shook her head. "This is ModPol *Defense*. They don't have that kind of jurisdiction here. They can kill us, but if they let us live, we're Terroneous's problem."

She left him there in the spotlight, surrounded by a ring of near-useless weaponry. Back in the tube chambers, she found Shadowdown had quickly taken to their new responsibilities of bringing people back to life after the longest journey of their lives since they entered this universe.

Nearby, Jax was giving directions to Wide-Mouth. The big man was actually listening to the gaunt B-fourean, following his gestures with intent and responding in tight nods. Then he went off to comply with the instructions he'd received.

Dava approached Jax. "How are they?"

"Oh," he said. A small flinch that she suspected he would never lose. Even at his best, Jax had become accustomed to living with fear. "They're good. Everyone is picking up the instructions pretty quickly."

She scrunched her face at him. "I didn't mean my crew." Though she admitted internally that it was good to hear. "How are the Earthlings?"

"Oh, of course. They are mostly okay. Vital readouts show a survival rate of one hundred percent. But I've never seen this kind of Xarp sickness."

She involuntarily clutched her stomach, then tried to surreptitiously brush her hand against her shirt. "It's old tech. The stasis tubes. And the FTL tech. They were out there for a long time."

He looked at her sideways. "It was like this for you." Not a question; an acknowledgement.

"Why are you here?" she said. "Some kind of guilt from growing up lucky?"

He narrowed his eyes. "I may have grown up lucky, but the past couple of years have not been so generous," he said evenly. Then he shook his head. "You're right though. Life in the domes is very different. I had to be thrown out of that life and dropped to the bottom. When I first came to Terroneous, I was starving. Literally. I didn't know it was possible to feel so empty. And cold."

She nodded. "I spent a few years in the domes. Even as an orphan, life is plush there." Her eyes lost their focus and she thought of Moses. Thought about what his absence felt like. Thought about how empty her life would have been without him. "But when I left, I wasn't alone." She looked at Jax again, the small twitches of the head and hands at every sound, and at every silence. No, she decided; he had not become accustomed to *living* with fear, as she thought. He'd become accustomed to overcoming it. "It must have been hard for you."

His head slid back, her sudden sympathy hitting him unexpectedly. Then he shrugged. "Point is, when my life came back together, I saw how it was out here – outside of the domes. How people worked together, helped each other."

He looked at his feet. "Even in Space Waste. Bunch of thugs, and they care more about each other than anyone in any dome cares about anyone else."

She blinked at him. A domer, envious of the ragged lives of gangbangers cobbling together shelter in the depths of space. A small part of her mind nagged at her to grasp the meaning of it. Something about how she should be thankful for the wealth of the intangibles. But she was suddenly exhausted. She wanted to go home. And there was none. There never had been, really. There had been shelter. There had been family. But there had not been *home*.

"What's next?" Jax said, breaking the anxious silence that had grown between them. "This new group of yours – Shadowdown?"

When he said the word, he looked into her eyes. He told her without any words that he knew what it meant. In the shadow of Moses Down. The galaxy had one less bloodthirsty gangster boss. And Dava had no keeper. Naming his shadow felt like a way of memorializing him, of promising to continue his mission. And yet, his mission was not her mission. His shadow was not for binding his will to hers; his shadow was for his passing. For moving on.

"I don't know," she said quietly. The question opened her up. Confusion twisted her guts. But it wasn't alone. Weightlessness. Warmth. Light. She was free. She was in control.

"Life on Terroneous isn't so bad," Jax said idly, as though talking to himself more than her. "Can't beat the food."

She smiled at him. The crack in her face was enough for what was building inside her to escape. She laughed, a ridiculous sound to her own ears. "No, you can't," she said.

Had the seed been planted in that moment? Or was it

already there, when Dava led Shadowdown into a one-way trip to the surface of Terroneous? She couldn't have expected to pack everyone into the black marias and zip back to the Space Waste base, to claim it for their own. Maybe she'd been gambling that 2-Bit could help her out. But she didn't think so. Something inside her wanted to bring her people to this place. *She* wanted to come to this place. A thousand Earthlings had just landed, and they too were lost. Without home. She could start it all over. She could step off the ark with them. A second chance at being a refugee; a capable adult instead of an orphaned child. A place without domes. A place that was hard, but free.

EPILOGUE

He hadn't heard that his mother had come to Terroneous until she was already there. She'd made it all the way to Stockton without a word. Knocked on his apartment door.

"Sylvia?"

"Stanley!"

She embraced him and after the shock of surprise, he returned it. Then a spike of fear. "What are you doing here?"

She brushed past him with a wave. "Is this your place? Did you just move in?"

"Huh? Uh, a few weeks ago," he stammered.

"Oh, Stanley, honey," she said with a playful glare. "You have to get some furniture. Where is your mother supposed to sit?"

Runstom pulled the only chair he owned away from the only table he owned and gestured at it. "What are you doing here?"

"I'm not in any danger," she said as she waved off the chair. "Really. Not any more than I would be anywhere else."

"But Space Waste," he started. The whole reason for the witness protection was to keep her hidden from the gang she'd infiltrated as an undercover detective. And they were all over the B-5 moon.

She waved dismissively. "Space Waste is no more."

"They just formed a new gang," he said, drawing the curtains on the only window.

"Moses Down is dead," she said. "The rest of them don't even know who I am."

He peeked around the curtain he'd just pulled. From the third floor of the old stone building, he could see his street. A gravel-and-dirt affair, it saw little traffic. The densest cluster of buildings lay to the east, in the center of town.

When he turned back, he saw her looking around the room. Saw it through her eyes. Drab gray-brown walls. An ancient holovid set in one corner. The table and the single chair, both made of local wood. A small door that led to a tiny bedroom. A couple of storage units, including a cold store for perishable food. A small cooking unit that had been pulled from an old starship and refurbished. Jax had asserted that it worked, but Runstom still hadn't figured it out.

The whole place was Jax's idea. He lived in another apartment just down the street. It had been a place to sleep, but Runstom couldn't bring himself to feel anything more. He had no idea how to make a home out of it.

The thought of Jax brought him to another thought. "Any other word ... in your network?"

She looked at him, her eyes hardening for a moment. "You mean about Mark Phonson. X." She looked around. There were no hidden bugs in a place like this. No tiny cameras or microphones. "I should be asking you."

He felt his face flush and he shook his head. "I think he's gone." Runstom had left Jenna Zarconi in full control of Comet-X. How long it would take her to kill the man, he didn't want to know.

"Well, so does everyone else, thanks to our favorite cop Jared McManus," she said with a sigh. "After you dropped him at Outpost Gamma, he planted himself at the bar and has been telling the story to anyone who would listen."

He cringed. "The whole story?"

She laughed. "Of course not. Not that I would know. But I do know that his version doesn't include Stanford Runstom."

He exhaled, realizing that he'd been holding his breath. "It's not the way I wanted it to end."

She touched him lightly on the arm. "Of course not, Stanley. You're a good person. And you were a good cop."

He pulled away, his throat tightening. "Well. It's done."

She broke the growing silence by tut-tutting at the book lying on his table. "The Art of War," she said. "I hope you're not too into that."

He swallowed, slightly embarrassed. "Just trying to figure some things out."

"A little advice," she said, brushing past him. "Forget war. Art stands alone."

He picked the book up, intending to put it away. Grunted and dropped it back onto the table, given there was no other place to stow it.

She walked to the kitchen side of the room. "Well, this is an affair," she muttered at the cooker. She looked over her shoulder at him. "Do you have any tea? Coffee?"

"Yeah, but I can't get that damn thing to work."

She rifled through his cupboards, calling out to

inanimate objects in the way she'd always done when he was a child. "Come on out, tea bags. Mugs, I know you're in there."

"In the back there," he said, too late. She'd already pulled out what she needed and was going to work on the cooker.

"Did you quit your job, Stanley?" she said, facing her work.

He winced. "Public relations wasn't for me," he said.

Victoria Horus had not been thrilled with his efforts on Terroneous. The Space Waste defectors laid down their arms as promised. By the time the Defenders had pushed their way to the ark, Dava and her gangbangers were helping Earthlings out of their sleep tubes. Nursing them back into consciousness. There was nothing left to defend. Runstom was certain the order from on high was to drive the gangbangers out, but Major Oliver called her unit off. She had the authority of the operation on the ground and made a call.

Threat eliminated, the Defenders didn't bother to stick around. Clearly not the plan that Horus and Newman had in mind. In fact, it had been the opposite. Dava and her new crew made themselves at home. Praised by the Earthlings for their generous assistance, a few Terronean cities offered them shelter along with the refugees. Word was, some of those in charge were fixing to offer Dava a seat on the Federated Security Committee. Why pay for defense services from ModPol when you have your own squad of rehabilitated gangbangers?

After the ark was safe, Runstom had taken a shuttle back to Ipo. One last debrief. Horus had finally broken that happy demeanor of hers and showed teeth. He could tell her heart wasn't in it. Runstom realized his boss really did like him.

Her priorities were off, but somewhere in there was a good person.

The chief operating officer on the other hand had been an asshole. The angrier Francois Newman got, the quieter his voice. He launched into platitudes about long-term conflicts and visionary goals. Goals that Runstom had fouled with his incompetence.

Runstom had resigned the following day.

The smell of actual tea woke him from his thoughts. Sylvia brought a pair of cups over to the table. She sat and took a sip. Then looked up at him.

"I heard some of the reports second-hand," she said. "Sounds like Terroneous won't be subscribing to ModPol services any time soon."

"Like I said." He felt a small grin grow across his face. "I'm just not that great at public relations."

She smiled and waved off his comment. "I heard Jansen came in from the cold."

Runstom grunted. He'd heard that too, but not from his bosses. "The gangbangers decided to let him go."

"Why is that?"

He shook his head. "I don't really know. I guess they just wanted it to be over."

She flicked at the book. "Something tells me there's nothing in there about the art of peace." She took a sip and breathed in, her face relaxing, content. "It's not achievable through violence, no matter how just."

He looked at the book. Looked through it, into nothing. There had been a tiny itch in the back of his head. Since his promotion. He mistook it for self-consciousness. For the feeling of being an imposter, the wrong man for the job. But only recently did he understand that wasn't it. It wasn't the job, it was the division. When he was in Justice, he understood the purpose. Righting wrongs. But Defense was different.

The itch was telling him he didn't want to be part of a war machine.

"I hate to be *motherly* about it," Sylvia said, breaking the silence with a crooked grin. "But do you have ... something else lined up?"

Runstom huffed, giving himself a taste of tea for courage. "Yeah, I guess I do. Something with Jax."

Her eyebrows lifted. "Really? Here on Terroneous?"

"Yes." He looked away from her, at the cooker on the counter that she'd managed to coax to life. "Actually, we could use some help."

"Oh?"

He looked at her again, unable to control the small smile cracking between his lips. "Yeah. I mean, seeing as how you're not in wit-pro anymore."

"That's true, I'm not," she said with her own sly smile, covering it with her mug.

He took a breath. Allowed himself to feel the relief that she was there. That it wasn't temporary. That he needed her. Accepting all of these things at once caused his vision to swim. He suddenly wished he owned more than one chair.

But then all that acceptance hit a wall. It churned within him, ready to push forward, but the wall needed resolution before it would break.

"Moses Down," Runstom said quietly. "I met him."

She twitched, a small flinch, and set her mug down on the table. "You did?"

"How do you know he's dead?" he asked, remembering her earlier words.

"Where did you meet him?" she said firmly.

He felt his shoulders slump under her parental glare. "In the zero-G prison."

She looked at him quietly. "Did he know you?"

He nodded. "Yes." Thought about the exchange with Dava over a comm. *Our people.* She'd repeated it. And there was Horus's comment. *Tell them about how your father was an Earthling.*

"Sylvia," he said. "Mom." The question stuck in his throat. Just as it had his entire life.

She swallowed, smoothing out the folds of her dusty dress. Lifted her head, a distant smile in her eyes. "His name was Bishop Down."

* * *

Stockton was glad to have their Fixer back. As soon as Jax made his first appearance at the public library, the word spread and his schedule quickly filled up. The throw-away dome tech that the Terroneans considered a luxury never quite worked right, but everyone knew the Fixer's magic touch could coax it into behaving. In fact, it seemed as though Jax's news exposure had compounded his reputation, and now everyone in town – and in all the neighboring towns – had a job for him.

It was good because it kept him busy; and keeping busy was the only way he got any sleep at night. Even when he slept, he often woke up elsewhere: in a dirty cot in a cramped Space Waste quarter, or on the cold floor of Phonson's torture room. It was on those nights that he'd fall out of bed, pick himself up off the floor, turn on the lights, and then recite the poem that was stitched into a framed piece of cloth that hung on his wall.

Though unexpected rain
churns soil into mud,
the harshest of storms
births more green than blood.

Some local farmer had given it to him, and it was apparently a popular bit of rhyme because he'd seen it around town and in other folk's homes. To Terroneans, the lyrics were about sustaining life in a harsh environment. The color green, he'd come to understand, was the color of healthy plants full of good vitamins. Food in the domes had coloring, but it was artificial and bright, like candy. To Jax, the once-life-support operator, the color green was an indicator that systems were happy, as opposed to the color red, which signaled a time to panic.

The only time Jax had seen more than one light go red while he was on duty was when the outer doors on block 23-D of a sub-dome called Gretel had opened, venting the life-sustaining artificial atmosphere and asphyxiating thirty-two people. The deaths that had fallen on his head, resulting in his arrest and later his fugitive status. That day so many lights had gone red, they created a streak like a wound cut through the middle of the panel.

All of that was over now, and Jax would read that poem to remind himself of that fact. He'd come through the storm and made a new life on Terroneous. He was doing more than watching machines keep people alive; he was actually helping people directly.

The previous night was sleepless, though for a completely different reason. Lealina was coming into town. She was still acting director of the Terroneous Environmental Observation Board, though a vote was expected any day now on whether to make that title permanent or to appoint another director. She'd seemed to make peace with the fact that the ultimate decision was out of her hands. Jax admired that about Lealina: she always gave her focus to her work and didn't let the things she couldn't control eat her up.

And she knew how to value her days off. This concept was a little easier for Jax to manage when he was on a schedule set by someone else, like it was in the domes. As a freelancer, he didn't know how and when to give himself a break. Fortunately, Lealina's schedule helped dictate Jax's schedule, as she could only get away from the remote facilities for a few days about twice every month. Which meant Jax had to make sure to keep those days clear from the tasty jobs of fixing other people's problems.

Despite being exhausted from lack of sleep, Jax jittered with nervous energy as he paced around the small train station. Though he must have annoyed the hell out of everyone there, they all gave the lanky B-fourean a patiently wide berth. The locals had already gotten used to his new routine. They knew there was no point in talking to him when Lealina was coming to town, and there was also no getting him to sit down and stop drinking so much coffee.

Other than Jax, the unassuming station was quiet and still. When the train finally arrived, the place transformed into a hive of quick activity. Other waiters greeted long-parted friends and relatives with warm smiles, but not much else. Reunions were efficiently conducted, and then life carried on. Jax didn't know if he'd ever become so blasé about seeing Lealina after weeks of drought.

The bright blues came through the door. He floated to her and embraced her.

Sometime later his mind came back to the present when she pinched him.

"Sorry," she said with an impish grin. "I really need to pee."

He let her go and after she used the restroom, they continued on to what had become another new tradition, which was to visit the public house across the road from the train station. It wasn't so much for the drink, though a little imbibing was welcomed by both of them, having finally got a break from work, but more that, they found before they attempted to do anything, they needed to sit together and share the intimate little moments of their lives since her last visit.

They ordered drinks and found a small table near a window where the orange-tinged light of Barnard's Star warmed their faces.

"Mm," she said after she'd taken a sip of some kind of blue-hued bubbly cocktail. "They didn't add a bar to your library yet?"

He'd chosen a light beer that was crisp and cool in his throat. "Nah," he said, smiling wide. He'd been telling anyone that would listen about the *Bibliohouse* back on Epsilon Eridani-3. "I'm not giving up yet, but I don't think it's going to happen."

"Maybe that's a good thing," she said with a laugh. "You'd never leave the place!"

"Ha, probably not."

"Actually." She set down her drink and pointed at him. "You probably need to open your own place. Your own library-slash-bar."

"Yeah, right."

She cut off his laugh with a narrowing of her eyes. "It's

not *that* bad an idea. I mean, are you going to freelance forever?"

He poked at his beer glass with the tip of a finger, feeling the wetness of the condensation that collected like a light fog. "Well. I don't know." He'd been trying not to think about it. The glut of work he had right now was not sustainable. It would dry up, and then he'd need to supplement it with something else.

"I'm sorry, Jax." She reached across the table and touched his hand. "I'm not trying to push you. I think you're in a really good place right now, all things considered."

"Yeah, I guess so."

"It's just that," she started, then seemed to turn the words around in her head before continuing, her eyes looking into the sunshine coming through the window. "On Terroneous, we have to learn not to get too comfortable. When you're in a good place – that's the best time to prepare."

He read the concern on her face, slowly understanding what she meant: things were good now, but it was almost certain there were still bad times to come. The ups and downs of life. She was trying to train him. This should have offended him, but the reality was that his sheltered, domed upbringing had very few ups and downs. In fact, it had been almost completely flat, right up until that day he had to watch helplessly as nameless vita-stat readouts went from green to red.

"I got a d-mail from my dad," he said softly.

"Oh." Her face twisted through a few thoughts, and he could imagine she was trying to decide whether or not it was a good thing. "He finally answered your letters?"

"Yeah."

The truth was that his father responded pretty quickly.

It had been Jax who'd delayed in sending the initial letters, despite having written them months ago. Written before he was abducted from Terroneous, into a notebook that he had carried everywhere and left in Lealina's care. He'd told her he was going to send them, and then one day told her he *had* sent them, hoping that the dishonesty would motivate him to carry forward the act and turn the lie into truth. It did, but it took him a while.

Of course, his father immediately offered him a place in his home on Barnard-3. Back in the domes; though the B-3 domes were a bit nicer than those Jax lived in on B-4. This was the thing that perhaps Lealina feared, that Jax might be tempted to go home. Back to the safety of the domes, back to comfort, back to the place where *survival* was a given.

"I wrote him back already," Jax said. This time he wasn't lying. "I told him he should come out and visit me on Terroneous sometime. I told him that's the best way to see me, because I'm not going back to the domes any time soon."

Her face broke into smile, and she tipped it to hide it, either embarrassed by her relief or ashamed that she was happy for his rocky familial relationships. "You think he'd ever come out?" she said.

Jax looked through the window at the dusty street. A young man was pulling a small, wheeled cart that contained some boxes and a small girl who sat atop the load. This was what passed for traffic in Stockton.

"I don't know, honestly," he said. He looked at her. "I hope he does. But I'm not going to be disappointed if he doesn't."

She met his eyes for a moment in silence, lips neither

smiling nor frowning. He read pity on her face and it made him feel small. He was trying to stand on his own. Not many people understood how hard it was for him. As he looked at her, Lealina's lips turned up slightly, small triangular wrinkles poking into her cheeks. It released a warmth inside his chest. She didn't understand him, but she was starting to.

"You're still considering David's offer?" she said before bending her neck to take a sip through the straw of her drink.

"Yes," Jax said. "I mean, I'm going to take it."

She read the tiny crack in his voice. "You're safe now." Her hand was still on his, and she gave him another squeeze.

He smiled faintly and nodded. David Granderson wanted to re-cut the documentary he'd made. The film that had caught Jax on camera, outing the then-fugitive's hiding place. Granderson hadn't known then, of course, and still felt guilty for his part in Jax's trials. But then again, guilt or not, Granderson never did a favor that wasn't somehow also profitable to him. So he offered Jax a deal: they re-work the film to include Jax's secret fugitive status. Now that it was no longer a secret, Granderson felt like he could tell a more complete story. Which Jax understood meant a more *dramatic* story.

But this time Jax would get official credit in the film, and he would get a cut of the proceeds. It wasn't going to be much – Granderson made sure he understood that – but there was a good chance that it would see syndication out to the other colonies, which meant what Granderson called "a bigger piece of pie". Jax had only had pie for the first time in his life a few weeks ago, and it had been so overwhelming with its mélange of tart and sweet flavors and crispy and gooey textures that it had taken him a full hour to finish it.

"I know," he said, taking a pull of his beer. "You're right. I'm okay. It's a good deal."

She pulled her hand back and crooked a smile. "Well, it's a shitty deal. But it means you'll be able to eat for a while."

She'd meant the remark to be humorous, so Jax tried to respond with a smile. But something caught inside him – a nothing caught inside him. A sudden emptiness; a memory of emptiness. An unforgettable emptiness. He never wanted to go hungry again. "Yeah, yes. I'm definitely going to take it. I'll call him tonight."

Her head slid back slightly at his sudden desperate eagerness. Then she cocked an eyebrow in that way that she did sometimes that made him want to pledge life-long servitude to her divinity. "Okay then," she said. He died when she added the playful smile.

"Oh," he said, suddenly remembering something. "I got a message from Dava. She's bringing in another group."

"Soon? While I'm in town?"

"Yep, day after tomorrow." He beamed at her knowingly. "I told her when you were going to be in town, and she timed it. She's going to have a couple of geologists and environmental specialists."

Lealina's face brightened. "Yes!" She vibrated in her chair. "Oh, I hope they're looking for work."

"They're refugees," Jax said. "They're *all* looking for work."

They ordered a second round and chatted about work. Lealina was desperately trying to find qualified people willing to work for very little money. The TEOB had managed to get a small increase in budget, but it came with a mandate to staff up. Jax filled her in on the random jobs he'd been doing. This was all part of their newly established ritual; it helped them enjoy their limited time together if they could unload all the work stuff right from the beginning and get it over with.

"Hey, how's Stanford doing?" she said once the work talk ran its course.

"Good," Jax said, holding out the word too long. "Settling in."

"He found anything yet?"

"Um. Well." Jax had a hard time meeting her probing eyes. "He's ... kind of starting a new ... a new project. And he wants my help."

"What is it?" She set her drink so she could lean over it and draw him in. "What does he want you to do?"

Jax drew a deep breath and blew it out. "I kind of already said yes."

* * *

Dava found Captain 2-Bit staring at an empty field of turquoise-colored grass. He didn't hear her approach, but he didn't flinch when she spoke.

"Captain. What ya lookin' at?"

Without turning to face her, he drew a deep breath through his nose. "Sorry, Dava. I still can't get used to this place." He threw a flat palm at the horizon. "I mean, look at it! So much land."

She crooked an eyebrow at him. "Weren't you born here?"

He huffed. "That was a long time ago, right? Spent too much of the last few decades in ships and in that rickety ol' mess we called a home base."

"Well. This is home base now," she said. "You spend as much time down here as you want."

He nodded slowly. "Sure. I will. I got some trustworthy pilots up there, right?"

She grinned at him. The old captain was ever-loyal to his duty. She could see his guilt at leaving his post commanding the *Longhorn*, even if only for a few days out of each month. "Also, I like to see you," she said. "Everyone likes to see you. But me especially."

"Why's that?"

"Because I need your advice on stuff."

They began to walk down a lightly worn path that led to the compound. Whenever 2-Bit came down to visit, she saw the place through his eyes. She saw the slow but noticeable progression from month to month. It was an empty stretch of plainsland, with the edge of a thin forest visible a kilometer or so to the north and a rough bunching of gray hills rising a few dozen kilometers to the west. Unclaimed land, until she'd claimed it. No one had bothered to settle it mostly because of the predatory animals in their area. They weren't much of a threat to well-armed humans, but they were hell on livestock. The aggressive grass grew thick and tall and made farming a pain as well.

But it was a perfect spot for her crew. They could train without disturbing anyone – the nearest town was a good forty kilometers down the road – and there was a spot just at the edge where they could land a shuttlecraft. Some of them hunted or grew vegetables for pleasure, but most of their food was shipped in.

Paying for it was a bit of a challenge. Most of them, Dava included, weren't used to managing money. They were used to stealing what they needed, then distributing it amongst themselves. But in this new home, they had to actually buy stuff. Which meant they needed income. The FSC had made her a deal. Shadowdown would act as the moon's militia, and she'd get a small stipend. They were mostly interested in getting her to keep the *Longhorn* in orbit as a deterrent. On the ground, theoretically they wanted her people to respond to any hostilities, but such a threat was mild at best. The stipend's size reflected the lack of threat, and it wasn't enough. She supplemented their income by hiring out crew to local townships as guards, deputies, marshals, whatever form of strong-arm they might be in need of.

She and 2-Bit approached the main camp. Most of it was still tents, but there were a few new buildings coming in. Much of the material was recycled metal from the ark, dragged across the desert in pieces. No one on the moon minded when Shadowdown claimed what was left of the trucks and ATVs that the Misters had brought to the fight.

Which was good, because they needed to get around. She spent a lot of time organizing multi-purpose caravans that headed into one of the towns to pick up food and drop off people. And sometimes pick up people.

"Less tents than last time," 2-Bit said. "Placement programs?"

"Working pretty well so far," she answered. They were still housing half the Earthling refugees at the compound. A couple dozen decided they owed her something and joined her crew. The rest of the thousand hadn't traveled six light years in a tube to do security. They had unique, forgotten skills and educations, and were needed elsewhere. So she worked with local governments to arrange introductions.

Meanwhile, word had spread quickly about their efforts.

Some Terroneans loved seeing ModPol show up only to get turned away at the end of the day. They wanted to be a part of that rarely-needed defense force. So they joined the caravans on the return trips to the compound. Dava and her best people organized training camps. Their numbers grew, which was good, because they had a lot of area to cover.

"Still getting new recruits trickling in," she said as they walked past a strip of field where a few yellow-skinned Terroneans were doing calisthenics to the rhythmic bark of Johnny Eyeball.

2-Bit smiled broadly. "I love to hear that commanding voice put to use. He's good?"

She joined his smile as they watched Eyeball standing tall like a pillar in the midday sun. "He's literally the most sober person I know. The atmosphere has been good for him."

"All these new recruits," 2-Bit said after a moment, giving her a look. "I'm kind of surprised."

She looked at him. "We need all the help we can get."

"You're not worried about picking up another mole?"

She sighed through her nose at the thought of Rando Jansen. His deceit had cost lives, and not only those of Space Waste. But when it came down to it, he was doing a job. He was a piece in a strategy. He infiltrated them because he was placed there by some ModPol intelligence agency. But also because Moses couldn't resist the inside information he promised. Moses was working the same kind of strategy, just from the other side. It had blinded him.

Some of the grunts aboard the *Longhorn* had tracked Jansen down during 2-Bit's mutiny. They stunned him, bound him, and were ready to space him. But 2-Bit had waited for Dava to make the call. She went up to the *Longhorn* to look him in the face, one last time. To tell him that Space Waste was no more. He'd won, in that sense. His mission a success.

And she put him on a lifeboat and sent him back to ModPol.

"No," she said. "I'm not worried about moles anymore."

They kept walking. Chatted about the weather, which 2-Bit was fascinated with. He yammered on about how he'd taken it for granted when he was a kid. When a light rain began to sprinkle them with tiny droplets of cold water, he whooped with delight.

They came to the center of the compound. "This is what I wanted to show you," she said.

A black stone, some kind of volcanic rock, glossy and glass-like but entirely without light. Found by a hunter, hidden in a crevice nestled among the distant hills. Extracted by the sole constructor-bot on the compound, despite the delay it caused in the build schedule. Then carved by a group of four artistically-inclined materials workers who spent every waking minute of their personal time fighting with the stubborn matter, coaxing form out of the formless.

2-Bit looked up at the resulting figure and whistled. "It's like it's him, but it's not him."

"They captured his essence," she said of the vaguely human-shaped statue; repeating a phrase she'd heard someone else use. Words she didn't know the meaning of until they were used to describe the piece before her.

"Down's Shadow," 2-Bit said, reading the plaque at the base. "Your idea?"

"None of it was my idea," she said, a tinge of pride in her voice. "Just a bunch of people that wanted to remember him."

He leaned in to her. "Do you realize what this means?"

She squinted at him. "What?"

"We have *artists*."

She coughed out a laugh, then felt delayed goosebumps run over her skin. *Artists*. They were the same people she lived with for years, fighting together, stealing together. Surviving together. And hidden beneath all that crime and violence and survival was something like *this*.

"Well, I guess that's what happens," he added with a sigh.

"What?"

He looked at her and shrugged. "You gave 'em a real home, right?" He suddenly jerked his head to one side. "God *damn*, that smells good. I'm starving for some real food."

She waved for him to go on without her and he trundled off toward the mess tent, wholly unaware that his words had rendered her unable to speak.

She looked at the statue. Felt the *essence*. She missed Moses so badly, she thought she would evaporate whenever the memory of him flooded through her. And the others that had been lost. Thinking of Moses always made her think of all of them. Of the way she felt when Thompson was torn to pieces in front of her. Of how she tamped down the emotions in the moment, only to have them overwhelm her later. Of how it made her miss her mother and her father. All of those shadows buried as deep as they could go, but somehow keeping them deep only made them closer to her innermost, truest self.

So she stared at the black stone and saw his face in its reflection. His toothy grin. The twinkle in his playful and scheming eyes. Remembered him. Remembered his cause. His sacrifice. His generosity. His love.

And at the same time, reminded herself that those things were in the past. His drive, his needs. When they were alive and kicking, there was never a time for something like *this* to come out. There were battles to fight. Systems to break. There was no place for some kind of ridiculous creative expression, like the slab that stood before her.

Would he like it? She wondered. She placed a hand against the smooth surface. Cool, and slightly wet from the light rain. Then she stepped back and looked around at the tents. At the new scrap-metal buildings taking shape. This life – this home – had been what he was fighting for. He just never understood that. He never knew how to stop the fighting and just *make a home.*

She smiled up at him, her face wet from the rain. She'd made a home. And whether he liked it or not, he was in it.

* * *

Sylvia Runstom picked up her d-mail. It felt like a weird activity, to have to walk to a building to physically retrieve messages transported between the stars by FTL drones. The infrastructure of the small towns of Terroneous was weak on the telecommunications side, and no one could trust their mail to be delivered by any local network without being snooped on. She admired the healthy level of paranoia on the small moon.

Not that there was anything interesting to read. Since she was no longer underground, most of her underground connections wanted nothing to do with her. Still, she had a few. Keeping in touch with the pulse was a habit she'd never be able to drop.

"Mrs. Runstom!"

She flinched. Another thing to get used to. She turned to a clerk who was rushing to catch her at the door. "Yes?"

"Message for Stanford," the young man said cheerfully. "Would you mind taking it to him?"

She grinned as she took the small box with the message chip in it. "Of course. I'm on my way to see him right now."

"Thanks, Ma'am!"

She couldn't erase the grin as she left. Everyone else had to come to the d-mail office to pick up their messages, and yet somehow in a short period of time her son had earned the kind of respect that meant people wanted to deliver his mail right to him. Or at least ask his mother to.

As she walked down the quiet street in the quiet town, she looked at the package. The sender code was on the outside, and though it was non-identifying, she recognized the first few numbers as a ModPol station origin designation. She knew she shouldn't, but ... those old habits. She looked at the WrappiMate on her arm and pulled up one of her databases. They were stale by months and growing staler by the moment, but she tried the code anyway.

"Major Lucy Jennifer Oliver," she said to herself. She allowed herself a mischievous chuckle. "Now why oh why would this young woman be trying to contact Stanley?"

Why indeed.

She cleared her screen and rounded the corner. Just a few more blocks. It felt good to walk, and she didn't miss all the metro-tracks that had been all over the new settlements on EE-3.

In some ways, she was surprised this was the place her son ended up. But in other ways, she would never be surprised. She gave up long ago feeling guilty for not giving him a normal life. What in the galaxy was normal, really?

He'd always been independent, but never in control. She could tell by his words, in those sparse letters he would send her over the years. Never in trouble, but never in control. He didn't come out and say it, but she knew the symptoms. Her life was the same. Always trying to get somewhere, to move forward, but within the parameters meted out by the job and the circumstances.

And now he was taking control. Full control. The feeling it gave her was terrifying, but overwhelming in joy and pride.

On top of that, he wanted her help. It was more than she could have hoped for when she came to this tiny backwater moon to seek him out. Her nightmare, which he could never fully understand, was officially over. She no longer needed witness protection. But that was only the official side of it. Unofficially, she had to look into those brown eyes of his and see Bishop Down. The olive-green skin did nothing to cover up the resemblance; it was hard for her to differentiate it from Bishop's black Earthling skin, especially when the eyes were so identical. She had to remember her betrayals, to everyone and everything. And she had to remember all the times she had to push her son away, how many times she had to hide truths from him. How she had to watch from a distance as his colleagues and superiors punished him for her choices, in all the little ways they could. Giving him the shit jobs, holding him back. And she was helpless to do anything.

Through all that, her son had kept his head down and worked hard. He'd been a good cop. They should have made him detective a long time ago. It was ModPol's loss.

The office was still getting work done on it, so she had to go around a ladder to get to the door. She was so intent on not banging her head, she hadn't seen the new lettering until it was right in front of her, and then it hit her. A wave of warm pride, like sun on her face.

Runstom and Jackson
Private Detectives

Acknowledgements

A great big thank you to the fine folks at Harper Voyager, including Natasha Bardon, Lily Cooper, and Simon Fox. Thank you so much for giving me the opportunity to tell this complete story across three books, and thank you for the support over these past few years. Also, I should throw in here: every cover in this series has wowed me and made other authors green with envy. Thank you, Ben Gardiner!

I'd like to thank all the people who have supported my writing in one way or another over the years. The following organizations have contributed something meaningful to my journey: National Novel Writing Month (NaNoWriMo), the Northwest Independent Writers Association (NIWA), Willamette Writers, Indigo Editing, the Wordstock Festival, Literary Arts of Oregon, WorldCon, OryCon, WesterCon, and GearCon.

And then there are the fellowships I've developed with authors over the years. Thanks for the support, to the Third Thursday Writer's group, the Speculative Fiction Write-in group at the Fort Vancouver Regional Library, the Codex community, and the other HarperVoyager writers I've connected with. You people are the best. Lastly, as always, a shoutout to the Writers With No Name: Brian and Wes, thank you for the mind-numbing libations and the mind-opening conversations.

I also want to thank my alternate-dimension family, the innovative and inspiring folks at AWS Elemental. I've gotten so much support and encouragement there, it's not fair to call it simply a "day job". In particular I want to call out fellow writer and all-time NaNoWriMo champion Duncan "Dunx" Ellis, whom I've had the honor to share a stage with on several occasions.

Cynthia: I know I never say it, but I owe you everything, Mom.

Jennifer: why does it feel like ten years of marriage is only the beginning? Oh right, because I will love you for all eternity. Thank you for being my universe.